LEVERAGE

JOSHUA C. COHEN

speak
An Imprint of Penguin Group (USA) Inc.

SPEAK
Published by the Penguin Group
Penguin Group (USA) Inc., 345 Hudson Street, New York, New York 10014, U.S.A.
Penguin Group (Canada), 90 Eglinton Avenue East, Suite 700,
Toronto, Ontario, Canada M4P 2Y3 (a division of Pearson Penguin Canada Inc.)
Penguin Books Ltd, 80 Strand, London WC2R 0RL, England
Penguin Ireland, 25 St Stephen's Green, Dublin 2, Ireland (a division of Penguin Books Ltd)
Penguin Group (Australia), 250 Camberwell Road, Camberwell, Victoria 3124, Australia
(a division of Pearson Australia Group Pty Ltd)
Penguin Books India Pvt Ltd, 11 Community Centre, Panchsheel Park, New Delhi – 110 017, India
Penguin Group (NZ), 67 Apollo Drive, Rosedale, Auckland 0632, New Zealand
(a division of Pearson New Zealand Ltd.)
Penguin Books (South Africa) (Pty) Ltd, 24 Sturdee Avenue,
Rosebank, Johannesburg 2196, South Africa

Penguin Books Ltd, Registered Offices: 80 Strand, London WC2R 0RL, England

First published in the United States of America by Dutton Books,
a member of Penguin Group (USA) Inc., 2011
Published by Speak, an imprint of Penguin Group (USA) Inc., 2012

3 5 7 9 10 8 6 4 2

THE LIBRARY OF CONGRESS HAS CATALOGED THE DUTTON BOOKS EDITION AS FOLLOWS:
Cohen, Joshua.
Leverage / Joshua Cohen.
p. cm.
Summary: High school sophomore Danny excels at gymnastics but is bullied, like the rest of the
gymnasts, by members of the football team, until an emotionally and physically scarred new
student joins the football team and forms an unlikely friendship with Danny.
ISBN: 978-0-525-42306-5 (hc)
[1. Violence—Fiction. 2. Football—Fiction. 3. Gymnasts—Fiction. 4. Bullies—Fiction.
5. Revenge—Fiction. 6. High school—Fiction. 7. Schools—Fiction.]
I. Title
PZ7.C662642 Le 2011
[Fic] 2010013472

Speak ISBN 978-0-14-242086-7

Designed by Jason Henry
Set in Melior

Printed in the United States of America

For Charles and Jane with all my gratitude.

To Karen with all my heart.

D A N N Y

The high bar's chalky bite threatens to rip the yellowed calluses right off my palms at the bottom of the swing, where the pull is heaviest. Thirty thousand fans in the Olympic arena muffle themselves as I approach escape velocity. On the upswing, all my pain, sweat, and years of practice drop away like spent booster rockets, pushing me even higher in my one shot at glory and Olympic gold. The crusty steel pipe, my companion and punisher, slingshots me past gravity's reach and I am a superhero in front of the adoring, breathless fans waiting to see if I live or die. I can fly, like a god, rising higher, twisting and corkscrewing through space, spotting my landing mat, tumbling weightless—

CRACK!

Huh?

Eyelids flutter open as brain reboots from a math-induced coma. My nose twitches at the scent of Old Spice aftershave. Mr. Klech stands beside my desk, ruler in hand.

"Having a nice nap, Mr. Meehan?" he asks, cracking the ruler on my desk a second time. I flinch. The classroom snickers. Mr. Klech always addresses us formally, using our last names like it's his own personal joke, like he knows how far any of us are from being actual adults.

"Yes. No," I offer, pretty sure one of those has to be the correct answer. Mr. Klech doesn't even wait. He's already waddling back to the chalkboard to complete the same equation I nodded off to first go-round: $(x^2 - y^2) + (z^2 + m^2)$ = something you—Danny Meehan!—will never figure out.

The only good thing about Mr. Klech's class is Glory Svenson, who sits in front of me. My eyes drift off the board full of math scribble and focus on Glory reaching up behind her to undo the black clip securing all that golden hair into a pile on top of her head. Set free, her hair tumbles down in perfect, sun-streaked ringlets that hit my desk and fan out over my algebra textbook. I inhale deeply and am rewarded with the citrus-mango aroma of her shampoo.

Summer still lingers in the air this first week of my sophomore year and, even with the windows wide open, the classroom bakes at a snoozable eighty-four degrees according to the doughnut-shaped thermometer by the light switch. Outside, you can hear the machine hum of John Deere tractor lawn mowers grooming the football fields. The sweet smells of cut grass and gasoline waft into the class, mixing happily with Glory's shampoo. Sure beats getting stuck behind Wally Peters's pimply peg-head in science or DuWayne Runyon's speed-bump Mohawk in study hall.

With eighteen minutes and forty-seven . . . forty-six . . . forty-five seconds remaining until the bell releases us, I begin tracing around Glory's spilled goldilocks to stay awake. I've got a pretty decent pencil outline going on pages 31 and 32 of my *Algebra for Life* textbook when the classroom door opens. A guy who looks like he's been through puberty three times—while I'm still waiting for my first shot—walks through the door with muscles stacked on him like blocks. The guy actually has side-burns and chin whiskers. Chin whiskers! Though he tries to hide it with an overgrown mop falling over his face, I can see a scar traveling from the outside corner of his eye down to his heavy jaw and a patch of skin on that same cheek mottled pink and white, with the rough texture of cauliflower.

The guy looks tough, setting off my internal alert. Everyone knows a guiding principle of underclassman survival is identifying dangerous upperclassmen. The fact that I don't recognize the new guy troubles me. He keeps his eyes down, like he's already been busted for something. Around the patch of weird skin and the long scar, his face—what isn't hidden behind his hair—starts to redden. He holds a green hall pass folded over a white note. Mr. Klech stops filling the chalkboard with coded al-Qaeda sleeper cell instructions and impatiently glances at, then pulls a double take of, the big intruder.

"Yes?" Mr. Klech asks with that tone teachers use to make even a simple question sound like a put-down.

The big guy won't speak. He walks toward Mr. Klech,

offering up the green hall pass and the white note. His other hand reaches up to rub the scarred cheek, shielding it from our gawking. His clothes look old but not retro, more like Salvation Army. Or asylum. He wears the long sleeves of his satin shirt rolled to the elbow, revealing forearms corded with muscle and—no joke—about the size of my calves. His longish hair rides over a shirt collar with lapels big enough to flap. His dark dress pants stop at his ankles, revealing white tube socks and vinyl Kmart sneakers. His clothes don't matter, though, because the guy moves with size and power and remains scary quiet. No way, no how, is anyone in that class going to laugh at him, not even Fred Calahan or Erik Berry, two varsity football starters. The closer he gets to Mr. Klech, the more he looms over our teacher.

Mr. Klech snatches the papers from the guy's hand and starts reading. The man-beast continues forward, putting himself between Mr. Klech and the class, eclipsing our teacher while a serpentine sound slithers out of him.

Glory Svenson's hair rises off my desk as she and the rest of us sit forward to listen.

"Sure, Mr. . . . your name, again?" Mr. Klech asks from somewhere behind the giant. With his back still turned to us, I hear the guy make a *kuh-kuh-kuh* and then a *buh-buh-buh* noise like he's attempting really bad suburban beatbox.

"Well, Mr. Brodsky—Kurt—welcome," Mr. Klech says, and steps back into my sight line. "Just have a seat over . . . hmmm, it looks like we're full up at the moment." Mr. Klech looks around the classroom. "You can take my seat up here for the next few minutes until we finish. I'll see about getting an extra desk for tomorrow."

The guy takes a moment to study the teacher's chair at the front of class and then shakes his head no.

"There's really no other alternative," Mr. Klech says. The new guy, Kurt Brodsky, isn't listening. He heads toward the back of the classroom, down my aisle, like a bull hauling logs. As he passes me I notice his right hand bunched into a thick fist, knuckles white, looking capable of splitting the thin wood of my desk with one solid punch. He reaches the back wall and then turns around, leaning up against it, watching us watch him.

"Mr. Brodsky, I prefer my students not stand during class," Mr. Klech says, clearly miffed. "I'd like you to take my seat."

"I'm sssssssssssssss," the new guy, Kurt, starts cobra hissing. Then his eyes roll up into half-scrunched lids, leaving only zombie-slits of white. "Sssssssssssssss . . ." His face grows rosy as the class twists in unison for a better view of him wrestling some demon word out of his mouth. You can tell he's getting angrier the longer it drags on. "Sssssssssssssss . . ."

Without warning he brings up his fist and swings it down into the back wall.

Boom!

"Sssssssssstaying puh-puh-puh-put!" he finishes with a heavy stomp of his big, vinyl, Kmart sneaker. His eyes unroll from his head and glare out at us.

Holy shit!

No one says anything. No one dares. We all turn back

around in our seats. Mr. Klech ignores the outburst and returns to the chalkboard. I forget all about Glory Svenson's hair. I pretend to understand the final problem Mr. Klech puts up on the board. I slouch down in my desk and hope that when Kurt Brodsky gets expelled for slaughtering a couple of underclassmen, it isn't my corpse they'll find hanging in his locker.

K U R T

Sometimes, sir, there's just a meanness in this world. That song lyric says more about most people than anything else I've ever come across. It keeps playing in my head as I stand in the doorway of my new algebra class with no choice but to let every student look at me, look at my dumb-ass shirt. Look at my face. My cheeks grow hot and the scars start to itch, uglifying me even more. Without the cover of a football helmet, the stares fire on me nonstop. And just wait until they hear me speak. A bead of sweat caterpillars along my brow as I hand the note and hall pass over to the teacher, Mr. Klech, putting my back between him and a whole class taking aim from behind their desks.

If Lamar were here he would turn it around: act like being the new guy was all a big joke, point at one of the students in front, or pick the best-looking one, and flip 'em the bird. He's as small as they come but I bet he'd step right up to the biggest cat in the room—besides me— and try to pick a fight, establish himself right away. Of course, Lamar'd get himself suspended within the hour, but he'd be dancing all the way out the school door. Without Lamar, I got no voice, no one who understands my eye-rolls. I got no one to show my sketches for that bike shop we'd own together. Without Lamar, I got no one to help me track down Crud Bucket after they release him so we can kidnap him and tie him to a chair in some dark basement and make him explain every single mark he left on us. As always, thinking of Lamar helps at first. Then it hurts.

I tried explaining to Oregrove's school secretary I've already taken algebra, but with each attempt my idiot tongue thickened even more. Her pasted-on smile told me she wasn't really hearing anything the big retard said anyway. She's leafed through my records, read my transcript, heard me speak, and now she's got me all figured out. The wadded-up disco shirt Patti pulled out of a plastic bag and forced me to wear ain't exactly helping my case, either. Being a coach's recruit is supposed to make me special. But someone coming from my situation, sounding like my tongue's juggling ice cubes, makes me a kind of "special" that caused the secretary to address me too slowly and too loudly. Those grades I got at Lincoln High don't mean nothing to her because Lincoln's more a holding cell than a school in her mind. Funny how Lincoln and Oregrove both share the idea of keeping me back a year, two even.

All the better to keep me humping that football up and down the field to win them a title.

"That coach of yours said he'd arrange us extra funding to help beef you up," Patti explains that first day she welcomes me into her home as my latest foster guardian. "You'll get a real good education at Oregrove. Your coach said they'll be able to highlight your skills, most likely get you signed for a full scholarship at a university. I don't have to tell you just how big a gift that is." Patti's no worse than the last four foster guardians since Crud Bucket, but her face keeps lighting up whenever she mentions—three times that first day—the *extra funds* Oregrove High School's coach promised her.

Walking into the sticky-hot classroom, I got nothing against my new algebra teacher, Mr. Klech, but no way am I sitting up front at his desk while all those eyes zero in on me. So I ignore him. I put my head down, remind myself none of it really matters, that it's all just a game created by adults: filling out forms, standing in line, finding your place, doing as you're told, and—most important—making sure if someone's cracking fists, it's you doing the swinging. Me and Lamar discovered that last one together. All those eyes watching me walk to the back of Mr. Klech's classroom can't touch me. Not like Crud Bucket. Not even close.

D A N Y

Not sure what's worse, yet: freshmen assuming I'm one of them or upperclassmen mistaking me for an accelerated supergenius fifth grader—minus the supergenius part. Dad's attempts to reassure me I'll eventually hit puberty always start with a deep sigh or yawn as he's leafing through a medical journal, then end with a distracted promise that I'll soon be a "pimply, awkward, screechy-voiced troll" just like my classmates.

Thanks, Dad.

I guess he's impatient on the subject because he's a doctor. No such thing as someone never hitting puberty, he says. But I'm not so sure. I've seen all his medical books and *American Medical Association* journals documenting super-rare disorders and diseases (like the diagram of this dude with a scrotum that must weigh about fifty pounds and the baby born with a brain outside its skull). I'm willing to bet that somewhere out there is a super-rare disorder where a kid never hits puberty. And someone has to be the victim of that disorder, so why not me?

Someone my size has to be rabbity to survive the school hallways; darting around even the smallest spaces, avoiding hip checks, shoulder jams, and clumsy attempts at wall smearing. The most dangerous time comes immediately after the last bell when dismissal feels a little like a prison riot.

Nikes laced tight for the Dodge & Sprint, I drop off some books at my locker, avoid a not-so-accidental kick as I pass the Hacky Sack circle, and then hurry downstairs to the team locker rooms to get ready for gymnastics practice.

Entering the boys' locker room is sort of like entering a dog kennel with extra butt-crack thrown in for good measure. A toxic fog of sweat-mildew-pee-fart-bleach turns all of us into mouth breathers. Prehistoric sweat accumulates on the floor and walls like old coats of varnish accompanied by the more recent animal stink of too many guys trapped in a windowless gas chamber. Add to this the guys who peel wet gym clothes off still-dripping bodies and stuff them directly into a dark, barely ventilated locker to ferment for a few days before unleashing them on the rest of us. Once weaponized, these T-shirts, jockstraps, socks, and shorts may cause bleeding from the ears, nose, and eyes. They get batted around like dead plague rats until they're either tossed in the garbage, rammed into a clogged toilet, or tied around the face of a small underclassman.

Vital facts: Of the three boys' sports programs in the fall season, football controlls most of the real estate. The varsity football team has its very own smelly locker room but the players enjoy slumming in the general locker room so they can terrorize the rest of us. The general team locker room is reserved for the junior varsity and JJV football teams. There are also two small, one-bench locker rooms off to the sides. The first is reserved for gymnastics. The second is reserved for cross-country runners. Those poor cross-country runners. Being a gymnast in a lair full of football players is rough, but not nearly as bad as what the cross-country runners suffer. Nervous as deer, they change hurriedly before scampering off in hopes of avoiding the alligator eye of a lurking JV football player angry he didn't make the varsity squad. The cross-country runners don't stick together in a pack like the gymnasts do—this is their biggest mistake.

I enter the main locker room just in time to spot a freshman cross-country runner, tiny as me, getting pinballed pretty good between three varsity football players. Distracted by their prey, the three miss me sneaking into the gymnastics team room to change. It's the same three varsity members who have stalked our lockers all week: Scott Miller, the Knights' starting quarterback; Tom Jankowski, his offensive tackle; and Mike Studblatz, a defensive linebacker.

In the gymnasts' locker room, Bruce Nguyen, our captain, sits on the bench, winding tape around his wrist while frowning. Already changed, he wears gray sweatpants and a black T-shirt with the sleeves cut off. He's a specialist on rings, which takes muscle. Bruce's biceps and shoulders look like someone's stuffed oranges and grapefruits under his skin. He could pose on the cover of one of those bodybuilding magazines, except he's only five foot two. As captain, Bruce normally offers a friendly greeting to all of us, but today he keeps to himself. I nod to the other guys and change fast, embarrassed by my nakedness. None of us can help overhearing what's going on just outside the team room.

"Hey, runt, if you're such a fast runner, how come Studblatz caught you so easy?" It's Scott Miller's voice. "You think a little runt like you should be able to represent our school?"

"Please . . . I'm going to be late for practice," comes the faltering voice.

"Think I give a crap? Think we care about whether you're late for your little jack-off session with all your pansy-ass teammates?"

"Please . . ."

The clank of metal tells me they just smashed him into the lockers. I know the sound well from personal experience.

"Please . . . let me go . . ." I hear sniffling now and know that sound equally well, know how crappy the bullying feels. But all I can do is be thankful it's him and not me.

"Lookit his skinny little butt in those shorts. Looks like a little girl. Lookit him shake. Tom, yank down his shorts. Yeah. Lookit. The runt thought he had a pubic hair until he pissed out of it. What kinda sport takes a boy without any hair on him?"

"Pl-please . . ." Little cries replace everything else. I make sure the drawstring on my own sweatpants is double-knotted. No one's going to do *that* to me. Bruce is still winding a roll of white athletic tape around his wrists—way more than he needs—to prevent bone splints. We have boxes and boxes of the white tape and a few of the guys use it up like toilet paper.

"Dipshits," Bruce mutters under his breath. Vance Fisher, Paul Kim, Bill Gradley, Larry Menderson, and I stand around, pretending to get dressed even though we're ready to go. All of us small in our own way.

"What does Coach Brigs feed his goons?" Gradley asks under his breath.

"Something you need a prescription for," Fisher answers.

"Come on, guys," Bruce says, and we follow him. We might be small, but we are a pack, and packs are a safe bet. We turn out of the room in time to find Tom Jankowski pushing the cross-country runner belly-down on the pine bench and Mike Studblatz yanking his shorts and jock-strap down past his knees. Scott Miller's snickering. The kid's face, turned sideways on the bench, is bright red. He sees us and he's not hoping for help. He's expecting us to join in the laughter and humiliation. That's how it works.

Bruce slows. "What the hell are you doing?" he asks the three varsity football players. That he says anything startles me and makes me proud of my captain all at once.

"Why do you care, pussy?" Tom Jankowski asks, daring Bruce to admit he actually cares. Caring is for the weak. Bruce shrugs his shoulders.

"I don't. But it's weird you like to pull down boys' pants," Bruce answers. "Maybe Chrissy would find that interesting, Scott. It would be a shame if the homecoming couple broke up because the quarterback likes feeling up freshman boys."

Scott's eyes narrow and so do Jankowski's. But they let the kid go. The boy tugs up his pants without saying anything and bolts out of the locker room.

"You faggots try spreading lies about this to anyone and you're all dead. You understand, Chink Kong?"

Bruce is Vietnamese-American, so Scott thinks his joke is really, *really* hysterical. Paul Kim is Korean-American, so I'm guessing both he and Bruce are laughing hard on the inside.

"Yeah, chink-faggot!" Jankowski echos like a toilet bowl fart. "Mind your own business."

"*I'm* the faggot?" Bruce asks, ignoring the chink part. His voice isn't so calm anymore and his face starts turning red. "Last I checked, it was you three playing grab-ass in the locker room." This gets Vance Fisher, our team's clown, laughing. Bruce is getting into dangerous territory. Jankowski and Studblatz are huge, but worse than that, they are just plain mean. And Scott, their leader, is cruel. You hear it in his laugh and what he finds funny—basically things involving torture. Jankowski and Studblatz step over to Bruce. We monkeys circle around the three gorillas, keeping our distance but not retreating. Larry Menderson sidles down the hallway toward the gymnasium, ready to run and call the rest of our team for help.

"Don't talk again," Jankowski growls. "You understand?" He pokes a heavy finger into Bruce's chest. As strong as our captain is, he looks puny compared to the overstuffed lineman, but as Bruce stretches his flushed neck to try to meet Jankowski's face eye-to-eye I can tell he is way past logic. If Tom pokes Bruce's chest again, it'll be like pressing a detonate button. I cringe as Tom pulls back his finger just enough to poke Bruce one more time in T minus three . . . two . . . one . . .

Click-click-click . . .

The sound of approaching football cleats on cement pauses doomsday. The man-giant, Kurt Brodsky, in a varsity Knights' football uniform—shoulder pads spanning across him like vulture wings—turns the corner and fills all remaining space and light. This time his eyes do not search the floor, but land like concrete blocks on every single one of us. His scars look wicked cool. He seems capable of anything.

"Suh-suh-Scott," he says, addressing Miller, somehow knowing he's the leader. "Cuh-cuh-cuh-Coach sent me to fuh-fuh-fuh-find you. Ta-ta-ta-told me to introduce muh-muh-muh-myself after delivering his muh-muh-muh-message."

Kurt Brodsky, either because of, or in spite of, his stuttering, has everyone's full attention. Miller, Jankowski, and Studblatz, faces full of confusion, blink dully and nod in unison for him to continue. Actually, we might all be doing that.

"Cuh-cuh-cuh-Coach suh-suh-said, 'Tu-tu-tell them suh-suh-suh-sonsabuh-buh-bitches if they don't have their asses out on that field in fuh-fuh-fuh-five minutes, they can ruh-ruh-run sprints until muh-muh-midnight.'"

"Who the fuck are you?" Jankowski woofs.

"Kuh-kuh-kuh-Kurt Buh-buh-Brodsky. Your new fuh-fuh-fullback."

Miller, Jankowski, and Studblatz all cock their heads as if hearing their master's sharp whistle. They push past us in their hurry to get back to their locker room and change into their practice uniforms, not bothering to wait for their new teammate.

KURT

There he is," Coach Brigs says, waving me into his office while his other hand holds a phone up to his ear. "Bibi, our future star has finally arrived," he tells the phone, winking at me, getting his fill of my face, taking in my scars without apology. He did the same thing—wink and everything—the first time we met. I try forcing a smile, but the best I can do is get the left corner of my mouth to lift a little. Coach gestures for me to sit down on an old vinyl couch with cracks in the seat cushions while he nods to something said on the other end of the phone. My butt hits the couch, and it keeps on sinking until I'm sure it's about to go clear through to the floor. When it finally stops, I'm almost squatting. My knees poke up toward my chin, making my high-water pants ride up even farther, almost to my calf.

"Bibi, that Jumbotron is going up in our stadium. I don't care if they have to slash the budget for those other sports to cover it. Hell, half of 'em aren't real sports anyways. Everyone knows our program generates the revenue. We subsidize the rest of them. Without football they don't exist. That Jumbotron is coming. Bet on it! My baby is coming. Tell the alumni association it's the best damn recruitment tool around. Hell, we'll have half the state scrambling to move into our school district to get their boys in our program. We'll beat the pants off any charter schools and double—maybe triple—state contribution revenue. Property values will go through the roof. And the school board'll get their cut in increased property taxes . . ."

I wait for him to finish his phone call and watch players pass by outside the large window made of shatterproof glass—the kind that has chicken wire sandwiched inside it—separating Coach's office from the rest of the varsity team locker room. Inside his office, the wall behind Coach Brigs's desk is filled with team photos going back at least two decades. Trophy shelves line two other walls, brightening the painted cinder block with cheap-looking gold figurines, all of them helmeted with arms cocked back to throw a football. The maroon and gold paint, the team colors, must've been applied right after they built the place, based on the gray murk dulling them now.

"It's about time we got our hands on you, son," Coach Brigs says after finally hanging up the phone. He stands up and comes around his desk, and it takes me a second to get unfolded from the couch. When I do he shakes my hand, gripping it hard and pumping it twice before dropping it to put his hands on my shoulders. He stands there staring at me, his eyes returning again to my scars before traveling over the rest of my body. "You been eating enough?" he asks. "You look like you might've lost some weight since last we talked in person. We got some great supplements. We'll get you on a program. Assistant Coach Stein will set you up. Need to make sure my soldiers stay strong and healthy."

I nod at him.

"Now, I talked with your foster mama," he continues, still eyeballing my arms and legs. "I told her I'd send you home with a little something to pass along to her, make sure she feeds you enough. We need big Knights on this team. It's a tough division. We got to take care of our own, you understand that, son? We are one family here. No enemies in the ranks, only soldiers and family. We gonna take care of you, now, Kurtis, because we expect great things from you. All of us. Not just me and my staff, not just your teammates, but your fans. You heard me, your fans. You watch the students' eyes light up when they see you coming down the hallway after we get a few wins under our belt. You walk like a hero because you are a hero in their eyes. You're going to be part of our great tradition of fine, upstanding men that others look up to and want to be like. And if you turn out to be a real star, like I got a hunch you will be, then the sky's the limit. You can have anything you want, just about. Great warriors deserve their just deserts." And that's when he finally takes his hands off my shoulders. He delivers his speech close enough to my face that I smell every cup of coffee he drank this week. Still,

I ain't about to find fault with his words. In one minute, he's offered me more than anyone else ever has.

Coach Brigs goes back around to his desk and opens up his very own locker and pulls out two jerseys: one white with maroon piping and numbers; one maroon with gold piping and numbers. Coach Brigs tosses me the maroon jersey while he holds up the white one, his fingers pinching each shoulder and spreading it open for me to read. Above the number 27 is the name BRODSKY running across the back. I want to think it's stupid and that it just makes me a dumb animal they've branded, but the fact remains that seeing my very own name on a team jersey— a real jersey, not something Lamar and I made out of old T-shirts and a permanent marker—is pretty cool. It *does* make me feel special. Playing for Lincoln, we never got jerseys with names.

"We expect nothing but greatness from you, son. And I know you won't let us down. Not one bit. Welcome to the Knights." And Coach Brigs flings the white jersey over his desk. I snatch it out of the air, this time feeling both ends of my mouth curl up into a smile that pulls on my scar. "Your locker number is the same as your jersey number," he says. "How's that for serendipity?"

I nod again, not really knowing what the word *serendipity* means, but promising myself I'll look it up as soon as I get a chance.

"Now, you missed our summer camp two-a-days so it might take you a bit to get into our system. Just go where you're told and do what me, Assistant Coach Stein, or the trainers tell you and you'll be just fine."

Without realizing it, I've brought the maroon jersey up to my nose as Coach keeps talking. I inhale the clean smell of brand-new fabric mixed with the toasty tang of the silk-screened numbers and name—my name—customized at a print shop. Coach Brigs stops talking for a second and watches me. That's when I realize what I'm doing. His eyes twinkle a little and it makes me feel . . . kind of . . . good. Foolish, but good.

"Now look here," he says, pulling out a plain white envelope from his desk drawer and handing it over to me. On its front is Patti's name in blue pen, but it takes me a second to realize it's her because the envelope reads "Ms. Dornf." "I want you to hand this over to your foster mama soon as you walk through that door tonight, you understand? It's sealed up and I'm the one who sealed it and I'm the one who knows exactly what's in it. So when I call her in a few days and ask whether or not she got my envelope, I don't want to hear her say, 'What envelope?' and it turns out that you were just another blockhead that forgot all about the envelope—either intentionally or accidentally. You go home after practice and you give this to her right away and you tell her Coach Brigs sends his regards and will give her a call in a few days."

"Yessssssir," I say, staring at the envelope, thinking it might be the most valuable thing I've ever been entrusted with.

"Now, I don't normally do this, but I am very aware of your situation, and it's partly for that reason that I have such high hopes for you, Kurtis. A boy coming from your station in life, to make himself into a fine, upstanding young man, well, he needs to be applauded and encouraged from time to time. And it's for that reason that I'm going to give you a little something here on the side to help you out. Now, this is just between us, you understand." And Coach Brigs pulls out a silver money clip and slips out four bills that I'm too nervous to look at directly. "And if anyone ever asks you, well, I never handed you nothing. I wish't it weren't that way but sometimes the bureaucrats get a little too stuffy with their rules when all someone is trying to do is help out a kid in need. This here's a little pocket money for you, to help you fit in, to help you adjust a little bit. Most of the kids that go to this school, God love 'em, are too spoiled to ever understand a single thing about wanting for something or going hungry or not getting the newest gadget or latest gizmo. I ain't giving you something these kids don't get ten times over from their coddling mamas and daddies already. That's why most of 'em couldn't even think of playing this game, even if they were the size of Godzilla. They're all too soft. Start bawling when Daddy even looks at them crosswise. But I've seen you play, Kurtis, and I know just how tough you are, son. You play like you got fire in your veins. I like your style. And I want to keep my soldier happy. So if you need to go out and buy yourself some new pants that fit you a little better, maybe a few shirts from the mall, well, this money is to help you do just that. Nothing much, nothing fancy, just a little something to help out."

He palms the money and clasps my hand again, shaking it firmly. When he lets go, the bills sit nestled in my grip. Still afraid to look, I slip them into my front pocket. Thankful and surprised by Coach's generosity, I can't help feeling it's more wrong than just breaking a few "stuffy, bureaucratic rules." I don't feel bad enough to give 'em back, though.

"And if you want a pretty girl to take you shopping for clothes, you just let your quarterback know. He'll introduce you to whoever you'd like to meet. You're in good hands now, son. We take care of our own."

"Sssssir. Thuh-thuh-thank you, ssssssir."

"I see someone raised you right," Coach grins. "Put those good manners in you . . ."

At night he'd come into our room, pants half unzipped, coiled belt dangling from his fist like a strangled snake.

". . . but no need to be so formal, son," Coach Brigs continues. "You can call me Coach."

I nod a few times to fill the silence. Coach slaps my right shoulder hard, like he forgot I'm not wearing pads yet.

"Now go get your stuff and get ready for practice."

"Yesssssssssir." I open his door to leave.

"Oh, yeah, one last thing, Kurtis," Coach says.

I wait.

"Scott Miller's your quarterback. He's a top prospect. Letters coming into my office almost every day asking my help to sign him to some pretty good college programs. Tom Jankowski's an all-state offensive tackle. Letters piling up for him as well. And Mike Studblatz is our all-division linebacker two seasons running. Big Ten coaches love watching him hit. These three are also team captains and they're thick as thieves. These are my boys and I will lay down my life, in a manner of speaking, for them because they give me every ounce of themselves on game day. But they've let all that recruiting sweet talk go to their heads this last year. Started showing up late for practice last three days in a row, ever since classes started. I don't know what they're doing but I'd appreciate it if you'd go find them, introduce yourself to them, and give them this message from me, word for word . . . "

DANNY

5

In the gym, I am somebody.

In the gym, school stops at the thick, fireproof doors, held back by air that tastes of chalk, turns spit into paste, cakes the inside of nostrils, and packs under fingernails in a white powder. Buzzing halogen lamps, hanging from the thirty-five-foot-high rafters, turn everything the pink-orange of a beach sunset. Wall-to-wall foam mats forgive my mistakes, offering no judgment, only a cushion when I fall.

"Gentlemen," Coach Nelson announces as the team starts warm-up stretches on the thin tumbling mats, "we're running sets today."

"Sets" are when my teammates and I throw ourselves through the air, battle gravity like X Games superchamps, and occasionally crash and burn. Drop a so-called real jock in here and watch them assume the fetal position while we blast through circus tricks they can't even figure out. The jungle of toys waits patiently for our arrival after school lets out. High bars, parallel bars, rings, pommel horse, vaults, and springboards. Here my secret plan—revealed to no one, not even Bruce—hatches:

1. State champion on high bar by junior year.
2. Team captain by junior or senior year.
3. State all-around champion by senior year.
4. Full-ride athletic scholarship.

Number four is the one that really counts. Number four makes it legit. Number four turns virtual daydreams into a lotto jackpot, lets me laugh at everyone thinking "Danny who?" while I start a new life in a man's body really fucking far from this place.

Full-ride scholarship. Full-ride scholarship. Full-ride scholarship.

I whisper the phrase three times every day while stretching, sending it out to the gymnastic gods, hoping they're listening.

"Danny?" Coach Nelson gets my attention. He sits among us in a hurdler's stretch, both arms reaching out to touch his toes. Coach Nelson knows way more about rock climbing than gymnastics but he does his best to offer tips and advice and makes a good spot-catcher if one of us is about to crash. He keeps his long hair pulled back into a ponytail and the weathered skin around his eyes is spiderwebbed with squint lines. Vance nicknamed him "Uncle Jesus" but he looks more like a retired special ops officer who's renounced all things military, because that's exactly what he is. He served over in Afghanistan, though he won't discuss it. Bruce told us that when he was a freshman—Coach Nelson's first year coaching and teaching at Oregrove after returning from the war—he had a buzz cut. Coach just never bothered cutting his hair again.

"You going to try that suicide catch again today?" Coach asks me.

"Yeah," I say, grinning, liking his description.

"Look, squirt. I don't think my heart can take watching you miss that bar again."

Cool, I think. My new trick must be pretty nasty if Coach's actually worried about me. He's the only adult I don't mind calling me squirt, either. He calls everyone on the team names like kid, squirt, half-pint, headache, peanut brain or—if he's in a really good mood—little shit.

"You're tough, Coach," I say. "You can handle it."

Just like Bruce is our team's master on the rings, I'm the team's master on high bar. I convinced my dad to pay for private club practice during the off-season, so, unlike most of the other guys, I train all year. Now, I'd never say this out loud, but . . . I'm pretty good. Of course, no one outside the gym has any idea, including, I think, my dad. It's okay. All that matters is the scholarship. That'll make it official.

"You're up, Danny," Coach Nelson calls to me. "It's okay if you want to skip the trick."

"No it's not," Bruce says more to Coach than to me. Bruce and Coach are standing below me on either side of the high bar. If I miss the catch, they make sure I don't do a head-plant into the mats. We have a spotting harness attached to ropes and pulleys that hang from the rafters, but the ropes get in the way for this trick. It's not the floor

L
E
V
E
R
A
G
E

30

I'm worried about smacking, anyway. Crashing into the high bar feels like being hit by a baseball bat. If you're lucky, it's not your face.

"Make it!" Bruce barks at me like a drill sergeant. I nod to him—*message received*—and kick up to a handstand on the high bar. Then gravity takes over. I help it by jamming hard through the bottom of the swing and looping back up around the steel pipe. The leather grips only partially dull the bite of the chalky metal digging into the thickened skin of my fingers and palms.

"You got it," Bruce encourages as my legs whip past him and Coach Nelson on my way back over the bar. "Hit it!"

I kick my legs harder, tighten my belly, feel air breeze past my ears and ankles. The torque is pulling at my grip, tearing at my hands, itching to rip me off the bar. I crank even faster.

"Easy, Danny," Coach cautions. Too late. I whip around the bar until I can feel my fingers about to peel off. At the top of the arc, I let go. I'm weightless, feeling my thighs powering me up toward the rafters, body fighting hard to break orbit while my neck cranes backward. I'm searching, searching as the world spins around me once, twice, I'm searching and throw my hands out, feeling, hoping, reaching . . .

My hands slap the chalky steel. My fingers instinctively grab tight and hold on. I caught it. *I caught it!* I'm back on the bar swinging down and up around again. *I did it!* My legs snap me up and over the pipe for a smooth follow-through loop.

Bruce howls for me.

"Hot damn, Danny!"

"I'll be an SOB." Coach starts clapping. "Pigs are flying somewhere."

I hear Fisher whistle and other guys clapping. I do one more loop and then let go, tossing off a lazy flip before floating down from the sky onto my feet. Bruce reaches me first, raising both arms for high fives. Two powdery chalk-clouds pop out from our slapping hands.

"Outstanding!"

"That was sweet, bro," Fisher adds. Chalk powder settles over his raven-black hair, turning it old-man gray.

Coach Nelson offers me a small salute. "You could clean up in state on high bar if you keep that up." Then Coach turns to Fisher. "Vance, you work a little harder, like Danny here, and stop worrying about your fake ID and maybe we could count on some consistency in your pommel horse routines."

Ronnie, one of two freshmen on the team and the only guy actually smaller than me, approaches as I'm pulling off my leather grips.

"That's one of the coolest things I've ever seen," he offers.

"Thanks," I say, feeling too good to ignore him like I usually do because he's so shy and small and sometimes the sight of him irritates me in a way I'm not sure I understand.

K U R T

I n full pads and helmet, with autumn still feeling like summer, the players around me pant like sled dogs ten minutes into the tackle drills. The sun's scorching and sweat's running off me like rainwater but I ain't winded like the others. Getting bigger, faster, stronger comes as natural to me as stuttering. When you got no money and home sucks, the free community gym and library are what's to do besides watching TV, and Crud Bucket pretty much ruined TV for me. He loved it; loved drinking in front of it, loved talking back to it as he drained a twelve-pack, readying himself for one of us, rotating us to keep the bruising spread out.

Back at the other place, I used to sneak over the neighborhood school's fenced field and run bleachers. Or I'd run wind sprints on their track. But mostly I hit the weights.

First time I ever tried it, I took to weight lifting. All I ever needed to know was that it made you bigger and stronger. And if you got big enough, you'd never suffer someone else's temper ever again. No matter where the state shuffled me, I could always hunt down a weight room, stack the plates, and make all that iron rise again and again, muscles screaming with that final rep, me pushing even harder, imagining all the hurt I'd visit on *Him* when I finally—

"Brodsky!" Coach Brigs barks, interrupting my favorite revenge fantasy. "You got cotton in your ears? I said I want you in on this drill. Need to see what my new fullback's bringing to the table." I nod, feel my helmet shift down on my forehead. "The play is twenty-one split," Coach continues. "You fake the handoff from Scott and open a hole for Terrence coming up behind you. Full contact. Let's see you create some space on the line."

"Yes, sir!" I holler. On the field, behind a face mask, I hardly ever stutter. Gnawing on my mouth guard, I line up off quarterback's left and glance over to make sure Terrence, the running back, is on my right.

"Studblatz! Peters!" Coach barks over to the other side. "I just gave you the play. Won't get any easier for a defense than that. I wanna see you two stuff this big ol' sumbitch!"

Scott Miller chomps out a hyena laugh. "Yeah," he echoes in a way I don't appreciate. "Stuff that ugly sumbitch!"

I find the back of Jankowski, our offensive tackle. He looks bigger than he did in the locker room. Glad he's on my side of the ball during real games. If he does his job right, creates daylight, then I won't have to. But this is a drill and Coach wants me to make a statement on my own. Guess it's his way of introducing me to the team.

Something I learned in foster care is that power and size matter. So does toughness. All three are like math variables. Increasing any of them is a good thing if they're on your side of the equation. Take Lamar, for instance. Not much size, not much power, but *lots* of toughness. He'd back down boys three years older than us just by clawing the air and spitting like a wildcat and telling them they'd lose an eye if they so much as touched us. No matter how bad he might have needed it, he kept his inhaler in his pocket until we were alone. Then, bent over, hands on his knees, wheezing hard but smiling like he'd just been handed the heavyweight title, he'd suck on his inhaler, look up at me, and shake his head. *Boy, look at those feet. You gonna be huge. Big as an ox one day. Just you wait. If I had your size, I could rule the world. I'd show ol' Crud where he could stick his thing.* Lamar talked that way all the time, talked as if for all his toughness and my big feet there wasn't a final variable neither one of us could ever match: cruelty.

I look across the line and see Studblatz and Peters itching to double-team me now that they know the play, both grinning through their masks, both hungry to flatten me, give me a real warm welcome. A shudder runs up to my skull, twisting my neck as an imaginary yoke comes undone. I stare back at Studblatz until the face under his helmet is the man that used to enter my room at night reeking of whiskey and cigarettes, belt buckle already rising, waiting to make its mark. The right toe of my cleat digs into the turf, creating a starting block. The world beyond me and him melts into the color of fire. The source of all pain, all hurt, crouches in front of me, begging to be snuffed out of existence.

Quarterback calls out his cadence, then lets loose one sharp cry. I hear no more. My thighs expand as I lower, understanding all about leverage and the physics of unearthing bodies. I bull's-eye him under his chest, aiming for that crease at his waist, feeling his legs crab-scramble too late. My shoulder catches his gut while Peters, an afterthought, tries wrapping me up at the calves. Peters catches a pumping knee under his chin strap and drops like a stone. My target ain't as lucky. Folded over the rising plank of my shoulder pad, his feet leave the ground as I drive him backward. Legs airborne, his feet kick in tandem for the ground. Rushing toward annihilation, I welcome the hug of gravity as our combined weight accelerates. I ride big boy onto his back, body-slamming him into the grass, his chest absorbing my shoulder, deflating like a used air bag. First sound coming through my helmet's ear hole is a satisfying "Ooofff!"

Pushing off him to stand up, Crud Bucket vanishes, leaving behind only the smoldering remains of Studblatz. He doesn't move. The wind's knocked out of him, maybe more. Terrence sprints past with the ball for about ten yards and then slows. No one's watching Terrence, though.

I feel and smell them: the pack. They watch me from under their helmets, not saying anything until their leader speaks. Unsure how to respond, they wait for a signal to attack or accept. Just like first day at group home.

"Jesus!" Scott Miller cackles. "I think Studblatz might be pregnant after that one."

Assistant Coach Stein runs over to Studblatz, kneels down to him, and shines a penlight in his eyes.

"My, my, my," Coach Brigs says, holding his chin in his hand.

"Damn, boy!" Pullman, one of the linemen, whistles.

"Walk it off, 'Blatz. Walk it off." Rondo, our center, chuckles.

Coach claps his hands to restart the team.

I am numb with release.

"Hey, man." Terrence jogs up to me and slaps me on the butt. "I got a feeling you and me are gonna be real tight. *Real* tight. Shit, man. I ain't no homo but you do that for me in the games and I'll be riding your ass all the way to the end zone and a scoring title."

Size. Power. Ferocity. Establish you have the most of all three and everyone leaves you alone. That's how you survive those places. And if you find a brother like Lamar, a brother you trust with your life, to watch your back, then you've doubled your odds.

D A N N Y

What the hell are you freaks doing in here?" Mike Studblatz challenges.

I was wondering the same thing when Coach Nelson led us into the heart of the gorilla cave. The varsity weight room is technically open to all team athletes, no matter what sport, but during fall season, the unspoken rule is no one comes in here except football players—until today. My eyes wander from Studblatz to another gorilla pacing in front of a mirror, holding thick dumbbells, pumping them up and down.

"Get some, bitch," Tom Jankowski huffs at his reflection, focused on the image of his log-arms bulging with each dumbbell curl, missing the nervous monkeys skittering past him, staying as close to our coach as possible.

Coach Nelson walks right up to Mike Studblatz and

yanks out his earbuds by their wire. Studblatz's eyes open wide in surprise and his mouth drops. Coach Nelson cuts him off before his little brain can think to speak.

"Careful how you talk to a teacher, Mike. I've just given you your warning."

Mike stands there—stupid—but doesn't say anything.

"Cool," Vance Fisher whispers, his eyes twinkling. Fisher is the type who likes trouble, even if it may lead to getting his ass kicked. About now most of the other gorillas have stopped grunting and heaving long enough to notice our little group gawking at them. We stick close to Coach Nelson and his protective sphere of adult authority.

Tom Jankowski stops cursing at himself in the mirror and drops his dumbbells onto the rubberized floor with a loud boom that silences the room. He turns to face us. "This is our house," he huffs. He doesn't look like he cares that Coach Nelson is an adult and a teacher and, technically, off-limits.

"Actually," Coach Nelson levels his voice at Jankowski, keeping it steady and strong enough to be heard over a few remaining clinks and clanks as other players rack their weights and gather around us, "this is our house, as well."

"Hey, Ted." Assistant Coach Stein steps into the free weight area from the connecting room where rows of bench presses lie like empty morgue tables. "What seems to be the problem?"

"No problem, Frank." Coach Nelson smiles and holds up his hands. "We need to work on some strength training, same as your boys. I figured now would be a great time to teach both teams a little lesson in economics and accounting while I'm at it."

"I'm not following," Coach Stein says.

"Let me explain," Coach Nelson replies. "I just found out our team's operating budget all but disappeared. That means no money for buses to our away meets and no money to pay the judges who score those meets. Found out the same thing's happening to cross-country and swimming."

"What's that got to do with my team's weight room?" Coach Stein asks. His players cinch closer around us. Like Coach Stein, I'm wondering what the hell Coach Nelson's talking about. So's everyone else. Tom Jankowski and Mike Studblatz are both breathing like draft horses and shifting their weight like they can't wait to stomp us. There's only one player not standing around, not paying attention, and it's the new guy, Kurt Brodsky. He's strapped into the squat rack machine, ignoring all of us while pushing up a warping bar of steel plates equivalent to the mass of a small planet.

"*Our* weight room," Coach Nelson corrects their coach. "Turns out all the money's gone to paying for that shiny new TV going up in the football stadium, that nifty new Jumbotron. So here's where the economics and accounting lesson comes into play. You gotta pay for what you take in the real world. Since football took our money, we expect football to start sharing some of the wealth. So we'll be using the weight room for the season."

We will?! I gulp. *No way I'm coming into this place again.*

"Like hell!" Studblatz shouts. Coach Nelson turns on him fast and moves close, jamming his finger up into Mike's Adam's apple. "Son, I already warned you about talking to your teachers in a disrespectful manner. Now, I'm not going to warn you again."

Coach Nelson's shorter than Studblatz but he's layered with wiry rock climber muscle. Mike Studblatz, as angry as he's getting, holds his tongue for the moment.

"This weight room is for *real* athletes," Tom Jankowski tells our coach. Jankowski keeps making his hands into fists and opening them like he's seriously considering taking a run at Coach Nelson.

"You're right," Coach Nelson counters. "And that's why I'm not sure my gymnasts should even tolerate you guys in this room. Everyone knows the weakest gymnast is a hell of a lot stronger than your average football player."

What?! What is he doing to us? I'm thinking. *He's going to get us all killed.*

"Ted." Coach Stein holds up his hands and he's chuckling.

"You have *got* to be kidding," says Scott Miller, the Knights' quarterback. He steps forward and just stares at all of us like we're insane. Except for Tom Jankowski and Mike Studblatz, the other football players seem more amused by our coach than anything. I don't think it's funny, though. We should not be here. We should be in the gym—*our* gym—working on sets.

"Tell you what," Coach Nelson addresses mostly Scott Miller and Coach Stein. "I'll make a deal with you right now. One of our guys against one of your guys on one exercise in this room. If our guy demonstrates superior strength—like I know he will—we come in here whenever we want."

All the football players—except Kurt Brodsky, still

doing his own Atlas-lifting-the-world thing—erupt with laughter. Meanwhile, Bruce and my teammates look like I feel—miserable and sensing impending humiliation.

"Coach?" Bruce cautions, but Coach Nelson holds up his hand to quiet him. My teammates look beyond worried and Ronnie Gunderson just may crap his pants. Only Fisher, a natural-born con man, appears relaxed. He's enjoying himself as much as the football players, like he senses where Coach Nelson is going with this whole thing. Wish he'd tell me.

"So whaddya say?" Coach Nelson asks.

"Coach Brigs isn't here to make any deals," Coach Stein says.

"Forget that," Scott interrupts. "This is easy."

"I thought you'd approve," Coach Nelson says to Scott. "Okay, I'll pick the exercise, something easily done in this weight room. After all, we don't want to take advantage of you fellas."

Snickers break out among the football players.

"You get to pick the competitors," Coach Nelson continues. "One player from your team and one from our team."

A new round of laughter erupts as dozens of football players' fingers start pointing at Ronnie and me. We're the smallest on the team and, they assume, the weakest. I'm starting to get angrier and angrier, mostly at Coach Nelson. I feel my face grow hot with embarrassment. Ronnie steps closer like he wants my company, but all I want is to get farther away from him. I hate him at the moment, hate feeling like they think we're the same. We're not the same. Ronnie's a punk freshman who just started gymnastics.

I'm aiming for state champion in high bar. I'm going to be a full-ride scholarship athlete one day. We're not the same at all.

"Deal," Scott Miller says.

"You all heard him, fellas," Coach Nelson announces like a carnival barker. "Deal. We've got plenty of witnesses, so neither side can go back on it."

"This sucks," Bruce gripes. Guess he's not in on the plan, either.

"Okay," Coach Nelson announces with a smile. "Pick your competitors."

"This is too easy," Scott Miller says. "Jankowski, crush these little girls and try not to yawn while you're doing it."

The weight room bursts out in full-throated laughter as ginormous Jankowski, layered with a thick slab of butterball fat, steps forward, his hands still clenching into fists. His arms, neck, legs, and butt are huge and can easily squat, bench, curl, throw, punch, kick, or slam any of us into oblivion. He's also got a hefty gut that overhangs his sweatpants like he's about seven months pregnant and due to deliver a baby keg.

"Solid choice." Coach Nelson smiles. "Now pick one of our guys—anyone you want."

Whistles, shouts, and woofs as more fingers aim at me and Ronnie like daggers.

"Pick the midget pussies, pick the midget pussies," one of the players shouts, meaning either me or Ronnie.

"Twin needledicks. Give 'em one of the twin needledicks." Someone guffaws. I feel abandoned, feel like no one in the world exists for me, feel like I did the day Dad told me Mom died. More than I hate all those football players, more than I hate Ronnie Gunderson, I hate Coach Nelson for putting me through this. I trusted him and he does *this* to me?

"That one," Scott sneers, his finger casually aiming somewhere between Ronnie and me as if either choice is a guaranteed victory for his side, so who cares?

"Danny," Coach barks. "You're up. Let's go."

I hope Coach feels my eyes burning into him, hope he feels my hatred boiling into his lungs, giving him tuberculosis as we speak. Teammates push me forward with that better-you-than-me sorry backslap until I'm almost pressing into Jankowski's sweaty, fat belly. The angry breath coming out of his nostrils streams down on me like hot stank.

"Okay, let's see, here. We pick the exercise," Coach Nelson says, steepling his hands together as if in great concentration. "Hmmm. . . ." He scans the large weight room before pausing for dramatic effect. The football players and my teammates quiet down with anticipation, waiting expectantly for the challenge.

"I've got it!" Coach Nelson snaps his fingers. "That one over there. That's it." All eyes follow where he's looking and we're staring at a pull-up bar bolted into the wall ten feet off the ground. "Hanging leg lifts," Coach says. "*That's* the challenge."

The football players just stand there, blinking, not exactly sure what hanging leg lifts are. No one does them except gymnasts. That's when I hear a lone laugh.

"Beautiful, Coach," Vance Fisher says, and keeps laughing. "Freakin' beautiful."

Vance Fisher laughs because he knows I'm going to win

this contest easy. Humiliation simmering into anger, I plan on stuffing all their faces with a crushing loss. But that still won't make right what Coach has done to me.

"What's a leg lift?" Jankowski asks. Coach explains it's an exercise for your abdominals. You hang from a bar and—keeping your arms and legs straight—lift your toes straight up until they meet your hands. You can do all the sit-ups and crunches in the world but unless you work this specific exercise, you won't be able to do it. You also need good flexibility in your hamstrings or you end up fighting your own muscles. With Tom's gut and, I'm guessing, zero flexibility he'll be lucky to even do one. Tom jumps up to hang from the bar. He tries and tries and rests and tries again. Once his legs hit ninety degrees, he has to bend his knees to bring them any higher. The closest he comes is doing a single rep with totally bent legs. His teammates try. Coach gives all of them a chance, anyone who wants to can step right up to the bar. Only Terrence, their running back, and Sweeney, their wide receiver, can muscle out two reps and three reps each.

"Okay, Danny," Coach calls me over. "Get up here and put these wimps out of their misery." He winks at me but I'm still not happy with him. For a second, I think about faking that I can't do it, either. That would make the football players happy . . . or at least less angry, and it would teach Coach never to take me for granted and think it's okay to get everyone laughing at me. I step on the perch and grab the bar and hang from it. Bruce and Vance are nodding at me, smiling. So is Ronnie. I look away from him. All my teammates are counting on me. Then I look up and see Tom, Mike, and Scott watching me, their eyebrows pinching together in confusion, waiting. I slowly, smoothly lift my legs with perfect form until my toes tap the bar.

"Come *on!*" Scott moans as I lower my legs.

I lift my legs up and tap the bar again, and again and again . . . and again, and again. I do eighteen toe touches with perfect form before dropping off the bar. The most I've ever done in one set. Bruce and Vance knock knuckles in celebration. Gradley and Steve are slapping my shoulders. Ronnie punches my arm lightly and I accept it.

"Damn! These little dudes don't play around," Terrence, a star player for the Knights, says. Some of his teammates are nodding their heads in agreement. "I gotta start working my core like that."

"You *TRICKED* US!!!" The yell is so loud it pushes my hair up on my head. Everyone stops. We turn and find Mike Studblatz, face the color of a plum, steam practically rising out of his ears. His eyes are wild and ferocious and I'm sure he's about to lunge into our group and kill me, Coach, Bruce, and Vance, though maybe not in that order. Studblatz heaves a hundred-pound dumbbell off the rack and lifts it above his head and then hurls it toward us. We see it coming and step out of the way and it crashes like a meteor into a metal calf-raise machine. The noise is deafening.

"*Mike!*" Coach Stein shouts, trying to regain control.

"You *tricked* all of us!" Mike fumes. He's pacing back and forth and thumping his chest. He gets under a shoulder press machine and presses up two hundred and fifty pounds. His thick arms tremble and spit froths at the corners of his mouth. His eyes bounce around like he can't focus. "You. TRICKED. US!!!" he repeats, and heaves the weight up again and again. "This is real strength. Not *that!*"

"Frank," Coach Nelson snaps at Coach Stein, "you better get hold of your players."

Coach Stein starts to move in between the pulsing Studblatz and everyone else. Mike Studblatz picks up two more dumbbells and begins military-pressing them over his head and staring at us, like he's proving something other than that he's an animal. I'm pretty sure whatever he's imagining involves dismemberment. Coach Stein only gets so close and then stops, seeming wary himself. The other football players watch but don't move. Finally Scott Miller walks up to Studblatz and puts a hand to his chest.

"It's okay, big man, the pukes cheated us, they won't be coming in here."

"It's not a secret why he's acting that way," Coach Nelson speaks clearly for everyone to hear. "Frank, I know what you and Coach Brigs are giving these boys. Someone's gonna get hurt if you keep it up."

"Worry about your own team, Ted."

"*All of us*, Frank, are supposed to be on the *same* team," Coach Nelson says, and then he faces the circled group of football players. "That crap some of you are taking to get big and strong is the same thing they feed hogs and cattle before they slaughter 'em."

"That's enough," Coach Stein says. Coach Nelson raises an eyebrow at him.

"Let's go," Coach Nelson tells us. "We'll come back when they've settled down."

As we follow him out, Tom Jankowski grabs my arm

and yanks me away from my teammates. Coach Nelson, up ahead, is leaving without me, doesn't see me. I glance over and see Todd Pullman holding Ronnie Gunderson, his arm twisted up behind his back. Tom's big hand swallows my whole neck and starts squeezing the life out of me.

"Bet you think it's real funny what you just pulled," he says. "I'm gonna remember this. You and your little pussy friends are dead. You hear me? Dead. We are gonna bury you." The threat comes at me in a cloud of sour breath, and I feel my body freeze up, glance over, and only see Ronnie Gunderson in more pain as Todd Pullman jams his arm higher up his back. Just then, I see Coach Nelson turn back into the room, glance quickly around, and our eyes lock.

"JANKOWSKI!" Coach Nelson barks so loud the whole weight room vibrates. The grip around my neck magically releases, and I bolt for my coach, grateful and hating him at the same time. I'm trailed out of the weight room not only by Ronnie but also by the laughter of the other football players.

K U R T

I'm veering toward a far corner table, away from as many
people as possible, when Scott calls me out. "Brodsky!
Hey, Brodsky!" he shouts across the lunchroom. "Get over
here!"

Sitting on either side of him, two beautiful girls giggle
while picking at a plate of french fries, sending a spasm
of panic through my belly. Across the table from Scott sit
Jankowski and Studblatz. Both twist their thick, pimpled
necks to watch me over their shoulders.

"Brodsky! Whatsa matter? You got no love for your
quarterback?" Scott yells, waving me over. "What's wrong
with you? Studblatz ain't angry no more, are you, Stud?"
The plan to eat and leave unnoticed dies as every single
person in the lunchroom stops chewing, talking, listening
to music, drumming on tables, joking, texting, or laugh-

ing to wait and see where I'll sit. "Come on, man. My fullback's got to eat with me. Team rule. Get your ass over here."

I'd hoped to go unnoticed by sitting at the empty end of a table mostly populated by goths dressed all in black with pierced faces and skin the color of vampire flesh. Thanks to Scott, they spot my approach and stare at me like *I'm* the freak. One of the goths, a girl with spiky black hair and shaved eyebrows, wrinkles her nose so harshly I automatically tuck my own nose into my shoulder for a quick armpit whiff.

"What?" Scott asks real loud. "You gonna sit next to Count Dykeula, instead?"

I stand there, deciding, feeling all eyes on me.

"Brodsky, I ain't asking again," Scott shouts even louder, pretending to cry. The whole lunchroom—his personal audience—snickers. "You're going to hurt my feelings." He'll go on, I can tell, unless I come to him. Surrendering, I change course toward my quarterback's table. Scott jabs the redheaded girl, the one leaning against his arm, with a sharp elbow to her side that makes both her and me wince.

"Cindy, make some room for our fullback," Scott commands. Cindy slides over a space while Scott pats the empty bench next to him. "Sit down, man. Sit!"

Cindy's eyes do a little dance while taking in my scars. I squeeze my legs between the bench and table while she gets her fill. After I sit, Scott drapes an arm over my shoulders and leans close, talking with a mouth full of french fries.

"Oh, yeah, man," he says, "make some room. Let this

boy eat. Stuff it down your throat. We want you nice and big. I hear Ashville's got a defensive linebacker—Tommy, what's his name?"

"Chandre," Tom Jankowski answers. "Chandre Jackson."

"Yeah, Chandre Jackson. What kinda ghetto-ass name is Chandre? Anyway, I hear Chandre chomps down on fullbacks for breakfast, puts a little skull on his helmet for every fullback or tailback or receiver he knocks out during a game. Ashville's coach gives him a little bone as a reward. You believe that? I mean, sheeyit! That's hard core, yeah?" Scott asks, now chewing up his burger. A fleck of meat or bun sprays my ear.

"But you put a lick on ol' Chandre Jackson like you did Studblatz here," Scott continues, "and we got nothing to worry about. In fact, I'd be willing to bet money that maybe you could lay superbad Chandre out cold. Maybe punch a little hole in his chest, pile-drive him into the turf, and make everyone's life a little easier. Whaddya think, Brodsky? You think you're man enough to put a lick on Chandre? Send him bawling back to his baby mama?" Scott asks.

Jankowski snorts at Scott's cartoonish accent. A piece of potato shoots out of his nose. I glance over at Studblatz, still ignoring me because of that hit I put on him my first day of practice. He chews his food so hard, jaw muscles pop from either side of his face like two fists clenching.

"Coach Brigs said you might need some tutoring," Cindy speaks up, her soft voice teasing me with what I can't have. My cheeks warm and the long scar itches.

"Awwwww. . . . Look, he's blushing!" Scott laughs out

a chunk of burger. "How cute! Our widdow fowbak is shy awound gwirls."

"Shut up, Scott." Cindy reaches behind me to slap him. My skin tingles where her arm brushes against my back.

"Hey, man, I'm just kidding. It's cool, you know?" Scott slaps my shoulder. "Cindy, help him with his homework . . . and anything else he may need. She's great at biology *and anatomy.*"

"Shut *up!*" Cindy reaches around me again; this time it feels like she lets her arm stay there for a moment.

"I'm fuh-fuh-fuh-fine," I say, addressing the mystery meat on my plate. "I guh-guh-guh . . ." I try saying *I get good grades* but that's never going to come out now. "I'm not su-su-su . . ."

"What?" Jankowski asks. "What's that?" A smile creeps across his mouth. Studblatz no longer has a problem looking at me. Or probing me for weaknesses. Sweat trickles behind my left ear. My fingers tighten and crack the plastic spork sitting in my fist.

". . . su-su-su-su-su . . ." The more I push, the more I insist, the more it shoves back. ". . . su-su-su-su-su . . ."

I'M NOT STUPID! my brain screams. My mouth won't obey.

"Speak up!" Studblatz snickers.

"That's not funny," Cindy says, coming to my defense, which makes it worse.

"Easy, chief," Scott says. "A touch sensitive, huh?"

"I duh-duh-duh-duh . . ." *I DON'T NEED ANY HELP!!! I DON'T NEED ANY TUTORING. I DON'T NEED ANYTHING.*

"Duh-duh-duh-duh-do you think you can sell seashells

by the seashore?" Tom asks. He and Studblatz both crack up with laughter.

"Shut up!" Cindy yips, then protectively lays a fragile hand over mine, her fingers perching like a hummingbird on top of my knuckles. I'm ready to swing, though it's my own mouth I want to punch out. Reach into it and rip out my tongue for messing everything up like it always does.

"Enough, guys," Scott says. "Big deal, Kurt. So you stutter. Who cares? Bet you're still smarter than these two meatheads combined." Scott jabs a thumb at Tom and Mike. "That doesn't take a lot, though. Relax, man. You're my fullback. You're family now."

As Scott claims me, Tom and Mike go back to stuffing their mouths. Cindy strokes my hand in a way that makes me want to curl up beside her if she'd let me.

"Studblatz doesn't even believe in reading, do you, Mike?" Scott asks.

"What's reading gonna do for me?" Studblatz asks back. "They don't ask you how many books you bench-press in the NFL draft."

I take a hard look at Studblatz and think he's kidding himself if he really expects to reach the NFL; that there's a million guys around the country, just as big as him if not bigger, all saying the exact same thing. Maybe it's all those recruiting letters messing with his head.

"That's the spirit," Scott adds, encouraging Studblatz. I chance a look at Cindy, notice her eyes are the color of tropical lagoons advertised on the sides of city buses in the winter. Her eyes meet mine, then tip toward my bad cheek. She says nothing but lifts her hand off mine and looks out across the lunchroom. The moment is over. I turn and watch Jankowski with his chin almost resting in his potato mush, shoveling it into his mouth. A thick trail of zits dots his neck like oozing pellet-gun scars.

Gross, I think, knowing Cindy's thinking the same thing about my face.

"Hey, man, we're having a party at Studblatz's place this weekend," Scott says. "We're hazing the JV players before the girls come over, so you gotta be there."

"We should be hazing *him*," Studblatz grunts, pointing the corner of his chocolate milk carton toward me. I take a bite of my mush and replay drilling him into the turf.

"We don't haze starters." Scott shakes his head and then claps his hand on my shoulder. "Especially star starters."

"He's new to the team," Studblatz counters. A bit of gristle tips off his lower lip and back onto his plate. Red boils, big as snails, fester from his hairline down into the collar of his jersey shirt. "He should be initiated." Studblatz stabs at his plate of food with his spork to make the point.

"He's only new because they stuck him in that zoo at Lincoln before Coach Brigs rescued him. It's not like he's new to football. He isn't getting hazed and he doesn't have to get initiated if he doesn't want," Scott says. "But he *does* have to come to the party. No excuses."

Tom Jankowski and Mike Studblatz don't look too convinced. But they go back to shoveling food.

"Hey, Tommy, you find that thing I wanted you to get?" Scott asks, changing subjects. "The critter?"

Tom Jankowski stops eating and stares dully until his brain kicks in behind his eyes. "Yeah, I got it," he answers.

"Caught it yesterday. Kept it out in the sun so it's starting to get nice and ripe."

"Good boy," Scott says.

"What are you talking about?" Cindy asks.

"Nothing you need to worry your pretty little head over, darling." Scott winks at her. Wish I even thought to wink at her—not that I would because she'd probably slap me—but just to even attempt it puts Scott way beyond the rest of us.

"That means they're up to no good," Cindy tells me. "Boys, boys, boys," she tsks.

Scott stands up, retrieving his long legs out from under the table. Studblatz, Jankowski, Cindy, and the other girl I never met all follow him.

"You coming?" Scott asks, waiting for me to get up.

I shake my head no, pointing to my plate still full of food. Scott shrugs. "Okay, see you at practice."

They move as a group, and Scott taps fists with a couple of JV and low-rung varsity grunts at different tables before leading his entourage out of the lunchroom. Watching them exit takes my eyes past the goth group again, all studying me like I just crawled out of a hole, which for them might actually be a bonus in my favor. Mohawk girl's mouth moves, talking to one of the others, but her eyes stay on me. Safety-pin-in-her-cheek girl nods back while observing me like she really wishes she had binoculars because the beast is eating his kill and that's a rare sight during safari. The two guys with them, dressed in long black coats even though it's about eighty-five degrees in the lunchroom, twist around to watch me, see I'm looking at them, and turn away. I dig into my food, wrapping an arm protectively around my tray, letting hair fall over my face, trying my best to create a curtain.

About a minute later, one of the goth girls sits down across from me holding a bag of chips and an armful of books. Her skin is baby-powder white like her friends', and her cheeks are flawless and I wonder if she understands the gift she's been handed. Heavy mascara and black eyeliner circle pale blue eyes. She dyes her hair jet-black but the blond roots are showing. For a second, I think she looks familiar, but I get distracted by her ears, each of which has about fifty-seven piercings. As she speaks, a glint of metal piercing her tongue causes a slight lisp. Makes me wonder how she eats. Or kisses.

"Kurt?" she asks, using my name like she knows me. Those blue eyes lock on mine, never drifting to my scars, not even for a moment. I nod at the question and duck my head. "Kurt." She repeats my name. "You don't remember me." She reaches up and pulls her hair back as if that somehow will explain everything.

"It's Christina," she says. "Tina. I was at Meadow's House when you were there. Well, only for a few months, thank God, before they transferred me. On the girls' side. Well . . . duh, of course on the girls' side. I mean, why would I've been . . ."

Meadow's House.

The name reaches out and clutches my throat and I can't breathe. It trips off her tongue—metal piercing clacking against her teeth as she pronounces it—and makes me ill. I push my plate away. Kids came and went from Meadow's House. The lucky ones were adopted. Others, like me and Lamar, just got stuck. Crud Bucket ran the boys' wing. He owned it and he owned every boy that passed through it. When the men in coats and ties asked me to tell them exactly what happened, I started from the beginning and didn't leave out a single thing Crud Bucket did to me and Lamar. I couldn't forget if I tried.

But no one at Oregrove is supposed to know about Meadow's House. No one. They told me that. No one will know about my past. They promised!

"I duh-duh-don't know you." I push the words out.

"I was there," she says, her mouth rising at the corners. "I remember you, Kurtis. I remember your friend," she says. "I couldn't believe what they said happened on the boys' side—"

"Nuh-nuh-nuh-nothing happened," I say, unable to meet her eyes. "Go buh-buh-buh-back to your friends," I tell her. "We duh-duh-don't know each other. I duh-duh-duh-don't know yuh-yuh-you." I press down on the table to get my legs out from under the bench. I rise up, getting bigger, towering over the little goth girl pouting up at me with confusion on her milky face. She's scrawny. Almost as scrawny as me and Lamar back then. Bad thoughts surface like swamp gas and I need to escape, to hustle to the weight room and start stacking plates and heave some pig iron until my memory fails—or my body does. Staring down at this girl, I want to grow even bigger, reassure myself that no one will ever hurt me like that again.

D A N N Y

First thing hits all of us is the smell.

A sickly sweet odor creeps up our nostrils; the type you whiff when driving past a crushed dog or pulpy raccoon on the side of the road, flies buzzing all over the bloated fur and gore. The larger locker-room area usually smells bad but not *this* bad. We have it all to ourselves since our team works longer and harder than any of the other sports and by the time we finish, everyone else has gone home. Coach Nelson made the right call, leaving through the front of the gym and sparing himself the whiff of death. As we head toward our team locker room, built off from the main room locker room, the stench only gets stronger.

"Damn, Paul." Fisher coughs. "You wanna start using

deodorant or showering or something? You're killing me here."

"Whatever it is, Fish," Paul answers, "it must've crawled out your ass."

"It's worse than that practice when Fisher ate only CornNuts for breakfast and lunch," Gradley says, waving his hand in front of his face. "Fisher, you been eating CornNuts again?"

Ronnie Gunderson, unlucky enough to reach our team locker room first, flicks the light switch and squeals— yeah, squeals—as he reels backward out of the room.

"Yuck!"

Ronnie—not to overstate things—is a tad sensitive, being a youth-camp Christian and all. One more reason I'm not jazzed about being mistaken for him, which happens a lot. I mean, besides being even smaller than me, Ronnie is, like, fragile—almost dainty. He never swears, either, which I don't trust. None of it would bug me that much if people didn't accidentally call me by his name and vice versa. Then, again, he bugs Fisher way more than he does me and no one confuses them.

"What's your problem, fairy?" Vance Fisher snaps as Ronnie backs into him. Fisher's face, like the rest of ours, is scrunched up against the smell. Vance pushes Ronnie out of the way and then stops in the middle of the team-room doorway like he's hit a glass wall. Curiosity drives the rest of us to push in past Fisher.

A dead squirrel, its belly split open and its guts hanging out, is nailed into the center of Bruce's locker. A scrawled note, smudged with crimson streaks and pasted below the body, reads WAIT ROOM IS OURS!!!

The squirrel's head is cut off and wedged into the middle air vent of Bruce's locker. Someone's also taken the trouble to smear squirrel guts across all of our lockers, making sure to wipe the goo over our locker dials so we'll have to touch it while spinning our combinations.

"Gross." Paul sighs, then spits into the wastebasket.

"Is there a waiting room in the school I didn't know about?" Vance snickers. "Dumb fucks can't even spell."

"Gee, I wonder who did this?" Bruce grumbles. He looks grim, as if he's just been told his shiny, new senior year is going to suck.

"Just a little varmint, fellas," Fisher says. He walks over to the squirrel and with his bare hands yanks the thing off the nail. It sounds like a shirt tearing. Then he pinches the decapitated head with his fingers and pries it out of the locker vent. He goes over to the wastebasket and tosses in the remains, surprising me with how he handles the situation. "That the best those goons can do?" he asks. "Shoot, this ain't nothin' compared to deer season. You field-dress a twelve-point buck sometime and that makes this look like someone sneezed on your sleeve." Fisher gives us his goofiest grin. "Ronnie," he says, "go make your frosh ass useful and get a heap of paper towels, wet them, and pump the hand soap on them. We'll have these lockers cleaned up in two minutes."

Ronnie does as he's told while the rest of us just stand there scratching ourselves, stuck until the locker dials get cleaned up. Bruce starts pacing a small circle in front of the bench, softly bumping his fisted knuckles against each other. "We ain't letting 'em get away with this," Bruce says. Something's churning inside him. The muscles of his neck, arms, and back clench into a hard shell. "No way I'm letting these wads think they can get away with this."

"Damn straight," Gradley agrees.

"We got to tell someone," Pete Delray, the other freshman, says. Bruce turns to him with a look of disgust.

"You go ahead and tell someone, Pete, and get back to me when they decide to do something," Bruce grouses. "School ain't gonna do shit to those guys."

"But—"

"No, we take care of this by ourselves," Bruce speaks over Pete's protest. "They think they're untouchable—especially Miller, Jankowski, and Studblatz. Well, we ain't a bunch of pansy cross-country runners. They're going to find that out."

"I'm liking what I hear," Fisher says, the only one of us who seems to be enjoying himself at the moment.

Ronnie Gunderson looks like he wants to disagree but Bruce holds a finger up to him, signaling *not now.*

"Okay, guys," Bruce says. "It's payback time." He reaches into his gym bag and pulls out his almost empty water bottle, upends it into his mouth, glugs down its remnants, and then slams it down onto the bench. "Who's got to piss?" he asks, his eyes burning with a fevered look I've never seen on him. He rattles the empty bottle. "Well, fill 'er up."

Because we've been sweating our asses off for the last three hours, no one's got a lot to contribute to Bruce's bottle until it's Fisher's turn. Vance Fisher takes Bruce's bottle into the toilet stall and tops it off. Then he calls for another.

"Come on, guys. I'm flowing here," Fisher yells from the stall. "Hook me up!"

"Where's he put it?" Larry Menderson asks.

"It's all that soda he drinks," Bruce says. "You're gonna rot your teeth, Fisher."

"This isn't right," Ronnie protests.

"Relax, frosh," Fisher says over the sounds of his stream. "Baby Jesus ain't gonna cry just because we're pissing in a water bottle. Check your Bible. It's not like we're breaking a commandment. You ain't gonna burn in hell."

"Pete, give Fisher your water bottle," Bruce says.

"Hurry, guys," Vance calls again.

"Why mine?" Pete whines.

"'Cause you're a freshman."

"So is Ronnie," Pete answers.

"Ronnie's too busy saying prayers for all our lost souls," Bruce says, then slaps Pete's shoulder. "Come on, man. Do it for the team."

Pete finally sacrifices his water bottle for the good of the counterstrike. By the time we clean up our lockers, dress, pee, and walk down the long basement hall toward the varsity football locker room, it's real late and nobody should be around except maybe a janitor.

Since they're freshmen, we let Ronnie and Pete stay outside in the hallway as lookouts. Bruce tells them to whistle real loud if they see anyone approaching and then hightail it out of there. Bruce leads the way in to the enemy lockers, shaking the pee bottle like it's a protein drink needing mixing.

"Okay, dickheads," he whispers to the empty locker room. "Time for a little justice."

We move in a clump, afraid and excited. If anyone catches us in here, we're dead. Bruce makes a V with his index and middle finger, and brings it up to his eyeballs, then points the V out to the surrounding locker room. Fisher, the deer hunter in our group, nods his understanding.

"Fan out, guys," Fisher translates. "Keep your eyes open for the captains' lockers." The skinny junior, lanky as a scarecrow, with a gap-toothed grin and crooked nose, devours the whole experience like candy. Usually I think of Fisher as a screw-off, with no plans after graduation other than opening a bait-and-tackle shop or maybe joining the marines like his older brother, on the condition they let him get high and sleep late. But right now, hunting down lockers with bottles of piss, Fisher impresses me.

Unlike Fisher, Bruce doesn't look excited or pleased, just angry. He's been fuming ever since we found the squirrel. No one's talking to him other than Fisher, his mission cocommander.

The lockers in the varsity room are triple size and each has a glossy label with a player's name and jersey number stenciled across it. This makes our mission easier. Me and Paul, too scared to wander off alone, stay together and find Jankowski's locker at the same time.

"Over here," I stage-whisper. Paul punches me in the shoulder.

"Shhhhhh," he says, and puts a finger to his lips. Bruce rounds the corner, shaking his bottle like mad, practically walking over me to reach the target. He hops up on the long bench running between the rows of lockers. He pulls open the spout on his squeeze bottle. Without a second's hesitation, he aims the spout up into the top vent of the locker and crunches hard on the plastic with both hands.

Phhhhththththththththththt . . . The bottle sprays up into the locker vent, its contents disappearing on the other side, unseen.

"See how you like it now, bastard," Bruce hisses. He seems to be getting angrier and angrier as he does it. The bottle gurgles and he tips it at a steeper angle, squeezing again.

Phhhhththththththththththt . . .

"Studblatz's is over here," Gradley calls softly from the next row. Bruce hops down off the bench and moves like a minitank, pushing past us to get to the next locker. He steps up on the bench and presses the spout up into Studblatz's vent.

Phhhththththththththththt . . . shake, shake, shake . . . *Phhhththththththththththth.*

"Refill," Bruce calls out. Fisher is there, handing over Pete's water bottle like it's an ammunition clip for a depleted machine gun.

Phhhththththththhhtthth . . .

"Found Miller's," Menderson calls out.

Bruce finishes the rest of the second bottle, upending it, through the vent slit in Scott Miller's locker. It feels good watching piss spray into the quarterback's locker. I bet that cross-country runner he'd been harassing would love to be here watching. I think we're done but Bruce pulls out a baggie from his pocket.

"The gift that keeps on giving." Bruce smirks as he pulls the mushy squirrel guts and pelt out of the baggie and squeezes it as best he can through the vent. It smells bad and I lift my forearm to press against my nose.

"Shit, dude," Gradley hisses. "Now they'll know for sure it's us."

"What are they gonna do?" Bruce asks him, and I see he's challenging all of us. "They gonna cry that we didn't play fair? That we used their own squirrel guts against them? They gonna cry to their coach? Screw 'em."

"You just shafted us," Paul says, and shakes his head.

"Relax," Bruce says, stubborn. No way he's admitting he went too far.

We hear a high piercing whistle. It's either Pete or Ronnie.

"Go, go, go . . . ."

We scramble around the benches, banging shins on the planks of pine and slamming shoulders on the thin metal corners of the lockers.

"Come on, come on. . . . Go, go, go."

Paul leads the way, shoving the door open, and we pile out into the basement hallway, expecting . . . the whole football team? A group of teachers? Cops?

Pete and Ronnie stand in the deserted hallway, eyes big as a baby Pokémon's.

"What?!" Gradley asks.

"Janitor down at the end of the hall, but he went into the boiler room," Pete whispers. That's enough for us. We sprint down the hall in the opposite direction, our sneakers squeaking against the smooth cement floors and the thighs of our jeans *vvvrrrping* with each stride.

Upstairs, Bruce stops us.

"Okay, guys. Wait!" he says. "We can't all leave in a big group. Too suspicious. Go to your lockers or hang out for a sec."

"Yeah, smart," Fisher declares.

"And not a word of this to anyone. I mean, *anyone*," Bruce cautions. "No matter what, just play stupid."

"Paul's got that covered," Fisher says. Paul shoves him.

"The squirrel's fair game," Bruce continues, still pleading his case, "but the piss will send them over, so don't say anything."

We're all breathing hard, partly from the run, partly from striking back and having a great secret that'll get us creamed if anyone finds out.

"Pete," Bruce says, "here's your water bottle back." He presses the empty bottle into the freshman's chest. Pete looks down at it, slowly grabs the bottle while his lips curl and his nose crinkles.

"You can't throw it out right away because someone might find it," Bruce warns, deadly serious. "This mission isn't over yet. You've got to hold on to it, rinse it out, and it should be good as new. I want to see you drinking out of it tomorrow in practice, you got it?"

"Wh-what?" Pete asks, his voice rising. I look at Bruce, thinking he lost his mind downstairs. "Bu-but you can't be . . . You're kidding."

"Yes, I am, freshman." Bruce clasps Pete's shoulder. "Throw that thing away off school grounds first chance you get."

Bruce looks at the rest of us, his eyes twinkling with victory. "Okay, not a word, guys. See you tomorrow. Good practice today."

K U R T

We play the Jefferson Patriots that Friday, our first game, an away game. We clobber them. Ain't even close and I still only know about half the plays we're running, since I missed all of preseason training camp. Coach pulls me out of the offense every other snap, then gives me strict instructions on the sidelines for the following play and then sends me back into the huddle.

The Jefferson fans are hopping mad almost from the start after Studblatz levels their quarterback on a linebacker blitz, forcing a Jefferson substitution. When they bring out the stretcher and call an injury time-out, Studblatz hippity-hops on the field like he's riding someone, slapping an imaginary ass, and pointing at the Jefferson bench. That's when the first volley of soda cups flies toward our bench. Studblatz just pumps his arms at the Jefferson fans, taunting them with a double-biceps bodybuilder pose. He's been supercharged all night. Miller and Jankowski, too. Has something to do with their uniforms not being washed or still being wet or smelling or something. Miller smells the worst, and no one wants to get close enough to ask him for details. The other two stink like piss. They stink up the bus on the way to the game, and they stink up the huddle during the game. The three of them boil all through warm-ups, grinding on their mouth guards and daring any of us to say a word out of place.

Once it's clear to the Jefferson fans that Coach is running up the score, garbage really starts sailing out from the bleachers, forcing us to wear our helmets on the sidelines.

"Brodsky!" Coach barks. He always wants me within ten feet of him so he can grab me, shout the next play, and snap-count into my face mask, then send me hustling out to the team with a slap on the butt like I'm a horse needing a giddyup. I scramble out to our midfield huddle. Scott Miller stands there, hands on his hips, impatient to get the play, impatient even if I'm traveling at the speed of light.

I meet him and we clank face masks while I repeat Coach's play just above the crowd noise. "Fullback draw, sweep right on three," I tell him. He nods and turns away from me to gather us into a circle and repeat Coach's instructions.

"You take this ball all the way to the goalposts, Brodsky, or I'm telling Coach you called his wife a troll." Miller snarls but then winks, leaving me wondering if he's joking. Because we're killing Jefferson so badly by the fourth quarter, some of his anger over the polluted uniform has evaporated. Not so with Jankowski. He reaches across the huddle and grabs my face mask in his hand, jerking my head into alignment with his gaze.

"I'm not clearing a trench so you can run five yards and fall on your ass." Jankowski grunts. "You want a little respect, rookie, now's the time to earn it." His eyes narrow at me, angry for no reason at all. When I wear my helmet and pads, all my scars feel hidden and my stutter mostly dries up. I feel powerful at these times and not willing to take much shit.

"You just make a luh-lane," I say, "or take the ball if you think you can do better. But Coach didn't cuh-call for a left guard sweep."

Jankowski just grunts again and releases my face mask. I hear Terrence, our running back, snicker. Terrence's been in good spirits ever since we increased our lead by four touchdowns in the third quarter. He started smiling in warm-ups and now the game is one big party for him. It helps that Jankowski and I have been smashing open the line of scrimmage all night, allowing him to rack up huge yardage. I think everyone expected to win, but not by this much.

"On three, ladies," Scott says. We clap once and break huddle. I line up two strides behind Scott's right shoe and scan the field. No wonder we're stomping Jefferson. Their entire line, except for one guy, Adams, is smaller than us. We might as well be scrimmaging against our JV team. Jefferson's defense sets up, but we've already broken them. Their helmets sag while they squat, waiting for the snap, expecting to get pushed around. Scott's been untouched all

K
U
R
T

night, hitting his receivers almost every pass and throwing two sweet connections resulting in touchdowns in the first and second quarter.

"Ready . . . set . . . thirty-five red . . . two eighty-seven . . ." Scott calls out the cadence. I let my eyes wander the whole line so as not to give away where I'll aim or even if I expect the ball. Jankowski drops to all fours, his butt big as a mule's, each thigh larger than a freshman, and awaits Scott's command.

"Hut," Scott barks, ". . . hut . . . HUT!"

The ball snaps up through Rondo's legs and into Scott's hands. He swivels around to make like he's feeding it to Terrence crossing in front of me but then jams the ball into my gut instead. I clamp down on it and steer for Jankowski's jersey. Jankowski's good to his word, blowing a hole through their line big enough to drive a car through. He single-handedly shoves three guys left while Peller tangles up Adams. I burn through the line break, twist away from a last-ditch hand clutch, and twenty yards of open field greet me like a prize. Jefferson's cornerback and safety, both downfield, are my only obstacles. I steam ahead, gaining momentum, expecting Jefferson's safety to try and cut me off, preparing for the hit . . .

Terrence comes out of nowhere, racing up from behind me, and slams Jefferson's safety right between the jersey numbers. Their collision slides past my face mask like rain on a windshield. Fifteen yards to the goal line and I'm still charging as the Jefferson cornerback dives for my knees. I power up into the air and hurdle his outstretched body, my foot nicking his helmet, but I go past otherwise untouched. I coast into the end zone and then jog back, tossing the ref the ball before Terrence leaps up into my chest and hugs me like we just won the championship. Then Rondo lumbers down to meet me and head-butts my helmet. A gang of teammates slap my shoulders and helmet and buzz around me all the way back to the bench. A few more soda cups come flying out of the bleachers, like an offering, and Coach Brigs is there, beaming at me.

"Good boy!" He smacks my helmet with his clipboard like maybe he's proud of me, except I got no experience with that, so I'm not sure how that looks. For a second, I try pretending he's my dad but it disappears, like trying to glimpse a firefly after the glow dies.

"Hey, Brodsky," Studblatz calls out, "looks like you might not be worthless after all."

"Brodsky." Jankowski stalks over to me. The other players move out of his way. "We might keep you around for a few more games." He pounds my shoulder pad with the meat of his fist.

"Nuh-nice hole you opened up," I say back.

"We can't give Terrence all the glory," Jankowski says. We both ignore his bad smell for the moment.

"Okay, that settles it." Miller comes over. "Looks like you're legit. But don't let it go to your head."

"I won't," I say.

"Now get ready to party," Scott says, pulling out his mouth guard, "because tonight we're kings."

"Guys, you may think you're alone out there, but you're not," Coach Nelson says from twenty feet up the rock climbing wall. It's on the north side of the gymnasium and Coach Nelson built it before I attended school here. He basically drilled and bolted hundreds of pieces of rock chunks to the brick wall to create foot- and handholds to simulate a cliff face for climbing practice. It goes all the way up to the rafters, thirty-five feet high. He offers a class in the summer to all students, but because we gymnasts have the inside connection and we're naturally good at climbing, he lets us climb the wall for fun a few times during the season and then takes us on a camping trip for real climbing in July.

"They say gymnastics and rock climbing are individual sports but I don't believe that for a second," Coach Nelson continues. He's dangling by one foothold and one hand-hold, letting the other side of his body swivel out into space while he looks down at us. "No man is an island," he says. "Do you know who wrote that?" he asks. While we chew on the question, Coach Nelson turns back to the wall and expertly scurries over and up another four feet. The harness clipped around his waist and thighs connects to two ropes that ripple as he moves. The ropes go up into the rafters through bolted pulleys and drop down to the floor, where Bruce is holding them. Bruce tracks Coach Nelson's ascent with a lifeguard's watchfulness.

Coach Nelson now dangles from only one small rock handhold, his Popeye forearm flexing as three fingers form a claw attaching him to the wall. He swings a leg and catches a small rock chunk with his toe, then holds the position like he's been spattered by a giant flyswatter.

"It's tempting to pretend you don't need anyone else, that your work and your score are yours alone," Coach calls down to us. "You pretend if you do poorly, you only hurt yourself, and if you do well, the glory is all yours." Coach Nelson grapples with a few smaller chunks bolted into the wall, then reaches with an outstretched hand for a piece of round stone that is beyond his splayed finger-tips. No way is he going to grab it—and then somehow he does and pulls himself another two feet higher. He's almost at the top now. "But glory is no fun if, when you look around, you have no one to share it with," he calls down to us. "Make no mistake, gymnastics is a team sport. We count on each other in this gym: to spot each other on tricks, to offer advice and guidance on better technique, to push each other to do an extra strength set, to lead by example. The judges count the three best scores, not just your score. Remember that."

I glance around at my teammates and every set of eyes follows Coach Nelson as he makes his way upward. Some guys sit on the thick vaulting mats, some stand, some work on their hamstrings and straddle stretch, but all faces tilt up to watch Coach Nelson's progress. Since everyone but Ronnie and Pete—the two freshmen—have attempted the wall climb, we know how impossible it is to do what Coach Nelson makes look so easy. Only Bruce has made it all the way since I've been on the team.

A small bell jingles.

"Most importantly," Coach Nelson calls down from the top of the wall, where his outstretched hand flicks the dinner bell attached to the rafter—good for a free KFC meal with Coach if any of us can repeat the performance—"you need your teammates to be around when you need help because just when you think you've conquered the world all by yourself, something comes along and sweeps you right down to the bottom . . .waahhh . . . oh . . ."

Coach Nelson begins waving his free hand theatrically and then slips from the wall. He plummets eight feet before the ropes on his harness snap taut. The pulleys squeak, and at the other end, Bruce's arms flex as the momentum of the winding ropes lifts his anchoring body four feet up in the air. Gradley reaches over to help stop the rope and pull Bruce back down to the ground.

"Good catch, boys," Coach Nelson calls down, seeming to enjoy hovering in the air in the harness. Paul Kim reaches for the rope after the fact and Bruce, Paul, and Gradley slowly play the rope out through their hands, lowering Coach Nelson to the ground. When his feet touch, he unclips the harness. He claps his hand on Bruce's shoulder. "Thanks again."

Bruce nods, looking like he just aced a test.

"If your captain can catch your coach, he'll damn well catch you," Coach Nelson says. "The old cliché is true. There is no 'I' in 'team.' You see a teammate needing help, you help him. You see a teammate goofing off—in the gym, in class, outside of school at a party where he might get hurt or hurt others—it's your responsibility to step up and help him." Coach Nelson cracks a grin at Fisher. "And, no, Fish, that doesn't mean help him drink more."

"Aw, Uncle Jesus."

"When old guys like me tell you backup's coming and they're on the way, that the cavalry is coming, they're lying," Coach Nelson continues. "No one's going to help you but you and your teammates. So, look around you. This is it. You guys rely on each other. This is your unit. This is what you have and that's more than most get, so consider yourselves lucky."

We look at each other, our eyes meeting, and I feel close to my teammates. They may not be gunning for a scholarship like I am, and maybe they don't and won't train as hard as I do, but they respect this sport and they respect me when I'm up on the bars. They want me to get good scores like I want them to get good scores.

"First two weeks of freshman season is, mentally, tough as it gets," Coach Nelson says. "You don't know anyone and you realize what we do in here is *hard*." We all start laughing. "Now that we're past the two-week mark and you haven't quit, I want to officially welcome this year's freshmen Pete Delray and Ronnie Gunderson to the team. Keep up the good work."

Coach Nelson walks over to a bag and pulls out two faded, really faded, cotton T-shirts old as dirt. They've been washed and worn so many times, the fabric is like tissue paper and the original silk screen is barely legible. FRESHMAN CAPTAIN IN TRAINING, the shirts read if you look close enough. Coach Nelson hands the shirts to Pete and Ronnie. Pete looks confused but Ronnie looks like if you squeezed him, soap bubbles would come out of his open mouth because he's so astonished he's getting the shirt. I can't help but smile watching Ronnie. It's how I felt last year when Coach Nelson handed me and Paul Kim the same shirts. We returned them (laundered) at the end of the season. I wore mine a lot. I mean, *a lot*. Way more than Paul did. Judging from Ronnie's face, he'll be wearing it every other practice. Coach's speech while he climbed the wall I didn't mind hearing again, either.

K U R T

Patti wastes no time using Coach's funds. Weekend after I hand her the sealed envelope Coach gave me, a moving van backs into her driveway and two guys in blue coveralls unload a fifty-two-inch-screen television that barely fits through her front door.

"Now we can watch you almost like in real life," Patti says, fanning the cigarette smoke that's drifting up between us. "Coach Brigs tells me they replay the Knights' games on the community access channel every Saturday afternoon." Patti takes a deep drag on her cigarette, squinting one eye as the ember glows hot red. "That coach of yours is a good man," Patti says, smoke leaking out her nostrils and mouth as she talks. "And so nice, wanting to know how we're making out."

I nod back to her. I like Patti mostly because she's harmless, far as I can tell. More important, she's got no angry husband, ex-husband, or boyfriend in the picture. Thin as a soda straw, she's the first foster guardian who doesn't make me flinch, even by accident. Lots of times I'll come home and find her asleep on the couch or smoking in front of the TV with all the lights out and a tumbler of whiskey on her coffee table, only the ice melt left in it. The smell of cigarettes and liquor can remind me of him, though, and make me shiver. At those times I'll kneel down beside her, take a good look at her face in the glow of the TV, and make sure she hasn't turned into him.

Sometimes I might catch Patti sobbing about her ex-husband, Earl, and what a dog he was, how he left her no choice but to foster kids for extra cash and how the kids kept complaining about how they were always hungry and so the state kept taking them away and how I was her last chance. I keep quiet when she's like that, not minding the sound of her whimpers so long as she doesn't turn into him, so long as I'm bigger than her. When she gets like that, I stop listening, start thinking about Lamar, about the time he told Crud Bucket to go to hell after the man came into our room drunk for the thousandth night. While Patti cries about Earl, I'll remember the way Lamar shouted it, like someone punched him in the stomach and he couldn't hold back the words any longer. *Go to hell!* Crud Bucket reached for him, then, reached both his neck and his arm in one stumbling motion. There's sounds that stick with you no matter what: Lamar screaming into his pillow. The soft pop of his collarbone while I scrunched under my blanket across the room. Dark silence broken by whimpers. It comes back real sharp whenever I listen to Patti cry over Earl.

"I'm guh-going to a party tuh-tuh-tonight," I tell Patti while the movers wrestle the big TV into her living room. "Wuh-wuh-one of the guys is picking me up."

"That's nice, hon. A grown boy like you needs to get out of the house." She busies herself with the movers, pointing to where they should set down the TV and asking them if they can hook it up to her cable box. I go into the kitchen and open the fridge. Thing's empty as usual. I grab a jelly container off the top shelf, then pull down some bread and peanut butter from the cupboard and make six PB and Js. I try washing them down with milk, but I make the mistake of drinking directly from the carton. The first curdled chunk hits the back of my throat like cottage cheese and I swallow before I have a choice.

Scott Miller rolls up in a muscle-heavy Camaro SS with a bulging engine hood and black racing stripes over golden body paneling. I don't really want him coming inside and meeting Patti, so I push through the screen door soon as I hear a honking horn followed by the deep rumble of a V-8 with four hundred horses pulling into the driveway.

"You ain't going to introduce me?" Scott asks with a smile that hints he might know something about me I don't really want known.

"Nah."

"Suit yourself, big man." He backs us out of the driveway, turns the car around, and at the end of the street, at the stop sign, asks, "See any cops?" Without waiting for an answer, he punches the gas. The big V-8 roars and Scott pops the clutch. Tires screeching, back end shuddering sideways, a cloud of oily blue smoke pours up from the pavement behind us.

"YeeeeeeeeHAAAAWWWWW!!!!!"

The bucket seat sucks me deep into its soft leather as we blast out toward the world.

"You like that?" Scott asks.

"Yeah," I answer truthfully. And then, for no reason, lean my head out the open window like a dog. The wind howls through my hair.

"That's the spirit," he shouts. I bring my head back in and see Scott reaching into the backseat to pull out a six-pack already missing a can. "Have one," he says, dropping the beer in my lap. "Maybe you'll finally lighten up."

I hate drinking, especially beer. Especially beer out of cans. Crud Bucket guzzled it like Gatorade before moving onto the heavier stuff. I pull a can off the plastic ring.

"Pass me one," Scott says. "Chug it quick. My pops wants to meet our secret weapon before we head over to the party. And don't tell him Mike's parents went away for the weekend."

I pull a second can off the plastic ring and hand it to Scott, then stuff the remaining three cans under my seat. Scott opens his can and downs it like soda. I take a small sip of mine and it tastes awful, same as it always does every time I try it, like dandelion weeds mulched in a blender and boiled into tea.

"Finish that bad boy. We'll be there in five minutes."

I take a big swig, trying not to taste it. I take another swig and another until it's almost empty. Good enough.

Scott turns onto a street with big white houses and nice lawns, some with little lawn jockey statues holding lanterns by the front door. "Look," he says as he fiddles with the radio dial, "we'll keep this short as possible. Just nod and smile and pretend everything he says is scripture. Then we'll get outta there."

"Guh-got it," I say, taking Scott's instructions seriously. With adults, I leave nothing to chance.

"There's that stern frown again," he says. "My dad's gonna freakin' love you. Hold on to that look until we leave. *Then* you can lighten up."

"Okay." As much as I hate the taste, the beer relaxes my tongue in a good way.

Scott unloads a belch that sounds like a blown speaker. He kills the ignition and the vibrations rumbling through my seat die. I've only just climbed out of the car when the front door of the house opens and there's Mr. Miller: buzz-cut hair, heavy shoulders, broad chest, and paunch belly. A can of beer and an unlit cigar sprout from his right hand.

"Let me get a look at our newest acquisition," he says by way of introduction. He wears a big, overly friendly grin to go with his XXXL Knights jersey, khaki shorts, and flip-flops. His eyes are watery. I think his nose is sunburned, but the closer he comes, the more I see that the pink is from little broken blood vessels, like Crud Bucket's.

"Brought him over, Dad," Scott says, "just like I promised."

Mr. Miller ignores his son and keeps honing in on me, stepping closer, getting right up in my face, and taking me in from shoe to hair. The way his gaze avoids the bad side of my face tells me he's working hard to ignore it.

"Lookit the size of you!" Mr. Miller says, then sticks the cigar in his mouth, shifts his beer can, and offers his hand to shake. I take it, feel his grip clamp down on my fingers, trying to grind my knuckles together. He won't let go, just keeps squeezing. His smile turns wicked while he waits for a reaction. I won't give him one. I won't squeeze back, either. Something tells me he'll take that challenge.

"Someone's been feeding you good," he says. "Got to get Scottie here on that diet, beef him up a bit." I think about the six PB and Js I chowed down, pretty sure Scott wouldn't be too happy with that diet. "Come on and grab a beer. Just one, though, since you're driving and doing God knows what tonight. Am I right? Huh? Right?"

"Dad, we should get—"

"God*dammit*, boy!" Mr. Miller lashes out at his son, ears and cheeks growing crimson to match his nose. "Don't interrupt me again." Mr. Miller shakes his head and turns back to me, blowing out a stream of air, and the redness fades. "My boy has trouble minding himself. Thinks he's the man in charge. Well, he may be the man out there with those little faggots and pussies, but around this house, there's only one big dog."

"Yes, sir!" I say, happy that the beer smoothes my reply and makes Mr. Miller seem more like a joke than a threat. I glance at Scott, catch his eyes narrowing behind his old man's back.

"You hear that, Scottie? You hear how he addresses me? Someone taught you good, boy! Someone brought you up right."

"Th-thank you, sir."

"I sure would like to meet the parents of such a fine, upstanding young man. Makes me proud to be a part of this mostly derelict human race."

"Dad, maybe we can—" Scott begins, but is cut off again.

"Boy, I am not going to tell you again about interrupting your old man! Now get on in there and grab all three of us a beer. Now!"

Scott goes into the house without another word and returns with the beers while Mr. Miller and I stand in front of Scott's car.

"Kurt, I sure did like watching you run and block last night. You teach Scottie some of those moves, make a man out of him. He thinks he knows it all. The boy don't know shit. What you lookin' at, Scott?" Mr. Miller asks. "You know they've been pampering you. You may be the star quarterback here, but once you walk on campus with the big boys, they will knock you on your ass. Am I right?"

"Yesssssir," I say, glancing over at Scott, see him glaring *at me*. Mr. Miller leans down to rest his beer on the fender of the Camaro, but the can slips off and falls to the ground.

"Ahh, for Christ's sake! Scottie, what the hell are you doing to me here, with this damn car? Can't drive a truck. Got to have some flashy fairy car with a fancy grille you can't set nothing on. Jee-zus, what's the point?"

"You liked it plenty when Rick bought it," Scott hisses.

"What?! Whaddid you just say?" Mr. Miller squares his shoulders toward Scott like he's preparing to box his son into the ground. "Blaspheme his name again, boy," Mr. Miller growls, pulling the cigar out of his mouth, readying for attack. "Go ahead. Test me."

"Have my buh-buh-beer, sssssir," I offer, knowing from experience angry drinkers can be distracted with more alcohol. Mr. Miller stands there staring Scott down while deciding something. Then he plugs his cigar back in his mouth, keeping his eyes set on Scott while talking to me.

"Boy, got some good manners on you," Mr. Miller says, his hand opening expectantly for the almost full can of beer I place in the circle of his fingers like a servant. He likes that. I can tell. "Scottie, you stick with this one. Learn some respect from him."

"Yes, *sir*," Scott says, voice brittle. His face turns raw red as his old man's while his jaw clenches and unclench-es. I swallow nervously. Mr. Miller takes a long pull from my beer, tipping the can up almost vertical, then wipes his forearm across his mouth.

"Okay, you two get out of here. And don't go knocking up a cheerleader. Don't think I don't remember being your age. But the wrong move with one of them girls will put you on the path to food stamps. You remember that and keep it in your pants."

Scott's already in the car, turning over the ignition, when I say good-bye to his dad.

"Nice meeting you, suh-suh-sir."

"You too, son. Can't wait to see you run against Mill-field High. You'll make fools outta those boys."

A quarter mile from his house, driving up the on-ramp to Old Highway 8, Scott punches the gas. The Camaro bucks, engine snorting, and presses me into my seat once again.

"Who's ruh-ruh-Rick?"

"My brother. My forever-perfect brother. Never did

a single goddamn thing wrong, according to my dad."

The speedometer needle climbs way past the legal limit. I wait for Scott to ease off the pedal. The flatbed of a pickup truck grows larger and larger in front of us. Just as we're about to ram it, Scott switches lanes. We rocket past it, chased weakly by the truck's horn.

"Suh-suh-suh-Scott. Ease up."

"Whatsa matter?" Scott asks, wearing his old man's wicked grin. "The big, upstanding, young gentleman scared?"

"It ain't fuh-fuh-fuh-funny."

There are two cars up ahead, running side by side, blocking both lanes. We blast toward both sets of taillights on a collision course. Scott glances over at me, then throws his head back in laughter. He re-grips the steering wheel.

"Grow some balls," he says. "If my dad saw you right now, squirming like a sissy, he wouldn't be so hot to kiss your ugly ass."

"Suh-suh-suh-suh-suh—"

"Scott. My name is Scott. Say it. Scott!" He shouts at me.

"Duh-duh-don't . . . ." I brace an arm against the dashboard, expecting the crash. The two cars ahead plug both lanes. Nowhere to go. No room between them; only grass ditch and ravine on either side.

"Suck it up, man!"

"Suh-suh-suh . . . Come on!"

Scott flashes his headlights and lays on the horn. "Out of the way asshole!" he shouts, refusing to slow. I reach for his arm but he jerks it from my grip.

"Suh-suh-suh-*Scott*!"

A second from ramming the back of the left car, he cranks the steering wheel. We shoot down into the grassy ravine, Scott's side sinking and my side lifting, threatening to flip. Tall grass whips over the hood, smearing the windshield. Scott wrestles the wheel, whooping loud. The Camaro munches hunks of earth while the floorboard bangs under my feet. Any second we'll hit an unseen dip and crater into the field or cartwheel end over end. Either way it'll finish in a fireball.

"How you like it, tough guy?" Scott shouts. "Still my dad's best friend?"

Both my hands clutch the dashboard. "Puh-puh-puh-please . . . suh-suh-*stop!*"

Scott yanks the wheel back toward the road. We ramp up the embankment; catching air, then land back on the highway at an angle, hitting hard.

Crunk!

Metal scrapes pavement and rubber squeals. Scott hits the brakes and we fishtail while he struggles for control. The Camaro straightens out, barely avoiding flipping into the opposite-side ravine.

My mouth stops working all together. Scott laughs but it sounds more like crying to my ears. "You should see the look on your face," he says, slapping the steering wheel. We slow to the legal limit. I wait for my heart to climb back down out of my throat.

Other than Scott asking me to grab him another beer, we don't speak the rest of the ride to Studblatz's house. I grab a can for myself and drink it fast, not minding the taste anymore, hoping only to feel a little less jittery. By the time we reach Mike Studblatz's house, most of my adrenaline's burned off, but my legs still feel wobbly.

At the driveway, Scott hits the horn, waits a second, then honks again, a long, annoying blast. "Okay, you passed the test," he says to me, turning off the ignition. Except for a few engine ticks, the car goes to sleep. "Not exactly in flying colors, 'fraidy cat, but we'll keep that to ourselves," he says. "In my book, you passed. *Now* you're a Knight."

"*That* was a tuh-tuh-test? You driving like a kuh-kuh-kuh-crazy man *was a tuh-tuh-test*?"

"Of course. Whaddid you think? I'm going to freak out and scratch up my paint job just because Pops gets a couple drinks in him and wants to trade sons? You think that's all it takes to work me up? Shit, that was nothing. You just saw my old man on his best behavior. You should see him when his team loses. Or hear him gush every time Jankowski and Studblatz come over. Or starts telling stories about Rick. I keep waiting for him to offer Tom and Mike's parents a swap for me."

I look down and see that I've crushed the empty beer can in my grip.

"Me, Tommy, and Mike decided you had to have some sort of initiation. You can't just party with kings and get the keys to all the cheerleaders' panties without a little suffering first. You got to pay some membership dues. But you're in now. You're golden."

Through the dirty windshield I watch the front door of the house open and Jankowski step through it. A train of bald boys follows him. I slowly realize it's the entire

JV squad and some of the benchwarming varsity players. Music comes thumping out of the house: heavy guitar chords, boom-boom beats, and some guy wailing like a banshee. The bald boys all wear dog collars with bone biscuits attached to them. Tom comes over and taps fists with Scott through the open car window, then casts a brief glance at me.

"So you got a plan for Sasquatch here?" he asks Scott, tipping his chin in my direction.

"Already implemented it," Scott says. "My boy here is solid. He passed the test."

Disappointment hoods Tom's eyes. "Aw, come *on*, man. We were *all* supposed to help."

"Too late, Tommy," Scott says. "Tell you what, though. Get the peons here to wash my car and scrub it down real good. We did a little off-roading on the way over. Some idiot drunk, going like a bat out of hell, ran us off the road on Old Highway Eight."

"No shit?" Tom asks.

"No shit," Scott says. "I need a drink. Come on, Kurt."

"Shit stains, your work is not done here," Tom hollers. "You want to be a true Knight? Then scrub this golden chariot spotless. Wash it with your tongues if you have to, just wash it. Now!"

Bald boys jump at Tom's command. They hustle to find rags, buckets, a garden hose, and soap. Whoever shaved them didn't worry about gouging divots of flesh from their scalps to get at the hair. Bloody scabs speckle every single one of their skulls. One JV kid has a swollen eye and cheek, and a bloody lip. Tom has a grip around the kid's neck, pushing him to his hands and knees. His skull is worse than the others. Fresh beads of red gleam all over his smooth dome.

"Goldberg, did you not hear what I just said?" Tom leans over, screaming right into the kid's ear. "How do you expect to even be considered for varsity if you can't listen to simple directions? Lick that wheel clean, Jewboy. Lick it!"

"Sir, yes sir," the kid answers. He sticks out his tongue and Tom, still squeezing his neck, rams Goldberg's face into the Camaro's tire.

"Lick it!" Tom yells, and the other bald boys start laughing. "That Jew-tongue better be black as coal when you're done."

"Thir . . . yeth . . . thir," Goldberg answers while his mouth mops the tread. Tom straddles the much smaller JVer while he's on his hands and knees, really smushing his face into the rubber.

"Just make sure it's spotless, pukes," Scott adds. "Brodsky, follow me," he says. "You could've done a lot worse for initiation than the ride I gave you."

I glance back one last time before following Scott into the house. Jankowski's bent over Goldberg in a way I know from Meadow's House, a way I won't ever forget. A sickening tickle works its way up my gut, my breath gets short, and I fight the urge to run away fast as possible. A camera flashes and I notice Terrence aiming his digital at the same scene that's making me sick.

"Smile, Tom," Terrence says.

"Fuck you, Terrence," Tom fires back, not bothering to get off Goldberg. I turn away and follow Scott inside the house.

"Have a real man's drink," Scott says, handing me a plastic cup that looks like Coke with ice. Anything's better than more beer. I glug back a big swallow of the drink before choking up the burning liquid and coughing out the rest.

"Attaboy." Scott laughs. "Jack and Coke'll put hair on your chest." He slaps my back until I finish coughing. "Drink up. The girls'll be here soon and I'm about to make you Mr. Popular."

I nod dumbly, feeling miserable, wishing I could escape to the weight room or get under my covers and read about places far away, in jungles where no people exist, only jaguars hiding in trees and river rafts and chests of gold.

In the basement, there's a full bar that Studblatz's tending. When he sees me and Scott, he smiles at Scott and dips his chin at me. Scott and Mike give each other fist pounds across the dark wood of the bar top and I'm surprised to find his fist waiting to bump mine. A razor, a can of shaving cream, and a blood-splotched towel sit on one of the stools.

"You're real lucky our quarterback likes you so much," Studblatz tells me. "Tommy and I been busting to shave that mop off your head, but Scott says you might be like Samson or something. He doesn't want to mess with your power accidentally, go shave you bald like the other numbnuts and find out you can't run the ball no more. Coach wouldn't be happy about that."

"He wouldn't be *happy* about that?" Scott asks sarcastically. "Coach'd be a little more than *unhappy*." Scott lets out a long whistle and raises his eyebrows at Studblatz. "If we messed with Mr. All-America's running game, Coach'd have our balls. And only *after* my dad finished skinning us first."

"They're here!" comes a cry from up the basement steps.

"Finally," Scott says. "The females have arrived."

"Let the games begin." Studlblatz smirks.

Girls! Soft, beautiful, girls float down the steps wearing lots of short, tight, and skimpy. They parade around the wood-paneled basement with flowing hair, bare tummies, dark eye shadow, and glossy-wet lips. The party's been spared from guy poisoning. Curvy beauties—bright eyes, soft necks, round butts, and luscious cleavage—mellow out the scabby scalps and fill the room with a scent that makes me want to lick the air. Everyone in the basement loosens up with their arrival. Except me. See, the shaved plebes look stupid but their hair will grow back. My scars and my stutter cling to me, embarrass me, like permanent BO.

The bald boys wear the dried blood on their hatcheted scalps like war ribbons, grinning proudly even as the girls touch them and go *ewwww*. Goldberg—bruised eye and puffy lip—must be done licking Scott's Camaro clean. He's in a beer chugging race with two other baldies.

From my bar stool in a dark corner, I watch the girls dance in little groups, sipping red- and orange-colored drinks through rainbow straws, flipping their hair from one shoulder to the other, throwing off their girl scent. A hungry knot tightens below my belly. Unable to approach the girls, they still give me hope and make me feel safe. No girl, no woman, ever caused me to hide or hunker down, expecting a beating. The swell of their thighs and hips, the creases in their laps, invite tenderness, not pain. Their boobs feel the exact opposite of pain. Even their shoulders are soft. Nothing about them can hurt you in the least.

I see how they glance at me, know I scare them.

A camera flashes in my eyes.

"Good one," Terrence says, then turns around, aims his camera into the room, and fires again. The room strobes. "Guaranteed, I'll have some great shots once the drinking gets in high gear. Might make the trophy page on my site."

"What site?" I ask.

"Greatest hits and misses," he says. "All the good stuff. Need a secret code to get to the page, though. Can't have some of it getting out there, you know what I mean." Terrence aims his camera at the butt of a girl I think is named Heidi. The camera flashes.

"Damn, she's sweet!" Terrence sucks in his breath sharply, then slaps my arm with the back of his hand. "You play your cards right, I'll let you take a peek at the site. Course you don't play your cards right, you may be the star of your very own what-were-they-thinking page," he says, laughing more to himself than me, like he's in on his own personal joke. He throws his arm around my neck and holds up the camera to point at the two of us and it flashes, so I'm blind for a few seconds. When I get my eyes back, he's showing me the camera screen. There's Terrence, mouth open in laughter, teeth gleaming, having the greatest time, and there's me looking like I just got pulled into a mug shot.

"I'll come back after you've had a few more drinks," Terrence either promises or threatens, wearing his big grin. "See if we can actually capture you with a smile on your face."

And then he's off, moving into the grooving bodies, camera flashing away, leaving me alone on the stool, watching.

"Kurt, get over here," Scott shouts over the music. He stumbles over and grabs my arm, towing me behind him toward one of the girl groups I've watched for the last hour. At least Studblatz's basement is dark and noisy, all the better to hide my scars and stutter. I let my hair fall against my jaw, covering it.

"Hello, ladies." Scott inserts himself into the center of the girl ring. They giggle as if he's done something brilliant. I wonder what that's like, to have that level of charm. Scott sips at his drink and twirls around for all of them to admire. They cheer. He can do no wrong. I stand outside the circle until Scott reaches out of the group and grabs my arm and tugs me into the center next to him. We are the bull's-eye of attention. I look down at my feet.

"I don't know if all you ladies have personally met our new star," Scott shouts over the music. "Coach recruited him," he continues. "You believe that? That's how good my man here is. Coach stole him from Lincoln."

"Wow," one girl shouts back. I imagine her rolling her eyes, but when I chance a peek at her, she's staring right back at me, the drink straw between her teeth while she winds the other end around her finger.

"That's right," Scott keeps hollering. "He's a terror on the field but just a gentle, misunderstood beast off it." Scott slaps my back. The girls titter. "Ladies, introduce yourselves to the man who's going to lead us all the way to a state championship."

"Really?" another girl asks, sounding genuinely curious, making it a record for the number of girls I've met who show any interest in the game. This girl keeps watching me. She takes a sip from her drink, then purses her lips while her eyes wander all over me in a way that causes springs to tighten throughout my body. She steps up to me and grabs the thumb of my hand and then laces her fingers between mine.

"My, what big hands you have, Mr. Wolf," the girl says, batting her eyes. She has to have seen my scars but . . . it doesn't seem . . . she doesn't seem to mind. She leans in until her bare stomach brushes the zipper of my jeans.

"You've got dangerous eyes," she tells me, barely above the music.

"Marcia wins the prize!" Scott hollers. "Mr. Wolf. I love it. Mr. Wolf. We've got a winner!"

That's how I get my nickname. That's how I meet Marcia . . . and Tammy and Glory and Mona and Jessica. Lamar slips into my head as I keep drinking, surrounded by all this beauty. He tells me to take what I can get because tomorrow everything could change.

With that thought, and lots of Jack and Coke, I end up on the couch and Marcia ends up in my lap.

"I saw you play on Friday!" she tells me, putting her mouth right on my ear to be heard over the music. She lets her lips rest there when she's through talking. Her fingers come up to comb my hair out of the way and then her tongue flicks against my lobe. I'm getting way too excited below and I try readjusting my pants but she's sitting there and no way she can't feel it.

"I hear . . . Mr. Wolf . . . you're the biggest . . . ," she says, and her lips travel from my ear to my jaw to my neck. Still kissing me, her fingers come up to trace the long scar running down under my eye. Her other hand reaches down between her legs and lands on the spot where I'm totally hard. "Are you the strongest, too?"

Throughout the basement bar area people are sloppy drunk and swaying to the music—plebes and varsity starters, cheerleaders and dance line girls. Just before I stop caring about anyone but Marcia, I notice Goldberg handing a drink to Tom Jankowski and Jankowski laughing and rubbing Goldberg's scabby, bald head like a genie lamp, like they've been best friends for life.

D A N N Y

13

"How'd your meet go today?" Dad asks. He pulls a slice of pizza from the cardboard delivery box resting on his lap. A long string of cheese attaches itself to his mustache. We sit on the couch, watching TV. I pull out a slice of pizza from my own delivery box balanced on my knees and bite into the soggy, hot goodness.

"Okay," I say. "Bruce scored a personal best on rings and I got best score on high bar. Fisher surprised everyone. He got second-highest score on parallel bars. But we've got no depth. Farmington High killed us."

"And why is that?" my dad asks, his eyes not looking at me, but watching the Friday night movie on TV, half listening to what I say. "Why no depth?" His hangdog expression deepens every year. The shadows under his eyes, which I never really noticed until after Mom died, progressively darken from lack of sleep during the week, so that by this time every Friday he looks like someone's given him two shiners in a fight. I think about answering his question by saying, *Well, if you ever came to a meet, you'd know our team has one, maybe two, good scores on each event but that we can't put up three solid scores on every apparatus and that's what the judges combine.*

But I don't say that. My dad has basically worked two full-time jobs ever since Mom died, putting in long hours and also volunteering his time at a free clinic. It's selfish of me to expect him to stop treating really sick people to make one of my regular meets. He says he'll go see me in the state meet if I qualify. He won't come right out and say it, but sports, in his eyes, should be more like a hobby, like chess, and shouldn't be taken too seriously. Especially if it gets in the way of grades. That's why my secret plan to get an athletic scholarship is so important. I play and replay the scenario of a letter arriving one day and me opening it and handing it over to him—an offer for a full-ride schol-arship. Then he'll understand why I spent all that time in the gym, why I pestered him to go to private clubs during the off-season. It won't be just a dumb hobby when I hand him that letter. It doesn't matter to me if he can pay for my education. *I* want to pay for it, show him I can do it on my own. Until that magic letter arrives, though, there's a little thing called math that keeps harshing my buzz.

"How's algebra going?" he asks, losing interest in his first question. *That's* what I have to work with here.

"We need more guys on the team," I say, ignoring the algebra question. "New guys get scared off when they step in the gym and see how much work's involved."

"Speaking of work, are you keeping up on your home-work assignments?"

"I mean, it isn't like other sports where you can just pick up a ball and start running or be competitive after doing it for a week. It takes a while just to put together a semi-decent routine."

"Hmmmm." Dad nods like he's being thoughtful but I know that means he's too tired to argue with me and too tired to keep talking past me. What he's really trying to do is catch what the lady accused of murdering her husband is telling the district attorney on TV. He has his ear tipped toward the screen while he chews, still pretending to listen to me. It's okay, though, because I do the same thing back whenever he starts lecturing me about getting good grades. The two of us have an understanding. The key is to not upset the all-seeing eye of Mom's ghost while we live completely separate lives under the same roof. In two more years it won't matter, anyway. I'll be out of here.

After devouring our individual pizzas, we both slouch back into the couch. The TV screen fades and Mom comes into my head—a memory of her leaning over me, holding a teaspoon of medicine under my nose, waiting patiently for me to open my mouth and swallow it. A warmth comes over me that I cannot hold and then it's gone. Mom once said you could put yourself in someone's head if you thought hard enough about them. She said memories of the dead meant they were out there, thinking about you, trying to say hello. Was she out there right now, thinking of me like I was thinking of her? Dad laughed when Mom told us her theory. We'd been eating breakfast in the kitchen after burying our cat, Pebbles, in our backyard.

Dad wanted to just bag it and throw it in the garbage but Mom insisted on a ceremony. Dad said Mom's theory was superstition.

After she died, he talked differently. Once, after I woke from a dream about her that was so vivid—about the three of us swimming together on the ocean, out at sea, and surrounded by shark fins . . . or dolphin fins, I was never sure which—he told me that she was still around and paying attention to us, and that was her way of talking to us. He said he dreamed of her all the time and looked forward to his sleep for that very reason.

I wonder if she's saying hello to Dad at the same time as me, if he's thinking of her right now on the couch, seeing her like I am.

"Dad," I ask, "are you . . ." I glance over and my question fades. Dad's eyes are closed and his head lolls at an angle that'll give him a crick in his neck when he wakes. His mouth hangs open. I turn back to the TV. After another minute he begins to snore softly.

". . . *dreaming about her?*" I whisper. I take the pizza box off his lap and put it on the kitchen table. Then I grab the comforter off the couch arm and drape it over him and put a pillow under his head. He never even budges.

K U R T

Monday practice starts with game film in the team room. I scratch myself while Coach plays, rewinds, freezes, and replays video of last Friday's game. While he talks, my eyes wander around the half-lit room. Judging from the looks of things, the other guys find game film about as interesting as studying the industrial revolution. Scott, though, peers intently at the TV monitor while scribbling in his notebook, bobbing his head along with Coach's game breakdown. I fan myself with a sheaf of plays I'm trying to memorize, flipping through them flashcard style, thinking: *If I put half as much effort into my vocabulary cards for Spanish, I'd be fluent by now.*

The TV screen goes black, the video finishes. The room lights flicker back on, causing a stir of bodies trying to wake up.

"Men, let's see if we can fix some of those errors I pointed out here," Coach Brigs says. "Hope you were paying real good attention."

Uh-oh.

"Drills, drills, drills," Coach goes on, standing in front of the TV, arms crossed in front of his chest, whistle around his neck, and folded papers stuffed down the front waistband of his shorts. "Practice makes perfect," he says to the room. "Out on the field in twenty minutes. Stragglers will be running laps. Afterward we'll hit the weights. Hard!"

Scott is still taking notes. I'm impressed.

"Move!" Coach snaps.

I get up first. Walking past Scott, I glance down at his notebook, expecting to see scores of X's and O's forming play diagrams and maybe some key concepts underlined with bullet points and notes in the margins. Instead, I see a sketch, a cartoon. Naked ladies climbing up and sliding down nine block letters spelling out "THIS SUCKS!" In one corner of the page, there is a mushroom cloud going off. In another corner, a spaceship shoots lasers and a stick soldier is machine-gunning air and a skull has a knife handle sticking out of its eye socket. Scott keeps the page tipped so Coach can't see it.

Twenty-five minutes later, Assistant Coach Stein is doing his best to drown out the team's lingering Monday blahs on the field. "Bust a hump! Bust a hump! Hustle! Hustle! Hustle!" Coach Stein shouts.

Except for Studblatz and Jankowski, the slouching line of yawning guys waiting for drill instructions stands like dozing heifers. Studblatz and Jankowski, though, they're more like werewolves patrolling the chalk lines, itching for any opportunity to rip apart one of the lessers. Studblatz never stops clanking helmets with whoever's nearby and pushing guys around like he's getting paid to herd them.

On the far sideline, older men—players' fathers—gather together and stand like coaches themselves. Some smoke, some chew tobacco, some chew sunflower seeds, others chew gum. Some hold cans of beer in little paper bags; others drink half-liter bottles of sports drinks like they're exercising right alongside us. They all seem to watch practice with faces full of worry and disappointment. Scott's father stands among them, a rolled-up newspaper in his hand, slapping it into the palm of his other hand like a billy club. Coach Brigs, I notice, never acknowledges the group of fathers. A squad car is parked nearby on the grass. Terrence tells me the squad car belongs to Jankowski's dad, a cop. Guess he makes his own rules about where it's legal to park.

Scott, hands on his hips, face mask swinging back and forth in an exaggerated "no," keeps cussing under his breath, as if the sight of turf and sun irritates him. His golden boy routine faded right after we finished reviewing game film. He must've continued drinking from Saturday's party straight through most of Sunday because his sweat smells like a brewery and he started dry-heaving on his way out onto the field. Still, he's got it easy since he gets to wear the red vest over his practice jersey. Only player that gets one. The red vest means don't hit or tackle him in drills or scrimmage no matter what because a quarterback is too valuable to ever risk injuring in practice. He's untouchable.

"I know you fellas don't need reminding that we've got homecoming this Friday," Coach Brigs speechifies. "God help you boys if we don't destroy the Millfield Bucks." Outside on the field, Coach Brigs communicates mostly through shouting that causes the veins running along his neck to bulge thick as night crawlers. "You understand what I'm saying, soldiers? I'm not concerned with losing because that is so unthinkable I cannot even tolerate thinking about it. No, I'm talking about not winning by enough. It's *our* homecoming. It's *our house*! You understand? I want to send a message to the entire division: You come to the Knights' field and you should be thankful if you walk out under your own power."

A grunt of agreement off to my left. It's Jankowski practically vibrating with Coach's words. He beats his chest with his fists like Tarzan. I'm not kidding. He actually beats his chest and he's not trying to be funny.

"That's what I'm talking about, boys." Coach slaps his clipboard, then points at Jankowski. "Tommy, you hear me loud and clear, don't you, son?"

"Yes, *sir*!" Jankowski bellows back.

"Good boy."

On the side of the field, the fathers offer no reaction to Coach Brigs's pep talk. Some of them cross their arms over their chests or adjust the bills of their baseball caps. Some spit because the chewing tobacco wedged into their bottom lip forces them to drain thick brown streams into the surrounding grass. Others spit because watching their own sons play seems to pain them with frustration even though they cannot look away from us, like viewing a bad car accident. I don't think Scott's dad chews tobacco.

Halfway through scrimmage, Coach Brigs blows his whistle like he's trying to pop it, then Frisbees his clipboard inches above our helmets. Leaves of paper flutter down on the team while the clipboard sails out to the twenty-yard line.

"No. No. No. *No. Noooo!*" Coach shouts, whipping off his ball cap and slapping it against his leg. He looks back up at us and the sight still pisses him off. "Goddammit, no!" he repeats. "What kind of pansy camp do you think I'm running here?"

We don't answer.

"Scott, so help me," Coach gripes, "you line up that slow under center again and I will sit you down, son, you understand?" The gate of Scott's face mask dips, telling Coach he understands.

"Studblatz, whatsa matter with you?" Coach taunts. "My niece tackles harder than that. If you want, I can get you a set of pom-poms and let you try out for the cheerleading team."

The image of Studblatz in a skirt and pom-poms makes me laugh out loud.

"You think that's funny, Brodsky?" Coach stares at me for what feels like a full minute.

Crap!

"No, sir," I say, shaking my helmet.

Coach wipes his mouth with the back of his hand, runs his fingers through sweat-matted hair, then yanks the ball cap back onto his head.

"Men, this isn't a joke," he says. "We face a serious attack on our good name this Friday. Our community is coming out to support us. Your families will be there to cheer you on, and if the best you can do is some half-assed job, then walk out right now. I don't have time for this." Coach slowly turns a full three hundred and sixty degrees until his eyes hit all of us. "Homecoming, men, is not some silly game. It is what glues our community together. It's what gives your little brothers and nephews—and, one day, sons—hope. It's what comforts your mothers, sisters, and girlfriends with the knowledge they are safe because they are in the capable hands of young men who aren't afraid to enter a battlefield, go head-to-head with the ene-my, and come out victorious. If you think this is anything less than the defense of all that is good and decent in this world, then go home. I don't need you. If you believe in what I'm preaching and want to enter a righteous war by my side, then take your dresses off, strap up, and start hustling."

More fathers gather along the sideline as they come from work, watching us with grave concern. They never stray from a ten-yard area, on the opposite side of the field, by the visitor bleachers.

After scrimmage, I ask Terrence why they never come closer.

"They're not allowed," Terrence answers quietly, way quieter than he normally talks, which is always loud and laughing. He glances around to makes sure others aren't that close. "Last year there was an . . . *altercation*," he says, making quotes around the word with his fingers. "Now there's a court order preventing parents from coming onto the field during practice beyond that point at the visitors' bleachers."

"An altercation?"

"Yeah." Terrence nods. "One of the dads was pissed off his boy wasn't in the starting lineup, so at the next practice, he punched out Coach Stein."

"Lucky thing Juh-Jankowski's dad's a cuh-cop," I say. "Coach Buh-Brigs must be glad he's here."

Terrence snickers. "Not exactly," he says. "It was Tom's dad that punched Coach Stein. He parks his squad car out here to let everyone know he's still keeping an eye on things, court order or not."

"Juh-Jankowski didn't start last year?" I ask, surprised.

"No way, dude. Tom was way smaller last year, before he started taking *supplements*." Terrence makes air quotes again. "He's beefed up a lot since then."

"You mean Cuh-Coach's suh-supplements."

"Yeah, his *special vitamins*." Terrence exaggerates the words sarcastically, then his helmet swivels, checking that no one is close enough to hear us.

"Good vitamins," I say from under my helmet. Terrence rolls his eyes at me and moves in close enough that our shoulder pads clack together. "'Roids, dude," Terrence whispers. "These boys don't play. They shoot the shit now. Get it from Coach Stein."

"You tuh-tuh-take them?" I ask, curious.

"Are you kidding?" Terrence asks, grabbing at his crotch. "And have my balls shrivel into raisins? Fuck no. I want the rushing title more than anybody but I don't play around when it comes to my dick. I keep it covered when I stick and I don't take nothing that makes it sag like a wind sock." He starts laughing again. "I got a reputation to keep up with the ladies."

"Shuh-sure you do," I say, giving Terrence a friendly shove. But I'm wondering just how much bigger I could get, how much safer I could make my world, if I took Coach's supplements. By the time we enter the locker room, it's all I'm thinking about.

D A N N Y

15

The hip check sends me bouncing into the lockers right before third period. I'm used to random body blows but this one catches me hard. I'm trying to shake it off when a heavy force slams me a second time from behind, pinning me face-first into the cold metal.

"Asshole," the voice grunts, "think I forgot about that stunt you and your coach pulled in the weight room?"

"No," I squeak out as a hand shoves my head, smushing my right ear against the fins of a locker's air vents. The hand presses harder, squeezing my skull and flattening my cheek, so my plea gets distorted. "Preesh jush let go."

"And think we're just going to forget about the piss on our uniforms?"

"Nuh-uh."

"Or you dropping that squirrel back in Scott's locker?"

Man, we—correction, *I!*—am screwed!

"You like wedgies?" the voice hisses as a hand reaches into my pants, grabs the back of my underwear and jerks the waistband up behind me. Feels like a rope's lynching my nuts and ass crack.

"Aaaaahh!"

Hanes tighty whities cut through my thighs as my feet leave the ground.

"Goddammitmotherfuckerassholeshitbucket!" I squeal.

"You like that?" The voice laughs huskily, and I'm gasping as the pain between my legs turns into something that makes me want to black out.

"Leave him alone," a girl's voice pleads.

"Go fuck yourself, raghead."

"Hey, assface!" Another girl's voice—not pleading, demanding—joins in. "Let him go before I kick my boot up your fat ass."

The wedgie slumps, dropping me back to the ground. Relief—sweet relief—floods my groin. I can finally turn my head to confirm that yes, indeed, assface is Tom Jankowski, the big blob I beat in Coach's leg lifts competition. Then I see a caramel-skinned Indian girl hugging her books to her chest, doing her best to come to my defense. Even scared shitless, even with my nuts throbbing from near castration by wedgie, I still can't help noticing the girl's long dark lashes and her large eyes. They're fearful, now, and her forehead furrows with fright and that makes me love her all the more. Her name is Indira. She's a junior, but compared to Tom, she looks like I do—a dwarf caught in the land of giants.

"What's that, dyke?" Tom asks a goth girl stepping

protectively in front of Indira and wearing steel-toed Doc Martens boots. Though she's not much bigger than me or Indira, goth girl looks like she might actually enjoy tearing Tom's throat out with her teeth.

"Tina," Indira cautions, still hugging her books with one arm while using the other hand to restrain her friend. *Don't hold her back*, I think. *Let her kick Tom's ass.*

"Listen to the raghead, dyke," Tom says.

"Why, you—" Tina starts, but Indira cuts her off.

"Tina, stop it," Indira whispers. Other students close in around us, sniffing blood and humiliation. Tom moves toward Tina and Indira, forgetting about me. He is rhinoceros-big. I thought guys weren't ever allowed to hit girls but something in Tom's face tells me he feels different.

"Real tough guy," Tina says loud and clear, not backing down an inch. She holds up her pinky finger. "That about the size of your little weenie?" she taunts. "That why you need to act so tough?"

Students around us start laughing.

Tom's forehead and cheeks go from white to pink while the streak of zits on his neck flames. He moves within punching distance as his hands turn to fists. If only I were the size of—

"*TRY IT!*" Tina wails loud enough to stop all other noise and movement. "Try it and I'll kick you so hard in the nuts you'll be coughing 'em out!" She shifts into a karate stance, her heavy boots planted and ready to kick a hole through drywall. Tom stops. His cheeks grow a volcanic shade of pink, eyes darting from Tina to Indira to me and then at the crowd of students. He's a giant, but Tina has everyone convinced she's tough *and* crazy. Indira just looks ill.

"What's going on here?" Mr. Warren, the senior chemistry teacher, demands. His jowls flap like a hound dog's as he waddles toward us. Mr. Adams, the geometry teacher, rushes up from the opposite side.

"Nothing," Tom grumbles, not taking his eyes off Tina. He's bigger than both teachers. Tina stays in her karate stance, ready to Bruce Lee the entire hallway. Mr. Warren puts his hand on her shoulder and she flinches it off.

"Young lady, that's about enough!" Mr. Warren snaps.

"Tell *him* that!" Tina screeches.

Damn! I think, admiring her more with every passing second.

"Sorry, Mr. Warren," Tom says through clenched teeth. "These three girls must've run out of tampons." He makes sure to catch my eye as well as Tina's and Indira's.

Asshole!

"Just get to class," Mr. Warren tells him. "And you"—he points at Tina—"are coming to the office with me right now. I won't stand for this type of behavior."

Tom's hallway attack ripples through me the rest of the day, distracting me even during our home meet against Waukasha Hills. I can't shake free of knowing how easily he could have destroyed me.

"Something bothering you?" Bruce asks me while we're rolling out the three large wrestling mats we use for the floor exercise event.

"Yeah." I grunt because the big wrestling mats are heavy

as hell and it takes half our team to get them unrolled and taped together. "I almost got murdered today, thanks to you."

"Me?"

"Jankowski wasn't such a big fan of our little piss stunt. Or the return of the squirrel."

"We were *recycling* the squirrel," Bruce corrects, snickering.

"It's not funny, dude." I sniff. We've got the first mat unrolled and are walking back to start on the next one. "Jankowski tried pushing my head through a wall," I say, not mentioning the wedgie part, "and then I had to get saved by two girls."

"Oh, shit, dude, that was you?" Fisher jumps in. "I heard two hellcats almost clawed Jankowski's eyes out in the hallway after he wedgied a freshman right up off the ground." Fisher slaps the rolled mat we're pushing, then bursts out laughing.

"I heard that one girl is a psycho," Gradley adds from Fisher's other side. "She tried to hit one of the teachers that came out to stop it. Or tried to bite him or something. Heard he has to go get an AIDS test, now."

"No shit?" Fisher asks, still chuckling. "Wish *I* had a girl like that hanging around, waiting to protect me. Did you get her number, Danny?"

I don't say anything, just push against the mat, trying to get it rolling. I'm trying to make sure my eyes don't tear up. I can't stand it when they tear up. It's like it proves I really am a baby.

"It's not funny, Fish," Bruce says. I can tell he's watching me as we unroll the big mat. "We'll get 'em," Bruce says quietly. "Trust me. We'll get 'em."

"'Course we will," Fisher says on my other side. "Count on it."

I wait for a second until I know I won't cry. "I don't want to get anybody," I mumble at the mat. "We get them, and then they get us or just get me again. It won't stop and they're way bigger."

"Danny, you can't just let them run around beating on you or some other kid and think they can get away with it," Bruce says, huffing as he puts his shoulder into rocking the third mat to unroll. "It ain't right."

I'm pretty good on floor exercise, even on wrestling mats that feel like tumbling on mud and give you no spring. Thoughts of what I should've done in the hallway against Tom, how I should've gotten out of the jam, what I could've said, fuel my body so I'm flipping and twisting in a full adrenaline rush. I bounce through my routine and finish without even realizing it, without realizing I nailed all my passes without a wobble. I bow to the judges and then look up into the bleachers. All seventeen fans in attendance give me a nice clap. That means my teammates' parents, Fisher's girlfriend, a lost teacher killing time, and a wayward janitor think I'm aces. I don't really ever expect to see my dad, but always hope maybe he'll show up and surprise me. He's not here tonight.

"Great routine." Bruce holds out a chalky fist and we touch knuckles. My whole meet goes that way: me killing on all my routines while all I'm really imagining is killing Jankowski. High bar is the last event and I'm last up. By now, I've imagined 197 different variations on how to completely torture and destroy Tom Jankowski if I were the size of Tom Jankowski. Or Kurt Brodsky. Walking over to the bar, escorted by Coach Nelson, I've exhausted all mental scenarios involving power tools, lawn mowers, sewage treatment plants, uranium pellets, bedbugs, exotic snakes, ferrets, piranha, Tina's boots, an Iranian women's soccer team, and, perhaps, a wood-chipper. I'm beginning scenarios involving large circus animals, clown suits, and shark chum as I stand waiting for the judge's signal that I can jump up and begin my best event. Absently, I glance over to my teammates, all clapping for me, and then my eyes wander out into the almost bare bleachers, maybe hoping Dad snuck in at the last minute.

"No suicide trick today, right?" Coach whispers. "It's not quite ready."

"No," I say out the side of my mouth, reassuring him. "No suicide. Not yet."

"Okay, good."

Out in the bleachers, all seventeen attendees have been joined by two more bodies. I make sure my eyes aren't playing tricks on me.

"Danny," Coach prods. "Judge is ready."

"Huh?" I ask, not paying attention because I'm seeing person eighteen, Tina, the girl who saved me today. But that's only half of it. Person number nineteen is Kurt Brodsky, sitting off by himself like mob muscle come to finish the job Tom didn't get to in the hallway.

"Danny." Coach puts his hand on my shoulder. "He's ready for you."

Oh, yeah, he's ready for me, I think. *He's going to kill me dead after this meet. Son of a bitch!*

"Let's go." Coach pushes me forward. I shake my head, raise my hand to the judge without seeing him, then leap up for the bar with Coach's help. Tom Jankowski leaves my head, replaced by Kurt Brodsky just sitting out there watching. And Tina, the goth warrior? What's up with that? My body drills through on autopilot while my mind races. I'm sailing around the bar smoothly, letting my arms and legs think for me. I could show them, show both of them I'm somebody. Show off for Tina, say thank you. And for Kurt and his Orcs, give him a message that I'm more than a kid they can beat on whenever they want.

I throw the suicide.

I place it right after my V-hinge grip change, add an extra two loops for speed, and chuck it without really thinking about what I'm doing until I'm upside down in the air above the bar and my mind finally wakes up, screaming *What the fuck are you doing?!?!?!*

A sharp intake of breath from somewhere below confirms I'm in trouble. Then everything goes quiet as I come out of my second somersault above the bar and blindly stretch my hands out hoping something connects and it's not my neck, nose, or lips. I'll even take a shoulder.

Chung!

The bar smacks the meat of my palms and my fingers snare it for dear life. My legs keep swinging down and back up. I think I hear the universe—that is to say, all nineteen people in the bleachers plus my teammates plus the other team plus the coaches and judges—release their breath at the same time, then hoot and whistle and start clapping. I finish with my safe full twist layout and hit the mat without a single misstep or deduction.

"Yeeeaaahhh!" Bruce hollers across the entire gymnasium. He's running at me full tilt, pumping his arms.

"Jesus, kid!" Coach slaps my back. "You really are trying to give me a heart attack. I thought we said no suicide."

"We did," I say, smirking. "I forgot."

It's the best score I've ever made on high bar, only a couple tenths away from the high score at last year's state meet.

"Scared me half to death, son," the judge says to me at the end of the meet. "But I can't wait to see that again at the end of the season."

Amid the fist bumps and high fives and backslaps that create a chalk cloud around me, I stare out into the bleachers. Parents and girlfriend are coming down to congratulate us on our first win.

Kurt's gone.

So's Tina.

KURT

Kurt." Coach Brigs stops me coming out of the showers. "Coach Stein and I would like a word with you in my office when you're dressed." I'm the last guy in the locker room, having stayed late in the weight room again like I always do. Best time of day, alone by myself, all memories demolished under stacks of iron, my brain quiet for a short while. Coach still being here catches me off guard. Shower flip-flops slap the bottom of my heels steady as a metronome on the way back to my locker while I wonder what I did wrong and what my punishment might be. I towel off quickly and head to Coach's office, the collar of my T-shirt sponging the damp from the ends of my slicked-back hair. Assistant Coach Stein sits on Coach's couch lazily lobbing a baseball back and forth between his hands.

"Hey, Kurt." He smiles, stops tossing the baseball, and

pats the empty space on the couch for me to join him. Coach Brigs is leaning forward in the squeaky chair at his desk, diagramming plays with one pencil while chewing on another pencil. He stops scribbling when I enter and pulls the other pencil out of his mouth. A country-and-western song plays quietly on an old radio on his desk.

"Have a seat, son," Coach Brigs says, opening up with a big smile. I must've done something pretty bad if he's giving me a world-class grin like that, like he can't wait to spring something on me.

"Kurt, it goes without saying that Coach Stein and I have been very pleased with your progress so far and your contribution to our team. Your work ethic is outstanding. Hell, Frank here won't stop talking about how you're the first one in and the last one out of the weight room every day. He doesn't need to brag to me, though, because I see it with my own eyes."

I glance from Coach Brigs to Coach Stein and realize I'm still standing. Maybe they aren't about to punish me. I slowly walk over to the couch and sit down next to Coach Stein, feel his grin beaming at me, warming the side of my cheek.

"Shoot, if every player on the team worked half as hard as this boy here, there'd be no question we'd be walking all over our opponents on our way to a state champion-ship," Coach Stein says, and slaps my knee. "Kurt, we all know you're dedicated with a capital *D*."

"You hear that, Kurt? You hear the way Coach Stein brags about you? He'll talk the same way when the scouts come calling, asking about promising players."

Are scouts already asking about me? I wonder.

"Now, I don't want to get your head so swollen that you get it stuck in the doorway when you leave," Coach Brigs continues, "but I do want you to understand just how much we value you. We recognize that great players are a rare commodity, that they come few and far between, and the greatest don't just happen, they're built. They're built through raw talent, dedication, determination, and a willingness to lead a team by example, show others they're willing to do whatever it takes to win."

All the compliments start to make me feel uncomfortable because I'm not sure where this is going. Getting smacked around sucks, but at least when it's happening, it makes sense, not like this, getting compliments for no reason.

"Kurt." Coach Brigs is still smiling at me. "Does that describe you? Are you a leader ready to do whatever it takes to win?"

I rub my hands on the knees of my jeans while I nod at Coach Brigs that, yes, I am ready to do whatever it takes to win. Coach Stein claps his hands together and it rings like a firecracker in the small office.

"I told you," Coach Stein says, like he and Coach Brigs had a bet on how I'd answer. "I told you this boy was on the same page and ready to step it up. Take it to the next level."

Coach Brigs and Coach Stein glance at each other, grins getting even wider, if that's possible.

"It warms my heart to hear this, Kurt. It really does," Coach Brigs says. "Because Coach Stein and I have plans for you. We think you can be our team's next great player. We're talking about building an offensive scheme completely around you and your skills and making you a star—not just on our team but in the whole state. We think you can be the engine that gets us all the way to state and wins us a championship. Whaddya think about that?" Coach Brigs asks, painting a real sweet picture for me while he slowly pulls open a side drawer on his desk.

I nod at him that I like the idea a lot.

"Good boy, Kurt. Good boy," Coach says. I don't mind how it makes me feel when he says this. Way better than getting a belt across the mouth. "Frank and I knew you wouldn't hesitate to step into the role of lead warrior. My hunch about you has been right as rain since the day we first scouted you."

I glance at Coach Stein, still beaming at me, nodding along to Coach's words. He keeps regripping the baseball between his first two fingers and thumb, like he's readying to whip a forkball through Coach's trophy case.

"Now, to get you to the next level, Kurtis," Coach Brigs says, "takes a new level of dedication." Coach Brigs reaches into the open drawer and pulls out a dark blue pill bottle with one of those childproof caps. He sets the bottle on the desk between us, closer to me than him.

"Coach Stein's got a guaranteed system for getting you even bigger and stronger than you already are."

"That's right, Kurt." Coach Stein nods. "This stuff is safer than aspirin when taken on my schedule. Put another fifteen pounds of rock on you in a couple weeks the way you train."

"Kurt, Frank and I wouldn't be approaching you if we didn't see the way you train, didn't see the hunger in your eyes already. That thing burning in you is a rare jewel. It marks you, makes you special, separates you from all the coddled kiddies I see nowadays who cry if their mama's not around to wipe their behinds. But you, boy . . ." Coach begins drumming his fingers on the desk near the bottle of pills as his voice drifts off like he's daydreaming about my training. The three of us sit for a moment, listening to his fingers.

"Kurt," Coach begins again. "That hunger you got can't be taught or coached or trained. I know you want to get bigger. Hell, I can sense it just sitting across from you right now. You feel it, too, don't you, Frank?"

"Sure do," Coach Stein agrees.

"Son," Coach Brigs continues, "I see an absolute warrior, an absolute monster, buried inside you just itching to claw his way out, just waiting to be unleashed on the field of battle, show this world how great a man he is. Are you ready to be that man?"

I think of Crud Bucket, think of all the things I could do to him if I got even bigger.

"Kurt, Coach Stein and myself, we want to do our part to help you realize your full potential."

"Nothing will get you there faster and safer with minimal side effects than D-bol," Coach Stein jumps in. "That's Dianabol."

I nod my head as Coach slides the pills closer across the desk to me.

"I'll give you a full schedule . . ." Coach Stein continues, but I've stopped listening. I'm imagining me, but even bigger, even stronger, imagining no one being able to hurt me ever again. Before I know it, I've pocketed the pills and both Coach Brigs and Coach Stein are slapping me on the back, offering me a path, offering me almost a guaranteed way out. Where I come from, that's bigger than Jesus Himself.

Walking under a halo, imagining a future mapped in the gold of Coach's promises, the bottle of D-bol pills cha-cha-cha-ing like Tic Tacs in my sweatshirt pocket, I almost don't notice the clapping until I'm past the gym door. Curious, I peek my head in. It's a gymnastics meet and it's pathetic. I mean, more gymnasts than fans? Really? Come on. It's funny enough, especially in my good mood, that I almost start laughing. Then something goes *boom* and a kid's flying off a springboard and over a vault like he's been shot out of a cannon. His body tumbles and twists through the air and then his feet pound the thick mat. First thing I think is how great that would be to do over a defensive line into an end zone. Another gymnast signals some judge I can't see from my spot in the doorway and he barrels down the length of the gym and hits the springboard like the first guy. *Boom!* This guy goes even higher and twists more than his buddy. He hits feetfirst but over-rotates and goes sprawling in a body skid across the mat. Everyone goes "*oooohhh*" but he bounces up like he did it on purpose, like it's a cartoon and he can't get hurt. He turns and offers a small head bow to the judge and jogs back to his team with a shoulder shrug.

I want to see more.

Trying to quietly climb the nearly empty bleachers is impossible; they groan under my weight with each step but I've got my pick of good spots. For the next hour I watch these monkeys throwing the craziest tricks, sometimes landing them and sometimes wiping out in ways that have *got* to hurt, even with mats. But the monkeys just smile or clap their hands together, same as how I do after taking a hit, never showing anyone's got the best of me. These guys are small, but fearless. Lamar would've fit right in with them. Makes me miss him while I watch the little guy from my math class—the tiny dude who's always nodding off and getting razzed by Mr. Klech—bounce and flip along the square of wrestling mats. His teammate—the Chinese guy ready to duke it out with Jankowski that day in the lockers even though he's half his size—gets up in the rings and owns them. He's holding poses on the rings—dangling in midair with arms sticking straight out from his body like a crucifix while his legs shoot forward—that would crush me or anyone on our team trying it. Then he's swinging in giant loops that turn into a blur of body twists as he flicks the rings away. When he sticks the landing, I suddenly wonder if maybe he *could* handle Jankowski.

Nothing beats the trick I watch my tiny math class buddy throw on the high bar, though. Dude is whipping around the bar like he's got rockets attached to his ankles. He keeps letting go and regrabbing the bar in different positions as if on a dare. Makes me nervous just watching. I'm not the only one, either. His coach stands under the bar the whole time, arms spread out, as if expecting the kid to burst into flame and he'll have to catch the pieces. Then the kid lets go, heading straight up, flipping above the bar and he's dead. I mean he's going to come straight down on the bar and snap his back. I open my mouth but can't yell. He's still flipping, still dead, as his body arcs over the bar and he's got no choice but to pile-drive his head into the floor from a drop of fifteen feet. His coach, arms raised, eyes wide, ain't about to break *that* fall. Then, like magic, the dude's hands reach out from this blur and snag the bar. A chalk cloud puffs and next thing I realize, the kid is back to whipping around the bar, unhurt. When he lets go a last time and lands without a crash, I finally let out my breath.

His routine ends the meet. I'm clapping mostly out of relief that he's not dead, but it's also pretty amazing. I should congratulate him, I think, him and his other monkey-mates. Then I spot that goth girl, Tina, the one from the lunchroom who claims she knows me. She's two empty bleacher sections over but heading my way. How long's she been here? Was she watching the meet the whole time? No way am I letting her bring me down with her shitty memories of Meadow's House. Screw that. I grip the pill bottle in my sweatshirt pocket and hop down the creaky bleachers, scrambling through the gym doors for a clean getaway.

Once outside the school building, I relax, pretty sure I've escaped. Crossing the student parking lot, partly blinded by a low-hanging sun, I sense someone approaching from behind a small herd of parked cars.

It's her, again. Tina. Even with the heat rippling off the warm asphalt, she's got on her black leather jacket and combat boots. Before she can open her mouth, I put a hand up.

"Juh-juh-just leave me alone."

"I was there, too," she says. "I remember you and Lamar and I remember Mr. Sanborn—"

I move on her real fast. So fast it surprises me. Surprises me how quickly my own anger can flash. *I don't want to talk about it!* My right hand reaches out and clamps her wrist, twisting it so she has to kneel down on the oily blacktop or risk breaking a bone. My other hand grabs her neck before she can scream.

"*Don't* . . . don't you ever muh-muh-mention his nuh-nuh-name. Understand? Nuh-nuh-not *ever!*"

Her eyes bulge as my hand tightens around her throat. All those little muscles and tendons between my thumb and fingers feel so, so . . . delicate . . . so easy to crush in one jerk. Such a simple way to silence her, keep everything a secret. Something boils up in me at the thought, something wicked. Something Crud Bucket would do . . . *Ever breathe a word of this and I'll cut you into pieces. Put you in trash bags. No one'll even notice you're missing. No one ever misses garbage.* His threat reaches me even now, even after all these years, from the time I caught him bent over Lamar, pants down. Lamar, who never backed down or gave in, crying in a way that told me Crud Bucket had finally found a way to break him.

Little goth girl struggles in my grip, eyes dancing wildly in search of mercy while shame, slick as Vaseline, coats my outside and insides—same as it does every day—with the failure and weakness that buried Lamar.

"Sh-sh-*shit!*" I let go of her neck before I accidentally squeeze it limp. She falls backward against the door of an old, rusty Subaru, clutching her throat, heaving for air.

"What's up your ass, anyway?" she snaps, hacking up

some lung and spitting so it lands next to my feet. "I mean, Jesus, I'm only trying to be friendly and you're, like, a dick."

"Suh-suh-sorry."

"You oughta be," she says, rubbing at her neck. "That first day, in the lunchroom, I couldn't believe it was you, how big you got," she goes on, acting like she didn't just call me a dick. "I mean, I knew it was you 'cause of your sca . . . anyway, you want to be left alone, fine!"

"I duh-duh-don't ruh-ruh-remember you at all," I say, though she looks maybe a little familiar beyond the piercings and eyeliner and dyed hair and black nails.

"Everyone here comes from such cush families and it's like I can't even tell people how I grew up 'cause they look at me like I'm a freak."

A puff of air escapes my lips while I let my eyes wander up and down her real slow. "Muh-muh-might be your costume," I suggest.

"I *am* a freak. I know. But now you're here and I thought, *finally*, someone in this place that'll know me. I mean, *could* really know me. Who gets it." Tina watches me as she says this last part like I'll suddenly open my arms and give her a big hug. I do nothing but roll my eyes. Of course she mistakes this as a signal to keep talking. "I was in the girls' quarters only for about six months, thank God, before they placed me . . . actually the first family sucked, but the family after that was okay and the one I'm with now is all right. They let me do my own thing. . . . Anyway, I remember you and some of the other boys at . . . the place. None of you talked much. We'd heard rumors about what Mr.—" I stop her with a warning finger. I'm not kidding about her speaking his name again or teaching her a lesson if she does. "About what . . . what's-his-name was doing to the boys over in your unit."

"They wuh-wuh-weren't rumors," I say, and I wobble for a second, trying to knock back the ugly taste rising up in my mouth. Tina's talking again but I'm no longer paying attention, finding it hard enough just to maintain my balance as I turn away.

". . . because I know what happened, I mean I was living the same situation—"

"No." I try cutting off the voice behind me since she won't take any type of hint. "No you wuh-wuh-weren't."

"Okay, but I'm here, now, to talk to . . . if you want. I don't mind. Really."

When I turn back around, Tina's sitting on the hood of the Subaru, rocking on her butt while clasping her knees up by her chest. She's gazing across the parking lot, toward the football fields. Her offer sounds stiff, like she's been practicing it since the day I left her in the lunchroom and nothing, not even the truth, is going to get in her way. The truth is that living at Meadow's House will never be something I want to talk about, even though Lamar and Crud Bucket sit on either of my shoulders all day, every day. The truth is that I have plans for Crud Bucket soon as I find him unguarded by the state. The truth is that since the day Lamar suffocated in that plastic storage bin, stuffed in there by Crud Bucket as punishment, my insides feel like concrete. The truth is that when they first blamed me for killing Lamar, they were partly right. I was sealed up in that plastic storage bin right beside him and the truth is that it's *me* who should've died, not Lamar. The truth is I keep waking from the same nightmare, throwing off damp sheets and calling for him, but there's no escape and no rescue coming. Never is.

So I go on, waiting for a sign that Lamar forgives me while I plan out ways I'll make Crud Bucket pay. Hard hits on the football field are sometimes the best because they feel deserved and relieve some of my guilt for a second. Explaining any of this—even if I wanted to—leaves me tired. And I never want to explain it: not to the detectives; not to the reporters; not to the teachers; not to the counselors; not to Patti; and especially not to the pathetic, powder-white goth girl rocking on the Subaru. That first wave of shame and anger evaporates over the warm asphalt but little currents remain, leaving me weak.

"Wuh-wuh-why were you in the gym?"

Tina sighs. "Kinda a long, dull story but I run the AVT club—Audio Visual Technology. Lame name, I know, and I was downloading some music for my friend Indira. When I finished up, it was late and I was walking by the gym and saw the gymnastics meet. There's this kid on the team who almost got wedgied to death today but Indira and I saved him. Well, mostly me—and I got three days' detention for it, too, fascists! Anyway, I saw him and I guess I was curious. Then I saw you and wondered why you were there and wanted to, you know, say . . . what I said earlier . . . before you almost crushed my larynx. Asshole!"

She hops off the Subaru and takes a feisty step toward me. "You fucking almost ripped off my head. Got anything to say?"

My anger is gone now. "Suh-suh-sorry," I offer again, meaning it.

"Better be," she huffs, and steps forward, then punches me semi-hard in the stomach. I flex so she hits stone. "Ouch!" She grabs the wrist of her punching hand. "Big ape!"

Watching her do this, for some reason I think of the time I'm riding in Sergeant Schmidt's cruiser, heading back from a full day of trial testimony about what Crud Bucket did to us. It's winter and nightfall comes early and Sergeant Schmidt pulls his cruiser over on a lonely stretch of road without streetlights. He makes me get out of the car, wind whipping and cold making me pull the hood of my coat over my head. He points up to the sky, tells me no matter what happens down on earth, the stars won't change for millions and millions of years. That I'm safe as long as I can look up and see starlight overhead. We get back in his cruiser and he takes me to my new boys' home. I'm wishing for night right now in the school parking lot so I can look up into the sky. . . .

"You deaf, too?"

"Huh?"

"I asked you how you're getting home." Tina says.

"Buh-buh-bus."

"The late-activity buses left an hour ago."

"City buh-buh-bus. The suh-suh-stop is by muh-muh-McDonald's."

"That's, like, a mile away. Who actually takes city buses?"

"Me," I say, shrugging my shoulders. "Suh-suh-suh-sometimes I have a kuh-kuh-car."

"I'll give you a ride."

"It's okay." I turn and walk toward the sun hovering

just above the houses across the parking lot, squinting against the light, feeling my stomach rumble with hunger as I leave Tina behind.

"Come on," she calls out. I don't answer, just shake my head no and keep walking. Coach's money sits in my pocket ready to burn on three Big Macs, maybe four. I'll chow them while waiting at the bus stop. I'm taking the first D-bol tonight. Any doubts I have about the pills fade, pushed out by thoughts of Lamar and how I should've saved him, how I'll get justice for him yet.

D A N N Y

Ronnie pisses them off but at least it's an accident. Bruce and Fisher have no excuse. Then, again, maybe it's all Coach Nelson's fault for dragging us out to tumble at the stupid homecoming pep rally in the first place.

"Come on, guys." Coach Nelson blows into his hands while our team tries to jump-start in the unseasonably chilly morning with some push-ups and jogging in place. Late fall expired sometime last night and now the threat of winter hangs in the air plain as the white vapor coming out our mouths. Despite the calisthenics, I'm still shivering in my dingy gray sweats.

"This is your chance to show off in front of the whole school," Coach says, "advertise a little for next season. It's your moment to shine."

"Advertising's for soulless corporate hacks," Fisher

says, hopping up and down with his hands tucked under his armpits. His nose is red and running from the cold and he stopped wiping at it with his sleeve, so his upper lip is glossy with snot. Coach arches his eyebrows at Fisher.

"Your choice," Coach counters. "Complain now or complain next year when they cancel the season because no new recruits came out for the team." Coach holds up three fingers on his left hand. "We lose Bruce, Gradley, and Jason next year. I'd like the team to at least stay in the double digits."

It's ten A.M. and the home field side of the football bleachers is packed with the entire student body, ecstatic to escape class for the morning even if it is only to attend a pep rally. They get to witness our illustrious homecoming king, queen, princes, and princesses (i.e., jocks and cheerleaders) parade past them on the track circle, paired up in the backs of alumni convertibles. Coach has got us playing court jesters, far as I'm concerned, filler entertainment for the official crowning of the king and queen and the yay-rah-rah for the football team—like they need more of it.

"Okay, we're up," Coach shouts above the marching band, which is in the process of forming the letter *K* on the fifty-yard line. I brace against a strong gust of wind that makes my eyes water, messes up my hair, and cuts through the cotton of my sweatpants.

"I've got severe ball shrinkage over here," Fisher yaps, opening up his waistband and looking down in his pants. "And I do mean *severe!*"

"Sure, Fish, blame it on the cold, buddy," Gradley says.

"I'd hate to get wet on a day like today," Bruce says to Fisher more than the rest of us. "Might catch a cold and die," he says, and the two of them chuckle, sharing some private joke.

"Bruce," Coach calls out. "Lead the way."

Without any of us actually getting warm or stretching properly, my teammates and I do about fifty back hand-springs on the uneven turf of the football field sidelines for our fellow students' entertainment. My wrists and ankles are not happy. The wind is swirling, and if anyone is clapping for us up in the bleachers, I sure don't hear it—especially over the brass horn blurts and snare drum snaps coming from the marching band. What I *do* hear is Scott Miller and Mike Studblatz taunting us nonstop as we set up the mini-trampoline right next to where all of the homecoming court jerks sit on the field.

"Hey, Munchkins, the yellow brick road's that way."

"These fairies are short enough to give a dude head standing up."

"Bet they get lots of practice doing that."

"You think dogs piss on 'em thinking they're fire hydrants?"

Most of my teammates do the right thing. They ignore them. Some of us use it as motivation. Menderson—our vault specialist—launches off the mini-trampoline, soaring over Scott and Mike's heads like a ghost before tucking into a simple front flip and touching down on the mat, easy as if he were stepping over a sidewalk crack. When he lands, I finally hear some applause from the stands. About time.

"Hey, dickweed." Studblatz curses Menderson. "Better watch where you're landing. You touch me and I swear I will pull your fucking arms off."

"Come that close again," Scott adds, "and I'll shove your scrotum up your ass."

Bruce sprints hard and hits the mini-tramp like he wants to bust through it. He flies over the royals while spinning seemingly out of control. He lands on the mat fine but close enough to Chrissy, the homecoming queen, that she jumps out of her seat with her arms folded over her tiara-wrapped head. Laughter and applause reach us from the stands.

"Try that again, little shit. Try it!" Miller threatens, pulling Chrissy into a protective hug.

"Relax." Bruce chuckles as he jogs away.

I go next. Not wanting any trouble, I do a nice clean lay-out twist, making sure I land as far from Scott, Mike, and the rest of the royals as possible while still hitting the mat.

"When did they let junior high kids on the team?" Scott asks me.

Prick!

Fisher jogs real slow down the grass lane and clown-bounces off the mini-tramp. He performs a very simple straddle split leap, his bright smile facing the stands and his ass aimed at the king and queen. In mid-flight, he peels off a fart strong enough to rip open his underwear and add a second to his hang time. Scott grabs the crown on his head as if checking that it didn't get blown off. After he lands, Fisher slaps his knee in a fit of laughter while pointing at the homecoming court.

"How's my ass smell?" Fisher asks them.

"Hey, shit stain," Studblatz yells. "Go crawl back to your sewer."

"I can't," Fisher says. "Your mom's there, sucking off

guys for spare change. She ain't bad. I gave her a quarter last night."

"Laugh now, funny guy." Studblatz chomps. The other royals are actually snickering, though. Fisher steps off the mat to let Leeson fly through the air. Leeson almost lands in Scott Miller's lap. Scott gives Leeson a shove.

"You're, like, a disgusting turd," Chrissy tells Fisher, which, judging by his widening grin, he takes as a compliment.

"Weak." Leeson critiques Chrissy's dig after righting himself from Scott's shove.

Fisher's in a zone, possibly amped up on a six-pack of Red Bull, and has no fear. He points at Scott. "Hey, king-man," he says, "last night, after I blew my load on your mom's face, she told me to remind you to take your steroids today. You, too, Mike." Every mouth in the royal court drops open as Fisher speaks the unspoken. With the wind and the band noise, our skirmish is too far away from the stands for anyone else to hear what Fisher just said. Still tittering, like even he can't believe what's come out of his mouth, Fisher takes a step backward, ready to cheetah his ass to safety as both Scott and Mike stand up like hungry lions, needing to kill. This is when fate turns on Ronnie Gunderson, who has the misfortune and bad timing to be the next gymnast up for a trick. He hits the mini-tramp just as Studblatz crosses the landing mat to chase Fisher. Seeing the big football player in his path, Ronnie, already sprung upward, yelps as his legs and arms spindle, clawing air in a vain attempt to stop his forward momentum. He lands in Studblatz's chest and arms in a full-on love hug. The crowd in the stands breaks out with laughter as little Ronnie momentarily clings to Studblatz like a scared kitten hanging from the mouth of a beast.

"Yaaagh!" Studblatz shouts, spinning once with Ronnie glued to him before hurling him onto the mat. I hear the crowd loud and clear now. They're cheering with full throats. Ronnie bounces off the mat and gets up on his feet as snarky whistles and claps sail out from the stands like unspooling rolls of toilet paper.

"You little shit!" Studblatz hisses at Ronnie. He must think our little freshman—like crazy Fisher—planned to land on him and make him look like a fool. Studblatz advances on Ronnie, ready to pummel him. Ronnie's eyes bug out and he scampers toward Coach Nelson, who's busy scratching his head over on the sidelines. Coach can't hear us but he knows something's up. Fisher's now jogging backward, halfway to Coach if he needs to run for safety, and flapping his arms up and down, encouraging the crowd to stay noisy, keep cheering and laughing. Scott, one hand holding his crown in place, takes a few steps toward Fisher but then stops. He must figure he'll look pretty stupid running after Fisher while wearing a cape.

"Numbnuts!" Scott shouts at Fisher instead.

"Jackass!" Fisher shouts back, then pivots so the stands of students and teachers can't see him grab his crotch at Scott and Mike and the rest of the royals. That's it for me. I'm out. So are my teammates. We flee to the sidelines and the safety of Coach Nelson. When we arrive, Ronnie's face is white as the clouds overhead and tears stream down his cheeks. He's shaking but I don't think it's from the cold. More like he just glimpsed the jaws of death waiting to clamp down and rip out his bones. Part of me wants to tell him to man up, that everything is over now, so relax. Part of me recoils from his naked fear and hurt, afraid his crying is broadcasting our team as "easy prey" to the rest of the student body.

"You're okay, Ronnie," Coach Nelson says, putting an arm on his shoulder, pulling him close to his side, making him face the field so fewer people can see his tears. It isn't exactly how we want to advertise for new recruits.

Fisher is staring out at the field with a big smile plastered on his face when Bruce grabs him by the elbow.

"Come on, man. We don't have much time," Bruce says, tugging on Fisher.

"Where you guys going?" I ask. Fisher, giggling, flashes me the peace sign in response.

Bruce puts his finger up to his lips and says under his breath to me, "Don't go anywhere. The real show's about to start." Then he and Fisher slip between a seam in the stands and disappear. The hollow space under the stands is an easy way to sneak out to the parking lot without being noticed. Except for Bruce's mysterious caution, I'm assuming they're both cutting class for the rest of the day. With a shrug, I turn back to the field and cup my hands to my mouth to warm them up. The stadium's new sound system distracts me as it announces the starting lineup of the football team in booming volume. I forget about Bruce and Fisher, try to ignore Ronnie, and stop blowing on my hands, deciding to stick them under my armpits instead.

K U R T

Mr. Brodsky." Coach pulls me aside before the start of that morning's pep rally. A freak cold snap has rolled in and sharp winds swirl with a nasty chill for this time of year, nipping at earlobes, noses, and fingertips until they're pink. The clouds bunch along like floating mountains and the sun hits my eyes with a clarity that stings. "You've been selected to wear our team's new helmet. The sponsors for our new Jumbotron went out and invested in some fancy helmet. Thing cost a small fortune but it gives the fans a player's-eye view of the game. Also lets 'em hear game sounds from the field brought to them by their favorite potato chip snack." Coach watches me for a reaction. I don't have one. I just nod.

Coach laughs to himself. "Aw, Kurt, I knew I picked

the right boy," he says, then tugs me closer and lowers his voice. "Look, son, between you and me, I'm not too keen on giving the fans all the sights and sounds from the field, especially since most our players cuss like sailors on shore leave. But we're still paying off that big ol' TV and those potato chip folks are writing us a nice fat check. So you're the safest bet I got. You keep doing what you always do. Hit 'em hard and don't say a word. Or at least don't cuss up a blue streak. Keep your mouth shut and put your hand over the mic anytime Studblatz starts teeing off near you. Think you can handle that?"

I nod to him that I can. Coach smiles at me and grabs my shoulder, then squeezes it.

"You're a fast learner, my boy. You keep it up." He jogs out to the field for the pep rally festivities while I climb up into the stands. Homecoming royalty on homemade floats wave from the backseats of convertibles chauffeured by white-haired old duffers.

No surprise, I guess, that Scott and Chrissy are homecoming king and queen. It's a snooze-fest except for the troupe of gymnasts backflipping down a whole length of sideline grass like human Slinkies. They're pretty fun to watch; funner than the marching band and way funner than studying Mike Studblatz's connect-the-dots face as he and Charline are chauffeured past the stands. Wish I could do those gymnastic tricks. Wish I could whip off a string of backflips in the end zone after scoring a touchdown. How cool would that be?

Homemade floats dawdle by us. One says HUNT THE BUCKS in big cardboard letters built on the flatbed of a red pickup with a real dear carcass dragging behind from a rope attached to its neck. Another says BLITZ THE BUCKS with the same type of cardboard letters on a blue pickup truck and two girls in football pads standing in the flatbed, throwing candy into the stands. In the cold, the candy hits us like rocks. The aluminum bleachers might as well be blocks of ice, numbing the backs of my thighs and butt.

Finally they get to the good part and the PA system announces the varsity starters for the game. As each name is called, the new Jumbotron spells it out in flashing letters with digital fireworks popping off around the player's jersey number. When my name comes over the loudspeaker and the Jumbotron flashes it big as the side of an office building, the students in the stands around me start whistling and stomping their feet. For me. The pom-pom girls even do a cheer using my last name. It feels like nothing I've ever experienced. It feels good. I walk out onto the field to stand alongside my teammates in front of the marching band. We line up in the center of the field, far enough from the bleachers that I don't feel like I need to hide my face. Scott and Studblatz leave their thrones to join us, Scott still wearing his red velvet cape and gold crown. *I am a part of this,* I tell myself, *a part of their circle.*

Ceremony finished, we head back to our seats. Scott and Mike go back to their royal court and wait for the convertibles to pick them up and take them for a victory lap. The marching band starts up again, playing loud and off-key, while the bass and snare drums chase a beat the horns don't hear. Doesn't sound like an actual song. Sounds pretty crappy, but who cares. I got my name spelled out on a Jumbotron. People clapped and whistled when they called my name.

I'm climbing back up into the stands when students around me point out on the field. I turn around and see two guys on a motocross bike racing over the football field behind the marching band. The bike's speeding for the homecoming court. The driver and passenger both wear rubber masks of . . . George Bush? The driver is wearing a backpack. Ten feet from crashing into the homecoming court, the driver does a wicked one-eighty skid that sprays a fan of dirt and grass across the king and queen. Passenger Bush hops off the bike and stuffs his hands in the driver's backpack. Passenger Bush pulls out . . . what looks like . . . water balloons and starts pelting Scott and Mike, rapid-firing them, the balloons bursting on Scott's face and Mike's chest. One hits Chrissy on the back as she turns away. The former president gets off three more pitches, hitting Scott and Mike again, before the last balloon sails out onto the grass. It takes Scott and Mike a second to get past the shock but now they're raging—and soaked—and they sprint for their attackers, but it's too late. Both Bushes are back on the motorbike. The rear wheel shreds a thick divot of grass and spits up a shower of dirt as the bike races off the way it came, leaving Scott and Mike wet, dirt-streaked, and grass-stained. The stands are howling again. Studblatz gets down on all fours and I see him punch the turf before grabbing clumps of it and hurling them toward the disappearing motorbike that's leaving an oily purple exhaust in its wake.

"How about an instant replay up on the Jumbotron?" someone shouts.

"First time George Bush got anything right!" someone else yells.

Guys near me start hollering: "Re-Play. Re-Play. Re-Play." By the time the teachers start dismissing us, the whole field rings with the chant.

D A N N Y

Are you crazy?!" I ask the both of them. "What were you guys thinking?"

"What was who thinking?" Fisher asks back, trying hard to appear innocent. Then a smirk creeps across his face and his eyes twinkle like I've seen when he's pulled a stunt before.

"Come on, Fish," I whisper, glancing from Fisher to Bruce, who's suddenly really interested in his notebook doodles and won't meet my eyes. "If I can figure it out, *they're* gonna figure it out."

"Figure *what* out, Danny?" Fisher asks, but he starts laughing and puts a fist over his mouth like he's coughing but that only gets him going more. I glance around, seeing who else in the library is watching us. It's study hall for some students, but I'm up here for lunch period, hiding out from football captains on the warpath since the water-balloon drive-by earlier that morning at the homecoming pep rally. Surprise, surprise I find Fisher and Bruce up here as well.

"I've seen your dirt bike before, dumbass," I say. I know Fisher doesn't care, but I expect Bruce to be more responsible. "Bruce, do you think they're going to just let the whole thing slide?"

Bruce, ignoring my question, keeps doodling until Fisher elbows him. That's when I see Bruce's shoulders start jerking with silent laughter.

"God!" I shake my head. "When they come to kick my ass, I'm snitching you guys out so fast . . ." I start to threaten, but drift off, knowing I won't. "Doofuses!"

"Relax, Danny." Bruce gets hold of himself. "You didn't do anything. You've got nothing to worry about."

I've got nothing to worry about. I've got nothing to worry about. I've got nothing to worry about. I repeat Bruce's words in my head during Mr. Klech's class. We're supposed to silently solve all practice equations on pages 63 and 64 of *Algebra for Life*, but I distractedly wedge the eraser end of my pencil into the textbook's binding and imagine the freshly sharpened No. 2 is a cruise missile seeking a target, set to launch.

With our school's rotating schedule, algebra is my last class that day, and when the bell rings, I sit and wait for everyone to leave first. My plan is to give it ten minutes and let the halls clear before heading to my locker and then go down to the team room. I've successfully avoided

Miller, Studblatz, and Jankowski all day since the pep rally.

Then Kurt Brodsky squeezes himself down into the empty desk next to mine.

Uh-oh.

The last of the students files out of the doorway. I close my launching pad and pile *Algebra for Life* on top of my blank work sheet and notebook. Mr. Klech is busy erasing the chalkboard, his back turned to us.

"Yuh-yuh-you and your friends were pretty fuh-fuh-funny today," Kurt Brodsky stutters at me without any introduction. By "fuh-fuh-funny," I take him to mean Fisher and Bruce's water-ballooning, and maybe even Ronnie accidentally landing on Studblatz. Since Kurt is neither smiling nor laughing, I also take "fuh-fuh-funny" to mean this giant's been paid in raw beef liver to mutilate all gymnasts and I'm first.

"It wasn't planned," I snivel, glancing toward the front of the classroom. Mr. Klech is still erasing, whistling now as he rubs away the day, totally oblivious to the murder about to occur in his classroom. Kurt Brodsky will punch me once with that huge fist of his and obliterate me, then walk out of class without Mr. Klech ever noticing. I grab the *Algebra for Life* book and slowly move it against my rib cage like body armor.

"Are fuh-fuh-flips hard to luh-luh-learn?" Kurt asks, leaning toward me as he stutters, like he wants to disguise what we're discussing from Mr. Klech—if Mr. Klech ever bothers turning around.

"The back handsprings? Hmmm. Not really," I say

while my inner voice urges me to keep talking and hold off the attack until Mr. Klech finally notices us. "I mean, you need to know some basics first but then, once you know how, they're pretty simple."

"You think . . . I could luh-luh-luh-learn how? Or do you have to be suh-suh-suh-small? Luh-luh-like you?"

"Being small doesn't matter," I snap, feeling my lip curl at the lame question. "You have to be strong," I say. "And limber." I frown at the big body hunched over the too-tiny desk. "You *might* be able to learn it. I don't know. *Maybe.*" I grip my pencil in case I needed to use it as a wooden stake. "Why do you want to learn it?" I ask.

"I wuh-wuh-want to do one in the end zone. After I suh-suh-score a tuh-tuh-tuh-touchdown." Kurt thumps a fist against his desktop like an exclamation point. "Muh-muh-maybe you could tuh-tuh-teach me."

Me?! Teach you?!?! Wait! You're not going to kill me?

Once I get over my relief, I have to admit that seeing someone as big as Kurt Brodsky scoring a touchdown and spiking the ball, then doing a back handspring—especially wearing all his football gear—would look pretty cool. And if I could teach him that and if others knew I taught him . . .

"Yeah, maybe I could." I nod. "It *would* be pretty sweet seeing someone big as you toss a handspring in the game." Kurt dips his chin along with me like we just figured out Mr. Klech's extra-credit question together. "You'll have to come into the gym," I say. "'Cause we'll need the mats, especially with you. And I'll need one of the other guys to help me spot you."

"I got puh-puh-practice same time you duh-duh-do," Kurt says, pinching his brows together. While he thinks, he props his chin on a granite fist. He barely fits behind the desk but he's all muscle, not fat. His jeans stretch tight over massive thighs, telling me he has plenty of horsepower to motor his body through a handspring. Not counting Terrence Mathers, the Knights' compact running back, or Deon Sweeney, their speedy wide receiver, Kurt has the best chance of learning a backflip out of all the football goons.

"How about tomorrow?" I ask. "We practice on Saturdays. It's an optional workout. Coach usually leaves early, so it'll just be me, Bruce, and a few of the guys. Me and Bruce can probably get you around safely if we team up."

"Ruh-really?" he asks, and the serious expression policing his face loosens a little. He turns his head farther toward me as we talk and I see the long scar peeking out from behind his hair.

"Yeah," I say. "It's worth a shot. We usually practice from ten to one. Come in around twelve thirty. Coach'll be gone by then. He's not supposed to, but he lets us lock up. I'll tell Bruce you're coming. The other guys'll be gone."

"Okay."

I glance toward the front of the room to see if Mr. Klech is paying any attention to us yet. Nope. He finishes wiping down the board and starts filling it up with more math crap for Monday's lessons. The nub of his chalk goes *tick, tick, tick* against the slate like a warning transmission. Warning . . .

Wait! My brains wakes up. *What if this is all a trap?!*

"If you're trying to set me or my friends up," I say through clenched teeth, remembering who Kurt's teammates are, "then . . . well . . . that's *bullshit*."

Mr. Klech's chalk stops *tick, tick, ticking.*

"Mr. Meehan, I don't know where you think you are right now but that language is not tolerated in this classroom. And don't the both of you have practice to attend? I'd appreciate it if you and Mr. Brodsky would leave now and allow me a few moments to myself."

"Sorry, Mr. Klech," I say, and mean it. My irritation with Kurt lingers, though, for no other reason than I know his team captains are a bunch of ass-licks. Kurt unwinds himself from the cramped desk and exits class without a word to Mr. Klech. I follow behind him.

"Danny," Kurt says as we walk down the hall, my head only coming up to his shoulder, "I ain't suh-suh-setting you up."

The school is clearing out fast. In the hallway, eyes from every grade, guy and girl, ping Kurt as they pass. Most dash away quickly but, as he and I talk, a few land lower, noticing me for the first time.

"All right," I say. "If you're serious about learning, I'll teach you."

That night, at our homecoming game, we kill the Millfield Bucks. Even better, we get to watch the highlights of ourselves up on the Jumbotron screen. Thing is unbelievable. My new helmet feels the same as my old helmet except there's a little silver eye at the front—same as on a camera phone—and the low bar on my face mask is a little wider for an implanted mic. Studblatz and Jankowski seem to grow bigger and angrier every game. Studblatz blitzs through Millfield's front line and wallops their quarterback so many times that the poor guy starts flinching and false-starting every time Studblatz even fakes a rush. The Bucks end up pulling their QB before halftime and replacing him with their bench guy. Studblatz is jawing on the field all game, calling the Bucks "the Fucks," raging about how he's going to choke 'em with his cock, make 'em squeal like pigs if they get him angry, their mothers and sisters are all whores, their brothers and fathers all suck dick. The usual. Whenever the wind changes direction, our sideline catches long strings of Studblatz's word charms like he's only a few feet away. Coach Brigs doesn't even blink at what's coming out of Stud's mouth. In fact, I think I see him even chuckle. He turns to me and raps his knuckles on my helmet, like he's knocking on a door.

"You see why I didn't choose Studblatz for the miked helmet now?" he asks me, and winks.

On offense, Jankowski and I pound through the line of scrimmage, opening holes so big that Terrence, our running back, practically dances through them, cackling as he scoots past us with the ball. Terrence is our biggest fan, since we help inflate his running yardage and scoring stats. With Jankowski leading the charge, I barely have anyone left over to block for Terrence. On the fullback sweeps, I bust straight through an almost open line of scrimmage practically unchallenged with only a puny Millfield cornerback between me and the goal. Through his face mask, I see his eyes grow real big at what's coming. Our collision's gonna hurt him a lot more than it hurts me. Tucking the ball securely between my forearms, I lower my head and right shoulder while he braces for impact. I give it to him. Impact. Our shelled pads clack and crunch as I power over him and continue down the field for a score, barely breaking stride. My teammates pile on me. The score is 37–7 at that point. The cornerback has to be helped off the field. On the Jumbotron screen is a replay of the view from my helmet cam. The whole stadium sees the cornerback's eyes grow wide on a face now the size of a highway billboard. Then it goes dark as I smash into him. Our collision and my grunt sound like thunder over the new speaker system ringing the stadium. Words flash across the Jumbotron: ALL ABOARD! THE BRODSKY EXPRESS BROUGHT TO YOU BY FRAYS POTATOES!

The final score is 52–13.

"Did you see Studblatz level eighty-one?" Scott stands on the benches in our locker room after the game. "That boy's still wondering what year it is. Man, we are rolling now. You hear me? We are rolling!"

Players start pounding their lockers like drums. I join in. Then Coach Brigs holds up his arms for quiet.

"That's right, boys," Coach echoes. "Your quarterback is exactly right." He's rubbing his hands together like he's getting ready to tuck into a flame-broiled steak. "Excellent team effort tonight. We keep up the hard work, nothing can stop our momentum." Coach slaps Scott on the butt for emphasis.

"Hoo-wah!" we chant in our best Marine Corps imitation. "Hoo-wah! Hoo-wah!"

Scott jumps down off the bench and drops a fist on my shoulder pad. "Nice blocking, Brodsky. And nice running. You keep that up, those recruiting letters will fly into Coach's office."

"Thanks," I say, liking his words. Scott pushes Tyson, a second-stringer, out of the way and straddles the bench to sit next to me.

"Me, Stud, and Jankowski are going up to Tom's grandpa's place tomorrow, going hunting in the morning. You should come, man."

"I kuh-kuh-can't."

"It's fun. Nothing better'n rocking with shotguns."

"Muh-maybe next tuh-tuh-time."

"What's so important tomorrow that you're blowing off your captains?" Scott asks.

"Tuh-tuh-training."

"Training? You train enough already, big guy. What kind of training?"

"Juh-juh-gymnastics. With their suh-suh-squad." I leave out the part about me wanting to impress him and everyone else by throwing a back handspring in the end zone sometime this season.

Scott's head pulls back like I just poked him in the eye. "Seriously?"

I nod yes.

"Studblatz," Scott calls out while locking me in his sights. His voice sounds light but his eyes flash like a cat with a mouse. "You believe this traitor? He ain't gonna go hunting 'cause he's hanging out with the midget-brigade gymnasts."

"You see those guys flip on the mini-tramp?" Tyson asks. "Man, that shit is cool."

"Shut the fuck up!" Scott cuffs Tyson across the back of his head hard enough that Tyson yelps.

I stand up and continue changing out of my uniform. Scott stands up, too, and I know he's waiting for me to buckle and say I'll come hunting with him instead. Problem is, the longer he waits, the more stubborn I feel. When I'm down to only a towel, he finally speaks.

"You need to get your priorities figured out." He talks softly, but his words are hard. "You got one team, one family, and it ain't those puny pukes, you understand? It ain't those disrespectful fucks! You figure that out or we'll figure it out for you."

DANNY

21

Only a handful of gymnasts ever show up for Saturday practice since it's optional. Bruce, being team captain, is always there and on time. Larry Menderson, Paul Kim, and Bill Gradley come mainly because they don't want to get razzed for being lazy even though they mostly lounge around on the crash mats, pretending to stretch. Fisher arrives an hour late sipping breakfast out of a Mountain Dew bottle. The surprise is that he shows up at all. Our two freshmen, Pete Delray and Ronnie Gunderson, come because Bruce hints—well, actually he outright states—they'll have extra strength sets the entire season if they don't attend Saturday practices. Coach ignores Bruce's intimidation tactics and compliments the two freshmen on their commitment to the team. Pete mostly fakes his way through the practice, taping and retaping his hand while yawning every thirty seconds. Ronnie works hard, though. He wiggles his thin torso up on the parallel bars and practices swinging between them like a pendulum, prepping for the day he'll be strong enough to swing up to a handstand. From the looks of things, that day is a few years off. His arms vibrate with the effort after a couple of swings and his face turns so red that he catches Bruce's attention.

"Ronnie, the judges deduct points if you squeeze out a turd during the event," Bruce says. "Relax a little." That Bruce pays Ronnie any attention means he thinks Ronnie shows potential. For instance, Bruce hardly ever bothers giving Pete any tips. Or, for that matter, Fisher.

"Ronnie," Fisher adds, "weakness makes baby Jesus cry."

"Don't joke about him," Ronnie mumbles, dropping off the P-bars, insulted.

Fisher mimics a Russian accent. "Baby Jesus want you strong like bull. You do sit-up, now, for sins."

"You got three more sets up there, frosh," Bruce tells Ronnie, ignoring Fisher. Bruce motions for Ronnie to jump back up on the parallel bars. "Scoop your legs on the bottom of the swing and keep your stomach tight. It'll help."

Only Bruce knows I invited Kurt to Saturday practice. He likes the idea, since befriending the biggest wall of muscle in school is usually a good strategy. I go to retrieve a decent crash mat in case Kurt actually shows up. Our gymnasium has a giant storage room with fifteen-foot-high doors big enough to swing open and swallow all the girls' and boys' teams apparatus at the end of the season. We also stow extra equipment and mats needed for our home meets as well as the judges' scoring stands, folding tables, chalk trays, plus dust mops and brooms for wiping down the tumbling floor before and after each meet. Thick mats of various shapes and sizes flop around the tightly packed cavern like bed-factory rejects. Coach Nelson nags us to stack them neatly but guys get lazy and start pushing them into any nook or corner that fits. Hopping over a foam cube before stepping under a double-parked balance beam, I grab a blue, vinyl-webbed, foam rectangle about the size and shape of a squishy, king-size mattress. I slowly heave and drag the thing out of the storage room. It's a workout just clearing the mat from the other junk, and once I get it out into the gym, I let the blue mat flop over on its side, sending up a wall of chalk dust that envelopes Fisher. He turns to me, coated in white and coughing. "Thanks, Danny." He waves his hand in front of his face.

"No problem."

A piercing whistle gets everyone's attention. Coach's got both pinky fingers in his mouth, blowing till our eardrums rupture. "Okay, no funny stuff," Coach tells us. "I have to leave early. Just finish your strength sets. No fancy tricks while I'm gone." Coach says the same thing every Saturday practice, like it's a surprise he suddenly has to leave early. He tosses the gym keys in a high arc toward Bruce, letting everyone know exactly who is in charge in his absence. Bruce snatches the keys out of the air with a one-handed, behind-the-back, showboat catch. I imagine making that catch next year when Bruce is gone.

About three minutes after Coach leaves, Gradley gathers up his gym bag, tosses off a "peace out," and heads into the locker room. Over the next fifteen minutes, the other guys, relieved of the label *first to leave*, trickle out of the gym. Fisher, still belching up Mountain Dew between turns on parallel bars, plops down on a crash mat, lets off a loud fart, and pulls on his street shoes.

"You want a ride?" he asks Paul Kim.

"Yeah," Paul answers, gathering up his bag.

Vance Fisher and Paul Kim are walking toward the lockers when Vance stops and calls to me over his shoulder. "Hey, Danny," he says. "I left a present for you in your gym bag."

"Dude, farting in someone's bag doesn't actually work." Paul shoves Fisher's arm. "It dissipates."

"It ain't a fart," Fisher says loud enough for me to hear. "Think of it more as a piece of the legend."

Since whatever Fisher left me can't be good, I'm in no hurry to investigate. Besides, I'm in the middle of my second set of pull-ups and I never quit strength sets until I'm finished. It's cheating otherwise. Cheating doesn't win high-bar titles. As soon as I drop off the bar, arms trembling, I forget my bag for another reason.

Kurt Brodsky's standing in the doorway. He steps cautiously into the gym, hands stuffed into his front pockets, moving along the wall as if trying to blend into the brick. When he sees me see him, he pulls out one hand and offers a halting half wave, then stops, as if awaiting permission to cross our turf. I can't believe he actually showed.

"Hey, Kurt," Bruce calls, hopscotching over mats, making his way toward the big fullback. "Heard you want to improve your end zone dance."

"Um . . . naw . . . er . . . muh-maybe . . ." Kurt's waving hand returns to its home deep in his front pocket. His eyes bounce from one piece of equipment to another, sweeping across our little jungle, taking it all in. Saying the plan out loud makes it sound kind of silly. I think maybe Bruce does it on purpose.

"Hey," I say, walking over to join them, "you stretch at all today?"

"Nuh-nuh-not yet."

"Well, come over to the floor mats and I'll show you a few stretches," I say, leading Kurt over to the thin, two-inch mats. "You ever stretch?" I ask.

"We suh-suh-stretch before fuh-fuh-football," Kurt says, kicking off his shoes and lowering his big body to the mat. Bruce rolls his eyes.

"You guys can barely touch your toes," Bruce says, shaking his head. "No offense."

Kurt stays quiet.

"You know, that's one reason Danny kicked Jankowski's ass so badly in the weight room that day. I mean, don't get me wrong, Danny's way stronger in his abs than Jankowski but he's also not fighting against his own tight hamstrings when he does those leg lifts."

Kurt just nods and sticks his legs out in front of him and reaches for his feet, imitating me, but he's straining and bending his knees. Finally he manages to grab a toe.

"Wow," Bruce says sarcastically. "What a champ!"

"Thanks." Kurt grunts.

Bruce, arms folded across his chest, chuckles. I can tell he approves of Kurt's answer.

Bruce and I take turns showing Kurt basic stretches before walking him over to the blue mat I dragged out earlier. If anyone else came in wearing denim jeans, Bruce would make them change, but it's Kurt Brodsky, so he lets it slide. Menderson—mouth open since Kurt entered the gym—sits watching the giant fullback with open fascination. He finally puts on his left shoe and zips up his gym bag and leaves us with a wave. Pete Delray pretends to work on pommel horse but he mostly sits on it while Ronnie diligently works sets of pullovers. I start thinking maybe Ronnie might make a good high-bar specialist like me.

"You got anything in your pockets?" Bruce asks Kurt, not bothering to wait for an answer. "Better empty them."

"Whoa! Almost fuh-fuh-forgot," Kurt says, and pulls out a no-frills cell phone, the kind everyone but grandpa had upgraded from last decade. "Juh-just bought it," he says, then sets it down on the floor next to the mat.

"Okay, let's get started," Bruce says.

Kurt's a good student. He listens carefully to our directions. All that brute power needs to be focused properly, torso aimed and limbs harnessed to serve the acrobatic task. I guess it's sort of like solving one of Mr. Klech's trajectory equations. Bruce and I stand on either side of Kurt, explaining how he has to lead up and backward with his hands, lock his elbows, and drive hard with his legs to push himself around to his feet again.

Once he understands what we want him to do, and after Bruce and I both demonstrate a dozen times, each of us pointing out things to watch on the other, we tell him to go for it.

"You mean just duh-duh-do it?" Kurt asks. "Now?"

"Yeah," Bruce and I answer at the same time. It's the

three of us, plus Ronnie and Pete, left in the gym. Pete lives close enough to walk home but Ronnie's stuck until we finish and Bruce gives him a ride.

"Here's what's going to happen." Bruce breaks it down for Kurt. "You're not going to trust us the first time and you'll be scared, so you'll half jump like a pussy and Danny and I will catch you, sacrificing our backs in the process, and muscle you over. That's your one freebie. Then you'll realize you didn't die and that it felt kind of cool. Then you'll jump really hard the next time—no more freebies, so you better—making our job easy. After repeating this process several hundred times, you might be able to walk out of here one day and into the glory of the end zone, blowing the minds of your fans and caveman teammates. Danny and I, now crippled from lifting the equivalent of a mountain gorilla, will hold on to the satisfaction of knowing we injected a certain amount of grace into a big, uncoordinated football player."

"He's coordinated," I say, defending Kurt. "He's a fullback."

Bruce snorts

"I'm serious," I say. "Ball carriers are excellent athletes." Kurt narrows his eyes like he's trying to figure me out, see if I'm setting up a punch line. I'm not. It never comes up, but I love watching NFL football. Rooting for, and being disappointed by, the Vikings on Sundays is one of the few things my dad and I do together.

"Maybe some of them are," Bruce admits, then tips his head at Kurt while looking at me. "Guess we'll find out if he's one of 'em."

"Wuh-wuh-what do you mean, 'fuh-fuh-find out'?" Kurt asks.

"Well, if you're gifted as Danny thinks you are, then no worries. But if you suck and we can't lift your dead-weight, then you do a head plunge into the ground and break your neck. No mat, no matter how thick, is going to protect against a head plunge."

"Bruce! Come *on*," I say. The last thing we need is to try to lift a huge guy too scared to propel himself. I snap my fingers by Kurt's ear, hoping to short-circuit Bruce's image. "As long as you jump backward with good power— no sissy stuff—then we'll get you around. Remember, it's easy to turn you. It's hard to lift you. So *jump*."

Kurt nods back at me. "Okay," he says. Bruce and I get on either side of him, each of us placing one hand on his lower back and one hand just above the back of his knee. Then we count to three. Kurt *jumps*! He jumps just like we told him. He jumps and we flip him easy and he finds himself back on his feet, his face pinking up with relief and victory. Then Kurt Brodsky's mouth broadens and a full smile warms his face. Didn't know he could even make that expression.

"Whoa!" he says, standing there. "That was puh-puh-pretty cool!"

"Of course it's cool," Bruce answers. "Why the hell you think we do it?"

"Can we tuh-tuh-try it again?" Kurt asks, and even though he is huge and Bruce and I are dwarfs next to him, he's the one who sounds like a kid busting to ride the roller coaster a second time.

"Yep," I say, proud of the secret gift only we can teach him. Ronnie claps for Kurt in a joyous way that makes me ashamed of all Fisher's religious teasing I snicker at. Pete skitters over to another mat to work on his handsprings, inspired for the first time that day. I nod at Bruce and then look up at Kurt. "As many times as you want," I offer.

As many times as you want turns out to be seventy-eight times. I count every single try. At first, Kurt bites his lips nervously and glances backward half a dozen times before each attempt. Every time he makes it around, though, his eyes expand with triumph. By the end, he's mastered the trick enough that he only needs one of us to spot him and whip his legs around. So Bruce and I take turns. And even Ronnie practices spotting him a few times. Pete slips out around handspring thirty-seven or otherwise we'd make him practice spotting Kurt as well.

"My legs are shu-shaking," Kurt says, surprised by his own fatigue, as if it can only come from lifting weights, tackling, and running.

"It's a good workout," Bruce says. "Coach has us do sets and sets to build our endurance."

"Probably beats ruh-ruh-running bleachers in fuh-fuh-full pads," Kurt admits, then notices the clock up on the wall. "I promised I'd have the kuh-kuh-car back an hour ago."

"So you're going to wimp out of the strength sets?" Bruce asks. "Typical football player. As soon as things get a little rough, they take off."

"That's a chu-chu-challenge," Kurt says, pulling on his shoes without untying them. "Next Suh-suh-Saturday. We'll finish in the wuh-wuh-weight room." Kurt hustles toward the locker-room door. "Suh-suh-see ya in math, Danny."

Bruce jumps up on the parallel bars and starts pumping out dips like a machine. I can tell he feels good about teaching Kurt. Ronnie finishes eating an orange and then starts his sit-ups. I kick up against the wall to do a set of handstand push-ups.

"The big guy left this," Bruce says, jumping down from the parallel bars and holding up Kurt's new-old phone.

"I'll give it to him on Monday," I say, taking the phone from Bruce with only the tips of my fingers, trying not to get chalk dust on it, and stuffing it in my gym bag. My hand pulls back as it touches something soft and squishy.

Fisher!

At least my hand's not wet. Or smelly. I reach back into my bag and pull out Fisher's surprise. It's a rubber George Bush mask; the one used in the water balloon attack on the homecoming court. Ugly as sin, the thing lies in my hand like a dead fish. Without thinking, I flick the mask toward Bruce in disgust. It flutters in the air and lands on the pommel horse.

"It ain't mine," Bruce says.

"Might as well be," I answer. I let the mask lie where it lands, too irked to go retrieve it. Instead I do another set of handstand push-ups followed by a set of dips and then squat-jumps. After the jumps, I decide I better drag the crash mat we used with Kurt back into the storage room before I get too tired to lift it. The thing is heavy and bendy and trying to guide it into tight spaces and shove it up against a wall is like trying to eat warm Jell-O with a knife. I get the mat halfway into the cluttered storage room before it snags on something and bulges every time I push. I lean it against the door frame and go inside the room. The bottom of it is caught on the steel base of the extra set of dismantled parallel bars that weigh about three hundred pounds. I scoot in between the metal prongs and then shimmy flat between the mat and the back wall, lifting up on the foam to unsnag it and pull it toward me. The thing is finally standing up in place but now I'm sandwiched between the back of it and a dark cinder-block corner. I start squeezing out of the back corner when I hear an angry voice, a few of them, yelling back and forth. My hearing is dulled by the mat pushing up against my head but I definitely hear Bruce yelling, wild and harsh, and then . . . Jankowski and Studblatz barking. Then Miller's voice, taunting, stirring up his dogs.

"You don't ever come into our weight room again, understand?" Scott Miller threatens. "Don't matter what your coach says."

"The weight room is our house," Jankowski huffs. "Our house!"

"He tricked us," Studblatz yells. "You ain't as strong as Jankowski. Those leg lifts are dumb."

"Go jump off—" Bruce's voice begins, but stops. Something thuds followed by the crack-slap of skin on skin. A scream—not Bruce—squelches into a gurgle. The sound flies into the storage room and swirls around me. It has to be Ronnie! I freeze in place behind the mat, still wedged into the corner of the dim space, my legs refusing to move.

"Scott, lookit this." I hear Studblatz's voice.

"Think this is funny?! Huh?" Scott demands. "Takes

some balls, little boy, letting that mask just lay around here like a trophy. Must make you feel good, huh? Soaking me and Stud at the pep rally in front of all those students?" Scott's raises his voice, getting more and more worked up as he speaks.

I hear a soft thud followed by a coughing groan.

"Not mine," Ronnie squeaks, his tinny voice scraping against my teeth. "I swear. The mask isn't mine."

"Nobody else here, needledick, but you and your captain," Scott answers. "Two of you on that dirt bike. Two of you here now and that mask just laying there for the both of you to admire. For you to jack off to, remembering your glory. Why's it just laying here?"

Don't tell him it was in my bag, Ronnie! Please don't tell him it's mine!

"Let go—" Ronnie's cry gets cut off by two more skin smacks.

Sneak out! my mind screams. *Sprint for the locker room! Race out to the hallway! Pound on the custodian's door! Holler for an adult—anyone!—to come back to the gym!*

My body won't budge. Not an inch. The mat pressing me into the wall insulates against the terrifying wreckage occurring outside the storage room. Ronnie's next cry is muffled, like a hand shoots over his mouth. Then I hear laughing. Mean laughing.

"Wait," Scott's voice commands. "Not out here."

After a pause, a smothered whimpering seeps through the cinder block-walls of the storage room, where I remain stuck.

"In here! Bring him in here!" Scott directs, his voice just outside the big doors. I retreat farther into the dark corner, burrowing deeper into the nook behind the mat, feeling the chilled concrete press up against my bare calves and arms. I tug the mat into my chest as goose bumps ripple over my skinny limbs.

A cry.

Ronnie's cry is now inside the room with me.

"Shut your mouth," Jankowski grunts, mere steps away from my hiding spot. Heavy breathing fills the room.

"You tied up the other one good?" Scott asks.

"Yeah." Studblatz's voice. "He ain't going nowhere."

"Shut that door," Scott bosses. "We got a lesson to teach."

My corner grows darker as the big door swings shut and only a single bare bulb lights the space. I peek one eye around the side of the mat. It's mostly dark and shadows but I see Scott holding up the rubber George Bush mask. He, Mike, and Tom stand over Ronnie, pressing him, stomach-down into a square block of foam, like they're getting ready to chop off his head.

"Know how much trouble you little shits cause us?" Scott asks. "Trying to take over our weight room. Pissing on our game uniforms. Soaking us at homecoming. Make you feel like a man wearing this mask?" Scott asks. "Riding in, embarrassing us at the pep rally? You like the taste of rubber?"

Without warning, Scott wads up the rubber mask and jams it into Ronnie's mouth while Mike and Tom keep him pinned down to the cube mat. Chuckles, mean chuckles, mix with Ronnie's choking. Scott suddenly looks up and searches the room. I turtle my head back behind the mat.

"Hand me that mop," Scott orders.

I look again and Ronnie's legs kick and thrash like he's trying to swim across the mat. Facedown, his head flips from side to side, searching for oxygen, mouth stopped up.

"He's begging for it!" Scott sing-songs. Mike hands Scott the mop and Tom rips down Ronnie's pants. Scott shoves the mop handle inside him. Even choking on the rubber mask, Ronnie screams and *screams* and *SCREAMS*!!! Beyond the storage room, no one knows, but in there with them, Ronnie's pain travels through my bones. The lone bulb casts shadows and spooks my eyes as Scott finishes with the mop handle and Ronnie's voice finally breaks in half.

"Do him!" Scott barks at Tom.

"*You* do him!" Jankowski answers back.

"I'll do him," Studblatz says.

"Keep him down, Tommy," Scott orders.

Scott pulls the mask out of Ronnie's mouth and then Tom shoves Ronnie's head so hard into the mat that it looks like he's trying to suffocate him. Ronnie makes only a dull moan as Mike gets on top of him and starts chugging. Tom lets go of his head and Ronnie weeps in short bursts, each muffled cry snuffed out by a hog grunt from Studblatz. Through all of it, Scott cheers on his teammate.

"Get some," Scott cackles. "Get some."

"See. If. You. Dis. Re. Spect. Me. Now," Studblatz huffs. I can't move my arms up to block out the sounds. They're pinned between the wall and the mat. As I'm forced to hear all of it, my nose runs and a sickness enters me like poison gas, burning out my lungs and brain.

"He likes it," Scott laughs, then directing Tom, "Give me that mop again."

"Please," Ronnie whispers, nothing left in him but the breath being pumped out by Studblatz.

"Shut your little faggot mouth!" Scott snaps, grabbing a handful of Ronnie's hair. In his other hand he draws the mop handle closer, forcing it into Ronnie's mouth. The sound of gagging fills my ears.

Please, God. Make them stop! Please, please, please, please, make them go away. Leave him alone. Please make them leave Ronnie alone. Pleeeaassssseeee . . .

The door to the storage room slowly pushes open. Kurt Brodsky stands there, his hands slowly forming fists. . . .

K U R T

22

My phone!

Only a couple of blocks from Patti's house, know-ing I'm late, I reach into my jeans' pocket for a time check on my phone except there's no phone. Brand-new and I've already lost it. Stupid! I just bought the thing at the mall three days ago, can only afford it thanks to the "walking around" money Coach keeps passing me and topping off with a bonus for every win I help us notch in our season. Damn! I know exactly where I left it, too. Took it off and set it down a few feet from the mat I'd been handspring-ing on most of the day. First phone I ever owned. Gone. Saleslady kept pushing the fancy models on me, said how they made me look sophisticated and cutting-edge when what she really meant to say was "not stupid." Her inter-est faded pretty quick when I chose the old-school model, the only one I could afford. And then I go and lose it after only three days. Dumb!

I wheel Patti's station wagon into the nearest driveway, throw it in reverse, then gun it back to Oregrove. I'm already late anyway. Patti's not too keen on loaning me her car, only gave it up after I told her Coach scheduled Saturday practice, and if I miss it, he'll dock the pay going into those little white envelopes he has me deliver every week. Not that I even have a license yet, but Patti never asks. It's best to just let her assume things.

When I get back to the school parking lot, one of the three cars I remember in the student lot is gone. Hopefully it's not Bruce's. Then I spot Scott's gold Camaro parked at the far edge of the lot, near the school's auto-mechanics garage. Odd. Thought they were going hunting today. Maybe they decided to get ripped in the weight room instead. Never a bad idea, far as I'm concerned. No time to be curious, though. I drive into the teachers' parking lot and slip into the *Reserved—Vice Principal* space nearest the building door. I hustle back downstairs, through the long basement hallway, into the team lockers and then push through the gymnasium door. The big gym's empty but the lights are still on.

I duck under the metal guide wires that anchor the steel ring stand and then skirt around the island of four-inch mats surrounding the pommel-donkey thingy. At the other end of the gym, near the vault where I'd practiced all those handsprings, the blue mat is gone. So is the phone.

Shit, shit, shit. Double Shit!

I open my mouth to call out for Bruce or Danny when I hear dampened voices and then . . . something . . . not . . .

good . . . something wrong. Something like a scream, but quiet, like a ghost screeching from under his grave. The gymnasium—halogen lights buzzing and no sun, no outside windows, no people—feels cold along my arms all of a sudden. Chalk dust hanging in the air starts scratching the back of my throat. There it is again . . . another . . . ghoulish wail . . . coming from . . . behind those big doors. Doors at least fifteen feet high, like closet doors in a giant's house, making me feel small all of a sudden and . . . then that sound again . . . I ain't imagining it. Ain't crazy. A moan—faint, tortured—coming from behind the giant's closet. My armpits chill, the sweat running down them turning into metal beads. My feet sink into the soft mats with each step. My thighs, fatigued from all those hand-springs, grow heavier, yet trudge in the one direction I want to flee. Everything in my body tells me to run, get out, go. I'll ask Danny about the phone on Monday. But my feet dissolve into those swampy mats, stagger me toward those big doors like I'm creeping down into his basement all over again, spying the "secret punishment" that first time . . .

. . . "breathe a word and you'll disappear," Crud Bucket grunts on top of Lamar. "People applaud when garbage disappears. You hear me? You hear me? Answer with a 'sir' this time or I'll go longer. Cops'll thank me if you and that bastard vanish. Give me a medal . . ."

"Huff, huff, huff, huff . . ."

That sound. Coming from . . .

". . . stop . . . please . . . stop . . ."

. . . behind those . . .

The giant doors are cracked open the smallest bit. As I

draw closer I no longer hear a ghost's voice. I hear Scott's voice. Then Studblatz's speaking in bursts like he's bench-pressing, ripping out his sets. Blasting his pecs with each rep. "How. You. Like. Me. Now?"

Except he ain't bench-pressing.

No.

He's dealing out Crud Bucket's "secret punishment" on a boy, the special torture that used to be just for Lamar.

None of them notice me push open the door at first. The little gymnast takes all their attention. Barely bigger than Lamar, his naked legs so skinny and pale it hurts just to glimpse as a trickle of blood stains the back of his left thigh. As I enter the storage room, a vacuum sucks out my insides. All I want is to run fast and forever away as my fingers close into a fist.

Studblatz, glancing my direction, noticing me, lifts his big, ugly self from the boy. Scott yanks the mop handle out of the boy's mouth and his eyes bug at being caught until he sees it's only me. Then a smile worms over his face like he understands me, understands what I want. He acts pleased that I've arrived. Ronnie, gagging, collapses backward to his knees while his arms and head slump against the foam block.

"You want a shot, Mr. Wolf?" Scott asks me, as if Ronnie is his to offer. Studblatz zips himself up and turns to watch me, gauging my reaction.

"You going to say som—" Jankowski, off to my left, starts talking but his voice and all sound die in a wall of flame. Gasoline races through my veins, ignites at my scars, and detonates every cell in my body. Unable to scream or breathe, unable to think, I will burn up unless I extinguish the pain. Unless I destroy them.

My fist cocks and finds the side of Jankowski's thick head. My foot bombs Studblatz's gut. My elbow blasts a chunk of Miller's shoulder. They come at me now. Like Crud Bucket did. Fists and feet pummel me. I return fire. I *rock* them. I *inflict*, bruising something, cracking something else. I heave a lifetime of damage and pain at them, teach them they can't do this. *They can't do this!*

They swarm me but I am no longer small.

Scott runs out. Studblatz headlocks me and Tom punches my sides until I stop him with a mule kick to his chest. Still collared by Studblatz's headlock, I scoop him up in my arms and ram the both of us forward into the cinderblock wall like I'm driving against a whole defense for just six inches. I back up and drive into the wall again, back up and repeat. And repeat. My head pounds but it's okay, it's just fine. Hurt is good as long as he feels it, too. I can endure a world of hurt. So could Lamar. One thing Crud Bucket taught us real good was how to absorb hurt. I dive the both of us into the cement floor; smashing my forehead and Studblatz at the same time, feeling Studblatz finally release me. I'm getting ready to make him real sorry when something heavy—a foot, maybe—smashes into my head, smashes me good, and things stop.

D A N N Y

Kurt Brodsky goes ape shit.

I mean, he *whales* on his captains, his shots thumping their bodies in deep, satisfying bass notes. Scott, his arm half punched off, crumbles into the shadows and roach-scuttles out of the room. Battered by Kurt's hammer blows, Tom and Mike try double-teaming their fullback but still can't break him. Strangling in Mike's headlock, Kurt blasts Jankowski with his foot, then scoops Studblatz up easy as lifting a child. He rams straight into the wall—once, twice, three times—before diving headfirst into the floor, smashing himself and Studblatz into the cement. Kurt is winning the battle until Tom goal-kicks him in the ear. After that, Kurt just lies there, eyes open but still. Studblatz and Jankowski limp off like wounded demons without uttering a single word.

Ronnie yanks up his sweats during the fight and curls into an armadillo ball, never budging. Even after Jankowski and Studblatz abandon Kurt on the floor, Ronnie stays put. He doesn't try to run out or crawl away or nothing. Just stays folded up, rocking a little, his lips moving but no sound coming out. And me? I stay hidden, hugging the edges of the thick mat, my fingers digging into the vinyl-webbed foam, my knees clamping together and my jaw aching from the jackhammer in my head. My teeth chatter uncontrollably. Are those guys really gone? Or are they coming back? Are they bringing reinforcements? Too useless and weak to help anybody, I hug the blue mat tight to my body, ready to stay hidden for a long, long time.

A moan, an awful moan like death itself, rears up from the floor of that cold crypt. Kurt's mouth releases the sound, opening up, giving his soul an exit. His eyes stare up at the ceiling but nothing is behind them. Then he starts to vibrate. His big body twitches, then grows rigid, then arches off the floor. The twitching turns to thrashing. I know from my dad's hospital stories that it's a seizure. Kurt needs help, needs to be restrained so he doesn't hurt himself. That prods me out of the dark corner. Casting an eye on the door, expecting them to come back any second, I squeeze out from between the wall and mat and jump on Kurt's chest, trying to pin down his big arms, making sure they don't lash out at the cement walls or steel-pronged parallel bar stand. It feels like wrestling a crocodile. His eyelids flutter and only white shows underneath them. I am locked in a struggle, making sure his soul stays put. It's the only fight I have even the slightest chance of winning.

Come on, come on, Kurt. Come on.

I grasp at arms big around as my legs while his belly bucks up, nearly throwing me. I glance over, needing help, but Ronnie's in another world, murmuring to himself. Kurt's chest pogos up and drops. His head conks against the cement floor like a bowling ball. I let go of one arm and reach for a two-inch mat near my feet, yank it over both of us, and slip it under his skull. He broncos one last time, trying to throw me again, but I'm not having it.

"Come *on*," I beg through gritted teeth.

Slowly Kurt fizzles. He lies still, again, eyes closed. I shift off him and put my ear to his chest, listen for his heart and breathing, and it's all there.

Thank you.

"Mmmmm . . . nuh-uh . . . no . . . Lamar . . . I'm not . . . wait . . . ," is all he says. Then his eyes slowly open—pupils big as marbles—and gaze around and I see that his brain is trying to work again, trying to put the pieces back together. He lifts his head up off the thin mat and winces. He notices Ronnie in a ball six feet away, and he squints while bringing up his right hand to massage his temple.

"Kurt?" I test. His eyes slowly come around to meet mine. "You back? You gonna be okay?"

"I . . . ," he starts, then stops. I can tell his head is killing him by the way he cradles it, like a fragile crystal ball, between both hands. He steals another glance at Ronnie while balancing his face in his fingertips, then rolls over onto his knees and elbows. "I tried, Lamar," he whispers to the floor. "I tried . . ." And then he gags, still clutching at his skull, spilling his stomach up onto the cement and part of the two-inch mat. I back up, pretty certain Kurt will live.

That leaves Bruce.

I scramble out of the storage room and race around a gymnasium full of hiding places. Mats drape almost everything: the ring stand, the high bar, the two sets of parallel bars, the tumbling mats, the mini-trampoline, the vault and runway, and the two pommel horses. Nothing catches my attention.

"*Bruce!*" I shout, panicking that those guys'll return. What they did to Ronnie means they could do anything. "*Bruce!*" Freaking out, I'm bounding around the gym without direction when I notice the broken seam between the four-foot-thick vaulting mats. One rises higher than the other. I grab the bottom corner of the elevated mat with both hands. Adrenaline shocks my muscles into heaving the car-size chunk up onto its side in a single pull.

Bruce lies underneath, sprawled on his belly, ankles taped together, wrists taped behind his back, wadded-up tube socks stuffed into his mouth. He rolls a quarter way and his eyes are wide open and bloodshot, his nostrils flaring for air. His face glows red where his hair isn't pressed to his sweaty skin. I rip the sock out of his mouth.

"*Goddammit!!!!*"

He rolls to his butt and sits up with his legs stretched out in front of him. His wrists are wrapped good behind his back, so I go down to his ankles, find a loose strand, and unwind the tape. As soon as his legs are free, Bruce gets his knees under him and stands before I have a chance to help him up.

"Hold on," I tell him. "Let me undo your wrists."

Bruce ignores me and instinctively walks toward the storage room. I trail behind, working on his bound wrists, tied together with about a half roll of white athletic tape. Rolls and rolls of it lie all around our gym.

"You okay?" he asks me, tossing the question behind him as he moves.

"Yeah."

"Where's Ronnie?" he asks, but seems to already know the answer from the direction he's heading.

"In the storage room," I say, still trying to undo his wrists. They used so much tape that it's formed a thick rope that can't be peeled away. I leave him and fetch a Swiss Army knife out of my gym bag. By the time I scamper back, Bruce stands inside the storage room, not moving, taking it all in, trying to understand the crime scene. The acid stench of Kurt's vomit rises up in warning. I go back to work on Bruce's handcuffs. The Swiss Army knife's miniscissor is no match for the gummy strands and Bruce loses patience. Still cuffed, he kneels beside Ronnie, while my puny scissors gnaw frantically at his gluey bindings. The mop handle rests only a foot away, its tip stained dark. The smell of crap and copper and vinegar mix over the sour fumes of puke. Ronnie's sweats aren't pulled up all the way. The elastic of his underwear bunches above the drawstring.

Kurt groans. Bruce casts an eye at him but stays with our downed teammate. "Hey, Ronnie? Ronnie? Hey, man . . . you okay?" Bruce coos. Then he snarls at me. "God*dammit!* Danny, get this shit off!" I finally snip through the last strands and Bruce's arms snap forward and grab Ronnie's shoulders and try to sit him up. Ronnie's somewhere between living and dead. His white skin now superwhite. His purplish lips barely move as they recite something—a prayer, maybe—too soft to hear. He shudders for a moment and Bruce pounds his back like maybe he's choking. He's not choking.

"What happened?" Bruce asks, locking me in a stare, accusing me of all this. I feel my mouth go dry, unable to speak a word of what I witnessed. I shake my head and glance toward Kurt, now slowly dragging himself up to his feet, using the wall for balance, as if he holds the explanation.

"I'm suh-suh-sorry," Kurt whispers. "I'm suh-suh-suh . . . I . . . I guh-guh-gotta go. I gotta get the car buh-buh-back. Patti wuh-wuh-won't let me . . . I'm suh-suh-sorry," Kurt keeps repeating. He places a hand on the doorframe to steady himself, then wobbles out of the storage room.

"Wait!" I shout. I leave Bruce and Ronnie and follow Kurt, circling him like a toy terrier does a bulldog. "You sure you'll be okay? You don't look so good. I can drive you. I got my license."

"I'm fuh-fuh-fuh-fine," he says, then trips over the edge of a mat but manages to stay on his feet. He keeps his right hand cupped to the side of his head where Tom kicked him. His left hand juts forward as if feeling its way in the dark. His eyes are half shut and half watching his foot-steps.

"But . . . but what about what happened?" I ask. "What do we do?"

"Got to guh-guh-get the kuh-kuh-car back," he repeats, zombie-plodding into the locker room, leaving me stranded with the nightmare back in the gym. When I return, Bruce has one of Ronnie's arms slung over his shoulder while he holds him up around the waist, walking through the gym, trying to collect both their bags and shoes. Dark stains bleed through the seat and back left leg of Ronnie's gray sweatpants. I feel sick and gross for even noticing.

"Ronnie, man, you're going to be fine. Just fine. We get you home, you'll be fine," Bruce semi-yells while propping Ronnie over his shoulders, pacing him across the floor, like he's only drunk and all he needs is some coffee and time to sober up. "You'll be fine. Those guys are gone. It's over, man. Over. You take a long, hot shower and you'll be right as rain."

Ronnie's glassy eyes tell me only one of them is hearing Bruce's words.

"Danny!" Bruce calls to me.

"Yeah."

"Do me a favor and wipe up Kurt's mess. Use paper towels and, hey, go ahead and use my towel if it's easier. Just throw it all away. Then lock up, all right? Keys are by the door. My towel is by the rings. We'll be up at the car waiting for you. Do it quick, all right? Real quick. I wanna get Ronnie back home. Let him shower. Forget this ever happened." Bruce's version of a reassuring voice is to talk real loud and not bother waiting for a response.

Ronnie isn't doing much of anything but letting himself be led around on his feet. His head droops, and he continues muttering words impossible to make out. It scares me how lost he seems. I grab the gym keys out of Bruce's bag and speed back into the locker room, then pull out a brick of paper towels from the steel dispenser. I soak half of them under the sink faucet, whiffing the odor they give off when wet, like the paper company mixes garbage with mouse poop to create them. I run back into the gym and grab Bruce's towel off the ring frame and head into the storage room.

Kurt's vomit is mostly clear spit-up, but it reeks. I drop Bruce's towel on it and push it around with my foot to soak it up. I follow that with the wet paper towels and then finish with the dry towels. Good enough. The cube-mat squats in the storage room like a trunk bomb. A white flash—Studblatz lying on top of Ronnie—burns behind my eyelids, won't be blinked away. I approach the cube-mat like it might go off, wondering if what just happened really happened, if evil can just blow up like that, out of nothing, out of a day that starts so good. As I stand over the block, taking in the mess they've left on it, my legs begin to shake. I back out of the room and then shut the big storage door, holding both Bruce's towel and the paper towels as far from my body as possible. I chuck them into the wastebasket in the locker room, then return for my bag and lock up the gym.

Ronnie sits in the front passenger seat of Bruce's old beater Volvo when I dash across the parking lot. His forehead presses against the passenger window while he chews on a fingernail. With the engine already running, I open the back door and drop into the seat.

We pull up into Ronnie's driveway and jerk to a stop as Bruce throws the Volvo in park before braking completely. He doesn't turn off the ignition. Ronnie's house is a brown L-shaped ranch almost identical to mine.

"You want me to come in?" Bruce asks Ronnie. The way he's leaving the car running, he doesn't want Ronnie to say yes. Neither do I. The key, right now, right this second, is to get as far away from here as possible, get home, and maybe help my dad mow the lawn or rake leaves or put up a new porch or reshingle the roof or walk the neighbor's dog or just about anything else in the world that takes place outside in clean air. The key is to do anything but sit next to Ronnie, thinking about what he went through this afternoon.

From the backseat, I will Ronnie's head to stop leaning against the window and for him to get out of the car.

"Ronnie?" Bruce tries again.

"No," Ronnie finally answers, his voice barely a whisper. "Thanks." He stays put, though, making no move.

Leave, leave, leave, leave, leave, get out, get out, get out, getoutgetoutgetout.

But he just sits there. He sits for a long time and no one says anything until Bruce speaks up again.

"Ronnie, take a long, hot shower," Bruce says. "Tomorrow's a new day."

"Yeah," Ronnie answers. The sound of his voice makes me want to tear off my ears. I'm sure, now, I can smell him, smell what they did to him. I have to get away from him.

I'm about ready to bolt from the car when Ronnie finally opens his door and gets out like he has a date with the electric chair. He never bothers looking back at us. Going up the two stairs to his front door seems to exhaust him. He just stands there in front of his house.

We waste no time waiting for Ronnie to finally go inside. I stay in the back, not wanting to delay our escape by taking over the prized shotgun seat. Bruce jams the gear into reverse, backing his car up, then gunning the Volvo until it screams and lurches as he slams the gear back into drive. I roll my window down, trying to get the wind through my hair. When Bruce swings into my driveway I already have the door cracked open. My right foot plants on the pavement before we've completely stopped.

"Danny?" Bruce calls.

I get completely out of the car, unable to sit for even a second longer. Only then do I turn around and lean in through the back window, forcing Bruce to twist around, his right arm wrapped around the back of the passenger seat, his seat belt stretching out to contain him.

"What, exactly, happened?"

The question makes me shift my feet, makes me want to hurl my bag out into the street and never go back in that gym—or the school, for that matter—ever again. How am I supposed to walk the halls knowing those three are roaming them?

"You saw his pants? The stains?" I ask, unable to explain it and not wanting to. "They did all of that to him. Laughing the whole time."

Bruce only blinks at me. I push away from the car door without saying good-bye. The old Volvo backs out. Its tires give a weak screech as Bruce leaves.

K U R T

24

I return Patti's car keys to the glass candy dish stationed
beside her Great Lanes Bowling ashtray on the kitchen
counter. Upstairs in the bathroom, I open the bare medicine cabinet and then search under the sink cupboard
for aspirin or anything else to help my headache. I find a
packet of powdered flu medicine that says it treats aches
and chills. Close enough. I rip it open and tip it into my
mouth, then cup water under the faucet into my hand. I
gulp back the lemony grit.

"Kurt?" Patti calls up the stairs. "Expected you home
earlier. Thought we agreed on one o'clock."

"We did," I call back, voice rattling my brain. "Coach
guh-guh-gave extra duh-duh-drills for next game."

"Can't lend you the car for practice, hon, if I don't
know when you'll bring it back."

"Wuh-wuh-won't happen a-guh-guh-gain."

"I don't want to upset Coach Brigs, though. If he thinks you need to stay longer, that's fine. It's just that I'd like to know, is all. You coming out of that bathroom anytime soon?"

"Yes, muh-muh-ma'am."

"You wanna watch TV with me?"

"Tuh-tuh-took a good hit tuh-tuh-today. Head's ruh-ruh-ringing. Gonna lay duh-duh-down."

"You okay, hon? Did Coach Brigs look at you?"

"It's nuh-nuh-nothing. I juh-juh-just need ruh-ruh-rest." Stuck words clang around my skull. Tongue thick, lips swollen, the stutter wears me out. Down the hall I enter my room and collapse on the junior-size cot, ignoring that my feet dangle over the mattress, and double up the pillow under my nonthrobbing ear. Bleached cotton prickles my face as I pull the sheets up over my head. I try not to think about the afternoon. I try to think good things instead: think about the party, think about kissing Marcia, think about the smell of hot popcorn as our team marches past the concession stand during home games. But somehow my thoughts keep coming back to Scott and Mike and Tom . . . which leads back to that boy, Ronnie, and what they did to him. Or I travel further back to Crud Bucket and what he did to Lamar and me. Finally a sort of dying laps across me little by little, until all thoughts disappear under a rising tide of black.

"Kurt?"

"Huh?"

"Kurt, hon. Can you wake up for me? I'm about set to

call the doctor pretty soon if I can't get you out of this bed. You need to get up. You been sleeping long enough."

"Wh-what time is it?"

"It's time you got up and got to school. 'Course you ain't gonna make it today and you got me more than a little worried." Patti's raspy voice salts the wounded slug meat of my brain. I squint against the sunlight streaking through the open blinds. Why sunlight? I went to sleep an hour or two ago. It should be evening.

"It's been two days, now, since you got up out of this bed."

"Tuh-tuh-two days?"

"That's right. You doing drugs?"

"No." I try shaking my head but that kills. "No duh-duh-doctor. Must buh-buh-be the fuh-fuh-flu. I'm buh-buh-better. Need ruh-ruh-rest is all. Will you kuh-kuh-call suh-suh-school?" I ask.

"Sure, hon. I will. But I'm gonna call the doctor for an appointment if I don't see you up by tonight, okay?"

"Okay." I shut my eyes again, my head still throbbing where that last kick hit me. Sheets don't smell like bleach no more. Smell sour with my sweat and breath. I pull them back over my face, pretend it's a tent, pretend I'm camping with Lamar out on a mountaintop, under the stars, feeling a million points of light glittering down on us, a million worlds around those points of light, all of them offering to take me away.

D A N N Y

25

Dad's snoring in the bedroom when the house phone rings. I've got *The Late Show* on TV, the radio's "Party Rock" DJ chattering at low volume, and *Grand Theft Auto* playing on the laptop resting on my knees. Lights burn in the living room, kitchen, bathroom, hallway, and dining room—basically everywhere but Dad's bedroom and the basement. I've never liked nighttime much, especially in the fall and winter when it keeps erasing more and more life from the world. Since the attack, it seems like night-time's always hanging around, never quite going away.

Since I'm supposedly sick, I can't let Dad wake up and discover me living like a frat boy back from college. So I grab the phone on the second ring and listen for his continuing snore. It's late. Too late for telemarketers. Fish or Bruce would text my cell. The phone call has to be bad.

"Hello?" I answer.

"Danny?"

I can barely make out the voice on the other end. It's wispy as my grandma's the year she died. I remember her skin was thin and crinkly as cellophane.

"Hello?" I repeat.

"Is that you, Danny?"

"Yeah . . . who is this?"

". . . Ronnie . . ."

Exactly the person I don't want to talk to right now. Or ever.

"Yeah?"

"I'm sorry about calling so late . . ."

He waits for me to say it's no problem, but I don't. Instead, I inch up the volume on the "Party Rock" radio station with the remote while reading the Top Ten list on TV.

"Sorry I wasn't at practice today," Ronnie says. "I . . . I stayed home." That he's apologizing to me for not going to practice after what happened makes my heart crumple, makes me want to weep into a pillow.

"Me too," I say. "I'm sick."

"Yeah . . . me too."

"I ain't going tomorrow, either," I tell him.

"Danny? Were you . . . did you see those guys . . . do . . . that stuff to me?"

I stare at the TV.

"No," I lie softly into the mouthpiece. "I was in the locker room getting water."

"Oh . . . okay. I thought . . . maybe . . . I saw . . . that you were in there . . . but that wouldn't make sense, either. Why would you be in the storage room watching?"

"I wasn't there. I didn't see nothing till Kurt beat them up good." I think my lie will help make Ronnie feel better, let him think one less person saw him attacked. One less person for him to feel embarrassed in front of at school.

"I called Bruce," Ronnie says. "He thought you saw what happened, but I guess he—"

"He's wrong," I cut Ronnie off, which is so, so easy to do. "I wasn't in there. I didn't see nothing."

"Okay, it's just that . . . It's just . . . I think . . . It's not clear anymore. I feel . . . I can't wash it off. Bruce keeps telling me to act like nothing happened."

"Sounds like good advice to me," I say, tucking the phone under my ear and going into the kitchen. I pull out a big carving blade from the knife block on the counter-top and repeatedly stab the point into the wooden cutting board. The motion soothes me. I like how protective the weight of the razor-sharp steel feels in my hand. I hear sniffling through the earpiece as I keep stabbing the cutting board, lifting the knife higher and higher before plunging it, trying to get the blade clear through the wood. I wonder if this is what it feels like to stab someone and hit bone.

"I can't get . . . it's like when you're . . ." Ronnie floun-ders. ". . . like a poison . . . need to boil it away . . ."

"What?" I ask, not that I want to understand him.

". . . washing doesn't help," Ronnie says. "It's *inside!*"

"It's over," I say.

"I'm not strong like you. I've—"

"Look, Ronnie, take Bruce's advice. Nothing hap-pened." The image of Ronnie on his knees, gagging, pol-lutes my head until I think I can smell him right now in the kitchen. I drive the knife blade deep enough into the cutting board that it stands straight up by itself, handle quivering a little.

"But—"

"Stop it. Just stop it. Get over it."

That's what I tell him. *Get over it.* I despise Ronnie at that moment. I despise how small and weak he is, and I despise that it was only luck and timing that kept the two of us from switching places in those awful moments.

"Ronnie, I gotta go," I say. "See you at practice." I hope he gives up and quits the team. Even better, quits school. I don't think I can stand the sight of miserable, pathetic Ronnie ever again.

"Yeah . . . okay . . . all right."

"'Night, Ronnie."

"Good night, Da—"

I hang up on him before he finishes. I put the knife and cutting board away and go back to the living room. I adjust the settings on the video game so I can't die and I have all the weapons and all the ammo and I start blasting everyone and everything: bad guys, good guys, innocent passersby, street signs, bar windows, cars, sky, planes, pavement. *The Late Show* returns from commercial and I wait for the audience to laugh on cue and trick me into thinking the world is still normal.

KURT

"Kurt?" Patti calls, while tapping on the bedroom door. The hinges creak, and without opening my eyes, I sense she is sticking her head into the room. "Kurt, hon. I know you're not feeling well, but there's a boy here insisting on seeing you, said he'll only be a minute, wanted to tell you something."

"Mmmm . . ."

"I asked him if it could wait, but—Now, just a second, young man,"

"Kurt?" asks a new voice. This one is feathery soft, ready to blow away if I bark at it.

"He's sick," Patti snaps, nicking my earlobes. "Can't you see that?"

"Shhhhhh, it's okay. It's fuh-fuh-fine," I say, wanting only silence and more rest.

"Hummph," Patti answers. My sleep-crusted eyelashes pull apart. Sunlight swarms past the curtains and sets on my eyeballs with stingers extended. A boy slips by Patti to stand before me.

"Kurt?" the boy tries again. He's the one right out of that nightmare a few days ago. My throat tightens as I barely tamp down a groan, then wrap both ends of the pillow around my head. The sight of him—so small, so frail—starts the skin under my left eye twitching. A fever chill runs up my neck and escapes through a yawn.

"Wuh-wuh-what?" I ask, hoping he'll just go away. Patti hovers by the dresser. "Patti, wuh-wuh-would you get me suh-suh-some wuh-wuh-water?"

"Sure thing, hon." She leaves the room and her footsteps fade down the staircase. I force myself to sit up, ignoring the high-pitched ringing in my sore ear. The whole room shifts, and then rights itself, like when I was drunk at the football party.

Ronnie stands there without saying anything. He pulls a knit cap off his head and starts wringing it in his hands. He takes a step toward the bed, hovering too close. It makes me want to curl up toward the wall. But I don't. Not yet.

"Thank you," he says. "For what you did."

I can't have this talk now, not ever. Can't allow it to come back up from the dead. "Got in a fuh-fuh-fight. Had nothing tuh-tuh-tuh do with you."

Ronnie bows his head, already whipped. He's got to toughen up if he's going to survive. Brush it off. That's how me and Lamar handled it.

"Duh-duh-don't thank me. Juh-juh-just move on."

"That's what Bruce says." He sighs. "Danny, too. Says he didn't see anything, that I should just forget it. But they didn't see it like you. Hearing them talk, I'm starting to think maybe I'm a little crazy, you know? Like, maybe, I imagined some of that stuff. But why would I?" Ronnie's still wringing his cap, strangling it between his fists.

The front of my head, the part facing Ronnie, starts to boil, like he's radioactive and causing it. "They duh-duh-didn't see anything 'cause nuh-nuh-nothing happened," I repeat dumbly, hoping he'll leave me alone. Ronnie stops strangling his cap and starts picking at the skin around his thumb. His lips are so chapped they're peeling. His tongue darts out, quick as a lizard's, to wet them.

"The thing is," he says as he brings a finger up to his mouth to chew on the already bitten-down nail, "I'm not sure anyone would even believe me if I told." Not only is my head boiling but my stomach starts bubbling. Ronnie is spreading his germs all over my bedroom, sickening me, making me fight off his flu, too. "Maybe if you, like, maybe if you told—"

"Shut up," I hiss. "Just shuh-shuh-*shut up*. Stop tuh-tuh-talking. You're fuh-fuh-fine, now. I got in a fuh-fuh-fight. But yuh-yuh-you're okay. Go home."

"Kurt?" Patti calls, her footsteps climbing the staircase. She can't return fast enough, far as I'm concerned. She needs to chase him out of my room, stop him from reminding me what happened. The walls keep shifting and my stomach sours. A pasty acid collects at the back of my throat. He's making me sicker.

Patti comes back into the room offering Ronnie nothing but a stingy squint while handing me a glass of water.

I down half of it in one gulp, wishing I could gargle it instead and spit out the foul taste Ronnie's brought with him. "How you feeling?" she asks me.

"Bad," I answer, telling the truth. I feel worse than bad. Ronnie, standing there, small and broken, makes me think of nothing but rottenness and how the world is sometimes so horrible that just staying under your bedcovers seems like the only right thing to do.

"Come on, you," Patti tells Ronnie, never bothering to learn his name. He turns to follow Patti out of my room like she's just slapped shackles around his wrists and legs, slowly winching him toward his destiny. We don't speak another word to each other and that's fine by me. I close my eyes and let the world slip away.

A hand resting softly on my forehead wakes me. "You don't feel warm," Patti says.

"Hmmm."

"Coach Brigs called," Patti says quietly. She lowers onto my cot, sinking the mattress in that spot so I tilt toward her hips. "Turns out there wasn't no practice on Saturday. I don't much appreciate being lied to, Kurtis. You understand?"

"Yes, ma'am."

"And what did I tell you about calling me 'ma'am'? Don't call me that. You call me Patti. I swear I am about to call an ambulance for you or take your butt down to the hospital myself if you can't get out of this bed by tomorrow. 'Course they'll accuse me of abusing you. I just know it. I don't want that, Kurtis. I really wish you'd get better quick so I don't have to take you to the hospital. You know child services will come knocking soon as I do that. And that'll be it. I won't get another chance to take someone in. I'll starve."

"I'm good. I am. Just nuh-nuh-need suh-suh-sleep. A little more suh-sleep."

Wednesday afternoon I finally sit up and bring my feet over the side of the cot. My head still throbs but at least I can look around the room without squinting against the light.

"Thank God, Kurt," Patti says. "I been praying for you."

"I ain't guh-guh-going in today," I say. I walk into the kitchen and open the fridge to get some OJ, but the fridge is empty. "I ain't guh-guh-going in this wuh-wuh-week. I ain't puh-puh-playing on Friday. Call Cuh-cuh-Coach for me. Tell him. I got the fuh-fuh-flu. Real bad. I ain't fuh-fuh-fakin'."

"I know, hon. I know. I'm just glad to see you up and about," she says, smiling at me through the ribbons of smoke tailing up from her cigarette. Her bloodshot eyes rim with water. "And I'm not the only one. Some girl, Tina, called and asked about you. I said you were sick and best not to come by and catch it herself. When you're better you can tell me all about this girl you been hidin'," she says.

I don't set foot into the school until the following Monday and so, except for the visit from Ronnie, I get away without thinking about the fight for a whole week. But I pay for it. I pay for it good, on Monday. That's when the world, with all its claws extended, pounces.

D A N N Y

Fake sick starts feeling like real sick if you do it long enough. Two days after Ronnie calls, I'm pretty sure I really have a scratchy throat and a temperature. Dad leaves so early in the morning and crashes so heavily in the evening that it's not until Thursday that he realizes I've stayed home all week.

"You're really that sick?" Dad asks me, taking off his glasses and rubbing his eyes. Where the frames usually rest on bridge of his nose, there remain two red dents, like emergency nostrils. Dad readjusts his glasses, then spends a moment studying me. "How do you feel, now?" He draws out the question in slow, weary words, as if stalling for time while trying to remember his son's name.

"Like crap."

"Well, what hurts?"

"Everything."

"Everything?" he echoes skeptically, then scratches his bearded cheeks. "Well, let me have a look at you." He makes me open my mouth and say "ahhhh" while examining my throat with his penlight. He feels the glands around my throat, neck, and armpits. His fingers are gentle. I try recalling the last time he hugged me, but another memory surfaces: the two of us flying kites together the summer before last on a trip down to the Carolina coast. He was tired even then but somehow that day—with the surf and sky and sun flowing over us—woke him up for a few hours. That day he stopped looking like a sleepwalker and more like how I remembered him with Mom. That day on the beach both of us somehow managed to forget for a few hours that Mom was dead and all we really had was each other. That was a great day.

"Well, you don't have any swollen glands and your throat and ears look good. Probably just a virus. Nasty stuff is always going around, you know."

"I know."

"So, you've been out all this week?"

"Yeah," I say innocently. "I thought you knew." I didn't exactly plan it, but every morning when my alarm went off, the first thing I imagined was running into Scott Miller, Tom Jankowski, or Mike Studblatz. Or worse—facing Ronnie. So I kept hitting the snooze button—Monday, Tuesday, Wednesday, Thursday morning—until it got so late the choice was made for me. Dad always leaves for his hospital rounds long before I get up for school, so I've been on the honor system for the last six years.

"I mean, Dad, *come on*," I say. "I've been in my pajamas every night you've gotten home."

"Hmmm . . ." His lips purse to one side and I know he's nibbling the inside of his cheek just like I do. "Well, do you need me to write a note for those four sick days?" he asks. "To take to the school office tomorrow?"

"Better make it five days," I say, then cough for effect and rub my belly like it aches, grimacing the whole time. "I'll take it in Monday."

"You wouldn't want to ruin your streak, I suppose." He scowls.

"Nope."

"What about all those skipped gymnastics rehearsals?" he asks, putting his hand around my neck. "Doesn't that mean you'll have to miss your team's recital this week?"

"They're not rehearsals. They're *practice*. And they're not recitals." I practically spit the word out on the floor. "They're *meets*."

"That's right," he says, tugging me into him by my neck, then ruffling my bedhead. "Practice and meets. Got it. And it's not your schoolwork and classes you're skipping. It's *your future*."

I can't really say anything back, so I don't. Besides, I like him rustling my hair.

"Well, you should get to bed if you're sick. Get your rest."

"I will," I say. "I'm just going to watch *The Late Show* first."

Friday, my last fake sick day, Coach Nelson calls our house. My own cell has been eerily quiet and that's fine with me. No news is good news. Staying home from school has taught me that when our house phone rings in the daytime I can expect offers to refinance our mortgage, order new life insurance policies, or subscribe to a dozen magazines. So when I realize it's Coach calling, I clear my throat and cough into the phone.

"Danny, sorry to hear you're under the weather," Coach Nelson says. "You and Bruce, both. Some sort of bug going around. Half of Coach Brigs's starters been out sick this week, too. Kurt Brodsky's still gone. Scott Miller, Mike Studblatz, and Tom Jankowski only returned yesterday."

"Something's going around, I guess." I clench the phone tight enough to break it while Coach lists the names: Bruce, Brodsky, Miller, Studblatz, Jankowski. All of them mashing into my ear. Only one name missing for a royal flush. Ronnie. Poor, miserable Ronnie.

"Yeah . . . well . . . I wish that's why I was calling." Coach Nelson pauses. "You get yourself healthy. Both you and Bruce. We miss you in the gym. Miss you gu—" and Coach's voice catches. The line goes quiet for a second. I wait, unsure what's wrong, somehow scared he knows about the attack, blames me for letting it happen, for not saying anything. Maybe he's angry about the vomit stench. Maybe I didn't clean up good enough and he can smell it. Did I leave the lights on? He'd be mad about that, too, threatening to take the gym keys from us. Maybe he never should have left us alone in the gym. Then Saturday never would have happened. My mind races while waiting for Coach to start talking again.

"This is real hard, Danny, and it ain't right doing it over the phone but there's no more time," Coach begins. "We had a team meeting today, gathered before the rest of the school heard the announcement."

"What?" He's freaking me out.

"There is no . . . there is no easy way to . . ."

Someone told. Ronnie told. Everyone knows. Everyone knows about the attack. Everyone knows! I feel equal parts panic and relief.

"Ronnie Gunderson passed . . . Ronnie Gunderson killed himself yesterday."

WHAT!?

"What? How? Where?"

"His father found him in the bathtub. Unconscious. The paramedics couldn't do anything for him."

"But . . ." I trail off, having no idea what to say next. My ear feels hot from pressing it to the receiver.

"You still with me, Danny?"

"Yes."

"I thought he was out sick. Like you, like Bruce," Coach says. "If I had even an inkling what was going through his mind . . . Danny, I'm going over everything and I'm . . ." Coach's voice fades. I hear him swallow over the phone and then sniff, as if he's holding back from crying. I've never heard a man cry before except in movies. Not even my dad has cried in front of me, even after telling me Mom died, not even at her funeral. Sometimes I got so angry at him for that, told myself maybe he never loved her like I did. Coach Nelson almost crying over the phone into my ear hurts as much as the actual news about Ronnie. It coils around my chest and begins to squeeze, accusing me of cowardice. I should have said something to someone. If I had gone to school on Monday and told Coach what happened, not pretended it never happened, not hated to think about Ronnie facedown in that room screaming his guts out while those guys . . . he'd probably be alive right now.

"Danny?"

"Yes?"

"We'll get through this," Coach says. "The school's already contacted a grief counseling service and—"

"Does Bruce know?" I cut him off.

"Yes. I called him first, wanted him, as the team captain, to . . . you understand . . ."

"I have to go," I say, then repeat it. "I have to go."

"Sure, Danny."

KURT

28

After a full week out sick with the "flu," I walk into first period on Monday shadowed by a dull headache; wondering how I'm supposed to set foot on the same field as Miller, Jankowski, and Studblatz and remain their teammate. Mrs. Helmsley, our English teacher and a tiny thing with arms like Popsicle sticks and a brittle voice to match, sets her chalk down at the board and pulls her eyebrows into a serious expression. "As you heard last Friday," she begins, "one of our students killed himself. I thought maybe we could take some time out of our regular class today to talk about it, if anyone wants to." She is met with silent, unmoving heads staring back at her. I'm massaging my temples, only half listening. "Did anyone know the student? Ronnie Gunderson?" she asks. A few heads shake no while the rest remain motionless as she struggles with the topic. Finally, a girl two desks in front of me raises her hand, then asks why he killed himself. Mrs. Helmsley lets her cheeks puff out, holding her breath for a moment, before releasing a long exhale.

"That, I'm sure, is a very complicated answer," she says.

"Who was he?" someone near me whispers while I press my thumbs under the top of my eye sockets, once hearing that was a way to stop headache pain. It's not working.

"No clue," someone whispers back. "Never met him."

It takes at least a minute before the news actually penetrates my bruised brain and I understand that Ronnie Gunderson isn't just some freshman I never met and too bad for him. Ronnie Gunderson is *Ronnie*. The gymnast. That kid. *Ronnie*. The one who helped Bruce and Danny spot me on back handsprings. The one . . . Scott offered up to me in the storage room, pants down . . . *"You want a shot, Mr. Wolf?"*

Absorbing the full hit of Mrs. Helmsley's news, my skull clamps down on my swollen brain. My head starts pounding and pounding and I know if I have to sit in that cramped desk for another second and pretend I don't know anything about why Ronnie killed himself, I'll maybe tear the desk apart, if not the room, to relieve the pressure.

I lurch up to standing, feeling the whole class tilt with me.

"Yes, Kurt?" Mrs. Helmsley asks, partly helpful and partly challenging. I wave her off, not really sure what might come out of my mouth if I try talking. Like maybe I'll blurt out that Ronnie Gunderson, the freshman nobody knew, was torn apart in a storage room and that's what killed him. The suicide came after. And maybe I'll stutter and stammer that our homecoming king did it. And maybe I should go find him right then and make sure, once and for all, he never hurts someone like Lamar— like Ronnie ever again. I walk up the aisle and out of the classroom, gripping my books tight, wanting to whip them as far down the hallway as possible as if that might help even for a second. Breaking things is all I can imagine, is all I want to do. It's all I'm good at. I suck at saving things, suck at saving people.

Outside the school, there's a spruce tree planted in the middle of the lawn near the edge of the teachers' parking lot. It's warmed up again, back to being early fall, and the sky is powder blue and the grass is emerald green and still soft and the leaves on the maples are starting to turn auburn and gold. It's a perfect day and I feel nothing but wet concrete churning through my blood, causing my tongue to taste clay while light and sound just turn to dirt. Brown dirt. All of it. Everything.

I reach into the spruce and grab smaller branches and start breaking them off the tree, twisting them down and back until they make a satisfying snap, like the spine of a small animal.

Dumb sons of bitches!

Snap! Snap!

Stupid, stupid, stupid . . .

Snap! Snap! Snap!

I stay outside hoping the sun might burn off some of the ugliness swirling around me, but it ain't working. When I finally go back inside, it's only to catch Danny in math, hoping he knows more, hoping he'll tell me Ronnie was already suicidal, that me pushing him out of my room—telling him nothing happened but a fight and it was all in his head—wasn't what killed him.

I get to algebra early and drum my fingers on the desk waiting for Danny to arrive. When the bell rings, there's still no sign of him. Mr. Klech starts diagramming on the chalkboard while everyone pretends to care or at least not fall asleep. I keep watching the door and waiting for Danny to slip in with a hall pass. Thirty-five minutes later, I give up. He ain't coming. And even if he does, I realize, he ain't about to offer any words that'll excuse me.

No one except me saw what happened to Ronnie in that storage room. No one. If I go down to the principal's office and tell the truth about what I saw, they'll accuse me of doing it. Accuse me just like last time. They'll tell everyone about my past. They'll start the rumors all over again; that I hurt Ronnie same way I did my best friend at Meadow's House before I killed him. That *I'm* the monster. Without Bruce or Danny seeing anything until after it finished, it's three against one; Tom, Scott, and Mike's story versus mine. Ronnie can't say different. *Ronnie is gone.* I try picturing Ronnie in the gym last week but I keep seeing Lamar instead, resting in his polished chrome casket, smile like a mannequin's. The memorial service attended by three news crews and more people than either of us ever met. Lamar's shiny, boy-size casket—the most expensive thing he ever got to own.

Algebra finishes. Mr. Klech sets the chalk down in the metal tray running along the bottom of the board. He rubs his hands together and gives us our assignment. I write it down, not paying attention, wondering, instead, how I'll get through the next hour, afternoon, day, year.

I'm back at practice that same day I hear the news, too weak-minded to quit, unable to imagine walking away from it, hating myself for showing up. Scott, Tom, and Mike are all yammering and jawing on the field, same as always. I mean to ignore them and expect the same back. But when Scott sees me, he jogs over and greets me with a fist thump on my shoulder pad.

"Hey, man, no hard feelings, all right?" he says in friendly tones. The helmet shades his face, making it hard to read him.

"Wuh?"

"My left arm's still aching after that shot you gave me." Scott lowers his voice so it barely clears his face mask. "Good thing you didn't hit my throwing arm, huh?"

I don't answer.

"But you wouldn't do that," he says. "Don't want to mess with our record. Mess with what we got going on here. That would be pretty stupid." Scott pounds my shoulder pad with his fist again, then jogs over to run passing drills with Assistant Coach Stein.

"Hey, bro," Tom yells over at me. "Starting to wonder about you, weren't we, Pullman?"

"Hell, yeah," Pullman agrees. "Glad you're back, man. That flu'll kick your ass."

The gate of my practice helmet, the one without the camera and mic, dips as I nod back at him.

"Just don't give it to me," Pullman says.

"Now that Brodsky's back, we can start slaughtering the

rest of the division again." Tom thumps his chest pads and then slaps the top of Pullman's helmet. "Without your daddies on the field, that last game was a little too close."

"We still won," Pullman answers. "*And* it was an away game. That's all that counts."

"You won by a field goal," Tom says. "A field goal. If you can't beat Farmington by at least ten, you should wear a skirt."

"My man is back!" Terrence calls out. *His* smile, at least, is genuine. I move closer to him, feeling safer in his zone. "Ain't too fun running behind your backup," Terrence tells me, then clasps his hands together like he's praying and tilts his helmet up to the sky. "Thank you, Lord, for giving me my stat boy back. You know how bad my yardage totals were last game? Please don't let Kurt go off and get sick no more, you hear?"

I hold out my fist. Terrence bumps it with his.

Judging from practice, you'd never guess my captains and me helped kill a boy. Wearing the red vest that makes him unhittable, Scott doesn't even have to protect his bad arm during scrimmage. Tom bullies every player within shoving distance during our drills, same as always. Studblatz, unlike Scott and Tom, stays away from me, but, for him, that's normal. As leader of the defensive unit, he always treats our offense as the enemy during practice. Halfway through scrimmage, though, I notice him favoring his right side, like his rib cage on the other side's real tender. *Good*, I think, pretty sure that's my doing.

"Brodsky, Miller, Studblatz, Jankowski," Coach Brigs calls out, "meet in my office after showers, gentlemen." Coach Brigs's tone leaves no room for negotiation.

I dawdle on the field, pretending to work on some blocking techniques and lateral steps so I won't have to change alongside those three guys. Once in the shower, I take my time, letting the water scald me, hoping it might help clear my head. I put off the meeting in Coach's office long as possible.

"You squeaky-clean, now, Kurt?" Coach asks, closing the door behind me. "I support good hygiene as much as the next guy, but let's not go overboard with the prima donna routine. It leads to softness. And softness is something I can't tolerate in my players."

Scott snickers while Tom grins knowingly like they've been discussing my softness with Coach the whole time. Along with Studblatz, the three captains sit on Coach's couch, their bodies packed tight between the armrests.

"Softness leads to problems, leads to trouble," Coach continues as he settles into the chair behind his desk. "Hell, that confused boy, Ronnie Gunderson—God have mercy on his soul—I heard was troubled with that problem. Soft." Scott and Tom, I notice, lose their smiles.

"It's a damn shame what that boy did to himself," Coach says, staring up at the top shelf of trophies in his office. "What a selfish, *selfish* act it is to take your own life. Can you imagine what his poor parents must be going through? I'm sad for his parents. I'm sad for his family. I'm not sad for him, though. For him, I feel only anger. I feel *contempt*. I don't have an *ounce* of pity for such a *cowardly* act." Coach squeezes his eyes shut as he stresses the words, then suddenly opens them again. "Maybe it's just as well he got culled from the herd early. Lord has a plan. He always has a plan. Bet on it."

I shift my weight in the small wooden chair, the only seat left in Coach's office.

"Now, boys, I bring up Ronnie Gunderson for a reason," Coach says. My eyes shoot over to Scott. He's holding his breath, same as Tom, same as me. Mike looks like he's just chomped down on his tongue. "What that kid did tore a hole in the fabric of our community. Do you understand? And what we provide our community on Friday nights is more than a ball game. It's a time for restoring faith in our future, of passing the baton from the strong of one generation to the next. So this ball game coming up is not just about winning and improving our record. It's about healing our community after suffering a serious blow, about giving our community something more than the failure of one soft, misguided boy to dwell upon."

I gaze down at my knuckles, examining the scabs left on them from the punches I threw in that storage room.

"You all might be asking yourselves why I'm not giving this speech to our whole team, why I'm privileging you boys with it all by your lonesome." Coach leans back in his chair until I'm sure the springs will snap and send him toppling over. He stays upright, though, drumming his finger on his belly, taking his sweet time shifting his gaze to each of our faces. "You boys, you did something weekend before last."

This is it. Here we go. It's all about to burst open.

"I don't know what happened or what you did, but I find it more than a coincidence that my four best starters all come down with the same bug that lays them all out for a week, risking an away-game loss to *Farmington High*, of all teams!" He keeps drumming his fingers on his belly.

"Meanwhile, not one other boy—not a single player on the team—missed class or is even remotely sick.

"You want to know what I think?" Coach asks us.

The only thing that calms me is watching Scott, Tom, and Mike actually squirm on the couch, waiting for Coach's next thought.

"I think you boys had yourselves a little party," Coach continues. "Maybe drank a few too many beers and decided to go for a joyride and got banged up enough that Brodsky was out with some sort of concussion, Studblatz now has bruised ribs, Scott has a bad arm—you real lucky, boy, it's not your throwing arm—and Tom's been limping during sprint drills."

Coach rocks forward in his chair, the springs creaking, and jumps up to attention. He leans over his desk, planting both arms on it like cannon supports. "I'm not even going to begin lecturing you all on how stupid it is to drink and drive and how lucky you boys are that you didn't—God forbid—hurt anyone other than yourselves and how lucky you are that you got by with a few scrapes, near as I can tell. I'm not going to start lecturing on how badly you let this team down when your own selfish need to party gets in the way of performing on that field with the body that you were fortunate enough to be gifted from the good Lord himself. I'll leave all that for now.

"What I *will not stand*"—and now Coach's face turns crimson—"is being lied to and told you were sick with the flu. I will not allow that type of deceit and disrespect, you understand? We are a team. We are a family. The whole community looks up to us and what kind of example are we providing when our own family is lying to its coach? Huh? *Look at me!* You boys aren't even smart enough to come up with a good goddamn lie!"

"Coach, we—" Scott starts, but Coach cuts him off.

"Don't you start jawing that oily mouth, boy!" Coach pounds the top of his desk. "You may be the quarterback—for now—but I'm the coach, you understand? You want me to keep talking nice to those recruiters—telling them all how you're such a great kid and asking your teachers to bump up your sorry-ass grades—then you better shut your mouth and listen up. I don't want to ever have another game where my four stars are out. We got a chance at going all the way to state this year and winning the whole she-bang! The whole enchilada! You understand that? I don't want anything standing in the way of our team forming into a cohesive unit, like soldiers under fire." Coach lifts a hand and drags it across his mouth before planting it back on his desk.

"I will not tolerate your lying to me," he says. "Do you understand?!"

We nod our heads yes.

"I can't hear you."

"Yes, Coach," we say.

"Good," he says, taking his hands off his desk, standing taller. "And you better hope, for your sakes, that you heal real quick. I don't want to hear a single excuse about you getting hurt on the field and it turns out it's one of these injuries that came from goofing off when you should've been in bed."

We nod again in unison.

"Now get out of here," Coach growls.

I stay sitting in my chair while the other three get up to leave. I can tell Coach what really happened. Tell him Ronnie wasn't soft. That he was destroyed by Coach's captains, tortured in that storage room without mercy until they broke him. There was no car accident. Just a fight to stop them. Stop evil. And I lost.

I sit there, mind scrambling, trying to come up with a way to get my mouth to talk fast and smooth, form the first words that'll lead down that path. Maybe if I was wearing my helmet, I could get the words out.

"Cuh-cuh-cuh-cuh-Coach?" I start. Tom and Mike have already stepped out of the office. Scott waits, though, like he knows what I'm thinking.

"You coming, Brodsky?" Scott asks, interrupting me. I glare up at him, then glance desperately at Coach, hoping he'll read my eyes, see I need to confess. "You heard the man," Scott drones like a radio ad, filling every moment with his voice. "He said get out of here and leave him alone." Forced laughter pummels the small office space, leaving no room for my voice. "We've given him a big enough headache for one day. He's sprouting gray hair even as we speak."

"You're a real comedian, Scott." Coach grunts, then waves the back of his hand at us. "Yeah, all of you, git!"

I feel my chance evaporate while Scott stands in the doorway, ready to keep talking, if need be, waiting for me to exit. When I do, he pulls Coach's door shut behind us. I move to get away from him but he stays in step with me.

"You better rest that head of yours, Kurt. We need you ready for Friday. Ashville won't be easy. They got a monster defensive linebacker, Jackson. He's going to try and eat all of us for dinner. We need to pull together, not let anything get between us."

"Uh-huh."

"There's no going solo on this team, Kurt. We got your back. You need to have ours."

"I've guh-guh-guh-got to guh-guh-go."

"You want a lift?" he asks. "I'm giving Tommy and Mike a ride home."

"No."

"All right." Scott shrugs, then dusts my shoulder like I might have dandruff, which I don't. "Now don't go making up stories about us, okay?"

I'm unable to speak, betrayed by my mouth, again, hating myself, hating my weakness, more than Scott, wishing Lamar, just for ten seconds, could come back and speak for me.

"'Cause you know me, Mike, and Tommy would never, ever lie to Coach or anyone else about what happened," Scott murmurs in my ear. "Tommy's car got banged up when all of us went drinking. Coach is too smart to trick. He saw right through us. Saw that we tried to cover up a car accident by pretending we had the flu."

Then Scott walks away, leaving me stalled there like a fool.

D A N N Y

That first Monday back in school since Ronnie's suicide, I've just sparked the Bunson burner in first period chemistry—pretty much the coolest part of the class is getting to play with fire—when the PA system's angry squawk interrupts my brilliant new scheme to melt Studblatz's face off.

"Please send Danny Meehan to the principal's office."

The students around me titter in unison.

"Busted!"

Any student unlucky enough to get called in front of Oregrove's school secretary will meet a stout old woman with an Aqua Net hair dome and puffy arms swollen up like boiled bratwurst. Mrs. Doyle harrumphs at you in greeting because she knows if you're standing before her, chances are you've been up to no good. Fisher brags that

L
E
V
E
R
A
G
E

214

he's called down so often Mrs. Doyle now lets him address her by her first name.

Today Mrs. Doyle comes around her desk and welcomes me like a long-lost relative from the old country. She lays cocktail-sausage fingers on my forearm and pulls me into her pork-roast bosom.

"Oh, Danny, such terrible news. Such terrible, terrible news," Mrs. Doyle repeats, hugging me tightly. She stuffs me into her chest, blocking out all sound and light. She releases me and then leans down to look me in the eye as she cups my neck. Tan makeup flakes her downy jowls and fills the crinkles around her eyes and mouth like flour, like she just baked a flesh-cake. "Principal Donovan and Coach Nelson wanted to meet privately with the team and see how you're all handling things since the announcement last week."

Mrs. Doyle leads me into Principal Donovan's office and then into a side room I've never had the honor of entering. The room contains a large circular conference table. My teammates are seated around it like morose hobbits. Coach Nelson and Principal Donovan talk in low voices at the far corner while sipping out of "I'd Rather Be Fishing" and "Is It Friday Yet?" coffee mugs. Fisher glances up at me and for once he isn't smiling. Gradley and Menderson doodle in their notebooks while Paul tattoos the side of his sneakers with a ballpoint pen. Steve picks out thread at the knees of his jeans. Pete Delray chews off a hangnail while training his eyes on the door as if waiting patiently to be excused. Only Bruce sits stone still, head dipping forward from the neck, awaiting a hangman's noose. The rest of the guys all seem to be pretty focused on their laps.

"You okay, kiddo?" Mrs. Doyle asks Fisher, laying a hand on his shoulder as she stands behind him.

"Yeah, Maude, thanks." Fisher reaches up and squeezes her hand as if she were his grandma. *Maybe detention isn't so bad,* I think.

After Mrs. Doyle exits, Principal Donovan begins his spiel talking about "tragic event" this and "sudden loss of life" that and how sad we all must be feeling. His speech sounds practiced and fake and I tune him out. Instead, I concentrate on Bruce and his glazed, vacant eyes sunk into bruised sockets. A squadron of pimples sets up camp in the hollows of his cheeks while an oily nose shines with the cold fluorescence of the room. Greasy bed-head mats thick, black hair against his left ear while the right side swells up into a frozen tsunami. Basically, Bruce looks like shit. He looks like he's been awake for the last four days, hasn't showered or slept, and is surviving on Coke, chocolate bars, and corn chips.

Like me.

Principal Donovan punctuates his speech with loud slurps of coffee. He finishes with something about "persevering in the face of adversity" and "continuing to be strong." I glance at Fisher, half expecting and half hoping he'll mimic Principal Donovan under his breath, but Fisher just sits there, bobbing his head in agreement with the principal's words.

"Guys, this is a hard, hard thing to grasp," Coach Nelson takes up where Principal Donovan leaves off. "I encourage any and all of you to say something at the service, to let others know how special Ronnie was and how much we'll all miss him. In fact, I think that might be something we'd like to do now, in this room, among friends and team-mates."

I look around the table at my teammates, knowing none of them—none of us—knew much about Ronnie except what he brought into the gym. He was a freshman and pretty shy and into reading quietly by himself. He'd worked hard, a lot harder than Pete, a lot harder than Fisher, and never complained about doing strength sets. He could've made a good gymnast in a couple years but who really cares about any of that stuff? He's dead. I mean, he's dead! That won't change tomorrow or the next day or the day after that. He's dead. Forever. No one knows him because his chance to show us is gone. And if it was me dead in his place, people would have the same problem trying to say anything special about me. What have I shown the world? Maybe Ronnie was a good friend to someone out there. His future, his promise, his potential had been taken away.

Fuck!

"Last year," Pete Delray, our team's other freshman, begins quietly.

"Go on," Coach encourages.

Pete starts describing how he and Ronnie dressed as Aquaman and Superman for Halloween a few years earlier but some big kids jumped them and duct-taped them to a tree. Left them there all night. What kind of story is that? It's basically a version of what happened to him in the storage room. Did he have "victim" stamped on his forehead? Why did everyone pick on him? He suffered enough. Without realizing it, I've got my hands over my ears and I'm humming to block out the rest of Pete's memory. Gradley punches me in the arm to shut me up. When I unblock my ears, Pete's stopped talking, but I still want to smack him in the mouth for even bringing up the Halloween duct taping.

"He was a gentle soul," Coach says, and I can tell he isn't very good at this type of thing because he pats Pete on the head like he's dribbling a basketball. "Sometimes others take advantage of that. But I don't think we should dwell on that part of him."

He was weak, I think. ALL people will ALWAYS take advantage of that. Not just sometimes. Scott, Tom, and Mike smelled his weakness. Took advantage. Never be weak or gentle. You have to be strong to ward them off. Big and strong. Like Kurt!

"I killed him." Bruce speaks so quietly it's barely above a whisper. "It's my fault."

"No, son," Principal Donovan corrects him as he lifts his coffee mug to his lips. "No one in this room killed that boy. That's preposterous." *Slurrrrp.*

"Feelings of guilt are normal," Coach adds. "I keep asking myself why I didn't spot signs in Ronnie sooner, why I didn't see what he must've been going through."

Because you didn't stay to lock up the gym! I fume. You left us there, unprotected! Anger overtakes me as the meeting continues. I feel no sadness, not even fear, just a white-hot rage at everyone around me.

"I've been racking my brain over the whole thing," Coach continues. "But I . . . and you . . . and all of us must understand that Ronnie's death was not our fault. It's not your fault, Bruce."

Wrong! I think. Bruce started the whole thing the day

he stood up for that stupid cross-country runner. Why'd he have to protect that dork? He wasn't on our team. He wasn't one of us. Let his stupid, skinny, cross-country teammates protect him.

"Funeral is set for tomorrow at noon," Coach tells us. "You've all got excused absences to attend."

By the time the meeting finishes, it's the beginning of third period. I don't feel much like going to algebra, so I skip. Schoolwork isn't really a high priority at the moment. I keep thinking about how easily Ronnie and I could've switched places that day and now he's dead. It could be me dead and not him. Just dumb luck separates us.

Those three still roam the hallways, laughing and shoving others around like nothing's happened. They know they're invincible. They can do anything they want. How am I supposed to go back into that gym? How am I supposed to ever go near that storage room again? Those three came in and they destroyed the one good place in school.

I skip practice that Monday. I find out later, so did Bruce.

K U R T

Crud Bucket first said Lamar's death was an accident. Then he tried blaming me. Everyone believed him in the beginning, just like he threatened they would. That's why Sergeant Schmidt, the same officer who pulled me out of Meadow's House soon as the ambulance left with Lamar's body, escorted me to his funeral with a firm grip on my elbow while I remained "under suspicion." Because of the hype, Lamar's funeral was packed with people neither of us ever met. TV news vans with roof-mounted satellite dishes double-parked in front of the church steps. It took a real pretty coffin, but Lamar finally got people's attention.

So did I.

Men with big bellies aimed shoulder-mounted cameras and fired blinding beams of light at me. As I went up the church steps, my legs tangled with Sergeant Schmidt's

L
E
V
E
R
A
G
E

and he yanked on me like a dog on a leash to keep the both of us from tumbling.

Orphan Killer Attends Victim's Funeral.

That was the headline sticks most in my brain, but there were others almost as juicy.

After the service, Sergeant Schmidt escorted me over to my next residence—the Lake Ondarro Residence—a boys' reformatory where the windows had gates on them; large, unfriendly men in green uniforms patrolled the hallways; and at night our room doors locked us in from the outside. Sergeant Schmidt visited me once a week, bringing sprinkled doughnut holes to share with the other boys on my floor to help me make friends. I was the youngest one in there and under special protection. Sergeant Schmidt told me he believed in me, knew I didn't do nothing wrong. By then Crud Bucket was on trial and Sergeant Schmidt had driven me twice to a courtroom to testify what all Crud Bucket had done to me and Lamar. I used to hope maybe Sergeant Schmidt would take me home, let me live with his family. They transferred me to my next group home after three months, one without gates and guards. Sergeant Schmidt had stopped coming around by then. When they finally found Crud Bucket guilty, the newspeople lost interest. No one wrote a headline stating *Orphan Kid Didn't Do It!*

Ronnie Gunderson's funeral ain't much by Lamar's standards. Oregrove has almost three thousand students but I see, maybe, forty people at the service. That morning, when I go to the school office to get an excused absence, the same secretary that dumped me in algebra narrows her eyes at me, sure I'm using Ronnie's funeral as an easy chance to skip class. Eventually, she hands over the pass, speaking extra slow and loud as she gives me directions to the church. I start to understand her suspicion when I see all the empty pews. Suicide's not okay, I guess.

Short boys in suits—the gymnastics team—sit up front just behind what must be Ronnie's family. I stay in the back, unsure if I should even be here. The long scar tightens like a zipper up my cheek. Sitting alone at a funeral gives you lots of time to think. The thing I keep thinking is that Scott would've never bothered Ronnie, never even thought to come to the gym, if I had kept my mouth shut about meeting the gymnasts there that Saturday.

A line forms to file past Ronnie's open casket. I'm at the end of it, trying hard not to scratch the bubble skin on my jaw. The closer I get, the more it prickles. Inside the casket, someone's posed a wax-museum boy to make him look like he's asleep. Just like at Lamar's funeral. It's stupid. They aren't fooling anyone.

"I didn't know they'd follow me," I whisper to him. *"Didn't know you were hurting that bad. I swear. I didn't. I'm sorry."*

Scott should be here. Mike and Tom, too. I'd shove them in the coffin with Ronnie, shut the lid and bury them, ask them how they felt now.

"Sorry," I whisper again. I go back down the aisle, fiddling with the funeral program I rolled up into a tube during the minister's speech. I drum it against my thigh, let my hair fall over my face, and watch my shoes until I reach my seat. I see little Danny walking up the aisle toward me and stopping at my row. He signals me to slide over for

L
E
V
E
R
A
G
E

him. The two of us sit quietly while an old woman with a cane stiffly hobbles up to the podium. She speaks but the microphone doesn't reach down to her mouth, so it sounds like soft owl hoots. Her free hand comes up to her old face and covers her eyes as her shoulders shake with grief.

Danny reaches into his coat pocket and pulls out my lost phone and hands it to me. "I meant to return this to you sooner, but . . ." Danny, speaking quietly, lets his voice trail off.

"Thu-thanks."

A recording of "Amazing Grace" begins playing and we both sit listening to the hymn.

"It's good you came," Danny says, speaking only after the song finishes. "What you did, how you tried to protect Ronnie," he says, "you should be proud. I wish . . . I wish I had done something like that, at least tried."

Danny starts nibbling his lower lip while fiddling with the Bible in the pew pocket at our knees. "I was there," he says out the side of his mouth while his face aims up toward the big stained-glass window bleeding deep violets, blues, and reds. "In the corner, behind the mat, scared they'd do the same to me if they found me," he says. He switches lips, biting his top one now, as he starts sniffling. "I didn't do anything to stop them. I didn't even try." Danny wipes at his nose with the back of his wrist. "But you came in and you didn't even think twice."

"You suh-suh-saw what happened?" I ask, astonished. "All of it?"

"Yeah," he says. "What they did to him . . . they deserved everything you gave 'em. And more. I wish they were dead, right now. Up in that casket. I'd spit on them and laugh. I swear I would. I swear." His nose is leaking good and he wipes it again with his wrist, then pulls the Bible out of the pew pocket and starts flipping through it. He dips his head and a teardrop or snot drop hits the thin paper, staining the Bible page before Danny can turn it. "Ronnie didn't even pee on their uniforms. He didn't water-balloon them. He wasn't part of Coach's trick in the weight room. He didn't do any of it. But even if he did . . . what those guys did back . . . was. . . ." Danny brings the cuff of his suit coat up to his face and wipes quickly across his nose and eyes.

"They thuh-thuh-think it's only muh-me that knows," I say. "They thuh-thuh-think they guh-got away with it." *And they have,* I tell myself. After ten days, I haven't said anything to anyone. Even worse, I'm still their teammate, afraid to tell the truth and take them on. Afraid I'll some-how get blamed for things all over again. I'm a worse cow-ard than Danny.

"I wish I was big as you," Danny says, putting the Bible back in the pew pocket and pulling out the hymnbook, flipping through its well-worn pages. "I'd get them."

"It's not suh-suh-so easy."

"It is. You proved it."

"How's Buh-buh-buh-Bruce?" I ask, changing the sub-ject.

"Awful," Danny reports. "He's convinced he caused it. Keeps saying it's all his fault it got this far." Danny flips through more pages. "Actually, that's kinda true."

The service ends and people are filing past us up the

aisle to leave. I glance over at Danny and do a double take. Tina, the goth girl, is passing our row, offering me a small wave. Oddly enough, she dresses less goth for the funeral. The dyed-black hair with blond roots is combed back into a bun and the piercings in her eyebrows, nose, and lips are gone. The ones in her ears are still there. With the raccoon eyeliner scrubbed off, she almost looks alive. And kind of pretty.

"Hi." She mouths the word at me as she and her friend, the skinny girl with the big eyes and wavy hair, keep moving up the aisle to the exit.

"Make sure you sign the guest book so Ronnie's parents know you came," Danny says to me as he stands up to leave. He takes a step and stops, turns back to me. In a lowered voice he says, "I won't forget what you did. You did your best to save Ronnie." Then he leaves to join his teammates.

Even though I feel miserable and mostly like a fake, what Danny says means something to me. I sit in the pew, trying to take comfort in his words. I want to believe I helped, but what keeps returning is how I pushed Ronnie away when he came to Patti's house. The sight of him turned my stomach and I wanted nothing to do with him. I was grateful the moment he left my room and I never wanted to think about him or what happened ever again. There is no getting around any of that.

When I finally get up to leave, I find the minister in the aisle waiting for me. He holds a Bible in front of him, resting it on top of his left hand as if it's a serving tray.

"Excuse me," he says. "We haven't met, but I believe

I know you." I'm waiting for him to see right through me and tell me I'm going to hell for abandoning Ronnie in his time of need.

"Were you a close friend of Ronnie's?" he asks.

I shake my head no.

"Well, that makes it an even finer thing that you came today and blessed the family with your presence and support." With his free hand, he reaches out to shake. I wait for him to collapse when we make contact, like he's just touched the devil himself.

"Pastor Manning," he says, not collapsing. "And your name is?"

"Kuh-kuh-Kurt," I say.

"Kurt Brodsky?" he asks. "Oregrove's fullback?"

"Yessssssssir."

"You're a fine athlete," he chirps, his face lighting up. "It's a real ray of hope seeing you here on such a sad day. I'm sure it means a lot to Ronnie's loved ones that you showed up to offer your condolences."

I shrug my shoulders, not really sure what to say.

"I'm one of the Knights' loudest fans in the stands. A certified 'Bleacher Creature.'"

"Thuh-thuh-thanks."

"After a tragedy such as this, the community thirsts for events that help reaffirm their lives, reaffirm the goodness in others, reaffirm that we are all working toward a higher purpose. You and your teammates offer all of us just such a hope. I pray for your continued success. You know, I can't think of a more soothing balm for our community than a championship, something for all of us to rally around. It would provide such magnificent healing. May God grant you and your teammates glory."

I scrunch the edges of my coat with sweaty palms and shift my feet.

"And may I add that it would be an honor to have one of Oregrove's stars attend our services on a regular basis. I pray we see you again in here."

D A N Y

31

In our first gymnastics meet since the attack, Bruce leads the team in mistakes, but I pull ahead in the vaunted "Bonehead" category. Luckily, there's only, like, eight people in the Farmington High bleachers to witness the carnage and no one's taping for YouTube. I'm not sure if the rest of the team has figured it out, yet, but neither of us wants to be here. After almost two weeks away from the gym, the skin on my hands has softened and my body feels clumsy. During warm-ups on high bar, I trick myself into thinking I'm fine. The chalky steel bites into my palms in a rough but familiar way, like a handshake from my mom's brother, Steve, who works construction. He'll sit smoking Pall Malls and drinking Budweiser at our kitchen table and tell me and Dad story after story about Mom when she was my age.

The high bar's handshake turns painful, though, after a couple more warm-up swings. My palms grow tender, then sting, then get hot the way they do before they blister and rip open. Worse, my timing is off from lack of practice. I miss my easiest release moves in warm-ups, splatting on the thick mats during both attempts.

"How about we keep it nice and simple," Coach suggests after my second crash. "Leave out the big tricks today."

"Sure," I say. Even the crash is unable to shake me from my weird dream state.

Bruce starts the downward spiral early, falling out of position two times on rings and stepping out of bounds during his floor exercise. The rest of us follow his example.

I'm signaling the judge and back on high bar. I can't remember what moves I agreed to take out. Wait! Where the hell am I in the routine?! I've just skipped most of my tricks. I've got to throw *something* before the dismount. Might as well be the big one. I don't really throw the up-and-over-the-bar suicide so much as simply let go and see what happens. What happens is the steel pipe slams into my chest just below my throat.

What happens is I'm shattering.

A flash-bomb goes off and the world spins and tumbles and there's Coach reaching out, trying to catch me, trying to stop me but the floor's going to beat him to it. I tuck my chin to my chest, trying to form a ball, trying to roll through the fall and keep from snapping my neck. The angle I hit at drives out all air as either my teeth or spine cracks like plates.

Silence.

I lie motionless, unable to breathe, unable to move. The first moments after breaking my neck.

"Danny? Jesus Christ! Danny!"

Coach's shouting above me. I feel his hands squeezing my arms as he aligns my body. I can feel him. *I can feel him?* I make a fist and wiggle my feet. I'm not paralyzed. *I'm not paralyzed!*

"Unngh." I gasp, the wind still knocked out of me. My teammates circle me, hover over me, their faces wrinkling into prunes of fear and concern. It frightens me. I've got to move. I have to be all right. I have to be all right.

"Just lay still, Tiger, I got you," Coach says, but I don't believe him. No one has me. No one can catch me. No one caught Ronnie. I roll to my side while fighting for air, feeling it slowly come back into me.

"Just lay back, dude," Fisher says in a voice I've never heard, a serious voice, and that scares the crap out of me.

I sit up. "Fuck you, Fish," I croak. My teammates start laughing. It's not that funny, so I think they're mostly relieved.

"Okay, little pill," Coach says, "I'm guessing you're fine, but why don't you just relax for a minute."

Turns out, I am okay, minus the giant horizontal bruise running across my sternum. We lose the meet. By a lot. Bruce and I both set personal worsts. We're untaping our wrists and stuffing sweats into our bags when Farmington's team comes over to our bench.

"We heard about your teammate," their captain says. He's a shaggy-haired, freckled guy named Oscar. I remember him from last season, plus he placed second on pommel horse in state meet. "We had a guy on the swim team do that last year," Oscar says. "It sucks. It really does."

We mumble agreement back at him while mopping our brows with T-shirt sleeves. Oscar and his teammates go off to tear down their equipment and move it out of the gym. Coach Nelson's over on the side talking with the Farmington coach and I'm pretty sure they're discussing Ronnie.

"Guys," Fisher says. "Let's go up to the quarry Saturday. Weather's supposed to be perfect, like a summer rebound. We'll do a little tribute or séance or something. For Ronnie."

"Water's too cold now to go swimming," Paul says.

"Then we don't go swimming," Fisher says. "We'll just climb this time. Coach'll lend us the ropes and gear."

"I like it," I hear myself say, picturing the one place still unpolluted by the attack. "The quarry's perfect." I've got a break-n-shake chemical freeze pack pressed just below my throat. I'm imagining the quarry forest, far away from school and the halls and classrooms and locker rooms and that awful thing that lives like a monster in our gym's storage room. "I'm in," I say. "Fish, I'm in."

"Yeah, me too," Gradley says, building momentum.

"Yeah, why not," Paul Kim says, and bumps Menderson, who nods that he's coming as well.

"What about it, Bruce?" Fisher asks. Bruce has been in his own world as much as me. He's either thinking about the question while he stuffs his leather grips into his bag and pulls off his socks or he isn't even listening. Fisher's about to ask again when Bruce finally answers.

"Okay," he says quietly.

There's one more person who needs to come with us up to the quarry, I decide. Showing Kurt the team's secret place is the only way I can think of to thank him for saving me and Bruce that day.

"I've got a piano lesson on Saturday," Pete says.

"So skip it," Fisher tells him. "It's not like you're going to be a concert pianist or anything."

"Did you just say concert *penis*?"

"Pianist, dumbass. Pianist."

K U R T

Men, tonight will be our toughest fight yet."

Coach Brigs begins his pregame locker-room speech only after we all settle in a circle on bended knee around him and his staff. "Our school, our community, our family and friends have suffered a terrible blow this week from a mixed-up boy too weak to face the doubts and fears that plague us all from time to time. I pray for Ronnie Gunderson's poor parents. I pray they withstand the awful cruelty he inflicted on them. I take little comfort in his eternal damnation since it cannot make up for the fact that his cowardice has placed a black hole of doubt in the hearts of each and every one of the parents out there in the stands tonight. Doubts that grow about their own children and what may become of them if they go down the wrong path."

Huh? It sure feels like an odd pep talk before a game. I glance around the huddle and see teammates with heads cocked to the side and eyebrows knitting together trying to make sense of the words. If nothing else, Coach sure has our attention.

"That is why," Coach continues, "it's up to us, here, tonight, to reassure not only your parents and families but our entire community. It's up to us, here, tonight, to show our neighbors how righteous soldiers, how good and decent men behave when faced with challenge and adversity. Righteous soldiers do not run. We do not hide or cower under our mama's skirts. We face that challenge head-on. We face our fears and overcome them. We do *not* lay down and die."

"Hoo-wah!" booms from behind me.

"Hoo-wah!" answers from across the huddle.

Could Ronnie really be in hell for killing himself? I doubt it. And, anyway, if he *is* there, then Scott, Tom, and Mike are surely joining him someday. I glance around the huddle, nervous the others smell my doubt. I tell myself I'm still here, still playing, because I don't want to let the team down by quitting. There's a part of me that knows better, though, knows that I'm scared of the consequences —from my captains, from Coach, and even from Patti—if I walk away. Guys nod along with Coach's speech like they really get him, but I see them do this with other coaches and teachers, too, even if it's a lecture about splitting atoms—which I guarantee none of us get at all.

"We've got a good game plan tonight," Coach says. "If we stick to it, we play hard, leave our guts on that football field, then we'll emerge victorious. We'll walk away heroes."

"Hoo-wah." Studblatz thumps his chest. Coach reaches out to him and slaps his shoulder pads.

"This man—this soldier—is ready to go to war." Coach grins. "Now, who else is ready? Ready to close ranks with your brothers? Ready to fight the good fight and show our community we cannot be broken?"

Coach's words ripple out across the huddle, ringing our bodies with electric current, connecting each of us to the other. "Hoo-wah. Hoo-wah. Hoo-wah," we chant, completing the circuit. The chant pulses from my throat down to my chest and belly. It tingles up over my scalp and crosses my shoulder blades. It no longer matters what I believe or doubt because my body believes and needs to belong. In Coach's battle, I—we—are all heroes. It's a lifetime away from feeling like dirt. I'll tackle a steel I-beam just to hold on to it a little while longer; I'll break my arm to keep it. For Coach, for the team, my body'll do anything.

"And now that we've got *all* our warriors back in the lineup"—Coach raises his voice above the chants—"I expect nothing less than a total ass whupping tonight."

"Hoo-wah!"

"Give me thunder out there!" Coach shouts. "And total decimation. I want to see body bags on that field!"

"Hoo-wah!"

"Bring it!" Tom howls, standing up to slam into a locker with his shelled shoulder. Studblatz stands next, raising his arms up to the gods and yowling until his face is pink as a squished worm. He turns and punches a locker with his taped and gloved fist, punches it again, like he's mad it won't hit back, punches it a third time.

"Men, you've got your orders." Coach pounds a fist into the palm of his hand as the rest of us stand up. "Bring home a victory. Nothing less."

"Kill 'em."

"No prisoners."

"Destroy."

"Go, Go, Go, Go GO, GO, GO, GO, GOGOGOGOGOGO!"

We hup-march out of the locker room and down the long hall, through the open doors, and along the grass path leading to our fenced field. The gated entrance has been rolled back for us. We build up speed as we near it, moving like an army in full attack. Scott slaps the top of Terrence's helmet, the signal for our running back to sprint ahead and lead the way through the big paper hoop with a giant *K* on it, smashing through it just as the new monster sound system growls like God Himself anointing us.

"Here they come. Theeeeeeee Knights!"

We rush the field through a boulevard of pom-pom-shimmying cheerleaders; the stadium lights turn their glossy lips bright as camera flashes. The bleachers are a sea of bodies all praying for us, all wanting us to win. I can feel their love from here as they spill over onto the grassy hill and press up against the fence. The Jumbotron leads them in a chant that swells me with pride, washes over me in waves of love and worship.

"KNIGHTS . . . KNIGHTS . . . KNIGHTS . . . KNIGHTS . . . KNIGHTS . . . KNIGHTS."

The sound vibrates from my balls to my sinuses as the helmets come down, the chin straps snap tight, and the mouth guards wedge under lips. Now it's easy to see everyone as a thing, a unit, a piece in a larger game. No Scott, no Tom, no Mike, no Kurt, no Ronnie. Shutting down and not having to think, just doing what you're told, feels like turning into a machine in a good way. It feels like relief.

Ashville is undefeated, same as us, and most likely we'll meet again in the play-offs. Their line matches ours in size and strength. Their defensive unit is led by Chandre Jackson, a linebacker rumored to be crazy and known for his vicious hits. Mean as Studblatz but faster, if slightly smaller. What he gives up in size he more than makes up for in velocity when he slams into you. They say he's already signed a letter of commitment to Ohio State. Across the line of scrimmage, while the cadence is shouted out, I peer into Chandre Jackson's face mask and see the whites of his eyes barely containing two dark pebbles bouncing furiously back and forth, searching for an opening, searching for any chink in our team's protection. Chandre Jackson's eyes are jittery with the need to hit someone.

By second quarter, Chandre Jackson has marked his territory, prowling up and down the line of scrimmage and just banging the hell out of Pullman, treating our midsize lineman like a revolving door. Chandre's too smart to match up directly against someone as big as Jankowski. Instead, he attacks at angles, going at the flanks, jigging and juking to slip between our linemen and get at the ball carrier. And if he can't slip through in time, he makes sure to lay a good lick on whatever sorry Oregrove player happens to be in his way. First play of the second quarter he dives into our backfield and wraps up Terrence before we have a chance to set up the blocking scheme. Terrence's legs are still pedaling the air when he's brought down on his back, Chandre sprawled on top of him, screaming into his face mask, asking Terrence if that's how he lets his daddy fuck him.

Coach knows all about Chandre Jackson and has prepared for him. The crux of his plan involves keeping me in the backfield to pick up any blitzes that break through our line and protect the quarterback as he passes the ball. I ignore the fact that our quarterback is Scott. With his helmet in place, it's not so hard. I have a job to do. Scott is only a chess piece. My job is to allow our piece to pass the ball safely, unhit by Chandre Jackson's chess piece. Twice he's broken through as Scott steps back to unload, both times coming from Scott's blind side. Both times I intercept him, lowering my shoulder, keeping my eyes on Chandre Jackson's hips—not taking the bait offered by his weaving feet and bobbing helmet—and plastering a solid hit on the guy. Both times Scott gets the pass off to receivers downfield for good yardage. The first time I heave Chandre over my shoulder, he thumps his fists on my back in a tantrum, frustrated I'm not allowing free shots on the quarterback. Only after the whistle blows do I set him down.

"Tuh-try again," I tell him.

"Boy," Chandre snarls, still itching to lay out our king, "you better hope I don't catch you with that ball. You get it and your ass is mine."

"Bring it."

I don't know there's a DJ up in the stadium booth remixing the words caught on my helmet mic until Ashville calls a time-out. That's when the Jumbotron fills with a cartoon potato chip snapping into pieces as the sound system rumbles with chewing noises. The game's Big Munch Crunch is brought to the fans by the sponsor—a Fray's potato chip. Then the screen fills with Chandre's face caught in my helmet cam's fish-eye lens just before I hit him. The hit booms like a road accident on the sound system and the DJ adds a freight train whistle. "Boy-Bring it! Boy-Boy-Bring-Bring-Bring Bring it! Boy-Bring It!" raps out from the stadium speakers as the DJ mixes mine and Chandre's words together with a beat under it. The fans go nuts.

"Damn, Kurt," Terrence tells me. "That rap's going to make you and Chandre superstars on iTunes." I nod, trying to hide a smile, trying to obey Coach's warning not to talk with the helmet on.

By halftime we lead 14–10. Still too close for anyone's liking. It's the first game I play as a Knight that feels like we might not control our own fate. Ashville makes us pay for any yardage we manage to scrape together with some wicked hits. Studblatz does his own share of prowling the line and smashing Ashville's offense, but somehow it feels like Chandre Jackson is striking deeper to the bone. Our starting linemen drag themselves into the locker room. Jankowski's breathing real heavy. Pullman bows his head like he's already beaten.

"We are a team and we are being tested, right here, right now," Coach hollers, smacking his rolled-up playbook pages across Pullman's shoulder pads. "They are going to wear us down and try to get an easy score at the end. You can be sure of it. Men, we have thirty minutes left and four points might as well be zero points, might as well be minus-four points. I want us to attack, attack, attack. We need to send them a message, cut off the head, hurt them. Studblatz, you've got to get to their quarterback. They are stuffing you up at that line like a virgin on prom night. Is that the best you got?"

Studblatz jerks his head as if Coach has finger-hooked him by the nostrils.

"Boy, you better up your vitamin intake if that's all you can bring. Those scouts are going to take back their offers if you're going to play like a girl all night. Now get out there and hit someone. Hurt someone. Hurt someone bad. You send a message. You let Ashville know this is our house. You understand?"

Studblatz, huffing, eyes going demonic, nods that he understands.

"You've got thirty minutes to prove to me that I'm not making a mistake, putting my reputation on the line with those schools, telling them how good you are, how you'd be a fine addition to their teams. You go out there and you bring me back a head."

"Yes, sir!"

"What?"

"YES, SIR!"

"Pullman." Coach wheels on our beaten lineman. "I don't care if you have to sucker punch those sons of bitches when they go past you on the double-team. Step on their feet, or leg-whip someone, but by God, if you keep letting half their defense slip by you, letting them dance past you like swishy faggots, and, so help me, one of them

hurts Scott, I'm making you wear a dress at Monday practice. You are not making your daddy out in the stands real
proud tonight."

"Yes, sir."

"I want you to hurt those bastards, you understand.
Hurt them!"

"YES, SIR!"

"Scott, good job so far. Good passes. Stay relaxed. Stay
focused. You're in good hands with Kurt, you understand.
Brodsky's making some beautiful stopgap plays. He's saved
your butt at least three times tonight by my count. Kurt,
keep playing hard, keep hitting."

"Yessssssir!"

As halftime ends, we jog back to the field in broken
clumps. The marching band horns blurt and the drums
crackle and thump as special teams take position for the
kickoff. Win or lose, I'll handle this game, I'll handle the
rest of the season just fine, I tell myself. That's when Scott
comes up behind me and slaps the top of my helmet.

"You keep picking up the slack, Kurt. Keep playing for
me, playing for the team, and everything is going to be all
right," he says. These are his first nonfootball commands
to me since the meeting in Coach's office. "We take care
of each other, right?"

I look at him without answering. He's too close and I
can see his face behind the mask.

"Brothers, right?" he adds. I still don't answer, not
because I don't want to, but because I cannot.

"You know what I'm talking about, don't you . . . Mr.
Wolf?" Scott slaps my shoulder pads, smiling at the nick-

name. He's got no right using it, got no right calling me by it. After everything that's happened, what they did to Ronnie. It's all just a joke to him. No big deal.

Just like that, my mind is back in that storage room, Scott holding that dirty broomstick while making me an offer. *"You want a shot, Mr. Wolf?"*

A light drizzle that started before halftime now comes down heavier, making the field slick. Chandre Jackson revs up across the line, still itching to inflict pain. Right from the start he bosses Pullman around, knocking him flat on his ass and then catching Terrence from behind in our own backfield, again, wasting the nice hole Jankowski has blown open in the line. My concentration crumbles while Scott's question keeps playing in my head. Static pours into my helmet's ear holes, and I don't know if it's the sound of rain hitting the plastic shell or maybe the water's shorting out the wiring to the mic and camera. I shake my head but the sound is still there, distracting me so I can't remember the snap count. Not wanting to be flagged with an offside penalty, I play it safe and decide to wait a half beat after the ball snap.

You want a shot, Mr. Wolf?

Something shifts.

You want a shot, Mr. Wolf?

The gods on the field grow angry.

You want a shot, Mr. Wolf?

Images of Scott and Ronnie bring up memories of Meadow's House. The rain-static creeping into my helmet's ear holes grows in volume. It reminds me of the sound duct tape makes—that *brrrraaaapp* sound—when it's pulled off in long strips from the tape roll and you can't move because you're cramped up tight in a plastic storage bin with your best friend, both of you smothering and that *brrrraaaapp* sound tells you you're being sealed into the box to be taught a lesson that you'll never, ever forget.

Chandre Jackson blitzes.

He sniffs out the pass, knows Pullman is broken now, and easier to slip past than an orange gym cone. With one head fake and a stiff arm, Chandre's by Pullman and accelerating, afterburners flaming. In full sprint, Chandre's eyes lock on our quarterback, anticipating the big hit, checkmating our king and tossing our team. Scott's busy rolling right, looking downfield for the deep strike that will stab Ashville in their heart. The gods place me on the center of the seesaw, allowing me to tip that balance either way. And all I can hear is, *You want a shot, Mr. Wolf?* And all I can see is Scott standing in that room, offering Ronnie up like a piece of meat.

Chandre Jackson blasts forward.

I move to intercept him, dipping low to catch his weight and cut him off at the knees. I lunge at a good angle but my feet slip on the wet grass. My legs shoot out backward, behind me. I go down quick, face mask planting harmlessly into the turf. The last thing I see is Chandre Jackson's graceful stride as he hurdles over me on his way to murder.

CRUNK!

The hit sounds like a refrigerator dropping out of the sky. I roll over in time to see Jackson wallop Scott at his most blind and vulnerable—with his throwing arm cocked back, staring downfield, about to launch. Jackson spears Scott just to the left of his spine, tagging his kidney. The impact snaps Scott's helmet backward while his arms spread outward in crucifixion, the ball dropping from his hand. The momentum lifts Scott off his feet and drives him down, down, down, shoulder- and helmet-first into the grass while Jackson rides along, making sure to add his weight to the landing.

Chandre Jackson roars. His triumph fills the night sky while the bleachers, the hill, the fans, and both teams suck air in together at the vicious hit. Terrence is the only one moving for a moment, scrambling to recover the loose, live ball and fall on it until a whistle blows the play dead. Jankowski wastes no time marching over and shoving Jackson in the back as boos rise from the stands like steam clouds. Both teams start moving toward each other until the refs blow their whistles like crazy and let fly with the yellow flags. When the players pull back from the scuffle, Scott's still lying on the turf, groaning.

"It's his arm!" Jankowski shouts, waving in the trainers. "His arm!"

By now, players and fans are standing around watching the slow-motion replay on the Jumbotron while the paramedics rush onto the field with a backboard. Each time the screen shows Scott taking the hit from behind, the fans boo. Part of me sees my failure to stop it. Part of me sees justice.

"It's dislocated," the trainers report to Coach Brigs, Assistant Coach Stein, and the rest of us grouped ten feet from Scott and the paramedics on the field. "Might be his collarbone is broken, too." The fans clap and whistle as Coach Stein and one of the trainers help Scott limp off the field clutching his bad arm with his opposite hand.

"At least it's not his throwing arm," Pullman offers. No one answers him. Except me.

"He'll be fuh-fine," I tell him, getting close enough that my helmet clinks his.

Chandre Jackson and Tom Jankowski are both flagged with unsportsmanlike conduct penalties. Warner comes in as backup quarterback. It's too late in the game and the score too close to test our backup's confidence, so everyone knows he'll be handing off the ball more than passing it.

"We need you to send a message," Coach Brigs tells me on the sideline, then explains what he wants. Same three plays in a row. Fullback carry up the gut, behind Jankowski's blocking. Coach wants—everyone wants—some payback delivered to Chandre Jackson. Same play three times in a row. Predictable. No surprises. A good way to clear out game pieces.

On the first handoff from Warner, it takes me a second to adjust to his timing. I find the hole in the line and bull forward. Gaining yards is fine. Administering punishment is more the point. Ashville's defense tangles me up after three yards and I find Chandre Jackson dragging me from behind, tripping me until I topple.

"What kind of pussy tackle is that?" Tom asks Chandre, standing over both of us, offering me a hand up to my feet. I take it. Then he spits on Jackson still down in the grass.

"Fat boy, I'm gonna take you down next," Jackson fires back.

The second handoff is smoother. I hit the line quicker and Tom, even angrier, blows out a hole easy for me to punch through. My knees pump high, feet stomping on blue Ashville jerseys falling under me. My helmet is a missile aiming in one direction, puncturing chest numbers, listening for yelps over the sound of the ocean now filling my ears.

The third handoff gives the crowd what they want. Jankowski rips open a good-size hunk of real estate for me. I clear the line easily, gaining momentum and building speed. Chandre Jackson comes into view, moving fast, but he has to stop me and all I have to do is pound him. Thighs driving hard, knees pumping, I aim through him, lowering my head, charging like a ram. A puff of breath escapes him, sounds like a hiccup, as he tries to wrap me up.

"Ooofff."

Chandre Jackson deflates around me, his body collapsing over my head and shoulders; his belly smears across my face mask like a bug on a windshield. I carry him like that for a few yards and then drive us both deep into the turf, plowing him under the dirt.

We both lie motionless for a second, the collision taking its time to chew us up. Then I push off Chandre Jackson's chest, stare at him through his face mask, see him trying to smile like it doesn't hurt, but we both know better. "Stay down," I tell him, "'cause more's coming."

"Fu . . . yo" is all he can manage.

"Sure," I say.

Coach uses me like a battering ram the rest of the game, unleashing me into Ashville's defensive unit to deliver more and more pain. Jackson stops prowling the line. He also stops his trash talk. He just plants himself like a soggy cat, waiting for me to nail him while the clock burns down. I can't pull oxygen into my lungs fast enough. My thighs tremble near the end, a few times threatening to stop working altogether. My brain aches from using my skull as a weapon. On more than a few plays, Ashville cornerbacks grind their cleats into my back or ankles while I lie at the bottom of a gang tackle. Hurt drives me into Ashville's line, where sometimes I harpoon a tackler rather than aim for open field. Hurt I know well. Hurt I understand. Hurt, in the end, can be counted on to always arrive. So hurt I rely on, knowing I can weather it better than most. I punch a four-yard carry into the end zone behind Jankowski's blocking. I drag Jackson, wrapped up around my hips, into the goal with me. That finishes it at 21–10.

"KNIGHTS! KNIGHTS! KNIGHTS!"

The hill and bleachers start chanting along with the Jumbotron words as the game clock winds down. And then the chanting—and the Jumbotron—change to something new, something I've never heard before.

"BROD-SKY, BROD-SKY, BROD-SKY!"

I lift my arms up like a prizefighter and the stands roar. Middle-aged parents, white-haired grandparents, junior high and elementary school kids, guys long past graduation clap and stomp and whistle. They love the hurt. They love the pain. They love watching it flow in and out of me, seeing me take it and deliver it. I walk toward the sidelines surrounded by my teammates, knowing I could lead them if given a chance. I glance up at the Jumbotron and see it delivering the same view of the stands I got and then the view changes to itself. The helmet cam is on. The DJ up in the booth must have switched it to a live feed. The fans are watching themselves and this brings another cheer. Guys jump in front of me, grabbing my face mask, twisting my neck, to get in front of the little lens and stick their finger up, screaming they're number one. My head throbs from all the earlier hits, feels like it might swell and get stuck in my helmet, but it's a small price to pay to hear those chants and get a few moments quiet from all those awful pictures haunting my skull.

D A N N Y

I sit shotgun in Fisher's van as we roll into the McDonald's parking lot Saturday morning. Kurt is there waiting, along with my teammates, and it secretly thrills me. He half sits, half leans on the hood of Gradley's sedan, massaging his temples in slow circles while the other guys loaf around the duffel bags, minicoolers, and equipment plopped at their feet.

"That big fucker actually showed," Fisher says, voicing my thoughts, if not my exact word choice. "Thought that was just bullshit about you inviting him."

"Nope," I answer, trying to hide my own disbelief. Fisher hand-cranks his window down and hollers out a greeting.

"Morning, boys!"

Menderson flips Fisher the bird. Kurt pushes himself

off Gradley's car hood and the suspension lifts about three inches.

Bruce sits in the back of Fisher's van, using the big cooler stuffed with ice, soda, burger patties, and hot dogs as a bench. Silent since we picked him up, he opens the back doors, now, and hops out like he needs air. Paul Kim, Larry Menderson, and Pete Delray pile into the back of the panel van, marking their territory for the long drive by throwing duffel bags, backpacks, and pillows over the scattered carpet samples Fisher uses as flooring.

"I call the left wheel well," Menderson shouts, jamming Pete with his shoulder and moving the small freshman out of the way.

"The space behind Fisher's seat is mine," Paul calls.

"Where am I supposed to sit?" Pete whines.

"The roof is all yours," Menderson says as bits of Sausage McMuffin spill out his mouth and tumble down his shirt.

Kurt moves slower than the others, like he's banged up real bad. I get out of the prized front seat and offer it to him.

"Take shotgun," I say. He nods, still massaging his temples, stepping up into the van, rocking the whole vehicle with his weight. More guys pile into the back and then Gradley takes the leftovers in his sedan. Fisher swings through the drive-through and orders a seventy-two-ounce Coke to go along with his half-finished thirty-two-ounce Mountain Dew.

"You guys ready to roll?" he asks. It is still super early for a Saturday and Fisher is the only one mainlining caffeine, so his question dies on delivery. We pull out of the parking lot and our convoy of two heads for the highway exit.

"Anyone guh-guh-got aspirin?" Kurt asks.

"Danny, you got anything for the superstar here?" Fisher asks snidely, then glances over his shoulder into the pit of groggy bodies trying to get comfortable on the jouncing floor. "Hey, dorks, any of you got aspirin?"

"No!" Paul grumps.

I nudge Menderson's ribs with my toe until he opens one eye. "You got any aspirin?" I ask.

"No."

"Soda's good for headaches," Fisher says, handing Kurt his giant tub of Coke. Kurt takes it. "I always get a headache if I don't drink a Coke in the morning before school."

I lean back against a rolled-up sleeping bag. There is no room for my legs with Menderson hogging the middle, curled up in a ball and snoring, so I prop my sneakers on his butt and shut my eyes.

"I've gotta piss." Paul yawns. I open my eyes and glance at my watch. We've been driving for an hour and a half and should be close to the turnoff. I sit up.

"You think *you* do?" Fisher asks. "I've got a hundred and four ounces of soda in me. I keep flashing my lights at Gradley but the bastard won't pull over."

Kurt has his jacket rolled up into a pillow and wedged between his head and the passenger side window. His mouth hangs partly open and I notice his eyes never really close as he sleeps, like he doesn't trust Fisher or the rest of us.

"Turn up here," Bruce and I say at the exact same time, then look at each other.

"You guys going to give me directions *now*?" Fisher

asks. "Unbelievable." Gradley's sedan flashes its blinker and we follow him, turning off onto the unmarked dirt road that begins the unofficial back entrance up to the state park.

Canary-yellow leaves feather the forest. Here and there, tree foliage the color of young cherries and ripe pumpkins breaks out to dazzle our vision. Sun streams through the branches and dapples the morning mist. Kurt awakens all of a sudden and leans forward to get a full view of the scenery moving past the windshield, blinking against the color and light.

"Where are we?" he asks without a single stutter.

"Top secret," Fisher says.

"It's Lorry State Park," I explain. "Sort of. It's awesome here but where we're going is even awesome-er. It's not marked on regular maps."

Gradley's car slowly leads the way over the rough gravel road and the inside of Fisher's van rattles like a shaking toolbox as we come to the first "No Trespassing" sign strung across rusted wire hanging between two oaks. I scoot forward to kneel on the transmission hump between Fisher and Kurt, grabbing each of their seats' armrests for balance. The gravel road slowly fades into a rutted forestry trail. The "No Trespassing" wire corralling the trees to our right drops away and after a couple hundred yards an even smaller path, barely wide enough for a car, veers up through the forested slope. No way could we have found it without first being shown, the secret passing down from senior to junior teammates every year on road trips like this one.

"Are we tuh-tuh-trespassing?" Kurt asks.

"Naw," Fisher says. "It's still owned by the quarry company or their family or something but they're not out here. Signs are there to keep 'em from getting sued if some idiot drives off the cliffs. This way they can say they were warned."

"Oh," Kurt says like he's thinking about it. Then, as the van slips and jerks along the leafy trail, squeezing between tree trunks and scraping past thicket and bramble, Kurt leans forward to better see out Fisher's dirty windshield. "Wuh-wuh-what cliffs?"

"Big ones. You'll see," Fisher says, wrestling the steering wheel and gunning the engine. The back end fishtails and then drops. Paul and Bruce both pop up and slam down against the rear wheel wells.

"Damn, Fisher!" Paul snaps. "Take it easy, willya?"

"Clam it!" Fisher snaps back. He's hunched over the steering wheel, gripping and twisting it while the engine whinnies.

Kurt props his left hand on the van's dashboard and peers intently out the windows as if we might drop off a cliff any second.

"You see flags nailed to the tree trunks, that means the cliffs are coming up," Fisher tells Kurt. Kurt glances at Fisher and then back out into the forest creeping by our window. The sun shimmers through gold and maroon leaves and points of light penetrate the forest floor like drops of honey. It's so beautiful it makes me proud.

"Wait . . . luh-luh-like that one?" Kurt asks, jamming his finger right up to the windshield and pointing to a faded cloth ribbon nailed to the trunk of an oak tree.

"Yeah, that's one," Fisher says, wrenching hard on the

wheel as he guns the engine. The back tires spin over soggy leaves before rubber grabs something solid and we lurch forward, almost rear-ending Gradley's car.

"That's only a yellow flag," Fisher says. "You see a red one, holler your ass off."

"Wuh-wuh-what if we muh-muh-miss it?" Kurt asks.

"We're fucked," Fisher says.

Kurt takes off his seat belt and cranks down his side window, all the better to spot flags and jump out the door. Suddenly he slaps the dashboard and points out Fisher's side. "Fuh-fuh-flag. A ruh-ruh-ruh-red one." Fisher nods but otherwise ignores Kurt. In front of us, Gradley's car pulls off into the bramble. Fisher squeezes the van past the sedan. Kurt's eyebrows pull together. "Ruh-ruh-ruh-red flag!"

"Got it," Fisher says, then throttles the engine. The van jumps forward. Kurt reaches over and almost rips Fisher's arm off.

"Ssssstop!"

"Okay, okay, relax." Fisher grins.

Gripping Fisher's armrest for balance, I raise off my knees to a crouch. I know exactly where we are and Fisher's a dick for scaring Kurt but part of me didn't think someone like Kurt actually gets scared. The clearing appears, just a simple opening in the forest. You would never know from our angle in the van that at the edge of the clearing, the world drops away over the side of a man-made cliff, dug out when granite paid good money.

Coming up from the back, stepping over the others and squeezing next to me, Bruce finally joins the living. "This is far enough, Fish," he says, stern as Mr. Klech. Fisher hits the gas one more time, watching Kurt while he does it.

Bruce cuffs Fisher on his head.

"Ouch!"

"Dumbass." Bruce cuffs him again for good measure.

"Just trying to give the big man a first-timer's thrill is all," Fisher says, and then throws the van in park and kills the engine. Paul opens the back doors and we pile out.

"Come on," I order everyone, unable to contain myself any longer. I have one of the climbing ropes coiled around my shoulder. Coach Nelson donated all his old climbing gear and ropes to the team. He taught us how to take care of the ropes, to never drop them on the ground and never walk on them, and how to wind them up properly to make them last longer. He taught us how to knot them, clip in and tie into our harnesses, and how to belay a partner. Since we're trespassing, he can't lead us on this trip like he does the big trip upstate in the summer. But this secret location, we're pretty sure, was originally handed down from him, though he'd deny it.

"Hold your horses." Bruce harrumphs like an old man, which I take as a good sign that he's coming around. I don't mind him cuffing Fisher at all.

"Kurt!" I shout back to the van. "Kurt, take a look at this." Paul, Gradley, and Menderson trail behind me but they already know what lies ahead. It's not them I'm interested in. "Come on, man!" I turn around and watch Kurt slowly getting out of the van, stretching his arms wide and yawning. He rubs the sleep out of his eyes and then puts a hand up to shade out the partial sun. He's so big. And, at the moment, *slow*—it's killing me—as if he can't waste a single ounce of energy, as if he needs to store it all up for Friday night games.

"Come *on*!" I shout, ignoring everyone else, anticipating his reaction.

"Coming."

Branches canopy overhead in gold and cranberry while the sun, rising higher, heating up, fights to punch down to the forest floor. Only at the edge of the quarry do you finally see the drop-off as the forest disappears, the sun bursts through, and light finally wins.

"Whoa!" Kurt exhales, peering over the edge, down the granite cliff to the water below. I clap my hands together as if I've conjured the magical scene change myself. I can't help it. Kurt now knows about the best place in the whole state because I invited him, because we chose to share it with him. Then it hits me that maybe Fisher's not so keen on anyone outside our group discovering it.

"Cool, huh?" I prompt. Kurt doesn't answer right away, just keeps looking out over the giant man-made canyon. I can tell the drop-off makes him wary because he refuses to move right up to the edge. It makes me feel strong watching someone as tough as Kurt be scared by something I think is so beautiful.

"Yeahhhh . . ." Kurt slowly answers, wiping his hands on his jeans. "Wuh-why's it here?"

"It isn't natural," Menderson says. "It's totally man-made."

"How far down? To the wuh-wuh-water."

"About eighty feet," Paul says. "If you walk the edge that way a couple hundred yards, the cliff lowers to about forty feet above the water." Paul points along the edge

of the forest that grows right up to the lip of the drop-
off. At the edge, the sky pours down in blue so bright it
hurts your eyes. It makes me want to thump my chest
and breathe deep, holding all that blue sky inside me. The
bridge of my nose starts to tickle under the strong rays and
I'm sure it'll be pink by the end of the day.

"Wuh-wuh-was the lake always here?" Kurt ask.

"No," I explain with a tone like I know what I'm talking
about, but really I'm only repeating what I heard on my
first trip up here last year. "They say the water's, like, two
hundred feet deep. It filled up with rain and runoff after
the quarry company abandoned the pit."

Bruce walks up with two coiled ropes slung over each
arm and a climbing harness in each hand. "Okay," Bruce
says, "let's give the big man here a little climbing lesson
before we send him over the edge." Bruce keeps sounding like his old self and, despite his being a dick to Kurt
earlier, I want to slap Fisher on the back as a thank-you
for his idea to come out here.

"I'm nuh-nuh-nuh-not going over thuh-thuh-that."

"The hell you aren't," Fisher says, his grin growing,
enjoying Kurt's discomfort. I take back my wanting to
thank him. Now I just want to shove him over the cliff.
"Going down in ropes is cake. It's climbing up that's hard."

"I nuh-nuh-never duh-duh-done this," Kurt says. He
takes a step back, eyes narrowing at me—at me only—as
if blaming me for luring him into a trap. I'm responsible
for this, for him.

"It's not that dangerous here," I say, lowering my voice,
feeling protective. "You're in ropes and someone is belaying you."

"Wuh-wuh-what's that muh-muh-mean?"

"It's French, man," Fisher says, like he knows any more than what Coach Nelson taught us. "Don't sweat it."

"It means someone's controlling your rope," I cut in, holding a hand up to Fisher's face to shut him up. "So if you slip or fall, you won't go anywhere, we've got you."

"But yuh-yuh-you guys are luh-luh-little. You kuh-kuh-kuh-can't buh-buh-belay me." Kurt's stutter intensifies, I notice. As he fights to speak, his eyelids fold down and his big shoulders ride up against his ears and it suddenly feels like we're all ganging up on him. I'm about to explain the pulley system of belaying that Coach Nelson taught us that allows a person to anchor someone much larger with not much effort, but Fisher opens his yapper first.

"Look, big dude, it's not a problem," Fisher says. "Besides, worst-case scenario is you fall and land in the water. You know how to swim, right?" Fisher doesn't wait for an answer. "You swim over to the rock path and walk back up here, no problem."

"Wuh-wuh-what iffffff I fuh-fuh-fuh-fall at the tuh-tuh-top?"

"Then just make sure you hit the water straight, feet-first, legs tight together, arms tight by your sides."

"And if I duh-duh-don't . . ."

"Okay, well, that's a *worst* worst-case scenario. I suppose, hypothetically speaking, if you hit the water from up high and landed on your back or side or stomach, you'd die. Water feels like concrete then."

Kurt backs away from us. His lips twist and his nostrils flare with the scent of a betrayal. It's the same face he wore the day he walked in on Ronnie's attack.

"That ain't going to happen," Bruce says, shoving Fisher out of the way. Bruce moves right up to Kurt just like the day he tried to stare down Jankowski in the locker room. "I guarantee you won't fall or hurt yourself, not even once, today. I swear it to you." Bruce says this and his voice shakes. "Danny and I invited you up here. Our arms'll rip off before we'd let you slip in the ropes. That's a promise. Right, Danny?

"Yeah," I say, my throat dry.

"You understand what I'm saying?" Bruce asks Kurt, not taking his eyes off him. Kurt nods yes. The strength of our promise is backed by the weight of our debt—something understood only if it's known who stopped the attack on Ronnie. Bruce hammers things right in a way I can only imagine. Makes me proud of him. Also makes me think I've got a long way to go before I'll ever be captain material.

"Can I get that same guarantee?" Gradley asks, and the other guys snicker.

"Bruce is kinda freaking me out." Paul titters.

"Hey, man," Fisher tells Kurt. "We don't invite just anyone up here. You've got to be U.S. Grade-A athlete. Not just a big fat ass in shoulder pads like Jankowski."

Even though it's a joke, the mention of Tom sweeps through the air like a whiff of dead pig. Bruce turns away and starts uncoiling one of the ropes. Kurt steps over to the quarry pit ledge, sizing it up.

"Okay," Kurt says after a minute of study and a long breath. "I guh-guh-guh-got this." And just like that, we are unstuck. Bruce tells Paul to go pull the cooler and hibachi grill out of the van. I scout trees to tie ropes around.

Global warming pushes back against autumn for the

day. The high noon sun bakes the granite wall while the surrounding forest blocks any breeze from cooling things off. It feels good, reminding me of the way things used to be, just a few weeks earlier, before everything changed. Most of us expected a chillier day and have dressed in layers: waffle long johns, sweatpants, T-shirts, jeans, and long-sleeve flannel. Within the hour, most of us have stripped down to long johns and T-shirts.

The hardest part about dropping down the side of a cliff in a rope, if you've never done it, is taking that first backward step of faith over the edge. You have to trust both the rope and the person securing it. That first step is also the best, the one that sends tingles of thrill and fear up your legs when gravity suddenly warps a little and the world tips ninety degrees and you're walking the cliff face like a gecko. Kurt, wearing a frown of worry, keeps tugging on the rope, testing its tension and resistance, as we all crowd around him, urging him over. He's already watched all of us go down and come back up a half-dozen times until he trusts that it's not all a trick. With his back to the quarry pit, the heels of his sneakers kiss the edge of the cliff.

"Okay, here guh-guh-goes," he says, still tugging on the rope. He takes the teensiest step backward, leaning his butt into the rope harness, trying not to actually go over the ledge until—he does! Bruce has him tight and Kurt, adjusting his legs, suddenly stands sideways to the earth, eighty feet above water smooth and black as obsidian. He takes another dainty step, letting out a little rope between his hands. His face, stone-serious with concentration, suddenly splinters along his mouth line. He takes another step, playing out more rope. As his head slowly sinks below the edge, me and the other guys step forward to watch his progress.

"That's it."

"Good job, man."

"You got it, big guy."

Kurt hops back in inches and then, as he gets the hang of it, pushes farther off the cliff, swinging out and lowering a few feet at a time. About twenty feet from the top, he tips his face up to us, wearing a big smile.

"You know suh-suh-something?" he asks. All of us are leaning over the edge, monitoring his descent. "Thuh-thuh-this is all right." And with that his legs thrust from the cliff face and he arcs out about eight feet, letting the rope slip steadily through the carabiner so he drops about ten feet before touching the cliff again.

Kurt howls and his voice bounces around the bowl of the quarry. We howl back, giddy for him. The first time rappelling over a cliff is a sensation you never forget. As soon as you finish, you want to do it again. It's as cool as doing a double-flip re-grasp on the high bar but it doesn't take years to learn. *We gave him this,* I think.

Over the next few hours, we set up several more rope trails along the cliff for guys to descend and then test themselves by climbing back up to the top. By late afternoon everyone is hot and tired. Guys stuff themselves on chips and soda waiting for the burgers and franks to cook over the hibachi grill. There's also a mini-bonfire roaring, supposedly for s'mores, but, mainly, because fire's fun to make. No one's paying attention when I come out of Fisher's van wearing old cutoff jeans and beater sneakers and nothing else.

"Hey, Kurt," I say as I walk toward the cliff, making sure I have his attention. He stops in midchew of a granola bar as I get nearer the edge. "This is the next step," I say. "Now you'll know we were never putting you in any danger." I need him to understand Bruce and I would never invite him up here to betray him. That we only ever wanted to thank him.

Kurt freezes while the other guys scramble over to watch the show. Bruce stays back by the hibachi to tend the burgers and franks. I catch his eye, though. His look says he's going to be really pissed if I kill myself.

The only way to jump off a cliff is to not think about how stupid it is.

I jump.

Air.

Sky.

SPEED!!!!

My stomach rockets into my throat as the updraft tries to peel off my face and ears. Falling for three seconds might as well be thirty seconds, might as well be thirty light-years for how fast it rushes past you, overloading your senses.

Sploosh!

A cold blackness slaps me in midscream, jolts my heart, jacks up my body. Arctic liquid jets into my nostrils, ears, mouth, eyelids. Numbing dark sucks me down, down, down and . . . slowly . . . slowly stalls. I'm deep under, hovering at the level of the dead before I'm released, allowed to gradually float upward. Seconds tick as I kick hard toward the light.

Surface.

Sucking for wind and air and sun and light.

Alive! Alive! Alive!

"God!" I scream through chattering teeth. I swim fast as possible to the edge to get out of the water and get warm, move, run like a conqueror.

Poomph.

I hear the hit and twist around, wait for a few seconds, and see Fisher pop his head up like a seal, then sling his hair out of his face with one quick head snap.

Fisher punches the sky. "That's for Ronnie!" he shouts, and everyone hears it and for the first time in two weeks hearing that name doesn't make me want to bow in shame. My teeth clack hard and, out of the water, I fold my hands under my armpits as I climb the steep trail of switchbacks fast as possible to get back to the top and warm up over the fire and put on dry clothes. When I reach the top, only half the team is there. The others have followed me over the edge or are about to. Kurt stands near the edge, watching us go over, craning his neck and guarding against the cliff somehow reaching up and snatching him over it.

He whistles as Pete jumps off.

"You going?" I ask, shivering, hopping from foot to foot and practically standing in the little bonfire.

"Naw," he says, shaking his head. "But muh-muh-maybe next time."

"Deal."

KURT

34

irst, you create a soothing place in your mind," Ms. Jinkle, the speech therapist, tells me. "Thinking about it should bring you only positive feelings and good energy. This will be your home base, your starting point as you try and relax. When you relax, you breathe slower and your tongue relaxes. Get to the soothing place first before attempting the word list I gave you. Remembering the breathing exercises we worked on, you'll focus on the soothing place, then record yourself speaking these words. Listen to yourself. Then repeat the list again. Five times every day, okay?"

"I duh-duh-don't have a ruh-recorder."

"You do now," Ms. Jinkle says, handing over an orange sheet of paper with my name filled onto it. It's a library loan request for a digital recorder. "Go get it now so you can start tonight, no excuses. They'll show you how to use it. Now, make sure you come up with a good soothing place," she says. "Okay, see you same time next week."

The meeting with Ms. Jinkle ends halfway through fourth period, so I'm walking empty halls toward the library and trying to come up with a good soothing place when my mind wanders back to the quarry.

I remember waking up in Fisher's van and staring out at a forest wrapped in leaves the color of cherry, banana, and apricots. And then walking up to the lip of the pit with all that blue sky, pink rock, and black water dizzying my head; trusting that itty-bitty rope and harness to hold me. Whole thing felt crazy at first, letting Bruce and Danny talk me into rappelling down that cliff. But once I took that first backward step over the edge—one of the scariest steps ever, just backing up over nothing, praying everything would hold—well, then, the world changed. All of a sudden, in one step, I'm kind of floating, like one of those hawks that sits on a draft, never even flapping its wings, but just hanging out, searching for mice or whatever. Eighty feet of air between me and the water and only my old sneaks touching the side of that massive stone slab. These monkeys poking their heads over the top edge, staring down at me, eyes big, grins bigger, chattering at my progress. Danny's grin the biggest of them all.

Tippy-toeing along the rock turns into steps and then hops and then I really start shoving off the wall. I swing out from the cliff face and swing back in while the rope sings through my hands. My legs dance over the granite in slow motion. I'm graceful in a way that's impossible in football pads and helmet. It's like being in a dream where you figure out the secret to breaking gravity. Everyone else is stuck on the ground, stuck in the gears, but you get to float above it, float wherever you want.

And then Danny, leaping without the ropes! I feel the corners of my mouth turn up, now, remembering Danny stepping off the cliff like it's nothing. Never seen anything like that. Couldn't believe how far he fell, just kept going until his tiny speck smacked the water and plunged beneath, trailing a stream of white bubbles. Felt like a whole minute before he surfaced. When his head *did* finally pop out, his high whoop bounced off the quarry walls, climbing the sky back up to us. Then the other guys racing to see who's next over the cliff. *Shwiff, shwiff, shwiff.* They go over the edge like teenage superheroes, laughing at something that would kill a normal person. Daredevil Danny jogs the trail up top, hugging himself and shivering, lips purple, teeth chattering, and water drops coating his lashes. He's wrapped in goose pimples, hopping foot-to-foot around the bonfire, and I half expect him to just step into the flames to get warm, since, if he can survive that jump, why not a little fire?

Sun was setting over the far edge of the quarry before we finish gobbling up the last of the hot dogs and burgers, then get the ropes, harnesses, and coolers packed back into the van. The whole time I'm thinking I'm on the wrong team, that I should've let the hooting tribe of superhero monkeys adopt me instead.

"Can I help you?" the librarian asks, shaking me from the daydream. I nod slowly, trying to remember why I'm standing in front of her. The tip of the librarian's nose points down at my hands while she peers at me over her reading glasses. When I pass her the orange sheet, her lips move like she's sucking lunch out of her teeth. She squints at Ms. Jinkle's handwriting and, after a minute, she hands the note back to me and points at a door along the wall.

"That's the AVT room," she says. "Tina's in there now. She can help you."

I go where I've been pointed. On the door of the AVT room hangs a printed poster, a mushroom cloud in psychedelic rainbow colors with the words AUDIO VISUAL TECHNOLOGY CLUB IS A BLAST! A sheet of paper Scotch-taped to the bottom of the poster welcomes students to sign up for the AVT club. The sheet is empty. As I walk into the room, I discover that the Tina the librarian mentions is the little goth Tina from Meadow's House.

"Oh," she says, seeing me before I can turn around to leave and come back another time. "Hi," she says, pulling off headphones big as earmuffs and dropping them around her neck. Her white face reflects electric blue from whatever's playing on her laptop screen.

I take a slow breath and step forward, handing her the orange sheet.

"Oooohhh . . . you must be special," she teases. "We only have three of these babies and you get one on permanent loan for the whole year. Lucky you!"

I scratch at my chin whiskers and nod, wondering if I can get the recorder and leave without actually talking.

"Actually this is a requisition for one of our old, dumpy models. But luckily you've got the inside connection. Me. I'm gonna hook you up with our deluxe model. It's smaller. You can clip it on your belt or even hang it around your neck. Best part is you can use it for your music. I'll give you a flash disk, too, so you'll have enough memory to hold a buttload of songs. You control playback and file searching with this button here," she says, and her pinky flicks over the little gizmo without actually pointing to a button.

"Wuh-wuh-where?"

"Wow!" Tina says. "He speaks." She reaches behind her and digs out a wire cable from a box full of flash disks and then plugs the recorder into her laptop while still talking. "Might as well give you all the goodies. I can hook you up with some of my music playlists—try and expand that jock brain of yours. Now that I'm thinking about it, I should send you the redubbed videos I've got. Not that you need more ego-stroking about your Friday night highlights but I've got some great edits—especially the one's I've synched up to . . ." And she starts listing a dozen bands, most I've never heard of.

"Wuh-what?" I hold my hand up, trying to halt her mouth. "Video?"

"Of your games, *duuude*." She drags this word out with a smirk and she might as well be saying "retard" or "shitbrain." "Which reminds me, I thought the point of the game was that the ball carrier avoids the tacklers? Not rams into the nearest guy with that box of rocks under your helmet. Last game, you may have given yourself early-onset Alzheimer's. I saw it—we all saw it—way too up close and personal thanks to that helmet cam. I have to admit those hits are acoustical magic when I pipe them through the new SuperPulse sound system. Fans love it, too. And we always give the unwashed cretins what they want, right?" She stops long enough to take a breath of air and then starts up again. "It *would* be nice if you'd work on your verbal skills—I'm not asking for a twenty-four hundred SAT score or anything but I mean, come on, throw me a bone. I don't need a Shakespearean sonnet, but give me something to work with beyond the occasional grunt. Think about it."

"You like fuh-fuh-football?" I ask.

"About as much as getting my period," she answers.

"Huh?"

"I don't like football," she clarifies before sliding a spoonful of yogurt into her mouth. "What I *do* like is single-handedly running the control board for our school's newly acquired Xenbro XB 5000 Stadium Big Screen with Super-Pulse sound system. You want bigger and better, you'll have to buy NFL tickets."

"That's yuh-yuh—" I start before she cuts me off.

"Yeah, that's me," she says. "I'm the DJ up in the booth . . . beeyatch!"

"Why?" I ask, meaning why does she do it if she hates football?

"Why? Are you serious?" she asks back, ready to laugh at how stupid the question is to her. "While Buffy and Chrissy are bragging that they led the cheerleading squad, I get to tell Harvard and Yale I ran the sound and light board equivalent of an outdoor rock concert on a biweekly basis. In fact, I may just skip college and set up my own production shop. Chrissy and Buffy will marry one of you no-necked, atavistic, knuckle-draggers and pop out pretty but dim-witted rug rats while I'm touring the world with the stars, being paid in euros and yen, and having people shudder in ecstacy every time my fingers tickle a soundboard. You and your buddies go on and break your heads open. I'll broadcast it and make millions. That's why."

She suddenly stops like she's trying either to catch her breath or get hold of her mouth before it runs off without her. She turns her attention back to her laptop. I hear soft clicking as her fingers massage the keys. She starts talking again but this time she keeps her eyes on her laptop screen.

"It's only me and Walt Hasting, our play-by-play announcer and the man that time forgot, up in the booth. Walt's about as useful and nimble around electronics as a mummy and he's got no idea what the hell I do. He nips from a whiskey flask the whole game, tells me how much tougher the players were in his day—which to look at him, I'm guessing was back before fire—and refers to me as 'devil girl.' But as long as I get in the 'Big Munch Crunch' plug from our sponsor and turn on the feed from your helmet mic-cam, they let me do whatever I want."

She stops typing and unplugs the recorder from the laptop wire. She also unplugs a flash drive sticking out from her laptop.

"Here," she says, handing the drive and recorder to me. "You'll like this stuff, and if you don't, you should. It might expand your brain—what's left after the concussions. It'll definitely expand your music horizons."

I take the recorder and flash drive from her and notice how warm her hands are when we touch. "The flash drive can plug directly in the recorder for extra music storage or to swap out songs," she says, and then reaches under her desk and passes me a nice set of earphones, similar to what she's wearing. "These have noise reduction with bass-boost. When you listen to track three, make sure you crank up the bass. It'll blow you away."

I nod.

"Also, the microphone is built into the recorder. The sheet you gave me said 'speech therapy,' not that I was snooping, so if you need to record your voice, all you have to do is hit this button here and you're good to go."

I nod again and heft the little device in my hand. It feels small enough I might lose it faster than my phone.

"If you need help using it, you can come back here and I'll show you. And I can give you more cool downloads once I refine your tastes."

"Duh-duh-do you hear everything in muh-muh-my helmet?" I ask, feeling suddenly exposed.

"That's right, my friend." She smiles in a way that makes me bring a hand in front of my crotch. "*Everything.*"

I gather up the dangling headphone cords and turn to leave with my new goodies.

"Wait, you've got to sign the sheet or I'll get in trouble," Tina says. "I get class credit for running the AVT club. If you don't sign for this stuff, Ms. Jinkle's gonna get mad."

She thrusts a sheet at me and I reach for a short golf pencil on her desk and start to sign.

"Seriously, track three will blow your balls off. It's that good. I'll slip another flash drive in your locker with more music."

"Okay," I say. "Thuh-thuh-thanks."

She rolls her eyes at me. "Don't mention it."

D A N N Y

35

When our doorbell rings, I'm expecting a neighborhood Mormon or Jehovah's Witness to take another
stab at converting our household, but Coach Nelson standing there is a surprise.

"Hey, kiddo, how ya doin'?" Coach asks. I'm not sure
this is a trick question since I've skipped practice again,
claiming to be sick.

"All right," I say, then rub my stomach and frown, hoping that conveys the proper amount of sickness to him.

"Your parents home?"

"No. My dad's still at work."

"You got a minute?"

I nod yes but keep my hand on my belly in case I need to
fall back on a quick escape excuse. Coach Nelson doesn't
make a move to come into the house. Instead he turns

around and walks back to his pickup truck with a gun rack in the back window and bumper stickers that read KILL YOUR TV and THOSE WHO CAN MAKE YOU BELIEVE ABSURDITIES CAN MAKE YOU COMMIT ATROCITIES. I follow him outside. He leans against the back part of his truck, not shadowed by our house and still catching rays from the falling sun.

"Heard you had yourselves a good time up at the quarry," he says while squinting out at the orange sky. He doesn't see me nod yes and I don't say anything. "A little bee told me you jumped off the cliff. First one over. Real gung ho. Figured Fisher or Bruce would be the first. Normally I wouldn't recommend that, but since you're still alive, consider me impressed." He turns his gaze from the sun to me. "Didn't know you had it in you. Fact is, it doesn't seem like something you'd do at all. Thought you were a little more careful than that."

"You mean *chicken*," I say, surprised by how angry I sound.

"Not chicken."

"And weak. Same reason you knew they'd pick me to go against Jankowski on the bet in the weight room. You knew everyone thought me and Ronnie were little weaklings."

"And you showed them all, didn't you?" Coach chuckles. "Never underestimate the power of underestimation," he says, and slaps the panel of his truck. He's the only one laughing. "We sure showed them." He stops smiling when he realizes I'm fuming at him.

"You set me up. Everyone was laughing at me that day. They couldn't wait to see Tom cream me."

"But you kicked his butt, didn't you?"

I don't answer back.

"You know the crazy thing about life?" Coach asks, and now he's looking off at the sun again. "On any given day, you have the chance to be a hero or a victim, predator or prey. Most times, circumstances are beyond your control. Other times, you got a choice but you think about it too much and you freeze up. Sometimes, though, you're forced to react and it's all instinct. May not make a damn bit of difference in a bad situation. But sometimes instinct squeezes the good out of you, forces you to be a hero before you even realize it. Danny, that day in the weight room, you were our hero. It was David versus Goliath in there and you nailed it. Now, what if I let you in on the plan and you listened to your fears, backed out before you even set foot in that weight room and had a chance to become a hero? I knew you were strong. I knew you'd win. I just had to make sure your brain didn't cheat your heart out of the chance to become a hero."

"I don't remember feeling much like a hero that day. Just tricked."

"Is that what's really bothering you?" he asks. "I mean, besides Ronnie's death? I understand you boys taking it hard but you can't just fall apart."

"I'm not feeling very good. I don't much feel like practicing."

"So that's it? You're just going to quit on the team?" He takes a second to glance at me before going back to squinting at the sun.

"I don't know," I say. Truth is, I never thought about

skipping practice as quitting on the team until Coach calls it that.

"Danny, I can't force you to come back. I *can* tell you that you're throwing away promise and talent every day you miss practice. Maybe no one's told you this lately but you're good. Real good."

This kind of talk embarrasses me, especially since Coach doesn't know the whole truth, doesn't know how I abandoned my teammate, let him kill himself because I *am* a chicken and I *am* weak.

"Danny, I've coached enough seasons, now, to recognize a kid that's got some talent. I mean, hell, you're only a sophomore and you got a shot at placing in the top three on high bar at state. I don't know why you suddenly want to throw it all away. You think Ronnie would want his death to make you do that?"

What Ronnie would want is for me to have spoken up for him when he was still alive. My stomach cramps for real at the thought. No faking necessary.

"You're on track to be a co-captain next year. The boys in that gym look up to you. What you do on that high bar scares and thrills all of us. You're one of the best advertisements our team's got, and not just for new guys, but to keep the guys we have now from drifting off next year. The way you've improved in the off-season, you could place top three *all-around* next year, too. Senior year, you could mop up. Maybe get a scholarship. I'll be happy to write some letters to schools. I've got a few contacts and it's not just from coaching."

Mention of a scholarship makes me feel real hopeful

and doubly guilty at the same time. As much as I want it, why should my dream be rewarded when I denied Ronnie's cry for help?

"But none of that is going to happen if you don't get your skinny butt back in the gym and start working out." Coach drapes an arm over the side panel of his flatbed, then turns to face me. "I was hoping your mom or dad was home so I could tell them what I just told you. Maybe they'd help kick your butt for me," he says, grinning.

"My mom's dead," I blurt. Coach's grin fades. In the orange glow of the sun, his stubbled face softens. I hate telling people because of this exact response, but I can't stand hearing him mention her like she's alive; sounds like he's teasing me even though I know he's not.

"Aw, hell . . . Danny . . . I'm sorry . . . I didn't know."

"It's okay," I say, even though it's not okay at all. But it's not Coach's fault, either. Not long after I break that news, he gets back in his truck, and when it starts up, the tailpipe pops like the muffler is about to snap off.

"We need you back soon as you feel better," Coach tells me, sticking his head out the truck window, and then he backs out of the driveway and leaves me alone.

KURT

You were named prep all-star of the week," Patti says first thing when I walk into the kitchen. She's drinking coffee at the Formica table, wearing green nylon track pants and a cotton hooded sweatshirt with a quilted Mickey Mouse on the chest. A cigarette with an inch of ash rests in the V of her fingers as she holds open the city newspaper. Her legs are crossed at the knee and one dangling house slipper lazily flaps against the heel of her hanging foot.

"I was?"

"Yup, right here." She rustles the newspaper. "Lookit that, Kurtis. Right there in black and white. I'm so proud of you. Coach Brigs must be real proud, too."

And there it is, a photo of me holding the ball and running up the center of the field, my jersey number visible and, really, the only way to tell it's me. Must have been shot from the stands the way it's aiming down. A little paragraph under the photo has my name in bold print announcing me as the male prep all-star athlete of the week. It has my stats and the team's 6–0 record listed as well. Next to my paragraph is the girl prep all-star athlete of the week, a volleyball player, Samantha Hanes, who led her team, St. Vincent Academy, to a shutout at some regional invitational meet in Iowa over the weekend. Unlike my photo, hers is a yearbook picture of her face. She's smiling like she's ready to devour the whole world.

"Pretty neat, huh?" Patti prompts.

"Yeah."

"Now, you sit down and I'm going to make you some eggs and toast. Or pancakes. Would you like pancakes?"

My stomach starts growling at the thought. "Yes, muh-muh-muh-ma'am."

I'm curious about when Patti went grocery shopping because, except for the toast part, we don't have any of that breakfast stuff. I know because I check all the time. Patti pulls open the fridge door and then I understand she's only had the idea right now.

"Hmmm . . ." Patti stands there, staring at the bare fridge shelves. "I got to start feeding my big boy a little better." She scratches a mole under her chin, then sticks the cigarette in her mouth. "Tell you what, Kurtis," she says while smoke rises up in front of her eyes. "I'll drive you to school today and we'll stop by Mickey D's and get a little drive-through breakfast."

"Yesssss, muh-ma'am."

"Kurtis, when you gonna stop calling me 'ma'am?'"

Patti drops me off at school with a belly full of Mickey D's pushing against the waist of my jeans. It's not the only part of me getting bigger. My shoulders and pecs have inflated from the gym, pulling my once-comfortable shirt tight across my chest. Feels like they've grown at least two inches in as many weeks thanks to Coach's pills. The soreness from all my weight lifting tells me my cells are gathering together and multiplying, layering over me in a protective shell, thickening, increasing my armor, making me that much harder to hurt. It feels good.

At my locker, someone's taped the same newspaper photo Patti showed me that morning. Little streamers frame the photo and CONGRATULATIONS, KURT!!!! is spelled out in red construction paper running the length of my locker. I look around, expecting maybe the decorators to be standing nearby but it's only the regular morning crowd of students. Lots of them call out "Hi" or "Congrats" or "Nice game." Everyone, it seems, suddenly knows me, like we've been buddies for years. Teammates like Terrence and Rondo spot me in the hallways and make woofing noises, then give me fist pounds. Mr. Samuel, my history teacher, even congratulates me in front of class. I'm not going to lie. I like it. I like every bit of it. I make it through four periods like that, riding this good-vibe wave, until I find Scott, Studblatz, and Jankowski in the lunchroom huddled together. Students I barely know are coming up and slapping me on the back and it feels like they're pushing me toward my three captains.

Approaching them, I see a moment's hesitation in Scott's eyes while he works out a tricky problem in his head. He finds a solution, though, because he raises an arm to wave me over. A smirk creeps into the corners of his mouth, a smirk that says our little secret makes me just as guilty and dirty as him. That smirk slows my footsteps and I almost veer right out of the cafeteria. Neither Jankowski nor Studblatz seems real happy to see me.

"How's our all-star prep athlete of the week?" Scott asks. Sarcasm slithers under the question. Not until I'm standing at the table do I notice the sling around his arm.

"That fuh-fuh-fuh-from Jackson's suh-suh-sack?"

"Yeah, juh-juh-juh-genius," Studblatz answers.

"Rrrrrrr-remember?" Jankowski asks me. "You let that black bastard get a free shot?"

"Wasn't his fault," Scott says. "Pullman's the one that totally pussed out Friday. Played dead all night."

"It buh-buh-buh-broken?" I ask, preparing for more fake stutters from Jankowski and Studblatz. In foster care, I always first tried ignoring teasers. If they kept it up, then I swung.

"Naw," Scott says. "Only dislocated. Once they popped it back in, it felt fine. But the doctors say after it happens, the ligaments get stretched out and it's easy to repeat. This is to get the ligaments to shorten up again."

"How long?" I ask, trying to keep my questions short and clear.

"They said it should be fine by game after next."

"Suh-suh-suh-sorry about that," I say. I guess I mean it.

"You sh-sh-sh-should be," Jankowski says.

"No worries," Scott says. "Long as we got our prep all-star of the week to carry the load." Chrissy and Tammy, sitting on Scott's side of the table, giggle at a piece of paper that Studblatz slides toward them. It's a cartoon sketch of a robot monster; has bolts coming out of its neck and drool spilling out its mouth. Its got long hair and two scars on the side of its face just like mine. A little balloon comes out of its mouth, saying, "BBBBBrodsky Duh-duh-Dumbsky." Something burns inside my nose, stinging my eyes. If Lamar was next to me, mouth moving at the speed of sound, tongue slashing and burning at full volume, the entire cafeteria would turn on them. Lamar'd know exactly what to say, dropping words like bombs until they were crying for him to shut up. But me? I just stand there and take it, big and stupid, trying my best to ignore the monster sketch. A perfect retard.

"Besides," Scott continues, casting an eye at the sheet of paper and then back up at me, pretending it doesn't exist. "We've got Robbindale this week. Our JV team could beat them. If Warner can't control a couple of easy handoffs to you and Terrence, then we don't deserve to win."

"We'll win," Jankowski says.

"Wuh-wuh-what if we only tuh-tuh-tuh-tie?" I ask, wanting to be smart-alecky like Lamar used to be. But my stutter makes the question—and me—sound stupid.

"We'll win because I'm willing it, you understand?" Jankowski says. "Only pussies allow the game to be bigger than them. Champions become bigger than the game." He's jabbing his spork through the air at me as he says this.

"You heard my man here," Scott says.

I leave them to line up for food. Thankfully, by the time I come back, they're gone. When I sit down, a new group of guys I don't really know clusters around me. We don't really talk because I'm not about to stutter for freakshow points, but whenever they catch my eye, they lift their chins and ask, "What's up?" I let my hair fall forward and keep my face dug into my macaroni. While I'm shoveling in the food, the plastic handle of the spork rubs against a string of tiny, puffy blisters bubbled up between my thumb and fingers. Souvenirs from the rock climbing trip up at the quarry. Danny and me compared hands after math class; skin on his palms tough as rawhide. The way he showed them off, you'd think they had a blue ribbon pinned to them. He laughed at my "dainty" blisters, said my new nickname should be "ladyfingers". I didn't mind at all. His laugh reminded me of Lamar's.

Out on the practice field that afternoon, Coach calls me in front of the other players and congratulates me on my newspaper mention. Scott roams the field out of uniform with his arm slung up, shadowing Warner, tutoring him on the quarterback assignments. Warner's helmet is bobbing and nodding at every little remark Scott makes. Jankowski still pushes guys around because he can, same as every practice. Studblatz rides Pullman all practice, at one point shoving him in the back and forcing him down on the turf, Studblatz straddling his throat. With Pullman's helmet between his thighs, Studblatz cusses him out, calling him a pussy wart for letting Scott get hurt. Neither the coaches nor the trainers attempt to stop him. The fathers on the sideline watch dully like gated livestock, all silently approving Pullman's punishment.

Studblatz keeps his jawing up all practice, working my nerves, firing darts into my head, sparking little embers in the back of my skull. Studblatz promises he's going to whip the fat off Pullman for how he played last game and teach him a lesson. Pullman's helmet dips low enough that his face mask almost touches his chest. The new layer of muscle—muscle the D-bol's given me—winds tight around my neck, strangling me, and I'm breathing heavy, needing to smash something to break the squeeze. Jankowski, Scott, and Studblatz have put Ronnie right out of their minds, gone right back to acting how they always do, not sorry in the least. Arm sling or no arm sling, the three of them strut around like the field's named after them. Like they own it. Like no one can touch them.

"We go fifty percent, boys, you understand?" Coach hollers before the scrimmage session. "We cannot afford unnecessary injuries before next game."

"Nice and easy, Warner," Scott yells from the sidelines to his backup. "No stupid mistakes." Warner looks over at Scott and again bobs his helmet in agreement. First play is a ZigZag Alpha Twist with a jet route. That means the quarterback fakes a handoff to me and I push through the line, staying on Tom's left shoulder while Terrence runs behind our blocking. The ball is snapped and I go half speed, meeting Studblatz across the line, putting my hands out to slow up to a stop.

Studblatz decides Coach's fifty percent isn't hard enough. He slaps my arms away and rams his shoulder into my chest. Those sparks Studblatz's jawing planted in my skull earlier light up again. Not liking his attitude much, I grab his jersey and jerk him hard to the left while stepping right. The string of quarry-climbing blisters along my fingers tear open. Studblatz tries to throw me but I sidestep again and shove back.

"Offensive holding, you dumb, retarded freak!" Studblatz screams, voice rising into a wild howl of crazy rage—rage he has no right to claim—flying past his mouth guard, past peeled-back lips. "Holding," he sputters, barely breathing now, eyes wild as a pit-dog sniffing the cut, smelling the wound. He claws the gate of my face mask and rips downward, twisting and shaking, dragging on my neck. I grab his face mask back and jerk sideways and down. We shove and tug, face mask to face mask. Words choke out of him, past the rubbery plastic he chomps through. His fury makes no sense, only triggers my own.

"Holding, you ugly retard," he hisses, tears flowing over his eyes. "You fucking retard! *Retard!*"

I hear a coach's whistle, feel the press of a gathering pack. Hands and arms encircle me, pulling me backward, but I ain't letting go. No way. I ain't letting go. Neither is Studblatz.

"Ugly freak retard!" Studblatz bleats. "You let Jackson through. I watched you. You let him get Scott on purpose!"

If not for our face masks, I'm sure he'd bite me.

"Ruh-ruh-ruh-Ronnie Gunderson," I stutter. "Ruh-ruh-ruh-Ronnie . . ." I yank up and down on Studblatz's face mask in a yes motion, forcing an amen from him. *"Ronnie Gunderson."* His name comes out perfect on my last try. Unlike Studblatz, I can breathe again. The pressure releases.

I let go. Teammates pry his fingers off my face mask and pull us apart. One of the guys holding back Studblatz is Jankowski and I know he hears me speak Ronnie's name. I'm glad. I should shout the name over and over and over until someone asks me what I mean and then I spill it all on the field for them . . . but I don't. I say no more.

"Water break! Water break!" Assistant Coach Stein yells, shoving between us. "Cool down, guys. We're all on the same team here. Save it for Robbindale, will ya?"

I feel a slap on my helmet, turn, and find Coach Brigs beaming at me with an odd look, like he's happy and mad at the same time.

"Now that's what I call fired up!" he says. "Brodsky and Studblatz are going to eat those Robbindale boys alive." He starts slapping other helmets with his rolled-up playbook, any helmet within reach. "That's what I want to see out here. That's what I call fire. Some of you think Robbindale is supposed to roll over for you because we're six-and-zero and they're one-and-five. Well, I got news for you. They're not going to roll over. We need to turn it up. You feel the heat coming off Studblatz? Coming off Brodsky? I want *that* type of intensity from the rest of you."

I jog back to the school, hoping my legs will stop shaking by the time I reach the water fountain. Once inside the basement hallway, I decide to peek in on the gymnasts for only a second and remind myself of something good, something better. Just for a second, I want to watch the monkeys swinging in their little forest.

D A N N Y

I'm doin' somethin' tonight after practice," Bruce mumbles under his breath. "A little payback." The two of us are stretching before practice on the thin tumbling mats at the far end of the gymnasium. No one but me is within earshot of Bruce.

"Don't you remember how all this started?" I mumble in reply. It's my first practice back since Coach's house call. I'm not really sure how I feel about returning. I know I'm glad to see Bruce in the gym. At first.

"They gotta pay," Bruce mutters through a locked jaw, staring across the gym at the storage room. "They gotta pay," he repeats. I haven't gone back into the storage room and don't plan on it. That's why I'm down at the far end of the gym, stretching, when Bruce joins me. He slides his arms behind him and slowly rocks forward to loosen his shoulder muscles. "Besides, this is nothing dangerous. We're just going to make sure Ronnie's not forgotten."

No!

That's what my brain shouts. *No, no, no! What are you, crazy?!?! Wasn't the attack on Ronnie and his suicide enough?! Do you want to start a whole new round with these guys? We are small. Scott, Tom, and Mike are huge. And wicked. They do as they please and no one ever says anything. And they know that.*

My brain motors on but my mouth won't budge except to nibble the skin on the inside of my cheek. Every single day since the attack is a nonstop loop of remembering all those horrible things that happened to Ronnie in the storage room. He isn't forgotten in the least. The attack opened my eyes: Oregrove isn't a school. It's a hunting ground. Scott, Tom, and Mike choose their targets at leisure and go unpunished. Teachers look the other way, say "boys'll be boys," and bust the the rest of us for showing up two minutes late to class. It's a place where someone small as Ronnie gets chewed up. Where someone small as me is supposed to keep quiet, smile for the yearbook photo, and graduate without spilling any bad secrets.

Scott hurts his arm and all anyone talks about is when he'll be healthy enough to play again. Cheerleaders—those beautiful, awful cannibals who shred each other without ever making a fist—practically faint when he walks by them in the hall with his arm in a sling. That's how it works for royalty. Everyone cares about Scott and his arm while Scott cares about no one. And meanwhile, Ronnie's still dead because of what they did to him . . . and what I didn't do. People like Ronnie, like me, exist at Oregrove for the royalty to devour.

NO! My brain shouts inside my skull. *Tell Bruce NO WAY!*

"What are you going to do?" I ask.

"Let's make this fast," I whisper as Bruce and I skulk down the halls.

"Don't sweat it," Bruce whispers back. "We'll be in and out like commandos." His energy is high again.

"Fisher should be doing this," I grumble. "He loves this crap."

"Why don't you tell him what happened to Ronnie, then," Bruce snaps, "and I'll make sure to invite him on our next adventure."

"There won't *be* a next adventure. This is it."

"Right," Bruce agrees. His plan, as explained during practice, is pretty simple, taking him less than a full sweep of the gym clock's second hand to break my will and convince me that revenge is my duty. That, by the way, is Step 1. Step 2 involves us leaving practice last, and together, like he's going to offer me a ride home. The school and the parking lot empty out by that time.

That leaves Step 3.

Bruce cracks the trunk of his Volvo and glances both ways, real suspicious, like bad guys do in detective movies. I think maybe he's joking until he pulls out two industrial-size permanent markers. The kind sold at art supply stores. The kind dumbasses use for tagging. He plants one in my palm before I can pull my hand away. It sits in my fist, feeling like a weapon, or, more accurately, like a get-expelled-for-life baton.

"Bruce . . ."

"Don't worry about it," he tries assuring me. "We'll be quick. No one's going to know."

"I don't think—"

"Come on!" The cutoff is harsh, letting me know he's done caring about consequences or what I think. I follow him back into the school, stuffing the triple-size permanent marker into my gym bag.

We make it down into enemy territory inside of a minute—the varsity football locker room. This is serious. Too serious to involve others. Graffiti is grounds for immediate expulsion, no questions asked. No one else can know what we're doing or be able to prove it. Bruce performs a speedy reconnaissance around the locker room to make sure we're alone. Trying to explain our presence in the varsity football locker room would be impossible.

Satisfied the place is empty, Bruce moves decisively. Sweet chemical toxicity fills the air once he uncaps the big marker. Tom Jankowski's locker is first. Bruce scribbles hurriedly but carefully, making sure the name is clear. He moves on to Studblatz's locker and repeats the message.

"Okay, your turn," Bruce says. "Hit Scott's locker."

I do as instructed, hesitating only a moment, since it's already too late by then. Too late to go back. I pull the cap off my marker, hearing it snap. I press the wet wick against the thin sheet metal. I spell the name down the locker just like Bruce did the other two:

R
O
N
N
I
E

G
U
N
D
E
R
S
O
N

"Let's go," Bruce whispers. "Their regular lockers are next." I nod, still inhaling the heavy, sweet, chemical scent of fighting back. We scoot out of the locker room, peeking out the doorway and looking both ways before scampering down the hall and upstairs same as we did the time we sprayed pee in their lockers.

I sort of know where each of their three regular lockers is based on where I spot them hanging out between classes and the decorations the cheerleaders paste on them for game Fridays. Bruce, having planned for this moment, knows the precise coordinates and we go in fast. I sprint to the far end of the hallway and peer around the corner to watch out for janitors, late-working teachers, or delinquent students (like us), while Bruce tags Tom's locker.

Finished, Bruce waves me toward him to the next hallway. Running past Tom's locker, I see that Bruce tagged it with Ronnie's name the same way he did downstairs. But this time he's added "Murderer!" across the top. A nice artistic flourish, I think, popping the cap off my marker. Next up is Scott's locker and Bruce tags it quickly. Studblatz's locker is last. Bruce jogs to the end of the hall and plays lookout at the corner while pointing at me to tag it. The fumes from the marker mix with my adrenaline and my head starts getting light. I write Ronnie's name in bold letters, pressing hard, breathing deep. Across the top of the locker, I write "Murderer!"

"Go, go, go," Bruce mouths, scooping the air with his hands as a signal for me to catch up. As I reach him, he grabs my arm at the elbow and tugs me behind him. We fly down the next hall. With my head so light, it feels like I'm floating for a moment. I kick at the brick wall for no reason. I get only a dull thud that hurts my foot. So I kick a locker instead and get the nice, satisfying clang I want. Bruce glances back at me with a frown.

"Okay, slow down." Bruce puts a hand out to slap my chest. "We walk from here."

"Yeah, okay."

"No reason to look suspicious. We just forgot something after practice and we came back to get it, right?"

"Yeah."

"I'll give you a ride home," he says.

In the car, I uncap the marker again and put the wick almost directly up my left nostril. I inhale repeatedly until I start feeling nauseous.

"That smells like shit," Bruce says. "You're going to obliterate all your brain cells."

"That's okay," I assure him, recapping the marker. "Some parts would be better if they were obliterated."

Bruce pulls into my driveway. My dad isn't home yet. "I'll see you tomorrow," he says.

"Yeah, cool." Everything feels nice and distant, including Bruce's voice, like it's all coming through a veil and nothing is that awful or bad. Nothing really hurts or seems dangerous, and places like Oregrove—where they cheer for guys who did what they did to Ronnie, where they crown them kings—are only a joke.

"Thanks for helping," Bruce says, tapping the capped marker I hand him against his steering wheel. "It's the least we could do," Bruce says. "It's still not enough. Not even close. But it's something."

K U R T

"You think it's funny?" Studblatz asks in my ear, so close his breath parts my hair. He and Jankowski sneak up from behind, flanking me on my way toward English class.

"What's fuh-fuh-funny?" I ask, swiveling my head side to side, failing to hold either of them in my sights. When I slow, they slow, keeping a half step behind me. The skin along my back prickles like wood ticks are crawling all over me. Tom Jankowski and Mike Studblatz hold the triangle formation while I walk through the north hallway, pretty much blocking anyone trying to get by us.

"Hear that, Tom?" Studblatz asks. "He's p-p-p-playing stu-stu-stu-stupid."

"Yeah, I hear him."

"Wuh-wuh-wuh-what's the joke?" I ask, hoping they'll tire quickly and go off to class.

"You tell us," Tom says.

"Huh?"

"Don't even try pretending you got nothing to do with it," Studblatz says.

"What?"

"Better take acting classes with the theater fags 'cause you really suck at it," Studblatz says. "Walk by our lockers. Walk by 'em, then keep pretending you don't know what we're talking about. It ain't no coincidence we got his name all over our lockers a day after you sputtered it at practice."

I shake my head, totally confused.

"Wuh-wuh-wuh-what?"

"Tommy's dad's a cop," Studblatz says. "You know that, right?"

"Yup," Tom confirms in my other ear.

"He found out all about you. Told us what you did. Be real interesting if the whole school found out you killed a kid in some orphanage before they threw you in psycho-kid prison."

This stops me cold. I turn around, the better to face my attackers.

"Aw shit, lookit his face." Jankowski elbows Studblatz, then points at me. "Surprised much?" he asks me. "Guess your little secret ain't so secret no more. My dad says only freaks come out of those kid prisons—I mean, 'juvenile detention centers.'" He says this last part making air quotes.

"And psychos," Studblatz adds.

"You a freak K-K-K-Kurtis B-B-B-Brodsky? Huh?" Jankowski taunts. "You a psycho-kid killer? Who's the killer now, huh, Kurt? You think they'll cheer for you when they find out you smothered some kid to death?"

"Tom's dad's getting ready to warn the other parents," Studblatz smiles. "Let the rest of 'em know what you are."

"Then maybe we'll decorate your locker like you did ours," Tom says. Their threat turns my legs to sand. I'm not sure I can stand up much longer, thinking about my past coming out, the truth getting twisted like it did the first time. All the students so happy to be my new friend will be just as happy to turn on me.

Tom reaches out and grabs my arm like he owns me, then pulls himself too close. "Who you think people are going to believe if they ever start asking questions?" he growls under his breath. "About Ronnie? About what happened to him? Your word against ours, stutter-man. Scott told us he fixed this with you already."

The bass beat of my heart thumps in my earlobes.

"I duh-duh-duh-didn't suh-suh-smother Lam-ma-ma . . . nobody."

"Neither did we," Tom says, still gripping my arm. "But you got a juvey record and my dad says that shit can get leaked real easy. Before you know it, it's just a Google search away."

"Psycho's word versus ours," Studblatz adds.

"And we don't got records."

"Who you think everyone's gonna side with?"

An underclassman gets too close to this ambush. He's trying to squeeze by us when Studblatz shoves him into a wall of lockers, shoves him hard enough that the kid ricochets off the metal and drops his books. The kid doesn't say nothing, just rubs his shoulder and bends over to collect his books. No one helps him or even notices, really. Sight's as common as chewing gum stuck to the walls.

"It's too bad Gunderson killed himself," Tom says quietly. "But we didn't have nothing to do with it."

Jankowski's still got ahold of my arm. His threats have taken the fight out of me. Studblatz steps closer and they box me into the wall, double-teaming again, ready to take another shot at me.

"Wuh-wuh-wuh-what do you wuh-wuh-wuh-want?"

"Take a look at our lockers before the janitor finishes with them. Then tell us you don't know nothing," Studblatz says.

"Here's a little warning," Tom says. "Teammate to teammate. You don't know what you're messing with. Our parents, our coach, our fans don't want to see us fail. They won't let you or Ronnie or anyone else get in our way."

Tom releases my arm. Him and Studblatz drift off into the hallway stream. I lean against a drinking fountain, gripping the white porcelain for balance, pressing the button with my thumb, pretending I'm thirsty when I'm really just trying to hold on while the sound of Lamar's panicked wheezing fills my ears. When the end passing bell rings I'm still at the fountain. Except for a couple kids sprinting to class, trying to escape a detention, the halls are empty. I finally shove off and plod toward Scott's locker, the closest of the three. A janitor wipes at the surface with a gray rag that smells up the area with ammonia. The rubbing is worthless. Only thing that's going to work is a coat of paint.

Ronnie's name runs the length of Scott's locker, spattering Scott the same way I'd done to Studblatz in practice yesterday. No wonder they thought I wrote it. I would've thought I wrote it if I were them. Worry creeps down my neck. My past is about to leak out and poison everyone here against me. I'll get blamed for Ronnie just like I got blamed for Lamar. My locker will get decorated but it won't be with football congratulations. It's starting. I can feel it. A dark force gathering and it can't be wished away. I trudge toward Tom's locker and then Studblatz's locker, whistling low with awe at the addition of the word "Murderer!" at the top. It has to be Bruce or Danny that did it. Maybe both.

I walk into English class late, wanting to pretend it won't matter what Mike, Tom, and Scott say, but knowing better. At least Bruce and Danny know the truth and have the will, unlike me, to tell it. If and when my captains spread their lies, maybe Bruce and Danny will defend me, working their mouths in ways I never could.

On the field for practice, Scott, still out of pads and not practicing, walks over to me. He carries a football in his unslung hand, flipping it up a few inches and catching it over and over.

"Hey, man, you should know that Studblatz and Jankowski get a little worked up about stupid things," Scott says, flipping the football again. "I told them you didn't write that stuff on our lockers. I also know you stick by your teammates. You wouldn't say something, or make up lies that weren't true. I told both of them that. You stick with your own. I know you, Kurt. Better than you think. I know you're loyal. They don't see that yet, but they will." Scott peers through my face mask like he's having trouble finding my eyes in the shadows of my helmet.

"Now work on your cross-step," Scott says. "I'll make sure Warner gives you smooth handoffs all game. But if Robbindale beats us while I'm on the bench, I'm holding you responsible, you understand?"

"Yeah," I say.

The way Scott smiles at you, it can make you almost forget what he did. He isn't just popular because he's quarterback. He carries something in his face, a switch he turns on and off. When he turns it on and aims his beam at you, he can make you feel pretty important, like, of all his friends, it's you and only you who really gets him. He hits me with that beam now. It's strong as the sun peeking through the rolling clouds and it's hard to hold the line and hate him when that smile feels like the only source of warmth you got.

After practice I hole up in the one place offering me a little control over my life. The weight room. Pumping up in Oregrove's state-of-the-art weight room is like depositing another check in my security account. Coach's pills increase the payoff, I'm sure, as I pop the D-bols and switch into sweats. Lamar and I used to do push-ups in our bedroom because that's all we had. At the next group home, they had a creaky weight bench in the basement and a few dumbbells. I got too strong for those. The last high school, Lincoln, had no money for fancy stuff. Not until I got here did I know what the good stuff was.

Sometimes I come in early to have the whole place to

myself. Nothing better than heaving up cold steel and feeling it submit. Now, *that's* power. That last set, pushing with all you got, watching that bar tremble above your head, knowing if you fail, that bar's going to slowly come back down on your chest and pin you—no better way to get your juices flowing. So you drive it up, partly out of fear and partly out of want, your arms vibrating with every last morsel of energy inside you cooking away. Your muscles boiling down all anger and hate into rivers of greasy sweat draining off through your pores until you're crispy burned and the winner in a not-so-small battle.

Under a helmet or alone in the weight room are the two places I can talk almost normal. "You got this," I tell my reflection, curling the dumbbells, fascinated with how my muscles grow and bulge to master the weight. "One more," I say. Or, "Bring it home, baby," or "Come on, now, don't disappoint me." I almost speak perfectly. It helps, also, to wear the headphones and play the music Tina copied for me. The recorder the school loaned me and that Tina upgraded cranks real loud, loud enough to blast away anything bad trying to grow between my ears. Rock the tunes at full volume and everything else—Crud Bucket, Lamar, Ronnie—disappears for a while.

By the time I finish in the weight room, my body is demolished. Exactly how I like it. I've got the showers and locker room all to myself. I walk down empty hallways still cranking my tunes, safe from having to talk to anyone, fumbling a hello or turning my scars away from a stare. I dial through my playlist, try some of the latest music Tina put on a new flash disk and slipped through the vent of my locker with a note attached.

Kurt,
If you liked the first playlist (and you would have if
you're at all cool), you'll DIG this one. Guaranteed.
Tina

Or:

Kurt,
Here's a vintage mix. Listen to it when you're sad.
If you want some songs for walking in the woods
on a rainy day, I've got an even better playlist. I'll
drop it off tomorrow.
Tina

I like Tina's playlists and her little notes. It can't hurt, I figure, dropping off requests back through her locker.

Tina,
I like "Demon" but the "Earth" playlist is too soft.
Can you make me another metal mix for working
out?
Kurt

I still haven't used the recorder for its original purpose: to record myself speaking words off the list Ms. Jinkle gave me and play it back and try to correct my stutter. I hate the sound of my voice, hate hearing my tongue botch everything. I sound retarded. I sound stupid. It's way better listening to wailing guitars and stomping drums.

DANNY

Every year since fifth grade, I've gone to Oregrove's home football games, not to actually watch the game, but to run around with packs of friends on the big grassy hill near the bleachers. That's where we'd play catch with the mini-footballs that half the boys brought; spy on older teens making out under the bleachers or behind the concession stands; tease the girls we thought were cute; and toss peanut shells and popcorn into dangling coat hoods of anyone who looked like a parent. Friday night games used to be the best part of the week.

Not anymore.

For me, the carnival atmosphere around the games has vanished. Watching the tightly packed stands and the mob on the grassy hill, I think maybe everyone comes to Friday night games not because they're that great, but because there's nothing else to do around Oregrove. And yet I'm still here.

I've come to watch Kurt play and cheer him on while hoping the rest of his team gets hit by an asteroid or drops dead from eating bad lunchroom corn dogs. It's not easy rooting *for* Kurt but rooting *against* the rest of the team; I'm still refining my system. For instance, when the big new Jumbotron flashes KNIGHTS!!! KNIGHTS!!! KNIGHTS!!! I refuse to make a peep. But when Kurt punches into the end zone and the Jumbotron starts flashing KURT!!! KURT!!! KURT!!! I holler loud as anyone until his name rings the stadium. Our shouts are drowned out only by the huge stadium speakers booming with the sound of an approaching freight train that ends with a long, loud whistle blast. ALL ABOARD THE BRODSKY EXPRESS!!! the Jumbotron flashes. In the last couple of weeks, the local sports news has buzzed over Kurt. I spot a few homemade posters in the stands: GO, KURT, GO! and #27 IN THE HOUSE and NOTHING STOPS THE BRODSKY EXPRESS.

Scott Miller stands on the sideline wearing his game jersey over regular clothes with his left arm in a sling. Hopefully, it's arm cancer.

I tagged along to the game with Fisher, but he's off somewhere with his shop-class buddies. They usually pregame in the parking lot with Schmidt beer and vodka-laced Gatorade. Once inside the game fence, they head off to the far north corner of the field and smoke weed. To find them, I just look for the cluster of black leather motorcycle jackets. Doesn't matter how cold it gets, they still wear them. In the springtime, they switch to jean jackets with the arms cut off over hooded sweatshirts. Most of them carry brass knuckles drill-pressed out of scrap metal in shop class. Fisher's friends are also partial to butterfly knives and nunchakus ordered online or out of the back pages of *Black Belt* magazine. What I've noticed is the football team doesn't mess with them. That single fact makes me think maybe I should start hanging out with them. Problem is drinking makes me sick and weed just makes me cough.

I lean against the chain-link fence near the end zone. The leather sleeves of my letterman jacket squeak when I cross my arms for warmth. I lettered freshman year, which is almost unheard of in any sport. It still makes me proud. Without the jacket on, though, I'd probably be mistaken for one of the junior high kids tossing the mini-footballs on the grassy knoll. I hug my arms tighter and the leather scrunches more. Part of me feels like a fraud, like I'm faking being a high school student. Real high school students don't cower in a corner while their teammate is getting attacked.

Warner, Scott's replacement, barks loud and acts like a starter and doesn't seem nervous at all. But Coach Brigs isn't giving him an opportunity to make a mistake by throwing a bad pass. About every other play either Kurt or Terrence, the running back, gets handed the ball and grinds forward a few yards—enough to keep moving the chains and keep their offense on the field. The two teams slowly progress up the field near the end zone. The Jumbotron fills with a helmet cam view from one of the Oregrove players. Either Terrence or Kurt, I think, from the backfield angle on the screen. On the Jumbotron, the line of opposing bodies might as well be a mountain.

Warner's cadence sets loose the two sides. Picked up by the helmet mic, the collision explodes over the stadium speakers loud as an atomic bomb. Kurt breaks through the pileup like a firefighter charging through flames, thighs pumping almost as high as his chest, crushing his way into the end zone. The Jumbotron shows a blur of helmets sliding to the side or falling away to reveal open grass and black night beyond the chalk lines. It's Kurt's helmet, I realize. The only one in the end zone.

The stadium fans rise up together from the bleacher seats in a solid wave of adoration. Teammates jump on top of him, slapping his helmet, slapping his shoulder pads, whooping and hollering. Cartoon fireworks burst off the Jumbotron followed by a slow-mo replay of him smashing into the end zone. This makes everyone whistle and stomp even harder. For a moment it's as if every person in the world loves Kurt.

They'll pull him in, I think, twist him around, and make him believe he can be as cruel to others as he wants and still be adored.

The final score is 28–10. The Knights win again. Their record remains perfect. Both Kurt and Terrence score two touchdowns apiece. The entire team swirls around the two players—Terrence holding his helmet, Kurt still wearing his—on their way back to the lockers. Parents and grandparents step forward to glimpse and congratulate them. I pull back from the whole thing. I notice no one's swarming around Scott—or Studblatz and Jankowski, who escort him like bodyguards. The three talk among themselves, forgotten by the fans and the rest of the team as it marches on ahead. The three of them look angry. I'm glad for my distance from them.

KURT

Tomorrow, we take you to the next level. Tomorrow, we prepare you to lead, bro.

Scott's promise nestles in my ear like a worm. *Rest up,* he instructs in the locker room after our victory over Robbindale.

Tomorrow, we turn you into a king.

I lie in bed staring at the ceiling when the distinct growl of a V-8 prowls to the end of Patti's street, sniffing a trail up her driveway. The Camaro honks twice but I don't move, even when my new cell phone buzzes. Only after the doorbell rings do I finally sit up, bring my sore legs over the side of the bed, and plant my swollen feet on the cold floor. My toes curl protectively. A couple of the hits from last night's game rang my bell enough that I skipped the victory party and came straight home to sleep. Today, my head's still ringing. Scott's words might only be scraps from a dream until I hear his car.

"Kurt? Kurt, hon?" Patti knocks on my bedroom door and it slowly creaks open. "That boy, Scott, is downstairs. He says something about taking you on a Captains' Hunt. I never heard of a Captains' Hunt. He said it's a tradition." Patti sticks her head farther into my room and stage-whispers, "I don't much care for Mr. Man's attitude, by the way."

I nod at her while working up the energy to stand.

"He said only current and future captains are invited," Patti continues, not whispering anymore but keeping her voice confidential. "Are you going to be captain of the team, Kurt? Why didn't you say something, hon? That's something to be real proud of."

It feels like a hundred dentist drills are tapping holes in my skull. A Captains' Hunt? Did Scott mention that to me last night? Honestly, everything is fuzzy.

"Uhhh . . ."

"You get dressed, hon, and sort it out with Mr. God's Gift downstairs."

"Kurt." I hear Scott calling up from Patti's living room. "Come on, man. You're messing with a sacred tradition. We got to go. Can't be late. I told you to be ready last night."

"That boy's too bossy for my tastes," Patti says under her breath. "I don't care if he *is* the quarterback. Someone forgot to teach him his manners."

"Coming," I groan. "Puh-puh-Patti, wuh-wuh-would you mind getting me some aspuh-puh-prin?"

"Sure thing, hon," she says. "I heard you were the reason we beat Robbindale. Two parents called me last night. Never even met them. They phoned just to tell me how good 'my boy' was." As she chuckles her lungs rattle with loose phlegm until it turns into a wet cough, then dies down. "I was planning a real breakfast for you today," Patti says. "I went out and got eggs and bacon and toaster waffles and I even splurged and got the real syrup, the stuff from trees. I was going to give my star a lumberjack breakfast like he deserves."

"Kurt!" Scott shouts up the stairs.

"Kuh-kuh-coming," I yell back.

"Hold your horses," Patti snaps down the stairs. Then to me she mutters, "Someone got distracted when they were raising that one."

"Can we have that buh-buh-breakfast tuh-tuh-tomorrow?"

"You betcha. I got to keep the Knights' star and future captain fueled up," Patti says, then lets me alone to get dressed. I sniff my jeans and T-shirt and they don't smell awful. I pull them on, pull a sweatshirt on next, then pull on a wool overcoat Patti got for me from the Salvation Army. I can't get my letter jacket until after the season finishes but it'd be too cold for it today, anyway. The overcoat's too tight in the chest and too short in the arms but it's the closest thing I have to something that fits. Going down the staircase, I lean hard on the handrail. My insteps ache. My thighs burn from overuse and blob-shaped bruises. My left calf pinches every time I take a step, reminding me how someone ground their cleat into it under cover of a gang pile. At the bottom of the stairs, Scott waits with both his arms spread out like he's expecting a sarcastic hug. His sling is gone.

"Hey, big man," he greets me. "Hell of a game last night. We missed you at the party."

"Yuh-your suh-suh-sling is gone." I point with my chin.

"Sure is, Sherlock Holmes," Scott says. "Not a moment too soon, either, before Warner starts thinking he actually had something to do with last night's win. Speaking of the win, there's a good chance you or Terrence might get prep athlete of the week. If you get it twice in a season Coach'll have to get a PO box for all your recruiting letters."

That's a sweet little thought, and despite my groggy brain, aching body, and the fact that Scott Miller stands in Patti's living room like he's the landlord, I give up a half grin.

"A Cuh-cuh-cuh-Captains' Hunt?" I ask.

"Yeah," Scott says. "It's tradition. Cold out today, though. Good thing you got that coat . . . but the bum you took it from might miss it."

"I heard that," Patti says, walking back into the living room with a glass of water and two aspirin. She narrows her eyes at Scott while handing me the pills. "Some people's children," she mutters. This fails to stuff his smirk.

"Thanks." I take the aspirin from Patti and swallow them with the glass of water.

"You need something to eat," she says to me and me only. "Can't take aspirin on an empty stomach."

"Wuh-wuh-we'll get duh-duh-drive-through." Now that Coach's been giving me even more money, drive-through's my breakfast of choice on weekends and even a few days before school. It's cheap and fills me up.

"Let's go, superstar," Scott says. "We need to get a move on." He's already stepping through the front door, so he misses Patti shaking her head back and forth at him. I hold up both palms in apology.

Patti sheeshes. "Sure hope this Captains' Hunt is worth it."

"Me tuh-tuh-tuh-too."

"You be safe, Kurtis," Patti tells me. "You guys won't actually be hunting, will you? Especially with that one?" Patti flips her chin to the doorway, meaning Scott.

I shrug my shoulders, not knowing the answer.

"I wouldn't trust him as far as I could throw him," she says.

Good advice, I think, and step out of her house, then get into the Camaro. Patti stays at the door, lighting a cigarette and retying her housecoat against the chill of the outside air.

"Your orphan-mom's a drag, huh?" Scott says once we're sealed inside his car. Soon as he backs out her driveway and turns around, Scott guns the engine and pops the clutch. The big tires squeal against the sleepy street, loud and sharp enough to scalp me.

"We'll make a quick stop for food and then you can settle in 'cause were driving about two hours north," Scott says. "Tommy's granddad has some land up there we're going to use."

"Fuh-fuh-for what?"

"You'll see." Scott glances at me, giving no hint. "By the way, you ever hunted before?"

"No."

"Well, there's a first for everything, right?"

"It's juh-juh-just us?"

"Whatsa matter, bro? I'm not good enough? I'm the benched quarterback and suddenly I'm chopped liver?" Scott asks in a voice that's mostly—but not completely—joking.

"Yeah," I answer back, mostly—but not completely—joking.

"Tommy's taking Pullman," Scott says. "Mike's taking Wally Peters and I'm taking you. Just the six of us. Time to pass the torch to the future seniors. Of course, technically, you're way beyond junior, probably way beyond senior, but that's our secret, right?"

Scott says this like he knows I've been held back in school because of being tossed around group homes. Only way he could know any of it is through Tom's cop dad digging up dirt on Meadow's House. Or maybe Patti and Coach have more heart-to-heart conversations than I realize. Maybe Coach confides in his captains. I ignore the comment as best I can.

"Don't fuh-fuh-fuh-forget to suh-suh-suh-stop for fuh-fuh-fuh-food," I stutter hard, and wipe quickly at the spit leaking down my lip. Scott takes his time watching me. I pull a twenty out of my pocket, part of the fifty Coach slipped me last night after the game.

"Son, you are the definition of a soldier," Coach said, bringing me into his office after the victory, shaking my hand, crumpling the paper bills into my palm. "Missing our starting quarterback, getting no blocking from our line, and you let it roll off you like water off a duck. You treat yourself to a nice dinner, feed those muscles. You deserve it. Next week, we'll talk with Coach Stein about your supplements. The D-bol's good but there's better stuff, more potent weapons, for you if you're interested in staying a champion."

Scott swings the Camaro into the drive-through lane. I order three pancake-and-egg breakfasts. Scott orders two Egg McMuffins. After we get our food, Scott smokes the drive-through, leaving a patch of rubber and a blue cloud fouling up the cashier's window. With his mouth open with raw laughter, the first bite of his Egg McMuffin lolls around his tongue.

As we drive, the distance between houses slowly grows until lawns turn into fields and finally give way to acres of fallow farmland. Rows of broken, brown cornstalks race along outside our windows, hypnotizing me.

"You got a big appetite," Scott says. "It get that way from the 'roids or you always eat that much?"

Scott's question surprises me. "I always eat thuh-thuh-this way."

"I eat lots but it picked up after I started popping. 'Course it ain't like Mike or Tommy. They're always shoveling the food in but that's 'cause they're into the heavier stuff. They're shooting the shit in their asses, now. Once I saw the needles and syringes, I was like, no thanks, I'll keep my pills, you can have your AIDS and shit. I mean, I don't need it that bad. Besides, quarterback's a finesse position, that's what Rick used to say. Game's mostly brute force but a quarterback's the thinker. Quarterback's an artist, he'd say."

"Who's Ruh-ruh-Rick?"

"Older brother. Never got to play quarterback. Coach made him a free safety. He owned that position, though.

Got four interceptions one game, ran three of them back for touchdowns. No one'll touch that record."

"Wuh-where's he puh-play now?"

"Now?" Scott repeats my question before answering. "Now he's dead. Got killed in Bumfuckistan. Dumbass signed up to fight the towel-heads even though he'd been offered a partial scholarship to the university. Said a partial ride was an insult. If that's the best they can do, he said, then screw 'em, he'd go with an organization that would pay his full ride. The army."

I don't say anything back, just watch the rows of corn zip past our windshield.

"You know the best thing about seeing all those recruiting letters come in for me?" Scott asks. "It's getting the chance to remind them about Rick, remind them they didn't offer him a dime even though he was twice the athlete I am. Didn't touch the pills, either. Totally clean. Dumb fucking schools don't know shit."

"Suh-suh-so you're ruh-ruh-rejecting all of them?"

"You think I'm an idiot?" Scott slaps the steering wheel. "Of course not. Just 'cause I don't like what they did to Rick doesn't mean I won't take their scholarship money. But it's fun making them squirm first when they call, acting like they're my best friend." Scott stomps on the accelerator. The Camaro races down the two-lane highway for a few miles before either of us speaks.

"Dude," Scott says, clearing his throat. "Where'd those scars come from?"

I finger the dashboard for a second, deciding what to reveal. Maybe it's because Scott tells me about his older brother, Rick, that I decide to do more than shrug. "Tuh-

tuh-too young to ruh-ruh-remember," I say, staring out at the rows of corn. "They tuh-tuh-tuh-told me a boiling puh-puh-pot landed on me."

"Yeah, right." Scott snorts. "After someone threw it at you."

I close my eyes, recall shouts and crashing glass and then a hand clamping around my neck, lifting me up, carrying me into the kitchen, holding me over a glowing stove coil. My memory drops off at that point. Remnants surface when I'm real angry or scared and the world around me erupts into orange-red fire. After the stove coil, the next thing I can remember were these new voices, different voices, and friendly adults surrounding me. I guess I was two or three at the time.

"Yuh-yuh-you're right," I answer.

"So you're saying your mom did that to you?"

"No." I shake my head, refusing to think that. "Puh-puh-probably the guh-guh-guy she was with."

"Your dad."

"Naw, he wuh-wuh-wuh-wouldn't do that to me."

"How do you know?"

I don't.

"Sounds like your old man and my old man would get along real good," Scott says. "What about the long scar? It looks like you were in a knife fight or something."

"That kuh-kuh-came later, at another puh-puh-place. The guh-guh-guy running it did it with a suh-suh-suh-scissors one night."

"No shit!"

"He tuh-tuh-told the doctors that my buh-buh-best friend did it to me and that I buh-buh-broke my fuh-fuh-friend's arm in a fuh-fuh-fight. They buh-buh-believed him. They always buh-buh-buh-believed him. Every time."

"That's pretty hard-core, dude."

"Yeah."

The food starts settling in my stomach, making me drowsy. I shut my eyes for good as the aspirin helps my head. The ache over my eyes simmers down to an irritating buzz.

"All right, sleepyhead, wake up, we're almost there." Scott jostles the sleeve of my coat. I open my eyes. We're still driving along a two-lane county road splitting patches of harvested corn, plowed dirt, and green grass. Grain silos sit off in the distance like fat missiles waiting to launch. Small herds of cows and sheep dot the green fields.

"In case you didn't know, shooting a cow while hunting deer or pheasant doesn't count," Scott says. "And that ain't no joke. The farmers around here get real ornery about their property and their livestock."

"Nuh-nuh-no cows. Got it."

The green fields crack open into bramble brush and trees. The cracks widen into little forests that spread farther and farther. The few leaves still attached to the trees are the color of old pennies. Scott slows and turns off onto a dirt road that seems more like someone's private driveway. A big "No Trespassing" sign is posted on a pole about fifty feet down the road. I remember the same signs strung along the trees up at the quarry. Wish we were heading there instead.

We drive another mile or so until coming upon Studblatz's red pickup and Tom's blue Mustang pulled over to the side of the dirt road. White vapors wisp out of their tailpipes while their engines idle. As we slowly roll past, I see Wally Peters and Pullman in the passenger seats. Scott steers us half off the road and my side settles into the embankment as we park.

"All right. Let's do this," Scott says. As I get out of the car, the brisk air slaps at my cheeks, picking at my scars. I button up the collar of my raggedy coat.

"You going to a funeral or something?" Jankowski asks me. "What kind of hunting coat is that?"

"Didn't know wuh-wuh-we were going hunting," I say, never mind I don't own a hunting jacket.

"Hey, Kurt," Wally Peters greets me. "My dad told me to tell you good game last night." Wally seems pretty happy at the moment. He's holding a can of beer. So are Studblatz, Pullman, and Tom.

"Thanks."

"Yeah, man, you dismantled their secondary," Pullman says, then slurps from his can.

I nod in reply since my stuttering seems to get worse around Studblatz and Jankowski and I'm not in the mood for their jokes. Scott opens his trunk and starts rummaging. Along with the spare tire squatting in the center, there's a Maglite, gas tank, sports bag, and a semi-deflated basketball. There are also two cases of beer wedged into the back corner and two long, skinny canvas bags, making an X across all the junk. Scott grabs the first canvas bag, silk-screened in camouflage green, and slides out a shotgun. He hands the heavy, cold thing to me. He grabs the other canvas bag, which is all black, and slides out his own shotgun. The only difference I notice between the two guns is the wood on his stock is a cherry red and mine is a plainer walnut brown.

"You boys ready?" Scott asks, resting his shotgun, barrel up, against the fender of his car. He reaches into the trunk to unwedge one of the beer cases when the barrel of his shotgun starts sliding along the Camaro's smooth molded fender. Scott stops it from tipping over with his foot, balancing on one leg himself. "Here ya go," he says, pulling out two beers, handing one to me. I put the cold can up to my lips and swallow back a big mouthful, hoping to wash down the alarm growing in my gut. The thought of drinking so early doesn't make me nearly as sick as I imagined. At least I've already had breakfast.

"Now, the point of any good hunting trip is to get really shit-faced," Scott says, cracking open his own can and sucking it down.

"Well, I'm about halfway there already," Wally Peters chortles. He'll be Studblatz's replacement after Mike graduates. Wally will need lots more size and the temper of a rabid wolverine to equal Studblatz.

"Yeah, me too," Pullman says. Pullman's been ass-kissing his captains ever since Chandre Jackson beat him up and put Scott's shoulder out of commission two weeks ago. Pullman knows he was manhandled all game. Might be my imagination, but I'm sure he's already added more bulk in just the last two weeks. I wonder if our coaches had a private meeting about the powers of D-bol with Pullman as well. To make up for the loss of Jankowski next year, he'll need something.

"Good," Scott says. "Okay, rule one is the future captains have got to drink twice what the current captains drink. You've got to show us your fortitude, show us you have what it takes. Show us you're men, not pussies. We've got plenty of beer here, so don't be shy. Rule two is you've got to bag something before we leave. Lots of pheasants in the fields just past this tree line. They'd look real nice on the mantel. But if you get desperate and we're all getting cold, then, there's plenty of squirrels and crows hanging out, too stupid to run or fly away. It don't get much easier than that."

"All right," Wally cheers. "Gonna bag me a mean ol' squirrel." He reaches into Studblatz's pickup and pulls out his shotgun from the gun rack mounted against the back window. He starts waving it around in a way that makes me real nervous. Studblatz frowns as he snatches the gun away from Wally.

"How about we get past our cars before you start shooting," he says.

"But that's the spirit, Wally," Scott encourages. "And I toast that. Drink up, men." Scott holds his can up to his lips and empties his first beer, Adam's apple working like a piston. Finished, he wipes his sleeve across his mouth and power belches. "You know what that means, right, future captains? You each have to finish two cans. Now let's get drinking." With a wink, Scott hands me another can, so I'm holding two. No way can I drink both of these this early, but everyone seems real interested in me at the moment. So I finish the first one, then make a face and belch. My headache does soften, though, I have to admit.

"Attaboy," Scott says. "One more to go. I'll even let you bring it with us."

I sip from the second can. "Guh-guh-gotta take a puh-puh-piss," I announce, and walk down the embankment to the trees. Facing the trunk of a big oak, I unzip and tip out most of the second beer onto the bed of leaves at my feet while relieving myself. I return, still holding my can, sipping air from it. By now everyone has a can of beer in one hand and a shotgun in the other. Except Scott. He holds a shotgun in each hand.

"Let's go," Scott says.

I grab a dozen beers out of the first case and stow them in the gym bag Scott tosses me. Both Wally and Pullman sling their own bags of beer. I don't know how many Wally's already had before we arrived but he's already weaving a squiggly path through the woods. I ain't real excited about walking next to him while he swings around a loaded gun at anything that moves.

"All right, here's where it begins." Scott stops us about two hundred yards into the thin forest. From this point, you can see the beginning of farm fields to our left. "Each captain, take your future captain off in a different direction. Stud and Wally, you guys head that way. Tommy and Pullman, you guys go due west. Me and Kurt'll go this way. Before we separate, another toast."

Scott slugs down his can and drops it, forcing me, Wally, and Pullman to each take two cans for ourselves. Wally upends his and swallows it down no problem. He's either going to be sick or pass out, but no way is he shooting anything other than a tree or a cornstalk or sky. Pullman drinks his first one a little slower, and while everyone focuses on him and Wally, I pour most of mine into the ground, pretending to tie my shoe. I stand up and tip the can to my mouth, swallowing what I haven't spilled, about a quarter can.

"One more to go," Scott says. Tom and Mike laugh. I drink half the next can and wait. Wally, it seems, isn't really worried about pacing himself, which fascinates the other guys. By the end of his second can, he stumbles backward as he's emptying it and falls on his butt. While everyone guffaws, I tip my can into the leaves. Pullman, too, starts to shuffle his feet while standing and swings his head around, trying, but failing, to track whoever's speaking.

"Okay, men. Go forth. Bring me feathers of fowl . . . or at least a squirrel pelt," Scott commands us. "Mike and Tommy, look after these guys," Scott says. "They're the team's future."

I'm guessing Wally's probably had a six-pack to himself already. Pullman maybe four or five. While I've emptied four, I've actually only drunk one and a half.

"Let's go, superstar," Scott says. He holds out the shotgun with the walnut-brown stock and I grab it like I do this all the time. The steel barrel is icy in my fingers. I watch Scott tuck his gun so the wood stock wedges under his armpit and the barrel rests over his forearm; his hands aren't even touching it. I imitate him. It's easy to carry this way and even lets me tuck my hands into my pockets to keep them warm. I figure shooting the thing just means pulling the trigger. Scott must be reading my thoughts.

"Shotguns are simple," he says. "Like a camera. Just point and shoot. It's a twelve-gauge, so you get a pretty solid shot pattern, about a foot across. There's a little safety switch by the trigger. See that?" He holds up his gun and shows me a little thumb lever that he slides forward and back. I examine my gun and find the same lever. "Push it forward and the safety is off," Scott says. "Now you can shoot. Slide it back and the safety is on and the trigger is locked. That's about it. Now time for another beer."

I dutifully reach into the beer bag and hand Scott a can and take one out for myself. Scott chugs it likes he's been in a desert for a week. I whistle like I'm impressed, my own can tipped upside down at my side, draining into the forest, while Scott's still drinking. When he finishes I bring my own can up and swallow back the remaining mouthful in my can. "You got one more to go," Scott reminds me. "Chugalug that bad boy."

I've got no choice with the next can since he's standing there watching me. I drink the whole beer and feel my stomach push out with air. I belch with gusto, like I'm calling out to a musk ox. Scott answers this by swinging his gun up into the air and not aiming or anything, just pulling the trigger.

KABOOM!

The blast punches my ears, almost leveling me. I hear nothing but mosquitoes buzzing for the next minute while my head tightens up. No way do I want to be near that again or shoot my own. Scott looks supremely satisfied, like he just taught my dumb ass how to make fire or something. Two *boom-boom*s answer us from the direction of Mike and Wally and then another *boom* off to our left from the direction of Tom and Pullman. Scott raises his barrel to the sky again. I juggle my cold gun and clap my hands over my ears just in time.

Kaboom.

Scott's gun arm jerks with the sharp recoil of the blast. My ears, protected this time by my hands, are still jarred, but at least the explosion doesn't hurt.

"That's the call of the wild, baby." Scott laughs. "Call of the wild." The last full can of beer I just finished starts making me feel light, but not light enough to fly away from him and the others.

"Give me another beer," Scott orders. He drinks this time without noticing I haven't pulled one out for myself. We continue walking through the woods. My hearing slowly returns. The ringing mostly disappears but the headache still hovers. After a while, I notice the sound of my footsteps again, crunching the dried leaves and snapping small twigs. The wind plays through the tree branches in shushing gusts that bring old leaves fluttering down on us like ashes.

"Where you going, superstar?" Scott calls out. I turn around. I've gotten about thirty feet ahead of him without trying. He walks a little unsteady, his gun tucked back under his arm, its barrel pointing down at the ground. "You trying to lose me out here?" Scott asks, then laughs at his own question. "I know this area real good and you're just the rookie. *You* should be afraid of getting lost. *Not me.*" I ignore him, turn forward, and keep walking, maybe even moving a little faster. "You're the one that needs my help," he calls out again. "You think you can just waltz onto my team—*my team*—and take it over? You think Tommy and Studblatz will stand for that? You've got to pay your dues, rookie. You think just 'cause I'm on the bench, that I'm not the team captain anymore? The recruiting letters are still coming. Coach told me so. So I don't need some freak shooting off his mouth and making up stories about me and Tommy and Mike. Hell, if it wasn't for me, you'd've never gotten lucky with Marcia. Those girls drew straws and she lost. She had to down four vodkas at Mike's party before I could convince her to go with you. And she'll fuck anything."

I say nothing. I continue walking, hoping he'll shut up. For about thirty seconds my wish comes true. Then it ends.

"Gunderson killed himself 'cause he was weak, like Coach said," Scott hollers out suddenly, like we've been discussing the suicide all morning. "Had nothing to do with us."

I stop for a second, but don't turn around. The sight of him, and that smirk I know he's wearing, will be too much, probably make me want to tackle him and pound his head against the nearest tree trunk. I hear the rush of alcohol in his words, hear how it slurs them together, hear how he's only able to speak Ronnie's name because of it.

"You know what you duh-duh-*did*," I shout over my shoulder plenty loud for him to hear. "You and Muh-muh-muh-Mike and Tuh-tuh-tuh-Tom. All of you know wuh-wuh-what you duh-duh-did."

"Is that a threat, Mr. Wah-wah-wah-Wolf?" Scott shouts back. He must have stopped walking because he sounds even more distant. I still can't bring myself to turn and face him. "Are you threatening to snitch on us? Because it's your word against ours. And no one's going to believe a murderer. We all know about you, K-K-K-K-Kurt," Scott taunts. "Tom's dad found out. You may be the superstar right now but no one's gonna believe a psycho's word against your captains'."

"Yuh-yuh-yuh-you *know* what you *did*!" I shout again, unable to help myself. Wanting my words to hit home, I turn around in time to find Scott about seventy feet back with his shotgun lifted and aimed in my direction.

"What *you* did, Mr. Wolf. What *you* did!" he yells, and I know it's coming then. I drop just as the blast roars out from his gun. Twelve-gauge shot rips the branches and leaves over my head.

Son of a bitch.

I lie there for a second, stunned, then hoist my gun up, intent on using it. I peek out from behind an old, rotted-out tree trunk and see Scott standing there, his gun tucked back under his arm, barrel facing down.

"Come on out, Mr. Wolf," Scott shouts. "It was an accident. Hunting accidents happen all the time out here. Especially when guys are drinking and shooting. Probably more common than suicide, I bet."

Son of a bitch! Son of a bitch! Son of a bitch! I stand up, my heavy cold gun trained on Scott. Slowly I walk toward him, keeping the gun as steady as my furious, trembling hands will allow.

"Don't be mad, now," Scott says. "It was an accident. I thought I saw a squirrel in the tree above you is all." He starts giggling. "I wasn't aiming for you. It just went off while you were near where I was aiming."

"Sh-sh-sh-*shut up*!"

"Look, it's okay. As long as we understand each other.

As long as you realize this is real serious stuff: you talking shit in practice, shouting the little fag's name at Studblatz, *defacing* our lockers. And remember, their captain doesn't even know what happened. Unless you told him. He didn't see anything. He was tied up under the mats. It's your word against all of ours."

"Yuh-yuh-yuh-you're wrong!" I continue walking toward him. His gun is still pointing down. I can't remember whether the safety switch is supposed to be forward or back, so I keep my thumb on it ready to flick either way.

"Wrong about what, Mr. Wah-wah-wah-Wolf?" Scott taunts, that smirk of his returning. I almost pull the trigger just to blow that smirk away forever. "About the fact that it was you that came into that room and did all those things to that little fag? That me, Mike, and Tom tried to stop you but it was too late? That you learned all that dirty crap at the orphanage where you killed that kid? Once you do somethin' like that you can't quit. You're a repeat offender. That's what Tom's dad calls it. And he's a cop. He knows how your sick mind works."

"Suh-suh-someone else was in that stuh-stuh-stuh-storage room. Hidden in the kuh-kuh-corner. Behind the muh-muh-muh-mats. Suh-suh-suh-saw all of you. He knows the truh-truh-truth and he'll tuh-tuh-tuh-tell it." My mind buzzes with possibility and threat. My clumsy words ricochet off Scott's drunk forehead and it takes a moment for him to consider them. Then he shakes off his doubt.

"*Sure* someone was in that room." Scott sneers. "They were using an invisible cape, I bet. Just hanging out, watching us drill that faggot and not saying anything, huh?"

"Duh-duh-duh-Danny Meehan," I spit. "Suh-suh-sophomore. Suh-suh-small as Ronnie. Afraid if he tuh-tuh-tuh-tried to suh-suh-suh-stop you, he'd end up like Ruh-ruh-Ronnie. Probably right."

Scott's face changes, doesn't look so smug as he weighs the possibility I'm not bluffing, then wonders how screwed he might be. Injecting that doubt and fear into Scott is worth spilling Danny's name; feels as powerful as casting a hex on Scott for how his lips pinch together and his cheeks turn white. "Duh-duh-Danny Meehan knows everything, suh-suh-saw everything. He'll tuh-tuh-tell the world. It's not thuh-thuh-three against one. It's luh-luh-luh-liars against truh-truh-truth. And I duh-duh-duh-did not kuh-kuh-kill Lamar. He's my buh-buh-buh-best friend. *Ever!* You duh-duh-don't know about that. Neither does Tuh-tuh-tuh-Tom's duh-duh-duh-dad."

A ripple crosses Scott's brow while he digests this new information. By now I've closed within a barrel length from him. When he starts to raise his gun, I leap at him, wrapping my cold fingers around the long steel barrel, ripping it from his hands same time it goes off.

KABOOM!

The barrel jerks in my grip as shot sprays off to my left. Eardrum feels blown and I can barely hear but I see Scott's eyes widen in fright. His empty hands rise to his shoulders like I'm sticking him up. His mouth opens and the sounds he makes are dull, muffled.

"Easy, Mr. Wolf," he says. "I was about to hand it over."

That name again! It's too much. I raise my own gun and aim it at the sky then pull the trigger. Nothing. I flip the safety switch and pull again. The hammer draws back and then clicks. Nothing happens. It's not even loaded. *Son of a bitch!* I'm such an idiot! They all know it, too! I throw my empty gun like a spear, hurling it as far as I can into the woods, aiming for a tree trunk, hoping to smash it. The gun misses, sailing harmlessly into the underbrush. I flip Scott's gun into my right hand and pull the trigger.

KABOOM!

The thunder splits my head wide open. My trusty companion, pain, wraps me in its arms. I pull the trigger again, ready to pull it ten more times, but the gun clicks dead. Deafness helps cocoon me. I swing Scott's gun like a bat and let go, watching it fly end over end into the forest. I holler loud as I can, but my own voice sounds distant and cottony to my beaten ears. I search the forest for an answer or even a clue. Nothing comes out to greet me except high-pitched ringing.

"We're guh-guh-guh-going home," I tell him.

"Shit. What about my guns?"

"Fuh-fuh-fuh-fuck your guns. You luh-luh-luh-lost them in an accident," I tell him. "Accidents happen all the tuh-tuh-tuh-time out here, ruh-ruh-remember? Often as three kuh-kuh-captains kuh-kuh-killing a boy."

Scott's mouth opens but nothing comes out. I drop his bag of beer.

"Let's. Go," I say, shoving him in the chest. He stumbles but keeps his balance. We walk a fast pace back to his Camaro. I'm tired of guns and beer and threats and fearing my captains.

"Wuh-wuh-we're leaving," I announce when we reach his car.

"But what about the other guys?"

"Duh-duh-duh-don't care."

"I'm not leaving."

"Then guh-guh-guh-give me your kuh-kuh-keys."

Scott changes his mind, gets his keys, and we take off. He weaves on the road, so I keep my hand near the steering wheel, ready to correct him. Sometimes I bark orders at him just to watch his reaction. He flinches when I do this and it makes me feel powerful, having something over the homecoming king and star quarterback. Making our great leader wince feels good. He won't control me. I'll control him. Telling him about Danny was stupid, I admit that. But I can't help it. Watching all that doubt cloud Scott's perfect face feels good. Let him worry and fear like the rest of us, if only for a moment. This isn't over and I'll pay for it, later. So will Danny. But for the rest of the ride home in that golden Camaro, I hold all the power and that's worth something.

D A N N Y

Vikings game starts in less than two hours and I'm still raking the yard. I promised to have it finished by the time Dad gets home from his Sunday rounds at the hospital so we won't miss opening kickoff. The air is cold enough for my nose to run, but the blue-sky sun bakes my flannel shirt so I'm unbuttoning it and my hair is hot to the touch. It feels nice. Raking up the coffee-and-plum-colored leaves goes faster when I pretend I'm collecting sloughed-off dragon scales. Once the pile's big enough, and it's already pretty big, I plan on falling into the crinkly bed like it's a crash mat before bagging the whole thing for the compost drop-off.

I've cleared most the front lawn when an old beater pulls into our driveway. The rusted-out car grovels for a new muffler and a sooty cloud trails from its exhaust pipe.

When it shuts off, the engine coughs a few times before finally giving up. Squinting, I lift a work-gloved hand to block out autumn's low sun hitting my eyes. I find Kurt stepping from the car. His visit is unexpected and sets off a mix of warmth and dread. My friend, my gut warns, is about to deliver bad news.

"You told him?!?!?" I shout and whine at the same time. "You told Scott I was there? That I saw what they did to Ronnie? Why? What were you thinking? Jesus, I'm dead. I'm dead. I can't believe this!"

"Cuh-cuh-calm duh-duh-down."

"*You* calm down. *You're* the one that told them I saw the whole thing."

"They're tuh-tuh-trying to buh-buh-blame me for it," Kurt says, as if that's a good enough reason to give me up. "Suh-suh-Scott suh-suh-said they'll tuh-tuh-tell everyone I'm a muh-muh-murderer. You and Buh-buh-Bruce have to stop tuh-tuh-tagging."

"Fine. We won't tag their lockers anymore. But you shouldn't have told them about me. I'm dead. They're gonna kill me."

"No they wuh-wuh-won't."

"Kurt, if they could get away with it, you know they would," I say. "You saw what they did to Ronnie, the way they enjoyed it, enjoyed torturing him. People like me and Ronnie don't matter to them. We're just obstacles to them, not . . . you know . . . people."

Kurt listens and then, after a long moment, nods his head. "Yeah," he says, agreeing with me in a way that I don't want him to, in a way that sends a shiver along my neck and scalp. I slap the rake against our fence in frustration. Kurt just stands there, hands jammed into his pockets, not helping. Then his head jerks as if a thought's come over him. I'm waiting, expectant, ready to hear some brilliant plan that's occurred to him that will save me, make everything all right. Instead, he walks over to my pile of leaves and steps around the edges. He crouches down, pressing on the top of the pile with his hands, testing its firmness and cushion. Satisfied, he stands up and turns his back to the pile, concentrates for a few moments, and then springs. His hands crash through the leaves and his legs whip over into a clunky back handspring. While he won't win any style points, he does make it safely around, landing somewhere between his feet and knees. Despite my building fear at the news he brings, I can't help but be impressed by his trick. He's really learned how to do a back handspring. It's ugly, but it counts.

"Whip your legs over faster and don't let your elbows bend," I say instinctively, not forgetting why he's come here but glad to distract myself for a moment. Kurt dusts off his hands. Leaf crumbs stick to his hair, pants, and shirt. He goes back to the edge and tries it again. This time he keeps his elbows locked like I instructed. He makes it all the way to his feet, finishing in a crouch. "Better," I say. Kurt nods at me from his squat in the pile, like some sort of Baby Huey five-year-old. The big bastard has the start of a smile on his face and I can tell he's pretty satisfied with his improvement. He does one more, just as good as the earlier one.

"Maybe you should come out for our sport instead," I say, leaning against my rake handle. Kurt wipes his hands along his jeans and shirt, then pulls stray leaves off his shoulders and knees. He steps out of the pile and walks up to me. He is still huge.

"Buh-buh-be buh-buh-brave, Danny," he tells me.

"Easy for you to say. You're the Incredible Hulk and I'm, like . . . Snoopy."

"Muh-more like Suh-suh-Spider-Man."

"I wish," I say, though I like that Kurt thinks that about me.

"Yuh-yuh-you like Buh-buh-Batman?" he asks, reaching into his jeans pocket and pulling out his cell phone, flipping it open. Guess he'd rather keep the phone in his pocket when he does handsprings than risk leaving it behind again.

"He's all right. Kinda seems like a pussy, though, without his utility belt and all his gizmos. I mean, if he's naked, he ain't really worth crap."

"We need a Buh-buh-Bat Signal," Kurt says, then explains what he means. I drop my rake and go into the house to get my phone.

K U R T

I leave Danny's house, not sure if I've helped or hurt. Probably hurt. I got no excuse for giving up his name except that it felt real good to watch those shadows of doubt and fear cross Scott's face. But that makes me responsible for Danny, now. He needs to keep his eyes open, but I need to be there for him because what he said about those three's the truth. They'll do whatever's needed to keep us quiet.

Driving home in Patti's car, I'm still picking bits of leaves off my shirt. Waiting at a red light, I flip open my phone wondering if the Bat Signal idea will work. I guess we'll find out since it isn't a question of *if* Scott will try something, but *when*. When will he have an opportunity? How will he get Danny or Bruce alone? I don't have any answers yet, but if I try and think like Scott, maybe I'll see his plans ahead of time. Scott's closer to thinking like Crud Bucket than I want to admit, and that scares me. As for my own plan to stop him . . . well . . . I can't really say I have one yet.

A scrap of leaf falls out of my hair and rests on my nose. I wipe it off, thinking back on my last handspring in the raked pile. It felt good, sparked the only decent idea I've had yet. Maybe I need to go back and practice that trick for a few more hours until I come up with an actual plan. Or maybe I need to hit the weight room to clear my head and give myself some more ideas. I can sneak through the janitor's entrance. I'd have the whole place to myself on a Sunday afternoon.

Red and blue lights start flashing just past the intersection, breaking my concentration. I'm holding out hope they're for someone else, but the siren lets out two short squawks and the cruiser slides up close enough to almost bump me.

This is bad. I still don't have my license. Patti's going to kill me. Gotta get out of here!

I stomp on the gas.

Patti's car doesn't like that idea one bit. Unlike Scott's Camaro, her car jerks and snorts and then sputters and there's no way I'm outrunning a cop car. I got no choice but to brake and pull over to the side of the road. As I turn off the car, I try thinking of a good excuse for why I don't have a license. I'm also trying to figure out why he's pulling me over. I didn't run the light. I wasn't speeding.

A sharp rap on the driver's window jolts me from my thoughts. The nightstick hits hard enough I expect the glass to spiderweb. I roll down the window, afraid to look at the officer. I keep my face aimed at the road and, in side glances, take in the blue uniform from chest to belt. No head. No knees. Mostly belly, badge, and the gun butt that one hand rests on while the other grips the nightstick.

"Kurt Brodsky," the voice says. Not friendly, not mean, more like a vice principal taking roll in detention. Not sure how he knows my name.

"Step out of the car," the officer tells me. He hasn't asked for my license yet. That's good. I think. I get out of the car, and as I straighten up, the squat officer with a bristly flattop and Oakley wraparound glasses prods my shoulder with the stick. "Go ahead and turn around, put your hands on the roof of the car and spread your legs."

"Huh?"

"Do as you're told," he says, assuming my confusion is defiance. Maybe I'd be better off if he did just ask for my license. I turn and put my hands on the rust-pocked car top. "Spread your legs. Wider. *Wider*. That's it."

Over my shoulder, I hear cars slowing as they pass us, trying to take in my bust for . . . what? I duck my head down, not wanting anyone to recognize me. The officer's hands quickly pat up the insides and outsides of my ankles, knees, thighs, and crotch then jump along my belly, armpits, and arms. I think he's done, so I take my hands off the car.

"Don't move, you hear me? Do *not* move. Hands back up on the car. Keep those legs spread." This time the solid end of his baton pokes into my lower back and then the thing whacks the insides of my knees to spread them wider. I move my feet farther apart. The baton swings up between my legs, tags me in the 'nads, tags me hard enough that I instinctively jump from the sharp pain and my hands come down to cup my nuts protectively. The sharp bite flowers into nausea.

"I said, don't move. You deaf, too?" A hand shoves me up against the car.

What the . . .

"Put your hands behind your back. Now!" I uncup myself. My chest is pressing against the roof of the car and I'm off balance. I offer him my hands behind my back, feel hard steel clasp first my right wrist and then my left wrist. The handcuffs click down until they're gnawing at my bone and that's when I break into a sweat.

"Whu-whu-what did I do?"

The officer doesn't answer, just grabs my right elbow and tugs backward so I'm no longer leaning chest-first against Patti's car. Still using my elbow to steer, he pivots me, then pokes his nightstick into my lower back, prodding me toward his cruiser.

Shit!

Traffic is definitely slowing to take all this in, so I dip my chin and let my hair fall in front of my face. He pulls open the back door of his squad car.

"Get in," he says. My heart's racing as I enter. He grabs the top of my head and tries stuffing me into the car faster than I can dip inside. The door slams and I watch through the cage divider and the windshield as he goes back to Patti's car and starts searching it. I have to sit forward because the cuffs dig into my wrists otherwise. I have rights, don't I? I try remembering what they taught us in civics class but don't know if I can ask for a lawyer yet. The officer scares me. It scares me being locked up, stuffed in a cage.

Reminds me of Crud Bucket sealing me and Lamar up, telling us he could do whatever he wanted. I'm starting to have trouble breathing and I think maybe I'll have a heart attack, the way my chest is beating in my ears. There's no legroom in the back, and with the windows shut, I can't get any air. There's no air. The officer's coming back and I want to offer him anything, tell him I'll cooperate but just let me out of the back of the car, *please.*

His door opens and I inhale deeply before he gets in and slams it shut. There's a shotgun racked in the front seat next to a computer screen. The police radio's squelching. I can't breathe. The officer's writing something.

"Puh-puh-please, suh-suh-sir. I'm suh-suh-sorry."

"You know who I am?" he asks, but he's staring straight out his windshield, not bothering to turn around.

Who is he? I don't know. I just know I can't really breathe and I think my arms are going numb and I really can't breathe.

"No, suh-suh-sir."

"Officer Jankowski, to you. Not 'sir'. I'm Tom's dad and I got a problem with *boys*"—he hisses this last word— "like you coming into our community."

Tom's dad.

"Offi-suh-suh-sir—"

"Officer Jankowski!" he huffs, and swings his arm up, banging the cage divider with his fist. I flinch from the rattle, feel as weak and small as when Crud Bucket used to come into our room at night.

"You and me, we got a problem," he says, still staring straight out his windshield. "First, you're trash. Pure white trash that's headed for jail one way or another and

I'd be happy as hell to send you back there myself. You understand? I'm going to protect this community from a common thug goes and kills some kid at a group home. Yeah, I don't give a rat's ass what your excuse is, so don't waste your breath."

I press my cheek against the side window, hoping maybe I can get some air through the crack. My panting fogs the glass.

"Second, Tommy tells me his locker was vandalized. Tells me you were in on it, trying to spread some sick rumors about him and Scott and Mike? I don't know what kind of crap is churning in that thug mind of yours but I won't tolerate it. Not for one minute."

"Wasn't muh-muh-me."

He bangs the cage divider again. "Don't give me no sorry-ass excuses! This is your warning. Right here. Right now. Not you, not anyone, is going to derail my boy's career. You so much as whisper another thing about him and I will be happy to pull you over and discover enough meth in that shitty car of yours to put you away for a long time, you understand me? *For life.*"

"Yesssir," I say, closing my eyes, still pressing my cheek against the window, still trying to breathe. I'll tell him whatever he wants to hear as long as I can get out of this cage.

"You know why I stopped you? Huh? Know why I put the cuffs on you and threw you in the back of my squad car?"

I sit, shaking, panting, unable to come up with an answer. He bangs the cage again and I flinch, then I refocus on trying to push my nose through the cold glass for more air.

"Well, do you?" he asks.

"Nuh-nuh-no, suh-suh-sir."

"Because I can." He chuckles. "Because I goddamn can. That's what you need to remember. If anything happens to my boy, I will take you down in ways that will make you wish you stayed over at Lincoln."

It's a long time after Officer Jankowski releases me and pulls away in his squad car that my hands are steady enough to drive. So I sit in Patti's car on the side of the road, gripping the steering wheel, wondering if maybe it wouldn't be better to keep driving as far across the country as her old clunker will take me.

K
U
R
T

D A N Y

Danny,
Meet me in the gym after school
Bruce

Weird.

I find the note crammed up into the vent of my locker after last class Wednesday, the beginning of a four-day weekend. Bruce doesn't write notes. He texts, like everyone else. So I text him asking him what's up with the note, but I get nothing back. The note means he's still scheming and he thinks I'll help, but he's wrong. I'm done provoking the monsters. Now I've got to stop him before he gets us targeted by the whole football team.

Wednesday's our last day of school because of teacher conferences the rest of the week. Teacher union rules forbid sports practices or extracurricular activities of any kind that need to be coached or supervised for the rest of the week—with the one exception being the varsity football game Friday. That means no gymnastics practice, no football practice, no theater rehearsal, no cross-country running. Nothing.

At the promise of four days off, students go nuts. Five minutes after last bell the halls transform into a sea of crumpled notebooks, old tests, torn folders, wadded-up paper towels, and anything else that can be dumped out of a locker like it's Oregrove's very own ticker-tape parade. Girls cluster in groups and squeal for no reason whatsoever. Cigarette smoke drifts out from a bathroom. Guys lay traps for littler guys, pushing us around in a fit of jailbreak fever. I keep to the side of the hallway, surfing the walls, preparing for random shoves with one arm extended as a bumper. Rondo Holmes, the football team's blimpy ball-snapper, sideswipes me. A locker dial bites into my hip bone and Rondo chuckles but otherwise lets me pass without incident. I make it to Bruce's locker, hoping to catch him there and avoid going down to the gym. I don't like going there alone anymore, can barely stand it during regular practice with the whole team there. I text Bruce again while waiting at his locker, trying to blend into the background as much as possible to avoid extra smacks, shoves, and squishes. After ten minutes I still get no reply and he's not showing.

Crap! I've got to go down there, keep him from doing something really stupid.

"Watch it, fat ass!"

I recognize the voice before I even look up from my

phone. It's that supertough goth girl, Tina, who saved me from Jankowski in the hallways. She's at it again. This time she's turning hellcat on Rondo Holmes. Unlike Jankowski, Rondo just looks cowed by the girl.

"You know who runs that Jumbotron, Blubber Boy?" she spits. "Me! I can put your plumber's crack up on the big screen next game, freeze-frame it for the entire half-time show. That will really win over the ladies."

Rondo drops his head and one of his teammates, Pull-man, starts laughing. Rondo shoves Pullman and moves off down the hall, trying to get away from Tina.

"Keep waddling!" she shouts after him. In the crowded hallway, the ones paying attention are laughing. I can't help myself. As she passes I speak.

"That was great!" I tell her. Tina's head flicks at me, eyes narrowed, mouth pouty as if readying to fend off another attack. She sees it's only me and her face softens.

"He deserved it," she says. "Blubber Boy shoved my friend into the wall." Then she smiles. She's got a nice smile.

"You're good at that," I say. "Sticking up for people. I . . . uh . . . never thanked you for that time in the hall with Jankowski."

"Yeah." She nods at me. "I remember thinking you were a total jellyfish after that."

Ouch!

Seeing my reaction, Tina puts her hand up to her mouth. "But then I saw you that night at the gymnastics meet," she races on. "You were flying through the air, doing totally crazy tricks. Better than any martial artist I've ever seen on TV. So if you can do all that stuff, how come you can't stick up for yourself?"

"I . . . uh . . . I don't know. It's not the same."

"Of course it is," she says, then totally switches gears. "I'm sorry about your teammate. I saw you at the funeral, but didn't get a chance to talk."

"Um, it's fine," I say. "I mean, it's not fine. I mean it's okay that we didn't talk."

"I saw you there with Kurt," she says. "He was at your meet, too. You guys pretty good friends?" she asks.

"Yeah," I say, unsure if Kurt would say the same. "He hangs out with me and Bruce and—"

Bruce! Down in the gym! Planning something really stupid as we speak!

"Bruce is waiting for me downstairs," I say. "Gotta go."

"Okay, see ya, Danny."

She knows my name? Cool.

"Bye."

Downstairs, the main locker room is empty. So is our team room. No sign of Bruce, so he must already be in the gym, drawing up revenge plans or pacing the vaulting runway, impatiently waiting for me, his plucky sidekick, to begin our next adventure.

The door to the gymnasium is closed, but I see light seeping under the crack, so someone's in there and has fired up the halogen lamps. Out of nervous habit, I check my phone for a text. Nothing. Doesn't make sense. I think, just as I push open the door, that it's strange I don't hear any music. Ever since the attack, Bruce habitually turns on the team's portable stereo soon as he enters the gym, especially if he's in there alone. Phone in hand, I walk inside, about to shout out his name while texting him at the same time.

My mouth stops.

Across the gym Tom Jankowski squats on a squirming body while Scott Miller stands above them with his arms crossed. It takes another half second to realize it's Bruce that Tom's sitting on, crushing him with his weight.

This time I don't freeze.

This time they won't get away with it. I'll scream bloody murder at the top of my lungs and race out of the gym to get help, get whatever teacher, janitor, or parent remains in the building—even if that means Mrs. Doyle, the old school secretary. I don't care if they call me crybaby or scaredy-cat. Name-calling can't touch the terror pissing through me. I can scamper faster than either Tom or Scott and they're across the gym with Bruce. I have a good head start. I'll be upstairs and have someone back down here in less than a minute. That's all Bruce has to survive for.

Run! my brain screams, spinning me around, preparing me to leap in a single bound the three steps I'd walked into the gym before spotting the ambush. I'll pull open the door, fly through the locker room and out toward safety . . .

. . . except a body stands just to the side of—and now in front of—the door. A big body. A big, mean body with an ugly face.

Studblatz.

He's there, waiting for me, waiting to spring the trap and cut off my escape. Studblatz reaches for my wrist but I yank my arm away and spin from the exit, head into the gym, buying precious seconds. Phone's open and I'm pressing buttons, initiating a final SOS before I'm overrun. No time now. Press send before Studblatz catches me and wrenches down on my arm, breaking my grip on the phone. As Studblatz yanks me toward him, smushing my face into the sour cotton of his sweatshirt, all I can do is pray the Bat Signal's been sent.

"We've been waiting for you, dickweed," Studblatz hisses. A thick arm locks around my head, flattening my nose into his side and rubbing fiber into my eyelids. Blinded, I make my free hand into a fist and flail at him. Might as well be swatting at sandbags. Studblatz laughs at the punches. He releases my head long enough to snatch my flailing wrist out of the air then pin both my arms against my body. I yank back frantically but his grip's too strong. My fright amuses him. Plus something more, something I recognize from the attack on Ronnie. Studblatz is excited. The way his eyes gleam should spur me to fight even harder, scream out, start kicking or scratching—anything! But his excitement, with its unspoken promise to enjoy my hurt, get off on my pain, petrifies me. The more I struggle and beg, the more his eyes light up. That's when my limbs start freezing in terror. Just like last time.

K U R T

Best thing about walking around wearing the big earphones instead of the tiny earbuds is everyone sees you ain't in the mood for conversation. Let your head dip and bob to the rhythm and that's even better, tells anyone watching that you're really feeling your music, having your moment, and you don't need someone coming up to you, interrupting your day, trying to talk. Ninety-nine percent of the world gets it, sees the big earphones and leaves you alone so you don't have to wrestle out a simple hello. Maybe you throw them a head nod, and keep moving, but that's all. Bet if I'd been wearing these the day Jankowski and Studblatz snuck up behind me in the hall, I'd have kept walking, never even noticed they were there, gone straight to class, and never worried about them telling the world I'm a murderer.

End of school looks different with the music switched on. When all you hear is the wailing guitar and pulsing drumbeats, watching guys punch and hip-check other guys is almost poetic, like a music video. People's mouths open and close, open and close, probably cussing, maybe screaming, maybe making plans, but I'll never really know and that's all right with me. I don't want to know. The music pulls me away, pulls me out of the actual world, turns everyone around me into players stepping in and out of my video. It's like a drug, I guess, though I never much thought about it, unplugging me from the world, altering reality—

A tug on my elbow steals my drifting attention. I look down and I see Tina, her mouth moving in almost perfect lip-sync to the wailing demon in my ears. I increase my head bobbing, hoping she'll get the hint—*I'M HAVING A MOMENT. CATCH YOU LATER!*—but she just tugs again. Then her hand actually reaches up and pulls off my left earphone. Man, she is bossy!

"Earth to Kurt. Come in, Kurt!"

"What?" I ask, annoyed until I remember it's her music I'm listening to on my recorder—which I still haven't used for its intended purpose. I lied to Ms. Jinkle, my speech therapist, last time we met, told her I left the thing at home. Truth is I started to record myself but couldn't stand what I sounded like, so I erased it, listened to Tina's mix instead.

"One of my mixes?" Tina asks.

"Naw. It's the muh-muh-Metal Slayer disc you ruh-ripped for me."

"Oh," Tina says, and I can tell she's disappointed I'm

not listening to her Walking in the Rain mix. "What are you doing for the long weekend?" Tina asks.

"Nuh-nuh-nothing. Lifting and ruh-ruh-resting up for the guh-guh-game."

"Wow! You're a crazy man!" Tina teases. "Who knew the jock life was so mind-blowing."

"Muh-muh-maybe I'll listen to yuh-yuh-your music," I add. Tina breaks into a smile, a real smile, not a defensive smile, and I'm glad I told her that.

"Really? Cool. I can make you some more, you know. I mean, I'll bootleg more metal crap for you, but you need to hear this new guy out of Toronto. His stuff absolutely flows. I'll have to listen to it with you, though, make sure your cave-brain is catching the nuances. . . ."

My phone vibrates in my pocket while Tina continues trying to persuade me my music sucks and hers is way better. I nod along, pretending she may have a point, as I pull out my phone and glance at the text.

ooo

The Bat Signal. From Danny's phone. Shit!

"Got to find Danny," I whisper, staring at my phone, texting him back.

I send a reply: Where r u?

"Did you say you're looking for Danny?" Tina asks.

"Yeah." I glance up at her, waiting for my phone to buzz, expecting it any second.

"That's funny," she says more to herself. "I just saw him a couple minutes ago. Said he's meeting Bruce or

something?" Tina ends this more like a question, like I'll
know where they're meeting.

"Wuh-wuh-where?"

"Don't know." Tina shrugs. "He just said downstairs."

Downstairs. The locker rooms? The gym?

Feels like a static charge fills the air as the hair on the
back of my neck begins to rise. Still no text from Danny.
"Guh-guh-gotta go."

"What is it with you guys, anyway? Everyone's gotta
go, like there's a big party happening someplace. What's
up with that?" Tina asks, but I'm already moving down
the hall, ignoring her. Some guy, wrestling with his friend,
backs up into me. I shove him out of my way, shove him
too hard. He bounces off the lockers but I don't stop to
apologize. No time. Something's wrong. The more steps I
take, the stronger the feeling.

D A N N Y

Studblatz clasps my neck with his meat-hook claw and marches me across the gym like a puppet. The tips of his fingers and thumb pinch deep, threatening to meet at my spine, forcing a squeal out of me. He laughs while toggling my skinny neck side to side. I pry at the iron grip, scrambling to keep my feet under me. His thumb and fingers keep drilling deeper until dark spots bloom in my vision.

It *kills!*

I scream.

Just like Ronnie!

"Stop! Please! Stop! Stop!" I whimper.

"Shut up."

The claw forces me toward Tom, Scott, and Bruce. A final shove whiplashes me forward. I trip over a three-inch mat and skid to my hands and knees beside Bruce. For a moment, all I feel is instant relief from that grip.

Bruce lies flat on his stomach, his face red from the pressure of Tom's weight. His eyes are scrunched half shut. Caught in his own world of hurt, he offers no recognition or explanation.

"About time you showed up, twerp," Scott says. "Glad you got our invite in your locker. Didn't want to start the party without you." The hyper-happy tone in his voice scares me as much as, if not more than, Studblatz's animal excitement.

"You're just in time, dipshit," Tom growls. "Your butt buddy is going to give us a little demonstration on how he uses the harness here."

Tom has Bruce wedged under him like a roped calf, sitting all his weight on Bruce's lower back so Bruce can do nothing but lie there gasping for air. Tom's not bothered, it seems, that Bruce might pass out.

"Yeah, we don't use things like that spotting harness in football. But maybe we should," Scott says. "Looks like fun."

Tom finally rises up off Bruce. I see they've already forced the harness around him before I arrived. It's a heavy canvas belt that normally cinches around the waist and attaches to two ropes hanging from the ceiling by pulleys. If you're strapped into one, you can throw any dangerous trick you want off any apparatus because another person can slow your fall—or even suspend you—by tightly anchoring the ropes. It works on the same principle that rock climbers use to catch each other if they slip off a cliff.

Whether they've done it on purpose or by accident,

the harness is wrapped around Bruce's thighs, and not his waist, where it belongs. Tom drags Bruce, still gasping for breath, by the ankles underneath the ring stand. Scott snaps the two guide ropes to the metal harness clasps and then Studblatz starts yanking down on the other end of the ropes running through the pulleys. The three of them move efficiently, like they know exactly what they want to do, like they've planned it. Or at least one of them has. Studblatz heaves down on the ropes, winching Bruce up into the air. With the harness cinched around his thighs, Bruce's center of gravity is awkward. He lifts off the ground legs-first, hung upside down, same way an animal carcass swings above the butcher floor.

"Sons of bitches," Bruce pants, meeting intimidation with anger, unwilling to give even an ounce of fear. His face deepens from pink to red as the blood rushes down into his head. His neck veins bulge and his eyes turn bloodshot. Studblatz keeps hoisting the rope, hand over hand, lifting Bruce higher and higher into the air, up toward the pulleys bolted into the gymnasium rafters thirty feet above us.

"You got something to say, tough guy?" Scott asks. "You want to brag about your little locker stunts? You really dig that stuff, huh? First piss, then graffiti. Nice touch calling us murderers. Make you feel tough hiding behind masks and words?"

Studblatz keeps heaving on the ropes, treating it like some sort of strength drill, until Bruce hangs twenty feet in the air, way higher than anyone is meant to go in the spotting harness.

"He looks like a pig we caught in a trap," Jankowski says.

"Here, little piggy," Scott taunts.

"Oink, oink," Mike snorts.

"Stop!" Bruce yells down, but it comes out more like a heavy breath. He reaches for the harness ropes and pulls himself upright but there's no way to hold that position, even for someone as strong as Bruce. After thirty seconds his thick arms shake and then slacken and then he's dangling upside down again, his face flushing back to deep purple.

"You!" Scott walks over to me. "Now would be a good time to find out how much you like to snitch. You *are* the type that likes snitching, right?" Scott asks, stabbing a finger into my chest. "See, we've got our own snitch and he told us you were in the storage room that day with Gunderson. Our snitch told us you saw everything, that you and hanging piggy here are going to keep squealing about us. That true?"

Had Kurt not already told me he was their snitch, Scott's question might have stunned me. At least I'm prepared. "He's lying," I lie myself. "I wasn't anywhere in the gym that day."

"That a fact?" Scott asks, then turns away as if considering my story. A spark of hope lights up inside me. Maybe I can talk us out of this, I think, tell him we'll never say a word. Tell him whatever he wants to hear. I can do this—

Scott spins around, his arm trailing like a whip, back of his open hand slicing across my face.

Crack!

"Lying son of a bitch!" Scott shouts. The slap spins my face toward the wall. "Think I'm going to believe you now?"

I reach a hand up to cover my scalded cheek, expecting a second slap, when Scott's attention diverts up to Bruce, who's loudly hawking up a world-class lung oyster. It sounds like he's scraping out the inside of his nose and throat. With the aim of a ninja, Bruce lets fly. A gob nails Studblatz on his head, thick and white as bird shit.

"Son!" Studblatz roars. "You are going to *pay* for that." Studblatz opens his hands. Bruce drops like a rock for about ten feet and yelps before Studblatz regrasps the accelerating ropes. Bruce's momentum on the speeding ropes snags Studblatz's big arms skyward as he regrabs them, lifting him a foot off the ground before his heavier weight settles him back down to the ground. Bruce comes to a stop but bungees as the ropes stretch and contract. He wraps his head protectively in his arms.

"Let's tie that little piggy up nice and high," Scott says, then jerks a thumb at me, "while we give this one our special treatment, since he liked to watch so much last time." Scott locks his eyes on mine while suggesting this to the others. My reaction must please him because a smile eases across his mouth as he lays a firm grip on my shoulder like I'm a bad pet in need of training. That's when I feel it in me—something really awful is going to happen.

RUN!

I feint to the left and cut to the right, slipping from Scott's grip, darting at an angle, never taking my eyes off the locker-room entrance across the gym. Halfway there, a solid wave rolls over me, throwing me down on the tumbling mats, pinning my arms beneath me and pushing all air from my chest.

Tom Jankowski's squatting on me same way he'd squatted on Bruce. He starts bouncing on me, forcing every last bit of air out of my lungs, threatening to crack my chest.

"Good catch, Tommy," Scott says. "Work him over."

"Can't . . . brea . . ."

"What's that, snitch?" Tom asks. "You can't breathe?"

Tom's weight finally rises off me, his hands grabbing me up like a rag doll and plopping me on my feet. I'm leaking tears and choking back snot, knowing what's coming, knowing what happened to Ronnie.

"Lookit him, crying like a little girl."

"He *is* a little girl. Bet he don't have a single pubic hair on that scrawny little body."

The three of them laugh as I try wiping away the slick wet veiling me in defeat. Bruce's face is dark purple by now, a thick vein on his forehead ready to burst. We watch each other for a moment and I'm not sure which of us thinks he's in a worse position.

"I've got a game we can play," Scott says, his voice all fake friendly. "Your arms must be tired, Stud, from holding up the dipshit."

"Naw, he's light," Studblatz says in a creepy-cheerful voice. "And this pulley system is a beaut!"

"Give the ropes to the little guy, here," Scott says. "Make him hold his captain up. Let's see how loyal he really is."

Jankowski yanks me over to Studblatz, who shoves the ropes into my hands. "Now grab on real tight, fairy," Studblatz growls. "You don't want your friend to fall."

Soon as they're in my possession, I slowly let the ropes

slip through my fingers, guiding Bruce gently back down to the floor.

"What the hell you think you're doing?" Scott barks. "We didn't say you could let him down. Pull him back up now or I'm going to smack you." Studblatz comes over and cuffs me on the head, then takes back the ropes and heaves on them until Bruce dangles even higher than he did the first time.

"*I'm sorry,*" I mouth up at Bruce. He doesn't respond. Studblatz forces the ropes back into my hand.

"You think he'll pass out in that position?" Tom asks Scott. "Being upside down that long?"

"Won't hurt him if he does."

"Guys, why don't you let him come down for a bit," I suggest. My throat's salty and raw. I start to let the ropes slide through my hands again. Studblatz gets in my face and I flinch. He grins, just standing there, enjoying the moment. Then he hauls back and slugs my shoulder, knuckles hitting deep to the bone. Feels like the socket's exploding. Beyond the pain, my fingers in that arm go numb. Bruce starts falling. I clutch at the sliding rope with my good hand, feel it burn through my callused fingers until I stop him with about eight feet to spare.

"He'll come down when we say so," Studblatz says, needing no excuse to nail me again. He hauls on the ropes, hoisting the limp body back up. Bruce's arms dangle uselessly; he's not even trying to wrap them around his head this last drop. He's fading, and if he hits the floor headfirst, his neck will snap like a dry branch.

"So let's see how tough you are," Scott says to me. "Let's see how good you are at sticking up for your friends. Piggy up there better hope you're more loyal to him than you were to Gunderson when you were hiding in that corner, watching us, probably beating off. What kind of friend are you? What kind of teammate?"

Studblatz and Jankowski snicker. The questions hurt worse than even the punch.

"It's not funny," I cry. Tom stomps over and spits in my face, then punches me in the chest hard enough that my heart hiccups.

"No one told you to talk." Tom cuffs me on the head. "Did I tell you to talk?" he asks. "DID I TELL YOU TO TALK?!"

There's nothing to say. Nothing to do but cower when Tom swings again and his fist targets the same shoulder Studblatz already pulped. A bomb goes off where he hits and the arm drops to my side. The only thing keeping me from letting go of the rope is screaming agony cramping my good hand into a tight fist.

The mangled arm hurts bad. Real bad.

"Please . . . please . . . let us go . . ." I whisper.

"Hey assholes," Bruce calls down in a strangled rasp. I silently plead for him to shut up, don't anger them any more than they already are. "I figured out why you all like to fuck little boys."

"Keep talking," Studblatz hisses. "Every word's more beatdown for you."

"It's 'cause all those steroids you guys take. You can't get it up anymore. You think scaring some kid makes up for the fact that you jerkoffs have limp dicks and no nuts? How pathetic is that? Homecoming king can't even get it up for his queen." Bruce tries to laugh but it comes out as a cough. His face is the color of a deep bruise and I think maybe his eyes might start crying blood, they're so red.

"You think that's funny?! You think that's funny?!" Tom shouts. He pushes me away and starts lowering the ropes. "I'm going to stomp the shit out of—"

"No." Scott stops Tom. "Hoist him up. Hoist him way up. Come on. See how tough he talks in a minute. See if either of 'em ever wants to snitch again."

"Knew you were too chickenshit to let me down," Bruce rasps.

"Shut up, faggot."

"I know you . . . are, but what . . . what . . . am I?" Bruce grunts.

"Let's just lower him," Tom says. "Kick the shit out of him."

I think it might be a good time to try easing Bruce back down again. I get him to about fifteen feet when Scott steps over to me and swings for my face. I duck.

Thunk.

Scott's fist bites into the top of my head, knocking me sideways as my skull absorbs it. Hurts a lot less than the shoulder punch or chest punch.

"God *damn* it! Little shit's got a stone skull," Scott says, shaking out his hand. "My fuckin' pinky."

"What a pussy!" Bruce huffs. Scott tucks his punching hand under his armpit and stares up at Bruce, pacing underneath him.

"Scott, let's get—" Tom starts.

"Shut up!" Scott snaps at his lineman, never taking his eyes off Bruce above. "You think you can talk to *me* like that?" Scott demands, still walking a circle around his prey. "You think someone like . . . *you* gets away with that, huh?"

"Scott—" Tom tries again.

"*I said shut up!*" Scott barks at Tom, glancing at him only a moment before turning his attention upward again. "Hoist this pig up!" Scott orders me. I only stand there anchoring my friend, not hoisting and not lowering. Studblatz shoves me out of the way and hauls on the ropes, cranking Bruce higher and higher until his knees, the top point on his dangling body, are almost even with the thirty-foot pulley bolts.

"That's it," Scott says mostly to himself before calling up to Bruce. "Still feel like a tough guy now? Huh?"

"Scott, come on, man," Tom says.

Scott ignores Tom, glances at Studblatz instead. "Mike, give the ropes back to the little snitch," Scott orders. "He still hasn't proven his loyalty."

Studblatz forces the ropes back into my hands.

"It ain't funny anymore," Bruce says. I can barely hear him up there. "Let me down. Danny let me down."

The rope slides slowly through my fingers like I'm reeling out line on a stubborn fish. We can wait them out, I tell myself. Just a little longer. Already, Jankowski's anxious to go. *Hold on, Bruce. Just hold on. Let them get their kicks and leave.*

"Luh-luh-luh-let him duh-duh-down," comes a new voice.

Kurt!

"Yuh-yuh-you've had your fuh-fuh-fuh-fun." Kurt's standing at the locker-room entrance, stepping cautiously into the gym as the door closes behind him.

"You again!" Scott spits. "Why are you always hanging where you're not wanted?"

"They got the puh-puh-point," Kurt says, ignoring Scott's question. "No one's gonna suh-suh-suh-say nothing, okay? Juh-juh-juh-just let him duh-duh-duh-down."

"Kurt." Bruce sighs weakly, and I hear the relief I feel. Kurt, body moving in a way his mouth won't match, steps over and around the mats smooth as a stalking lion. He slows up when he reaches Tom, as if not to startle him. Scott eyes Kurt, his mind calculating, I can tell, trying to keep the plan on track despite the interruption. Scott reaches a decision, steps toward me, and punches my bad shoulder.

Fire erupts at the spot in my arm where muscle has turned into gristle. I won't let go of the ropes, though. I *will* pass the loyalty test Scott thinks I've already failed. I will pass.

"Come on, Suh-suh-suh-Scott," Kurt calls over Tom's shoulder. "No one's suh-suh-saying nuh-nuh-nuh-nothing. Bruce and Duh-duh-Danny wuh-wuh-won't talk. Thu-thu-that's the end of it."

No one moves.

"Bruce," Kurt calls up to him. "You won't suh-suh-say nuh-nuh-nothing, wuh-wuh-wuh-will you?"

Bruce, barely conscious now, gives the slightest head shake, agreeing not to say anything.

"See?" Kurt says. "We go about our buh-buh-business. Act luh-luh-like nuh-nuh-nothing happened. Luh-luh-let him down. Guh-guh-go home. We got a guh-guh-game in two days. Coach ain't guh-guh-gonna be happy with you wuh-wuh-wasting time on these tuh-tuh-two. Luh-luh-let's go."

Kurt has them. I can feel it. He's saying all the right things. My good hand, cramping from holding Bruce up by itself, slowly loosens and the rope starts easing ever so slightly through my fingers. This time it will work. I can lower Bruce while Kurt keeps talking in his calm tone, even with his stutter, lulling his three captains. It will work. But the pulleys need oil. I've got Bruce down to about eighteen feet when my stiff fingers let too much rope slip past them. The pulleys let out a sharp squeak, breaking the soft hypnosis Kurt's casting over the gym.

Scott looks up, sees how much I've lowered Bruce. His eyes do a triangle from Bruce to Kurt to me and something in him goes off.

"Did I give you permission to let him down?!" Scott screams in my face. *"Did I?!"*

A camera flashes same time as a thing—a fist—slams up under my chin and my knees wobble. Then darkness roars up over me like a summer twister, covering my eardrums and eyes, stripping me of everything but failure, weakness, and defeat. The world howls above me in fury as I topple over, knowing I've let go of the rope and Bruce is falling . . .

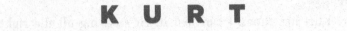

Bruce falls without a cry. Just like Lamar. Both of them sneaking out of the world without complaint. Only sound is the clack of teeth when Scott sucker punches Danny, throwing an uppercut to his chin. Second sound, as Danny tips over, is his skull gonging against the steel base of the ring stand. Then those rope pulleys squeaking loud as hamster wheels once Danny lets go, dropping Bruce headfirst from the gym rafters . . .

When Crud Bucket duct-taped me and Lamar inside that storage tub as punishment, you'd think I'd've known exactly when he stopped being alive. Packed tight as twins in a belly—face to armpit, shin to hip, shoulder to ribs—the only sound in that cramped blackness after we both stopped blubbering was Lamar's rhythmic wheezing. He's the one told me to use my belt buckle. Use the metal tong, he said, puffing to keep my shirt out of his mouth. My arm couldn't straighten to reach the buckle, so Lamar slid the belt off me, then fed it up to my trapped hand. All the while he's breathing like oily rags are stuffed into his lungs. When I got the second hole punched through, I told him to relax because I'd drill enough holes to turn that plastic tub into a spaghetti strainer. His wheezing quieted soon after, like I'd calmed him down. I'd just finished the twelfth hole, started on the thirteenth, when the jeans around my bottom knee got wet. Then that smell. Piss. I'm working like crazy to get holes punched and here's Lamar pissing on me like it's a big joke. It wasn't funny. I told him so. *Stop pissing on me, fucker!*

I got to lie with him like that for a day before Crud Bucket cut through the duct tape, unsealed the tub, and peeled the lid off. I'd punched four hundred and thirty-seven holes before that lid came off. Four hundred and thirty-seven. I *told* Lamar I'd turn it into a spaghetti strainer. I *told* him. If he just waited, is all . . .

A force—a bomb blast—blows me forward. Arms outstretched, I try to catch a body falling from the sky, attempt the impossible, try to save Bruce, try to make it up to Lamar, make up for the past. I drive into Bruce's dropping body like he's a tackling dummy, wrapping my arms around him, changing his direction from down to sideways. His legs tangle over my shoulders as we crash forward across an eight-inch mat. Bruce lands on his back as I somersault past him. Good chance he's got the wind knocked out of him. Might've even broken a collarbone or busted a rib, but I've stopped him from hitting his head and snapping his neck.

It'll do.

D A N N Y

I'm lying on a mat. A blue mat. In a gym. In our gym.
My jaw aches so bad I feel it in my ears. The back of
my head must have a railroad spike pushed through it.
Shouts and curses zing back and forth above me. Thick
legs and sneakers step over and around me, sinking the
mat near my body, jarring my jaw, sending out waves of
hurt. I blink, wonder how I got sand in my eyes, because
they're gritty. Haven't risked turning my head to find out
who the legs and sneakers belong to.

A hand descends from above and rests on my forehead.
A dusty T-shirt pats my nose. Then two hands slide under
my arms and start lifting me.

"Danny, let's go, let's go. Now. *Now!*" It's Bruce's voice.
I think. It's higher and trembling like a scared kid's, frantic
sounding, more like mine. A freaked-out kid is channeling

Bruce's mouth, like Ronnie back from the dead, warning me. "Let's go. *Come on!*"

"Guh-go!" a different voice pushes. I know that one.

Hands—Bruce's hands—grapple me, dragging me backward out of the gym, not giving me a chance to get my feet under me. My heel snags a mat, pulling me out of Bruce's grip, and I fall on my ass. Bruce yanks me back up into a semi-drag and my feet shuffle along for the ride. Everything's fuzzy. Kurt's back is to us, arms outstretched, warding off . . . those . . . three. I lose sight of Kurt as Bruce tows me through the locker-room door violently enough that I think I must've somehow caused all the trouble.

"We got to get out of here. We got to go. *Now!*"

"But what about . . . what about Kurt?"

"He can take care of himself," Bruce half yelps. "Those psychos are his friends." I've never seen Bruce flat-out scared and it terrifies me. They've turned him into *this*? It must be hopeless.

"Hurry up, Danny. Let's go!" Bruce's still got hold of me though my legs are working again. We make it out of the locker room and start down the deserted hall.

"We can't just abandon him," I say. "We've got to help him."

"They almost killed me! Do you understand?" Bruce gives a single, violent head snap like he's whipping wet hair out of his eyes. "They *tried* to *kill me!*" he says, like he's only now realizing it. "No more. I'm not dying. I *will* get a gun, though. I swear to God. I *will* come back with a fucking gun and shoot those fuckers."

"We can't leave Kurt."

"*You* save him," Bruce calls over his shoulder as he

skip-walks ahead. "Not me. Anyone even talks to those three, I don't speak to them anymore." Bruce's pace is losing me. "I'm outta here. You coming or not?" Bruce asks but he's already at the end of the hallway. He turns the corner, leaving me alone. By the time I climb the stairs, my head's throbbing bad and Bruce is nowhere in sight. The hallways are empty except for "school's out" celebration trash littering the ground. My legs weaken. I'm not going to make it out of the building before those three finish Kurt and get ahold of me.

Get out! Get out! Follow Bruce!

Kurt's dying right now, downstairs in the gym.

Go! Go!

I kick a wadded-up ball of paper out of my path. Then I turn down the main hall and jog toward the principal's office. The door is locked up tight. So is every classroom door I kick.

"Somebody!" I yell. "Somebody!" I yell again. "Where the *fuck* is a teacher when you need one!?" I ask the empty hallway. "Fuck, fuck, *fuck*!!!" I holler, knowing this *has* to conjure an adult out of thin air ready to stuff a bar of soap in my mouth and assign me a week of detention. I mean, I *always* get busted for cussing. *Always!* I take three slow breaths, waiting.

Nada!

"Im-fucking-possible!"

I jog down the hall, my head pounding.

"Help!"

KURT

"What part of this don't you get?" Scott asks me as if I'm genuinely confused. I keep my arms out, hoping to hold the three of them off while Bruce and Danny escape. "You're with us," Scott says. "Not them. We're your team. Not them. *They're* the enemy. They're trying to destroy us."

"Think you can protect those little shits forever?" Jankowski asks. "Think we won't get them?"

Studblatz takes a step to the side, ready to go around me. I shift with him, promising to cut him off, and he stops but jabs a finger over my shoulder. "Those little fuckers are dead! You hear me? Dead!"

"Your little Danny boy needs the Ronnie treatment," Scott says. "Tom, think we should nail that snitch like we did Gunderson?" Scott asks over his shoulder, never taking his eyes off me.

"Yeah," Jankowski answers. "Bet he'd take it like a champ."

I wince at the words, feel my guts knot.

"Whatsamatter?" Scott asks me. "You sorry you missed out on the fun the first time?" Then, louder, to Tom and Mike, "Maybe he wants Danny for himself." Studblatz laughs like a hyena and Scott's pleased with his joke. The three of them close around me. I take a step backward, my arms still out, like I'm setting up for a pass rush.

"Hell, you're just jealous," Scott taunts. "Studblatz, tell 'em. Nothing better than popping fresh meat like Gunderson. Best way to keep 'em in line."

"Gotta keep 'em in line," Studblatz repeats.

"Whaddya think, Tommy? Think Kurt should try it?"

"Probably has already."

"Awwww, lookit. Our big fullback's crying like a little bitch."

"Big, fuckin' baby!"

"Worse than Gunderson when we shoved it up his ass."

Tom's chuckling. I'm having trouble keeping them in sight because everything's starting to blur no matter how much I blink and wipe at my eyes. An old smell fills the air, smell of Crud Bucket's sour breath in my face, threatening to kill me if I ever tell I caught him on top of Lamar. The smell of his sweat and breath and my fear—it's all back here now, under my nose.

"Come on, Kurt. So we popped Gunderson's cherry. Big deal," Scott says. "We didn't tell him to kill himself."

That's on him. I mean, that's *weak*. Like that Darwin dude said, survival of the fittest, baby. Ain't that right, Tommy?"

"Amen," Jankowski answers with a grin. "Survival of the fittest, baby!"

"Shit, yeah," Studblatz agrees. "Gunderson wanted it. Loved it. Know how I know? He never fought back. He cried but he barely struggled, never escaped. That's how they act when they secretly want it."

"Here's the deal," Scott says, raising his voice like he's playing for an audience, setting up a punch line. "No one's ever, *ever* gonna believe a fuckin' word you say once we get done with you. Nope." I bring an outstretched hand back to my face, quickly wipe the tears from my eyes, but they keep coming, keep streaming down my cheeks. "They'll want to know how come the *orphan killer* is loose at Oregrove. Tom's dad tried to warn Coach, but you're still around and Ronnie Gunderson paid the price."

"Fuckin' A," Studblatz says.

"I mean, everyone knows it takes a fuckin' monster to fuck a kid with a broom," Scott hisses. "And when they hear you sputter and blubber, big strings of drool coming out that fucked-up face . . . sheeyit, boy. K-K-K-Kurt B-B-B-Brodsky ain't gonna be such a hero anymore, is he?"

"Kiss your scholarship offers good-bye," Jankowski adds.

"Yeah, fugly," Studblatz says. "And when we get through with him, you can add that little faggot, Danny, to your victim list."

"Go find your little friends," Scott says, and then spits on the mats. "Go pretend you can save them. And tell 'em we're waiting for 'em. Tell 'em we'll get them alone, eventually, so they better learn how to man up and take it!"

"Hey, K-K-K-Kurt." Tom juts his head forward. Spit flecks the corners of his mouth. "How come you're not sssssssaying nothing? Cat got your tongue?"

Studblatz howls at the joke.

"Yuh-yuh-you suh-suh-suh-said it all," I stutter, still backing up, never taking my eyes off them. When my shoulders bump up against the wall, I startle, then reach out for the door, pull it open, and hurriedly retreat through the locker room the same way Danny and Bruce left. Soon as I spin forward, I run out the building, past the parking lot and down Plymouth Lane. I keep running until I'm at least a half mile away from school, until I'm sure none of them are coming for me, until I can't run no more. All alone, I bend over, hands on my knees, puking my guts out, my throat burning.

Only then do I press the stop button on my little digital recorder.

DANNY

49

I come across the world's oldest janitor. Thin as me and my height with white hair pomaded back against skin as tanned and creased as old cowboy boots. A pack of cigarettes sits in his chest pocket and one cig rests behind his left ear. His stitched name tag reads GENE. He is pushing a dry mop through hallway trash like a snowplow. Gene's pretty much a fossil but he's still an adult. Not even Scott would commit murder in front of an adult.

"Help!" I call out, rushing toward him. He's wearing earbuds and I don't catch his attention until I'm standing right in front of him. He pulls out one earbud, irritated, then does a double take, sees something in my face that worries him. I touch my chin and my hand comes away sticky and red. "Help," I repeat. He nods, pulling out his other earbud, and follows me. Gene doesn't move fast.

When we finally reach the gym, I take a deep breath and step aside to let him enter first, not ready to face whatever horror it might hold. I half expect to find Kurt's beaten body, bloodied and unmoving, lying on the mats.

"No one's in there," Gene reports when he comes back out. "Place is empty."

"You sure? You check the storage room?"

Gene nods. "See for yourself, son. Now I got to get back. You better clean up. You tell the principal what happened."

"Uh-huh."

I step into the gym. Lights are still on but the place is empty. Whole place gives me the creeps and I'm leaving when I see a wink of silver metal on the pommel horse. My phone. Propped up on the chalky brown leather. Set there so I'll find it easily. I jog over, grab it, then get out of the gym and fly out of the school. I'm jogging home, looking over my shoulder, expecting a car to race up any minute, when my phone beeps. A text from a number I don't recognize. Doesn't take more than a second to narrow down the texter, though, or figure out who wants me reunited with my phone so I can receive their uplifting messages.

U R DED!

K U R T

She meets me in the parking lot of McDonald's, the only place I can think of that isn't school and isn't Patti's. Only place that feels safe. Since I sent her the text, I've downed two Big Macs, two cheeseburgers, a large fries, a large Chicken McNuggets, a large Coke, and an apple pie. Her pip-squeak Toyota zips into the parking lot and I'm moving to it, coming up on the driver's side before it even parks.

"Kurt," Tina says, cracking her door, her face opening up into a smile. It's a great smile, I think, wishing I didn't need her for anything but the smile. I'm about to speak when the passenger door opens and her friend Indira steps out. The little car's got an oversize stereo and a woman's voice mewing from the speakers about lost kisses while a piano plunks low keys. Why'd Tina bring a friend? A flame of rage licks across me. I grab Tina by the elbow and roughly pull her out of the car. I don't mean to, but can't help it.

"What the . . . ?" Tina starts to speak, confused.

"Tina?" Indira asks meekly.

Shit! Shit! Shit! "Kuh-kuh-come alone!" I say, glancing over the roof of the car at Indira.

"Jesus! If you want to ask me out on a date," Tina snaps, "McDonald's won't do and you'll have to ease up on the groping. Also, you'll have to—"

"I nuh-nuh-nuh-need . . ." I cut her off. ". . . yuh-yuh-yuh-your help." Those four words are hard as hell to string together and it's got nothing to do with the stutter. The way I grew up, you don't ask people for nothing. All it does is let them know you're soft. Weak. If they know you're soft, they don't help. They attack. But this time, I got no other option. There's no other way.

"Yeah, right!" Tina rolls her eyes. "You want *me* to help *you*. Is this a joke? Am I being punk'd right now?"

"I nuh-nuh-nuh-need . . ." And all that has happened that afternoon and the memories it brings back up in me and the bad future it threatens me with—all that wells up inside me until Tina and the world beyond her melt. Lamar's nowhere to be found and this thing is coming whether I want it to or not. "Yuh-yuh-yuh-your . . ." I try. I really try to hold it back but it won't be held back no more. It claws its way out of a crack in my heart and this . . . this . . . *thing* blasts up out of me, part moan and part sob. It embarrasses the hell out of me, laughs at me and my muscles, tells me they won't ever, ever make up for what I let happen to Lamar. Stutter or not, no words can explain how awful and scared I feel. All I can do is turn away and thump the roof of that stupid car.

And then Tina's arms wrap around my waist, hugging me, holding me even though she is small and I am big. Another sob crashes out of me and I almost pound her car again in frustration. I hold back. I let my heavy arms settle around Tina, pulling her tight into me like she's the last life vest in the angriest ocean. I bury my face in her jet-black hair with the blond roots and cry like the big baby Scott claims I am, cry like I haven't done since Lamar left me behind in this world.

DANNY

Phone's beeping so much with incoming text threats
I turn it to vibrate, set it on the kitchen table, and
watch it slowly buzz-crawl across the lacquered wood
while I eat a bowl of Cocoa Puffs for supper. When it gives
off the long *brrrr* of an actual call, I pick it up. I don't
recognize the number, but know it's not one of the three
football captains that don't seem to ever sleep, judging on
how often they like to remind me I'm going to die.

"Huh-hello?"

"Danny?" a girl's voice asks.

"Yeah?" My answer more of a question. What if it's one
of their girlfriends, luring me to talk before they hand off
the phone to Scott or Tom or Mike?

"It's Tina," she says.

"Oh, uh, hi," I say. *Why's she calling me?*

"Kurt just left. We've been talking for a long time."

"Uh-huh . . ."

"Danny, he told me everything."

". . . about?"

"Danny," she sighs. "I know. I know everything."

My phone beeps while she talks and I know another text has just come in, waiting for me to read it.

"So what?" I ask, annoyed now. Why the hell did Kurt tell Tina?

"Danny, Kurt needs your help. He won't admit it, but he's scared. Probably as scared as those bastards are."

"Those bastards," I say, "are not scared."

"Yeah, they are," she says. "They'll never call it that but they're freaking out that you guys are going to finally tell the truth. And they should, because you are."

"Trust me," I say. "I know scared. I know freaking out. Those guys aren't it."

"Danny, there's a way to fight them and make it all stop but we need you to make it work."

"Me?"

"Yeah, you," Tina says. "Kurt needs you, Danny. He needs you to help him speak up. It's about time, don't you think?"

My phone buzzes again with another text. I stir the rest of my soggy Cocoa Puffs around in my bowl, my hunger completely disappearing.

"I don't know."

"Remember you thanked me for sticking up for others," she reminds me. "It's your turn, now. You owe it to Ronnie. You owe it to Kurt. Jesus, you owe it to the whole school. At the very least, you owe it to yourself."

"I'd rather keep as far away from those three as possible."

"How's that working out for you so far?" she asks. "Or Bruce?"

"Bruce just wants to shoot them," I say.

Tina laughs.

"I'm not joking," I tell her. "I think he might do it. And I'm okay with that. Seriously," I say, and realize I'd like nothing more.

"I've got a better idea," she says. "One that doesn't involve murder."

"What makes you think you can outsmart them?"

"Uh, I'm a girl and they're boys," she says. "By default, I win."

"How about we stop the stupid schemes that only seem to piss off these guys more and more," I suggest.

"How about you listen to what I have to say," she suggests back.

As I'm mulling this over, the phone buzzes with another incoming text. I guess I don't have much to lose.

So I listen to Tina. My phone keeps beeping with new messages as she talks. In the end I'm not sure if the text threats convince me or Tina does, but eventually I agree to help her help me and Kurt.

"One more thing," Tina says. "Give me Vance Fisher's number."

After hanging up, I stir my soupy cereal some more. I glance at my phone. Twelve new texts in the last hour.

SPIT OR SWALLOW?
SNICH GOING DOWN

U CANT HIDE
DED MAN WALKING
U R DED MEET

I stop reading after five and delete the rest. I'm feeling more and more anxious, and it hits me, again, how scared and lost Ronnie must've been during his last days. He asked me for so little—just to tell the truth, tell him what I saw—and I turned away from him. God! I wish I could have that last phone call with him back, wish I could do it all over again.

"*I'm so sorry,*" I whisper over the table, acting as if Ronnie is sitting across from me now. "*So, so sorry. I'll make it right. I swear.*"

The texts keep coming.

HOME ALONE?
DADDY CANT SAVE U & MOMMYS DED!
TIMES UP
NOK NOK
HERE WE CUM!

The hungry growl of a big engine rolling into my driveway makes me bolt for the front of the house. I lock the doors and shut off all the inside lamps and TV. It's night out and a supercharged Camaro sits in my driveway, its headlights blasting our house. I peek out from behind curtains drawn across our front-yard picture window. I call my dad's cell but it goes to voice mail. Figures. The Camaro reverses at an angle, tires rolling across our lawn, so the headlights hit the picture window. Then it stops.

Without thinking I dial Coach's number, which he gave us after Ronnie died. The Camaro's high beams flash on, pentetrating our house's lace curtains like X-rays. Coach's phone is ringing . . . and ringing. . . . *Come on, come on, pick up!*

Outside I hear the Camaro engine rev like it's getting ready to drive right through our house. I chance another peek around the curtains, see the passenger door open and Tom Jankowski step out.

Shit!

"Hello?" Coach Nelson's voice answers over the phone.

"Coach! They're trying to kill me!" I pant. "Right now!"

"Huh? Danny? Is that you? What's wrong? Where are you?"

Tom's throwing something. I hear it thud against our garage door. He throws again and again and more thuds pelt the side of our house. One slams against the picture window I'm standing next to, hits a foot from my head, and cracks the glass. I see the outlines of a smashed egg, lit from behind by the car's headlights, running down the pane of glass. The car's driver's side door opens and Scott steps out. Then Mike Studblatz gets out. They're both holding baseball bats, walking straight toward the window.

"Coach, they're—" Fear catches my throat as I realize they're about to shatter the thin glass and come grab me.

"Danny, tell me what's wrong, kiddo. Talk to me."

Our neighbor's outside house lights come on across the street and their dog, Judo, starts barking. Mike, Tom, and Scott freeze, spin around, then jump into the car. The Camaro backs out, wheels spinning on our lawn, leaving a single black track of torn-up grass. As it flees the crime scene, the Camaro's back tires flame our street with a smoky screech loud enough to wake the entire neighborhood, alerting everyone to the fact that my world is totally exploding.

"Danny?" Coach is still on the line.

"Uh . . . sorry, Coach," I exhale. "I, uh . . . I'm having a nightmare. I'm sleepwalking. Must've dialed your number by mistake. I'm awake now."

"Sleepdialing?!" Coach scoffs over the phone. "You on something right now?"

Yeah, I think. *Fear!*

"Maybe you want to talk for a while?" he tries. "You sound pretty scared. Where's your dad?"

"I think . . . I think I'm okay." Now that the Camaro has left, I start feeling foolish for panicking and calling Coach. "My dad's doing late rounds at the hospital."

"I think I should speak with him when he gets back. Have him call me this week. Tell him anytime."

"Okay, sure," I say, knowing I'll never pass on the message.

K U R T

Chugging back toward the huddle, I scan the fence line for Danny but find no sign of him in the sea of fans. I glance up at the enclosed control booth at the top of the stadium, wonder if Tina's watching me right now. Oregrove supporters are out in force tonight for the last home game before a string of away games to finish out the regular season. Scott shouts to be heard over the crowd noise. To stay warm, fans of all ages hug themselves, hop up and down, break out into chants while clapping gloved hands, wave big foam #1 fingers, and hold up homemade signs with player names markered on them. They call out to us as if we'll answer their personal requests for more defense or to fire up.

I take it all in, pretty sure this will be the last time I'll ever have fans pulling for me. Come Monday, after

Tom's dad makes good on his threat and after my three captains see to it everyone misunderstands my past, the only crowds waving at me will be ones carrying pitchforks and torches, trying to run me out of town.

Terrence slaps me in the belly to get my attention, then points up to the Jumbotron. "You paying them or something?" he asks me. In big flashing letters the Jumbotron reads: BRODSKY EXPRESS! COMING AT YA!!!

"Who you blowing up in the booth to get all the attention?" Terrence asks.

"Tina," I tell him without a single stutter.

"No shit? That little Dracula girl runs that thing?"

GO GET 'EM! the Jumbotron flashes.

"Hey, Brodsky," Scott barks at me. "You want to join us here or you going to paint a picture?"

"Wake the fuck up, Brodsky," Tom growls.

In the huddle, I can't bring myself to even glance at those two, so I focus on the tops of my shoelaces while scuffing the turf with my cleats. The Columbus Bears are decent but we're still leading by two touchdowns with only a minute left before halftime. If we win tonight, our record will be good enough to give us home field advantage in the play-offs. The sellout crowd knows this, makes noise, in fact, like tonight's game is the state championship.

"Okay, play action reverse on three," Scott tells us. "Terrence, stay sharp 'cause their nickel package is weak on the left flank and you can bust for some yardage. Pullman, hold your lane. Tommy, drive that cocksucker, sixty-seven, into the ground for me. He's been up in my grille all night."

"Got it."

"On three, on three," Scott repeats. We all clap our chapped hands once—part ritual, part signal we understand the play—then break huddle. I glance up at the Jumbotron again like I got a tick. A cartoon chorus line of dancing hot dogs wearing top hats and twirling canes tells us they're ready to be eaten in four-packs at the concession stand. I try to refocus on the game but it's hard. As we set up and Scott shouts his cadence, my eyes wander off number 79, my blocking assignment, and begin searching the crush of fans along the fence one more time, hoping he hasn't backed down, hoping he won't leave me hanging.

Where are you? I wonder.

"HUT!" Scott grunts. I drive forward into the line, smashing into oncoming shoulders, helmets, and arms, feeling the wall of bodies in front of me slowly give, slowly shift left. Terrence squirts past with the ball, gaining six yards before the Bears' secondary drags him into the grass. The play's barely been whistled dead but Terrence already has his head cocked toward the Jumbotron, ready to watch himself in slow-mo instant replay. The crowd stomps and claps its approval.

"Damn, I *do* move beautifully." Terrence sighs in appreciation.

As we huddle up, Sweeney, a wide receiver, comes sprinting onto the field, relaying Coach's next play to Scott. Scott's helmet swivels side to side in an exaggerated no and spit flies out past his face mask. He walks into the huddle with Sweeney trailing.

"Okay, fullback sweep left on two," Scott tells us. "Brodsky must be giving Coach hand jobs again to get these plays," he tells the rest of the huddle while his eyes skip past mine. I reach down and pull up my socks, then adjust my knee pads, notice none of the guys laughing for Scott. "I don't know why he hasn't given up on you yet."

"This is bullshit!" Tom slaps his thigh pads then spits at my feet.

"Shut the fuck up, Jankowski," Terrence snaps. "Start blocking for a change and maybe Kurt'll get some yardage."

"Mind your own business, Terrence, or I'll give my guy a free pass at you."

"Tell that to Coach"—Terrence jabs a finger almost into Tom's face mask—"and I'll be laughing when he benches your fat ass."

"Enough, ladies," Scott speaks. "Fullback sweep left on two, on two," he repeats. We clap and break huddle, then set up into position. My rushing's sucked all night because Scott's purposely holding on to the ball a fraction too long when handing off to me, messing up my timing, and Jankowski's throwing powder-puff blocks whenever the ball's coming to me. To be honest, I don't much care anymore. One way or the other, it's over for me. All I want to do is smash something.

"Ready!" Scott barks, lining up under center. I cast one more glance at the fences, come up empty in my search for him. I crouch down, fire up the ignition, feel the power thrumming across my thighs, big turbines winding up, approaching takeoff.

"Set . . ." Scott calls out, his voice fading in a gust of wind and crowd roar. I chance a last look downfield, past the wall of scrimmage, think I see him now. He's there, waiting. He's so small . . .

"Hut."

. . . like Lamar . . .

"HUT!"

Launch!

Going supernova slows everything around me, expands my vision until I'm watching the field from all angles. Scott steps back from center and baits me with the ball. My arms clamp around it like a bear trap, ripping it from his hands, allowing no chance for mischief. I spot Tom slipping to the ground, untouched, letting his man—54— leap over him into my path. Like my last three carries, Tom's unblocked defender will lock me up in the backfield for a loss of yards. I prepare for the inevitable . . .

Bam!

Terrence—lined up in the backfield with me—cuts off 54, buying me a half second. It's enough. I stop dead and break right, against the traffic of bodies sweeping left. The wall clears and a field of almost pure green waits for me to dance over it. I plant my foot for the sprint downfield, already seeing the end zone as I cross it, when something cracks my kneecap, pushing it backward. Feels like a jagged icicle stabbing me there, shattering against the bone. I collapse across the lone body below me—Jankowski. Son of a bitch has leg-whipped my knee under cover of the scrum.

While the game clock ticks down I lie there in the grass clutching my knee. Cold sweat trickles along my neck as I sit up and try to slowly bend the leg, testing it. I yank off my helmet in frustration and slam it into the turf.

"Give him room. Give him room," Scott shouts, then squats so close his face mask jabs my cheek. Wincing as I keep trying to bend and flex my leg, it takes me a second to realize Jankowski's on my other side. The two of them block out all the others.

"It's only gonna get worse." Scott speaks just loud enough for me to hear. *"You done crossed the wrong bulls and now you need to learn your place."*

"You're fucking finished, retard," Tom hisses. *"Finished!"* He's smiling at me through his face mask. They both stand up and back away, letting the trainers and Coach get to me.

"Son, where's it hurt?" Coach asks. He's pulled off his baseball cap and his face creases with worry. Not sure if it's for me or for how he'll replace me, but I don't much care. I'm grateful for his presence. The pain in my knee eases a little. The wind whips past my sweat-dampened hair, chilling it, as anger and fear swirl within me. Our plan starts to feel as worthless as my knee. It isn't enough, I realize. Doesn't matter what we come up with. Scott, Tom, and Mike won't stop. They'll keep coming.

The trainer gets my arm around his neck to help me stand up. I just want one good lick on them. One lick, let them know how it feels to really hurt, for once. Then I'll go into hiding. The crowd claps and hoots as the trainer and Rondo ease me up to my feet. With my arms draped over their necks, I limp off the field.

By the time Rondo and the trainer help me to the sidelines, the rest of the team's jogging toward the school building for halftime. I'm able to walk by myself now. My knee feels loose, like it's been stretched out the wrong way. I worry it might decide to go the wrong way again and snap in half. I glance up at the Jumbotron but there's only cartwheeling potato chips and a blizzard of popcorn kernels telling everyone the concession stand is offering a family pack for $15.99.

At the fence exit leaving the playing field where we're supposed to meet, there's no sign of Danny. *I did see him*, I tell myself. *Or I think I saw him*. Maybe it was only Lamar, again, in my head. I limp on toward the school, deciding to go through with it even if he bails on me. My doubt, my fear, dissolves under the realization of what's been done to me again and again, over and over. Right now I don't care about being trapped in the back of Officer Jankowski's squad car, I don't care about Scott's threats, don't care if the world thinks I'm a murderer. I'm doing it. Fury burns off the rest of my worry. I'm going to give it to them.

DANNY

I can *do* this.

I *can* do this.

I can do this. I can *do* this. I can do this IcandothisIcandothisIcandothis . . .

Who am I kidding? This is insane! I'm dead. I'd rather catch the high bar with my teeth than go through with the plan. How did she talk me into this? What part of this did I think would work?

You owe it to Ronnie! You owe it to Kurt. You owe it to yourself . . . to the school.

Nope! Still not working. Dammit! I blow on my hands to warm them up, then jam them back into the pockets of my letter jacket. The cold turns the leather of the arms stiff as plastic while I pace the school parking lot, trying to work up the nerve to go down and buy a ticket, then mix with the herd cheering on the Knights, cheering on a football team with three captains capable of murder.

They're also cheering for Kurt, says a voice in my head, sounding suspiciously like Tina's. I keep pacing, hoping to gather up some courage, wish I'd taken a big chug from Fisher's special Gatorade cocktail when I had the chance, before he left to go meet with Tina. Too late now.

Go down there now, you little pussy!

I force myself to walk to the gates, pay for a ticket, and mill about with the crowd. The smell of buttered popcorn floats through the cold air. I could buy some popcorn and then leave. Say I got food poisoning from the popcorn. I wanted to go through with it but couldn't because I was throwing up. That last part would be the truth, anyway. I'm ready to hurl every time I think about going through with it.

"Danny!"

I practically jump out of my shoes at my name. I turn, see Coach Nelson wrapped up in a big parka with a black knit cap pulled low over his head. He's walking toward me, his face grim. "I'm worried about you," he says as he reaches me, squinting in a way I've never seen from him. He doesn't trust me, I think. Sees me as a little off. I don't mind. Wary means there's fear, means there's some respect. Maybe "class psycho" isn't such a bad label. Beats "class loser" or "class victim," I think.

"I'm fine," I try assuring him.

"Danny, that phone call, that was no accident. Something's terrorizing you. I've been around the real thing enough to recognize it when I hear it," Coach says. "Now, tell me what's going on."

Maybe it's because standing in the cold surrounded by thousands of cheering fans makes me feel small, makes my problems feel insignificant, that suddenly talking about Ronnie is simple. Maybe it's because holding the secret so long has exhausted me. Whatever the reason, I open my mouth and say, "You don't know the whole truth about what happened to Ronnie." Coach watches me, waiting for more, and I'm about to continue when the big stadium speakers crackle to life.

"Number twenty-seven, Kurt Brodsky, is hurt on the play," booms over the stadium sound system, so strong and clear, even down where we stand on the grass, that it could be the announcer's standing just over my shoulder. "We have an injury time-out on the field."

"Kurt's hurt," I tell Coach like that explains everything. I start walking toward the fence line near the end zone.

"Danny, you're acting erratic. Both you and Bruce . . ." Coach fades off for a second, like he's thinking about something. "Did you come with Bruce?" he asks. "Is Bruce here?"

"No," I say. "Yeah."

"Danny!" Coach grabs the arm of my jacket to stop me.

"No, I didn't come with him," I clarify. "But he's here, somewhere. He texted me he's coming," I tell him.

"Has someone been scaring him, too?"

Well, I think, *if stringing him up like a gutted hog counts, then, yeah, they're scaring him.*

"Is he . . . are you two planning something?" Coach asks, and this time he's a man I don't recognize as he yanks me into him, staring into my face for an answer. Maybe wary respect is more than I bargained for. "Does he have a weapon?"

"I don't know," I say, though I'm pretty certain the only weapon Bruce has on him tonight is the baby Swiss Army knife attached to his key chain. My answer isn't one that reassures Coach.

"Text him," Coach orders me. "Tell him to meet you here at the concession stand. Do it now so I can see."

This isn't part of the plan.

"Coach," I tell him. "I have to go."

"Really?" Coach asks. "Where do you have to go?" He's not loosening his grip on my jacket sleeve.

As the half ends, the football team jogs from the sidelines through the fence opening; their footfalls, as they near us, buffalo heavy and blind, driving toward a cliff. The crowd parts for them, gets out of their way or risks being trampled. At first I think I've missed Kurt but then I see he's being helped off the field by a trainer and another teammate, that he's only now crossing the track ringing the field as the rest of his teammates leave him behind. The trainer and other teammate finally leave Kurt and jog on ahead as Kurt limps alone through the fence opening. He's met by a crowd of fans slapping his shoulder pads and grabbing his jersey, trying to touch any part of him, hoping some of him rubs off on them. They're drawn to the star fullback like a magnet.

D
A
N
N
Y

393

K U R T

E very other step, a bur deep inside my injured knee
pricks like a rodeo spur. I snort in the cold night air,
fury blowing out my nostrils in jets of steam. It's all I can
do not to hobble ahead through the forest of arms and
hands reaching out for me and windmill my helmet like
a war hammer until I brain my captains. Lamar's phan-
tom rides my shoulder, egging me on, reminding me what
he did for me, how he took the blame that night I broke
Crud Bucket's stereo and TV in Meadow's House. I was
the one playing with the football in the sitting room when
I smacked into the console and knocked the whole thing
over in a huge crash. To protect me, Lamar told Crud
Bucket that he did it. Crud Bucket put both of us in that
plastic tub to teach us a lesson. Duct-taped it. Sealed it
up. Airtight.

L
E
V
E
R
A
G
E

You ain't gonna take his shit no more, Lamar whispers.

I ain't gonna take his shit no more, I agree.

You're gonna get them good for me, Lamar commands. *You owe me that, Kurt. You owe me!*

I owe you, I agree. *I'll get them good for you, Lamar. I promise!* The crowd presses in thick and my knee ain't making it easy to move. I pull my helmet back on, feel the weight of its protection, and my tongue loosens a little. I'm ready to hurt someone, hurt them like they keep hurting me.

"All right, men, just keep doing what you're doing," Coach says, wrapping up his halftime speech. I've waited patiently for him to finish before I begin. I can always tell when he's finishing his pep talks because he starts adjusting his baseball cap and resetting it on his head. "We're wearing Columbus's front line down. We play hard for another thirty minutes and the game is ours. We can clinch home field advantage tonight for the conference play-offs, so no letting up. No relaxing. Our next two away games will be tough, so we need to keep the momentum going right through the rest of the regular season and into our first play-off game. We do that by winning here tonight. No excuses. Okay, let's get ready to head out."

I raise my hand.

"Yes, Kurt?"

"Suh-suh-suh-Scott wants to suh-suh-speak."

Coach cocks his head at me, confused. "Well, then, why doesn't Scott speak? What's he need you to tell me that for?" Coach looks over at Scott, who quickly glances from Coach to me and then over at Jankowski and Studblatz.

"I don't know what he's talking about, Coach," Scott says, shaking his head at me like I'm crazy.

"Suh-suh-Scott wants to suh-suh-speak," I repeat. Hiding under my helmet's not helping my tongue so much now, because the anger's rising.

"Kurt, you take a hit to your noggin as well as your knee?" Coach asks with a frown. "I ain't got time at the moment for these hijinks. Now, speak your mind, boy, or pipe down!" By now, the whole locker room's watching me. The small stereo that Tina lent me and that I pulled out of my locker before Coach began his speech has been dangling by my side, partly hidden by other players' legs, butts, and pads. I lift it up to my chest with the speakers facing into the circle of teammates, coaches, and trainers. I press play.

"Studblatz, tell 'em. Nothing better than popping fresh meat like Gunderson. Best way to keep 'em in line."

"Gotta keep 'em in line."

"Whaddya think, Tommy? Think Kurt should try it?"

"Probably has already."

"Awwww, lookit. Our big fullback's crying like a little bitch."

"Big fuckin' baby!"

"Worse than Gunderson when we shoved it up his ass."

"Hold up, now, son." Coach shakes his head at me in confusion while raising his hand like he's patting the air.

"Come on, Kurt. So we popped Gunderson's cherry. Big deal. We didn't tell him to kill himself. That's on him. I mean, that's weak."

"What in God's name are you playing?" Coach shouts.

Like the rest of the team, it takes him long seconds to fig-ure out what he's listening to and even then I'm still not sure he knows. It seems pretty plain to me. Why isn't it clear to the rest of them? The other players stand quietly, scratching themselves, adjusting themselves, as their eyes go from the floor to Coach, to Scott, to me, and then to each other. Their faces are blank, impossible to read.

"Shut that shit off!" Scott screeches. He's shaking. I've rocked him. It feels good, like landing a solid body blow. I lock eyes with him through my face mask and crank the volume until I risk snapping off the knob in my fingers.

"Gunderson wanted it. Loved it. Know how I know? He never fought back. He cried but he barely struggled, never escaped. That's how they act when they secretly want it."

". . . everyone knows it takes a fuckin monster to fuck a kid with a broom."

"Kiss your scholarship offers good-bye."

"Kurt, is this some kind of prank?" Assistant Coach Stein asks. "It's not funny! What's wrong with you?"

". . . and when we get through with him, you can add that little faggot, Danny, to your victim list."

"Go find your little friends. Go pretend you can save them. And tell 'em we're waiting for 'em. Tell 'em we'll get them alone, eventually, so they better learn how to man up and take it!"

"That ain't me. That ain't us," Scott shouts. "That's a fake! Sick freak."

"I don't know what kind of game you got going on here, Kurt," Coach breaks in again, "but that's enough."

"It's nuh-nuh-nuh-nuh . . . not a guh-guh-guh—"

"Brodsky's gone off his meds, Coach." Scott cuts me off. "What's up with you, retard?" he asks me. "Huh? Speak up, freaktard!"

"Coach," Tom speaks. "Kurt's a freakin' nut job. My dad told me he's loony, he tried to kill a kid."

"Shut it!" Coach snaps. "Shut it now! That's enough from all of you."

I try speaking but my mouth stops working. Helmet or no helmet, I got too much to say, too much to tell. But it's all here on the recording. All they got to do is listen. Just listen. I press the stop button, hit the back button, and hit play again. I'll play it again, and again, play all thirty-eight seconds Tina edited together for me—thirty-eight seconds that rip your guts out to hear. Why aren't they getting it? Why aren't they seeing it? Where's Danny? He'll explain. If Coach and the team hear it again, they'll understand. They have to understand.

Assistant Coach Stein steps across the circle and reaches for the stereo, grabbing the handle. "That's enough, Kurt," he says, trying to snatch it away, but I hold on and we're both tugging on it.

"Shut it off, dumbass!" Scott yells. "Go back to prison."

"Thuh-thuh-they ruh-ruh-ruh-ruh . . ." I stammer. It's all there, all the evidence of what they did to Ronnie. All they have to do is *listen*. "Duh-duh-Danny!" I cry out. He should be in here now. This is his part. It doesn't make sense to them. It needs explaining. Where is he?! "Duh-duh-duh . . ." He ain't here to explain it. He's left me. Abandoned me.

Like all the rest.

Every time.

"Kurt," Assistant Coach Stein grunts as we tug-of-war for the stereo, "I don't know what beef you got with Scott but this is—"

"Thuh-thuh-thuh—"

"Enough!" Coach bellows. "Shut off that goddamned machine and be done with it. We got a goddamned game to finish and I don't know what the hell the idea is here distracting this team with this . . . this . . . vulgarity! Now get ready to get out on the field and win this game!"

Danny! WHERE ARE YOU!!!

Coach has his arm extended, waiting for me to hand over the stereo. I glance over and see Scott sneering in triumph. Tom and Mike watch me with narrowed eyes like rats trying to see past a trap. The rest of my teammates only look confused. They drop their heads, avoiding my eyes, pretending the insides of their helmets need adjusting. It isn't going at all how we planned it, how Tina described it. They're supposed to hear the recording and all would be explained. And Danny would come in and speak the truth, finally, tell the others what they did, shame my captains until they walked away forever. But it's not working. I've failed. Danny's abandoned me. I'm all alone, about to be destroyed.

"Thuh-thuh-thuh—" I stammer.

"Not one more word!" Coach shouts. "You hear me?!"

Even after I text Bruce a second time, Coach Nelson won't let go of my arm. Bruce says he's on his way but the crowd by the concession stands is massive and meeting here isn't exactly the best spot to pick. I glance up at the stadium clock, see that time is running out. My choice is being made for me just like I wanted but, somehow, I'm not feeling relief. Another five minutes pass and still no Bruce.

"Coach," I try. "I gotta use the bathroom."

"Me too," he says. "Soon as we see Bruce, we can all go."

"Coach, come on!" I'm about to start my superwhine when Bruce pops up in the crowd. Finally!

"Bruce!" Coach calls to him. Bruce sees Coach and looks surprised but not startled, not like he's hiding a secret. When Bruce walks up to us, Coach lets go of me so he can get his mitts on Bruce.

"Now, look—" Coach is talking to Bruce but I don't stick around for the lecture. Hoping I'm not too late, I slip behind the first two fat bodies mooing past me, then zip through a mass of people traipsing back to the stands carrying Family Pack snack treasures. The area is stuffed with slow-moving bodies. It's easy for someone small as me to squeeze through the gaps and weave around bellies and butts unnoticed. I've had years of practice doing it.

Jumping off cliffs begins with a single superscary step into thin air. Only way to do it is to not think about it. That's how I pep-talk myself while dashing toward the school entrance, rushing down the hallway, and arriving in front of the closed varsity locker-room door. Only way to enter that locker room is to open that door, take that first step no matter how terrifying, worry about falling only after you can't turn back.

Problem is I'd way rather jump off another eighty-foot quarry cliff than walk through that door. Chances for bodily harm are much higher here tonight.

No mistaking it, I hear Kurt's voice on the other side and then the recording. I hear Kurt's voice but it's locking up. Then that coach of theirs roars like a grizzly. I'm supposed to go in there?! Then Scott is shrieking, wild and raw, bringing back flashes of the cruelty he's only too happy to inflict. My back presses firmly against the opposite wall.

Go in there now!

I remain right where I stand, unable to move. The sounds coming out of the room—all heavy and brutish, could be from a cave full of bears about to square off. It's no place for a pip-squeak like me. I mean, I'm just a little monkey. What the hell can I accomplish? My role in the plan starts to feel ridiculous. Kurt can handle himself in there. But me? Are you kidding? I know he said he'd protect me, but how's he going to do that against thirty guys?

My feet move . . . but they're going in the wrong direction. I'm shuffling down the hall, away from the locker room. Kurt's played the recording. That's good enough. That's truth enough. Let them know we have them recorded. That's all that we really came to do. Expose them. He doesn't need me. What good am I going to do at this point?

"Duh-duh-Danny!" It's Kurt's voice, and it doesn't sound big or angry or tough. It sounds like a cry for help. It frightens me. How can I help him? If someone big as him is in trouble, I'm dead. My feet keep shuffling down the hall. The closer I get to the end of the hall, about to leave the building, get back out in the cold night air, put distance between me and them . . . well, that should make me feel safer, make me feel better. But it doesn't. My steps get heavier.

"Aaagh." I jam both fists deep in my jacket pockets in frustration.

One step, a voice whispers to me. One step. Just take one step. Don't think. Just step.

I turn around and take one step. Then another. Then another. My feet are light and my heart races the way it does when I know I'm about to leap off the cliff or let go of the high bar or hit the springboard and fly over the vault. My steps turn into a jog and then I'm in front of the locker-room door and I'm pulling it open and stepping inside, smelling the rank air. I'm in that moment of suspension before the speed and velocity of gravity overtake me, turn me into a missile. As I turn the corner, see the helmet and pads and body armor of the first players, I know the ground is racing up to greet me, promising a painful landing, no crash mats in sight. And then my mouth opens—not to scream but to fight. To protect Kurt. To be his and Ronnie's voice.

"Y ou *better* listen to him," cries a small voice just as I'm about to give up and hand over the stereo to Coach. "All of you listen!" Big bodies part and there is little Danny pushing his way past beefy arms and legs, coming toward me. I reach out and grab his elbow like it's my last chance at a lifeline, tug him the rest of the way into the locker room until he stands in front of me, facing the circle of football players, ready to blast them all with the truth.

"That recording is proof," Danny scolds the entire locker room. "So you better listen real close." Coaches, trainers, and players alike blink in surprise. You can practically see them all thinking the same thing: *Who is this kid?*

"All of you," Danny continues with my hand resting on his shoulder, letting him know I got his back. "Your captains—Scott, Tom, and Mike—they . . . *raped* Ronnie Gunderson. I saw it with my own eyes! I witnessed it! That recording's them admitting it. You all heard it! Don't pretend you didn't."

Danny pauses a moment and, in the shocked silence, I hear him swallow before continuing. "And Ronnie Gunderson—*my teammate*—killed himself because of it. Coach, that recording is their confession. It's real. It's the truth! Kurt's not playing any sort of trick." Danny's head tilts and I can tell he's watching Scott, now, as he says this. Scott's left eye starts twitching and his lips peel back from his teeth. Mike and Tom both start bouncing like they're getting tasered.

"Jesus H. Christ!" Coach's face turns a deep red as he points a finger at Danny. "Son, you realize what you're accusing these boys of?! I goddamn guarantee I'll string you up myself if this is some sort of twisted joke."

"He's sick!" Scott shrieks, high-pitched, uncool. "The little faggot's sick in the head!" Scott lurches for Danny. So does Mike. Assistant Coach Stein puts an arm out and stops Scott, but Mike is still coming. I let go of Danny's shoulder, cock my arm, ready to slug Studblatz, when Terrence and Rondo step in between us and shove Mike back over to his side of the circle. Danny remains untouched.

"Scott used a broomstick on Ronnie Gunderson. I saw the whole thing." The words stream out Danny's mouth fast as the demon inside can shovel them, like Lamar's spirit—or maybe Ronnie's—is working with him to get the truth exposed. ". . . and Mike stuck his . . ." Danny keeps going, not risking even a pause for air. ". . . Ronnie begged them to stop. They laughed at him while he screamed—"

"Look, you little . . ." Coach sputters, face splotchy. Instead of finishing his sentence, Coach slaps his cap against his leg, then starts running his other hand back and forth over his scalp like he's shampooing his thin hair.

"You heard them on that recording!" Danny shouts. I place my hand back on his shoulder. Bodies start shifting and rustling but otherwise my teammates hold position, obedient to Coach, as we've all been trained.

"You're going to believe this little turd?" Scott pleads. No one answers him. Tom and Mike still don't speak, just keep lightly bouncing. "They're making it all up," Scott goes on, his voice tightening, trying to shake off Assistant Coach Stein's grip but Coach Stein isn't letting go just yet. Scott tries catching the eyes of all the downturned faces. "Guys, who you gonna believe?" Scott asks.

I want to know the same thing.

"That's it!" Coach barks, like he's regained his balance. "All of you. Get out there. Halftime's over. We got a game to win. Enough nonsense. *Get your asses out there now!*"

One thing stuttering's taught me is sometimes speaking is overrated. Sometimes you can say it all without uttering a sound. I grip Danny's shoulder, hold him in place against the outgoing tide of bodies. The two of us a little sandbar in a moving stream of limbs and pads and helmets. Scott, Tom, and Mike notice us and they hold back as well. No way is Scott letting me and Danny get Coach alone.

In a minute, the locker room is empty except for the seven of us—both coaches, all three captains, Danny, and me.

"Boys," Coach tries again. His voice is quieter, but it

ain't softer. He's real close to blowing again. "I'm asking—no, I'm *telling* you—for the last time. Get out on that field."

"It ain't over yet," I say, without a single stutter. I feel Danny's shoulder broaden, straightening up.

"Yeah," he adds. "It ain't over." Then I feel him turn to Coach. "You can't play them. Not after what they did. It's wrong. What they did is unforgivable. Ronnie killed himself because of it."

"Shut up!" Scott jumps and Coach Stein regrabs him, tugs him back. I've never seen Scott completely berserk; it's as if a dozen snakes slipped under his skin. Coach Stein's battle to restrain him gets help when Tom shifts over to contain Scott.

"You'll lose the team if you play them." Danny keeps going, his words working on Scott like acid drizzling down on his flesh, melting him. I squeeze his shoulder, letting him know I won't let anyone get at him, not even Coach. "They know the truth, now. The team knows. You know. The team won't play for them," Danny pushes.

"Boy . . ." Coach begins, about one second from exploding on Danny, when Scott beats him to it.

"*So what?!*" Scott wails. "So what if we did do it? No one's going to say shit! Except you." Scott reaches over Coach Stein's arm and aims a dagger-finger at Danny. I feel Danny flinch. Coach reels his head toward Scott like he's just taken a hit to the jaw. "The *only* mistake we made," Scott hisses, snakes slithering faster under his flesh, taking over his body now, "was not finding you in that storage room and doing you the same way we did your little friend. *That* would've taught you never to speak up, boy!"

"Shut up!" Tom barks at Scott, shoving his co-captain backward. Tom's eyes saucer with alarm and he turns to Coach. "I didn't do nothing," Tom tells Coach.

"Yeah, sure, you didn't do nothing." Scott laughs like a crazy man, his eyes rolling around the room. "Just held the little shit down for us while we broke him."

"You're the one that shoved the broom up him," Tom yells at his co-captain, jamming his finger in Scott's chest.

"Back off me!" Scott hisses at Tom. "Go shove Mike around. He's the one couldn't wait to whip out his dick on him." Scott's eyes circle wildly as he deflects Tom's accusation. "He's the *real* homo."

"I *AIN'T* NO HOMO!" Studblatz roars, swinging his helmet by the face mask into the nearest locker. The room booms with the noise. "It was you told me to do it!" Studblatz blurts. "You *told me* to do him."

"And you fuckin' loved it," Scott spits at Studblatz, his words nasty as cobra venom. "Everyone knows you're a faggot. Had a hard-on for that twerp soon as I mentioned it."

"Shut up!" Tom growls, his eyes dancing between Scott and Coach, waiting for an unseen force to crush him. "I didn't do nothing. I didn't touch him. I only held him down. Scott and Mike are the ones nailing him."

For a moment all is silent as Coach Brigs puts his hand against a locker and slowly sits down on the pine bench. His mouth hangs open like he wants to shout, but can no longer speak. The hand clutching his cap has crumpled it into a ball with a bill. His other hand comes off the lockers and lies across his chest like he's hearing the national anthem. Mouth still open, unspeaking, he drops his cap on the bench while his other hand begins rubbing his chest in a circular pattern. Maybe he's having a heart attack.

"What in God's name have you boys done?" he finally asks, his voice more a croak.

"God didn't have nothing to do with it," Danny says.

"Shut the fuck up!" Scott pushes past Tom and moves toward Danny. I step in front of Danny, ready to meet the attack, but Coach Stein grabs Scott by the elbow and spins him around.

"You take one more step toward him," Coach Stein says, "and I'm going to shut you down, Scott. Don't care if you're eighteen yet or not. I will take you down, right here, right now, you touch a hair on that boy's head."

"Frank," Coach Brigs says. "That won't be necessary." Coach slowly stands back up off the bench. His hand stops massaging his chest and it comes back up to smooth down the thin wisps covering his shiny skull. He's not looking at any of us as he speaks, but staring off somewhere only he can see. "We've got a game to play. A game to win. I'll—we'll—deal with this afterward. Let's just go out there and finish this one."

"There's nothing to take care of," Scott insists, and now he sounds like himself—calmer but still threatening, like he knows something the rest of the world doesn't. "That recording don't prove nothing. Recordings can be edited and fixed any which way. It's still these two freaks' word against ours. You try punishing us, Coach," and here Scott turns his attention back to Assistant Coach Stein, "I'm going to make sure the world knows all about the little vitamin program you got going on here. In fact, I'll blame everything on those pills and syringes that everyone's favorite coaching staff"—Scott pats Coach Stein's shoulder—"has been encouraging us to take." Scott's smiling again. "I bet the school board, the news, the state, would love to hear all about our D-bol, Deca-d, and Nandro connection. And we'll spill everything. Trust me. They won't hire you for school janitor once we get done."

Damn! I think. He *is* smart; smarter than me or Tina or Danny. Even smarter than Coach. He's smarter and he's going to get away with all of it.

"But—" Danny starts and stops, unable to come up with anything else to say. I pull him back to me. I know when a fight's finished. I learned that one a long time ago. There's but one thing to do if you can't beat them and you sure as hell can't join them. You walk away.

"Coach." I speak up. "I can't puh-puh-play alongside them. I'm done," I say. Then I look over at Scott through my face mask. I take a big breath and let it out, see his eyes, still spoiling for a fight. I got to give it to him. He's wicked, but he's a wicked genius.

"You win," I tell him. "It's over. You all wuh-wuh-win. I wuh-won't saying nothing. But I ain't puh-playing alongside you no more. It's over. Danny wuh-wuh-won't talk no more, either." Studblatz crosses his arms, glaring at me but keeping quiet. "Tuh-tuh-tell your dad not to huh-handcuff me nuh-nuh-no more," I say to Tom. "Tell him I don't wuh-wuh-want no more trouble."

My stutter's coming back hard in defeat.

"Better not," Tom says, growing courageous again now that he knows Scott's engineered their escape. "'Cause he told me he can make you go away forever if he wants."

I squeeze my eyes shut as I tug gently on Danny's shoulder to retreat with me. He doesn't resist. It's over and I want to get out of here, never see this place again, maybe drop out of school. I can't go here no more.

"Kurt . . ." Coach Brigs calls, and with my eyes still shut, his voice sounds brittle and old, and for a second, it makes me think he's cried in his life at some point. "Son, we need you . . ." he starts to say, but I don't hear the rest because Danny and me are out the locker room and down the hallway. The only sound as we walk is my plastic cleats crackling against the concrete. My knee stops pinching, I realize, as Lamar settles back down on my shoulder for a moment, fanning my neck in warm wingbeats.

It's okay, he whispers, then lifts off again, setting the both of us free.

I am moving through the school doors, cutting across the outer lawn spilling over with crowds of fans, hoping to slip past the field where I'll never play again. I had a feeling it was going to end badly like this. Flushing my supply of D-bol down the toilet before the game seemed not only right, it seemed like fate. Why take that crap when it only helps me help the people that don't care about me? Enough!

"Kurt, hold up," Danny calls. "Wait!" But I'm still going, don't even realize how quiet it is out in the stadium and along the grassy hill or near the concession stand. That the band's not playing, that there's no music coming out of the new speakers. That no one's cheering or even talking. That everyone's silent.

The Jumbotron screen is so big that even from this distance I can see it clearly, see that it's broadcasting a view of itself as if someone's pointing a camera at it.

Someone is.

Me.

The view on it is coming from my helmet cam.

"Whoa!" I whisper, except it doesn't come out as a whisper. My voice rolls across the entire field, the concession stands, the grassy knoll, and the stadium, like a gust of wind.

"Whoa!" I repeat, loud, amazed.

This time, my voice is a hurricane.

D A N N Y

Thanks a lot, Tina!

Thanks for convincing me to risk my life for the most completely ridiculous, totally stupid plan of all time! How did I imagine any good would actually come from confronting pure evil? And in its own locker room?! God, was I high when I said yes to this?

Kurt, bad knee and all, is leaving me in the dust soon as we step out of the school.

"Wait up!" I shout. That's when I realize I don't need to shout. The outside is quiet. People are standing around same as before but no one's goofing around or even talking. It's spooky weird, like everyone turned into a zombie at halftime. I'm about to ask Kurt if he notices anything when I hear his voice whispering over the stadium sound system. It's coming at me from all angles. Then a second time, even louder.

"Whoa!"

Kurt stops and turns to face me as I catch up. Beneath his helmet I can see his eyes widening in surprise.

"That sounded like you—" I start to say, except I hear my voice coming over the speakers, echoing across the field. "What's going on?" I ask him, but my voice, amplified, asks the entire stadium the same question. Both of us stare at each other, frozen, not saying a single word more, wondering how long his helmet's been on. Then I hear the footfalls coming up on us. Kurt's eyes shift off me, look over my shoulder as I turn to see Coach Brigs and Coach Stein, tight-lipped, ignoring us as they hurry past, late for their own game. Scott, Tom, and Mike are ten yards behind their coaches, jogging loosely with their heads held high, triumphant, as if they've already won the state title game. When the three of them reach us, Scott, barely slowing, points his fingers at Kurt like a gun. Victory makes his smile large.

"Remember, shitbags, our little secret," Scott says, ego so huge that the words coming from his own mouth block out the sound of them rolling across the stadium through Kurt's helmet mic.

None of them makes it far into the surrounding zombie crowd before the first bags of popcorn dump down on them like snow. Then the first full cups of soda get flipped over on them, dousing them in freezing slush. The two coaches and three captains get corralled together by the mob and raise their arms, trying to shield the onslaught of Family Packs of nacho chips drizzled in melted cheese and cups of ice. Large pretzels sail toward them like Frisbees. As the mob builds, their path is blocked and they get stuck before even reaching the entrance gates to the stadium field.

The Jumbotron stops broadcasting Kurt's helmet cam. Instead, one single word fills its entire screen.

BOO!!!

The crowd responds. They boo. And boo. And boo. Anything the crowd can get their hands on sails down out of the stadium bleachers—mostly soda cups and more cardboard Family Pack trays but occasional hats and scarves and rolled-up paper programs flying out like snowballs.

The Jumbotron works the crowd, flashing a new message.

GET OUT! GET OUT!

And the crowd takes up the chant. Coach Brigs, Coach Stein, Scott, Tom, and Mike are surrounded, shoved, pushed, and jeered until they get steered back toward the school. Angry adults—men and women—try to get at them, shouting in their faces, reaching out as if they want to rip off parts of their bodies.

Kurt pulls off his helmet and dangles it at his side. We look at each other, smiling, amazed, guessing what's happening, hoping it's true.

"Let's guh-guh-get outta huh-huh-here."

"Wait," I say. "Let's enjoy it for a moment." I breathe deep. "Whatever's going on, it's a beautiful thing."

Kurt nods and turns to take in the sight while I start jogging backward around him in circles, delivering a series of shadow punches at the air. "We won!" I shout, jabbing right, left, right. "We beat them. Suckers!" I jab out with two more lefts and a right cross before repeating the offer I made the day I was raking leaves and he came to warn me.

"Kurt, you can join our team, now," I suggest again. "Screw football. You'll be the biggest gymnast in all of recorded history. I'll teach you."

"Muh-maybe," Kurt says, not making any promises. I'm ready to pester him more, certain my idea is great, when something catches my eye. The football team. More precisely, the entire Knights football team charging toward the two of us, trampling through the slowly parting crowd like rampaging wildebeests, ready to avenge the downfall of their captains and coaches.

"Ohhhhhh, crap!" My voice rises as I ready to scamper out of there. Kurt grips his helmet by the face mask and hefts it, ready to swing it against the first wave of the attack. He spreads his feet wide, planting himself.

"Kurt, come on!" I squeak. "Can't fight them all."

"No one's puh-puh-pushing me around nuh-nuh-no more," he says. "You guh-go."

"No!" I say. *Wait! What did I just say?* "If you're not going," I tell Kurt, "then I'm staying." Kurt nods but doesn't look my way because they're almost here. Kurt crouches, battle helmet ready for the slaying, his free hand braced on his knee as he waits. I imitate him, then scrunch my eyes as they come at us, moving fast, Terrence, their running back, leading the charge.

As my maiming rapidly approaches, the sound of hoofbeats fills my ears.

K U R T

Kurt!" Terrence barks. "Let's go!"

Terrence, leading the entire football team, pulls up short before steamrolling over Danny and me. As the rest of the team arrives, they surround us, closing in, the white steam from all their panting filling the cold night air. I feel Danny's foot set in the turf next to mine. He's covering my blind side.

"Refs said we got three minutes to get on the field or we forfeit the game," Terrence explains. "We didn't work our asses off all season so we can quit the last home game and risk not clinching the top play-off slot. So let's go. Now."

"Yeah!" Rondo woofs.

"Let's go!" Pullman shouts.

"Game ain't over, Brodsky. Come on!" DuWayne grunts.

"Buh-buh-but . . ." I start, then Terrence cuts me off.

"Kurt, those three have been pricks since our Pony League days," Terrence says. "If even half of what we heard is true—and I don't doubt for a second it is—they don't deserve to wear this uniform. If they go after you, they go after all of us. If you can't trust your teammates no more, if they don't got your back, you ain't a team."

"*Yeah,*" I hear Danny whisper beside me.

"Clock's ticking, guys," Warner says. "Down to two minutes to get a team on that field. Kurt, we need you to bring it home."

"We're asking nicely," Rondo says. "Now, come *on!*"

"They're right," Danny says quietly to me. "Finish the game." I glance down at him, see he's serious. I heft my helmet up over my head, then pull it down and lock the chin strap in place.

"Good man!"

"Knew you'd come through!"

Terrence raises his own helmet to the night sky like a torch. "Who are we?" he asks.

"Knights!" my teammates answer back.

"Who do we fear?" Terrence asks us.

"No one!" we answer.

"Whose house is this?" Terrence shouts the question.

"Our house!" we tell him.

"What's our name?" Terrence asks.

"KNIGHTS!" we answer back.

DANNY

59

Coach Gayle, the wrestling coach, has been plucked out of the stands to substitute for Coach Brigs on the sidelines and make the game official in the nick of time. The Oregrove Knights take the field under an umbrella of chants from the crowd led by the Jumbotron—KNIGHTS! KNIGHTS! KNIGHTS!

I can't help myself. I start chanting as well, cheering for my school, cheering for my team, and most of all, cheering for Kurt. I'm hollering so loud I almost don't hear the phone chirping in my pocket. I recognize the number, answer it.

"You pulled it off!" I shout into the phone above the chanting.

"I told you girls are way craftier than boys," Tina says back.

"Why didn't you tell us the whole plan?" I ask.

"And take a chance you two would screw it up somehow? Or you'd think about it too much and chicken out?" she asks me. Through the phone, I can hear her giggling. "I've found with boys, the less said, the better. The only guy conniving enough to trust is Fisher."

"Fisher?" I ask "Are you kidding me?"

"How do you think I was able to run Kurt's helmet cam live the whole halftime?"

"So the crowd saw everything?!"

"Everything!" she confirms. "This stadium heard every word and saw everything going on in that locker room. No way I'd be able to broadcast the whole thing live without old man Walt out of the booth. So Fisher came in at halftime, told him his car was on fire, and then locked the door when he left. It's only me and Fish in here at the moment and now Walt's pounding on the door to get back in. He'll have to wait. Fish's helping me run the soundboard now."

"You are *amazing*!!!" I whoop.

"I know," she says. "Watch this!"

The Jumbotron starts flashing.

WE ♥ KURT!!!

"Okay, that's a little much," I tell her.

"Danny!" a voice shouts, and I turn to find Coach Nelson and Bruce walking toward me.

"Gotta go," I tell Tina, and hang up.

Coach Nelson's face hasn't changed since I escaped him earlier. He looks angry. Bruce looks tired.

"I'm not too pleased, you running off on me," Coach

starts, "but I guess you had more important matters to attend to."

I glance from Coach to Bruce, trying to read either of them, trying to figure out what I'm supposed to say.

"Why didn't you boys . . . I wish you'd told me, told *somebody* sooner. There's no excuse for what they did, you hear me?" Coach Nelson says. Bruce hangs his head like this is his second scolding. "No excuse. They're going to be in a world of hurt. And so is that dipshit dad of Tom's. I'll make sure of that. Of course, I'll have to get in line, judging from the looks of things."

I jam my hands into my coat pockets, wish I'd spoken sooner, but know that at the time it felt impossible, felt like speaking was a death sentence.

"Danny." Coach Nelson steps closer and puts his arm around my neck, headlocking me in a hug. "What you did tonight, what you faced down in that locker room, took more courage than most people ever muster. Being a hero usually isn't much fun. It's terrifying, most of the time, right up until the point you make it out safe. It's being scared to do the right thing and doing it anyway. You remember that next time you're frightened."

Coach Nelson lets me out of the headlock and I step back, embarrassed but not really minding the hug. "Now I need you to do one more thing," Coach says, and this time he grabs Bruce's neck and pulls him closer so the three of us make our own little huddle. "I need you both to come back to the gym—no more missing practice. You lead by example. Face whatever demons you've got about coming into that place and start working hard again."

Coach reaches up and grabs my neck, bending down so he can look both of us in the eye.

"Deal?" Coach asks. I glance at Bruce, who nods his head.

"Deal," Bruce says.

"Deal," I agree.

K U R T

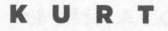

There's less than two minutes to play and we're up by ten points when Warner takes the snap and feeds me the ball. I follow my lead blocker in the line, Ben Yallese, substituting for Jankowski, and he smashes open a nice hole for me. Eight yards later, I've punched through the end zone with my legs charging hard. The referee's whistle tells me what I already know. Touchdown. My knee still pinches, but adrenaline's great for dulling the pain.

I toss the ball to the ref and let my teammates jump on me in celebration. When they finish and jog off the field, I have the end zone to myself for only a moment before we need to kick the extra point. Now's my chance.

I lift my arms up in preparation.

D A N N Y

61

Kurt Brodsky scores a last touchdown to ice the game and the stands erupt as his teammates rush him in hugs and helmet slaps. As the team jogs back toward their sideline, though, Kurt stays in the back of the end zone. He raises both hands high up in the air, pauses, then lowers his arms as if prepping and . . . and . . . flings himself backward while his legs power his big body up and over. Kurt Brodsky, in full helmet and pads, does a supremely ugly-beautiful back handspring that barely gets him around to his feet again. Awful landing aside, the handspring is still pretty cool. The stadium explodes all over again as the stunt is lovingly captured by Tina in slow motion up on the Jumbotron. He still needs to keep his elbows locked when he throws the trick, but I'll make sure to remind him sometime before the championship game.

"He made it!" I whisper.

"*We* made it!" a boy's voice, no longer mine, corrects me before vanishing forever.

ACKNOWLEDGMENTS

Fortunately for me, manuscripts still get plucked from slush piles by dedicated agents and acquired by great editors. *Leverage* was one such manuscript. To all aspiring writers out there I offer this small bit of advice: Be tenacious! Never give up! Keep the faith! This book's journey began with the wonderful Catherine Drayton of InkWell Management taking a chance on my manuscript. It continued with that great editor I referenced, Julie Strauss-Gabel, acquiring and further shaping the story. Along the way, *Leverage* received wonderful support from Patricia Burke at InkWell Management and a very real vote of confidence from two fine gentlemen, Stanley Jaffe and Dan Rissner. A big "Thanks" goes to the hardworking staff at Penguin/Dutton for helping make *Leverage* even better than I thought possible. Everyone else that I mention here has either supported, inspired, encouraged, or influenced me while I pursued the hard work of writing to get published: Mom & Dad Cohen (this goes without saying, but I'm saying it anyway), Karen Gayle (ditto), Barbara Cohen, Mohammed Naseehu Ali, Charise Hayman, Melannie Gayle, Denise Pinkley, Nathan Trice, the Gayle family, the Colonnese family, the Burch family, David Brind, Kent Frankstone, Michael Jones, Suzanne Lampl, Gary Laurie, Ben Speaker, and Stephen (Mr.) Schwandt.

QUESTIONS FOR DISCUSSION

1. In *Leverage*, the character of Ronnie not only endures a physical assault by upperclassmen whom he hardly knows, but he also endures taunts from one of his own teammates. Why is it harder, sometimes, to stand up to taunting or harassment from members of one's own team or clique or from friends or siblings than it would be to stand up to the same taunting or harassment from strangers?

2. In *Leverage*, technology is used both as a tool of the bullies (e.g., when the football captains torment Danny by sending him threatening text messages on his phone) and as a way to bring the bullies to justice. Do you feel that technology will eventually help to eliminate bullying or continue to contribute to the problem?

3. In your own experiences and/or awareness based on what you have read or seen in the news, do you think cyber bullying is becoming a bigger problem than physical bullying? Which one worries you more?

4. In your opinion, how much did "'Roid Rage" contribute to the bullying done by the football captains at Oregrove High School in *Leverage*? Would the football captains' bullying have been as extreme if they didn't take steroids? Is steroid use a problem on any of the sports teams in your school?

5. In *Leverage*, is the character of Danny ultimately a coward or a hero? Can someone be both a coward and a hero?

6. In *Leverage*, is it easier or harder for Kurt, who is physically imposing but has trouble speaking and frightens people, to confront the intimidating behavior of a group of bullies than it is for little Danny?

7. What would you have done if you were in Danny's shoes, witnessing the assault on Ronnie? Would you have kept quiet as long as Danny did? If you were afraid that no one would believe you if you revealed the truth and that your safety was in danger, what else might you have done to get help or justice?

8. Why does it seem that bullying stops after high school? Do you think that is a true perception? If it is true, what happens to people's attitudes and actions after high school to make bullying seem to disappear?

9. Is the violence depicted in *Leverage* too strong for readers under a certain age? Or is it better for young readers to gain exposure to the "ugly" side of human behavior through the safety of a book in order to avoid falling prey to such situations in real life?